# POOR THINGS

'By any standards, this is a marvellous, endearing book: a virtuoso feat of literary ventriloquism that projects literary voices from Hogg to George ("Flashman") MacDonald Fraser, while preserving its author's own dogged anarcho-socialist decency'

*New Statesman & Society*

'Mr. Gray contrasts the political and moral bleakness of contemporary Britain with the civic energy that characterized the best of Victorian values, now lost. He underlines the harm done to Scotland. *Poor Things* is a political book. It is also witty and delightfully written . . . Attention to Victorian Glasgow with its civic fountains, domestic interiors and medical schools gives the book texture. It is the characters, and strangely enough its phantasmagoria, that give it life'

*New York Times Book Review*

'A master of pastiche and collage in words and pictures, Gray has found a way to perfectly evoke a cracked, slightly out-of-balance sense of reality'

*Newsweek*

'Witty and delightfully written . . . Attention to Victorian Glasgow with its civic fountains, domestic interiors and medical schools gives the book texture. It is the characters, and strangely enough its phantasmagoria, that give it life'

*New York Times Book Review*

## BY THE SAME AUTHOR

### FICTION

Lanark: a Life in Four Books
1982 Janine
Something Leather
A History Maker
The Fall of Kelvin Walker
McGrotty and Ludmilla
Mavis Belfrage
Unlikely Stories, Mostly
Lean Tales (With Agnes Owen and James Kelman)
Ten Tales Tall and True

### NON-FICTION

The Book of Prefaces

# POOR THINGS

## EPISODES FROM THE EARLY LIFE of ARCHIBALD McCANDLESS M.D. SCOTTISH PUBLIC HEALTH OFFICER

EDITED BY
ALASDAIR GRAY

---

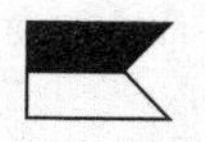

MARINER BOOKS
*New York Boston*

The author thanks Bernard MacLaverty for hearing the book as it was written and giving ideas that helped it grow; and Scott Pearson for typing and research into period detail; and Dr. Bruce Charlton for correcting the medical parts; and Angela Mullane for correcting the legal parts; and Archie Hind for insights (mainly got from his play *The Sugarolly Story*) into the corrupted high noon of Glasgow's industrial period; and Michael Roschlau for the gift of Lessing's *Nathan the Wise* (published in 1894 by MacLehose & Son, Glasgow, for the translator William Jacks, illustrated with etchings by William Strang) which suggested the form (not content) of the McCandless volume; and Elspeth King and Michael Donnelly, now of the Abbot House local history museum in Dunfermline, for permission to use some of their earlier circumstances to reinforce a fiction. The shocking incident described by Bella in Chapter 17 was suggested by the Epilogue of *In a Free State* by V. S. Naipaul. Other ideas were got from *Ariel Like a Harpy*, Christopher Small's study of Mary Shelley's *Frankenstein*, and from Liz Lochhead's *Blood and Ice*, a play on the same subject. Three sentences from a letter to Sartre by Simone de Beauvoir, embedded in the third and fourth paragraphs of Chapter 18, are taken from Quentin Hoare's translation of her letters published by Hutchinson in 1991. A historical note on Chapter 2 is extracted from Johanna Geyer-Kordesch's entry "Women and Medicine," in the *Encyclopaedia of Medical History* edited by W. F. Bynum. The epigraph on the covers is from a poem by Denis Leigh. The author thanks a close friend for a money loan which allowed him to finish the book without interruption.



FIRST MARINER BOOKS PAPERBACK EDITION PUBLISHED 2023.

*Designed by Alasdair Gray*

Library of Congress Cataloging-in-Publication Data has been applied for.

ISBN 978-0-06-337468-3

24 25 26 27 28 LBC 14 13 12 11 10

*Poor Things* might just imprint itself on the Scottish imagination of the 1990s as indelibly as *Lanark* influenced the 1980s ... the voyage is a teasing delight - and at times very moving ... Can a man "make" a feminist? It is the final riddle of a mesmerizing mind game in which not even the heroine, and certainly not the author, can be trusted. Only Gray's readers can provide the answer - and they are lucky, lucky things indeed' - **Scotsman**. 'If Gray had been content either to create a female Frankenstein or to give a new zest to the legend of Dr Jekyl and Mr Hyde Poor Things might have been a funny and original tale. ... But he has loaded his novel with false historical references and larded it with his own gruesome drawings. ... These are the ravings of second-rate characters in a second-rate novel?' - **Sunday Telegraph**. 'Not since Harry Harrison's *The Channel Tunnel, Hurrah! has* a work of light fiction amused me as much as Alasdair Gray's *Poor Things*. Gray, like Harrison, uses science fiction to resurrect England's Empire at its most spacious and gracious. Unlike Harrison he satirizes those wealthy Victorian eccentrics who, not knowing how lucky they were, invented The Emancipated Woman and, through her, The British Labour Party - a gang of weirdos who kept hugging and dropping the woolly socialism of their founders until Margaret Thatcher made them drop it for ever. The heroine of *Poor Things* is an oversexed blend of Eleanor Marx, Annie Besant and Alice in Wonderland. She meets her match in Harry Astley, the best type of English Conservative whose habitual reserve hides a warm heart and formidable intelligence. She is suitably punished for rejecting him by marriage to the spineless working-class Liberal who tells the story. A whole gallery of believably grotesque foreigners - Scottish, Russian, American and French - assist in her downfall, but my favourite character is Mrs Dinwiddie. This lightly sketched portrait of a faithful family servant stands comparison with old Nanny Hawkins in *Brideshead Revisited*.' - **Private Nose.** 'Although it is pointless to accuse a novelist of getting his facts wrong, it is hard to see why General Blessington (who supported home rule for Ireland *and* the Transvall) is presented as the worst of British Imperialists. This and similar inauthenticities makes *Poor Things* yet another exercise in Victorian pastiche, a fictional genre which deserves to be neglec... ntury or two.' **The Times Literary Implement**. 'Was Bella Victoria really ... a bizarre scheme hatched to get her away from her ... t. 'Those who, like me, are ... ht, and not just because ... int, it is at least as witty ... *on* and *The Island of Dr.* ... cs of sexual behaviour. ... greaty deal more than ... **Spectator.** 'Gray's ... t excitement. It is a ... good value too?' - **The Independent**. ... cus, Glasgow, a surgical genius used human remains to create ... reads in part the opening paragraph of the Editor's introduction to *Poor Things*, the Editor in question being the Scots novelist Alasdair Gray. And so begins the most erudite, inventive and entertaining novel I have read this year. Bella's innocence is a source of great fun and high drama, yet it also provides Gray with the opportunity to make powerful moral points. 'You need not believe this ... ' This phrase echoes around the entire edifice, for in the novel every assertion is contradicted, every argument challenged. Fact and fiction, history and literature are stitched together and animated in that 'Frankenstein method' known as post-modernism. Thus Gray remains true to his own fictional tradition, while employing the devices of older and (frankly) more accessible ones, to write this dazzling book. - **Harpers and Queens**. 'Gray is a notorious scribbler, doodler, all-round maker-upper and social anarchist ... It comes hard on those of us who have experienced the responsibility and loneliness of office to hear from people of Gray's ilk that generosity, benevolence and ordinary common sense are missing from the political process?' - **The Glasgow Herald**. 'Alasdair Gray is a true original, a twentieth-century William Blake who designs and illustrates his own strange fictions. *Poor Things* ... In this playful but profoundly serious novel, the alchemic effects of love and invention are the only consolation for us, 'poor things', helpless in the flow of historical fact.' - **The Observer.** 'The feeble state of English literary criticism has been demonstrated yet again. I refer to the recent kow-towing of London book reviews before the most recent product of that intellectual hooligan, Alasdair Gray.' - **The Skibereen Eagle.**

<u>erratum</u>

The etching on page 187 does not portray Professor Jean Martin Charcot, but Count Robert de Montesquiou-Fezensac.

Dr Archibald McCandless (1862-1911) was born in Whauphill, Galloway, the illegitimate son of a prosperous tenant farmer. He studied medicine at Glasgow University, worked briefly as a house surgeon and public health officer, then devoted himself to literature and the education of his sons. His once famous epic, *The Testament of Sawney Bean*, has long been unfairly neglected, and his wife suppressed the first edition of his greatest work, the autobiographical *Poor Things*. Recently rediscovered by the Glasgow local historian, Mike Donnelly, this weird narrative is as gripping as Hogg's *Confessions of a Justified Sinner*, and in 1992 received both the Whitbread Award and the *Guardian* Prize.

Alasdair Gray, the editor, was born in Riddrie, Glasgow, 1934, the son of a cardboard-box manufacturer and part-time hill guide. He obtained a Scottish Education Department Diploma in Design and Mural Painting and is now a fat, balding, asthmatic, married pedestrian who lives by writing and designing things.

FOR MY WIFE
MORAG

# INTRODUCTION

The doctor who wrote this account of his early experiences died in 1911, and readers who know nothing about the daringly experimental history of Scottish medicine will perhaps mistake it for a grotesque fiction. Those who examine the proofs given at the end of this introduction will not doubt that in the final week of February 1881, at 18 Park Circus, Glasgow, a surgical genius used human remains to create a twenty-five-year-old woman. The local historian Michael Donnelly disagrees with me. It was he who salvaged the text which is the biggest part of the book, so I must say how he found it.

Life in Glasgow was very exciting during the nineteen seventies. The old industries which had made the place were being closed and moved south, while the elected governors (for reasons any political economist can explain) were buying multistorey housing blocks and a continually expanding motorway system. In the local history museum on Glasgow Green the curator Elspeth King, her helper Michael Donnelly, worked overtime to acquire and preserve evidence of local culture that was being hustled into the past. Since the First World War the City Council had given the local history museum (called the People's Palace) no funds to buy anything new, so Elspeth and Michael's acquisitions were almost all salvaged from buildings scheduled for demolition. A store was rented in Templeton's carpet factory (which was soon closing down) and to this place Michael Donnelly brought troves of stained-glass windows, ceramic tiles, theatre posters, banners of disbanded trade unions and all sorts of historical documents. Elspeth King sometimes gave Michael manual help with this work, as the rest of her staff were attendants sent by the head of the city art gallery in Kelvingrove and not paid to retrieve objects from dirty, unsafe buildings. Neither, of course, were Elspeth and Michael, so the new and very successful exhibitions they put on cost the City Council little or nothing.

While passing through the city centre one morning Michael Donnelly saw a heap of old-fashioned box files on the edge of a pavement, obviously placed there for the Cleansing Department to collect and destroy. Looking into them he found letters and documents dating from the early years of the century, the refuse of a defunct law office. A modern firm had inherited what remained of the old business, and thrown out what it did not need. The papers mainly concerned property dealings between people and families who had helped to shape the city in its earlier days, and Michael saw the name of the first woman doctor to graduate from Glasgow University, a name only known to historians of the suffragette movement nowadays, though she had once written a Fabian pamphlet on public health. Michael decided to take the files away by taxi and sift through them at leisure; but first he called on the firm which had put the boxes out and asked permission. It was denied. A senior partner (a well-known lawyer and local politician who will not be named here) told Michael that his look through the files had been a criminal act since they were not his property and intended for the municipal incinerator. He said every lawyer was sworn to keep a client's business private, whether the lawyer inherited the business or not and whether the client lived or died. He said that the only sure way to keep old business private was to destroy proof that it had happened, and if Michael Donnelly saved any part of the heap from destruction he would be charged with robbery. So Michael left the heap as it was—except for a small item he had casually pocketed before learning this was a crime.

It was a sealed packet inscribed with these words in faded brown ink: *Estate of Victoria McCandless M.D. / For the attention of her eldest grandchild or surviving descendant after August 1974 / Not to be opened earlier.* A recent hand using a modern ball-point pen had scribbled a zig-zag line through this and this underneath: *No surviving descendants.* The seal of the packet had been broken at one end and the paper torn open, but whoever did so had found the book and letter inside so uninteresting that they had thrust them carelessly back—both protruded and the letter was crumpled, not folded. The arch-thief Donnelly examined this closely in the People's Palace store during a tea-break.

The book was 7¼ by 4½ inches and bound in black cloth with a grotesque ornament stamped on the batters. On the fly-leaf someone had scribbled a sentimental verse. On the title-page this was printed: *EPISODES FROM THE EARLY LIFE of a SCOTTISH PUBLIC HEALTH OFFICER / Archibald McCandless M.D. / Etchings by William Strang / GLASGOW: Published for the Author by ROBERT MACLEHOSE & COMPANY Printers to the University 1909.* This was not an encouraging title. Many shallow, gossipy books were published in those days with names like *Leaves from an Inspector's Log* and *The Opinions and Prejudices of Frank Clark, Barrister.* When the author paid the publisher for them (as here) such books were usually duller than those for which the publisher paid the author. Turning to the first chapter Michael saw a typical heading of the period:

CHAPTER THE FIRST

*My mother—my father—Glasgow University and early struggles—portrait of a professor—a financial proposal, rejected—my first microscope—an equal intelligence.*

What most interested Michael Donnelly were the Strang illustrations, all portraits. William Strang (1859–1921) was a Scottish artist born in Dumbarton, who studied under Legros at the Slade School of Art, London. He is known nowadays for his engravings rather than paintings, and some of his best work went into book illustration. A doctor who could pay Strang to etch pictures for a privately printed book must have had a larger income than most public health officers, yet the Archibald McCandless whose face was on the frontispiece had not the look of a rich man or a doctor. The accompanying letter was even more perplexing. It was from Victoria McCandless M.D., widow of the author, telling the descendant who never existed that the book was full of lies. Here is part of it:

*By 1974 . . . surviving members of the McCandless dynasty*

*will have two grandfathers or four great-grandfathers, and will easily laugh at the aberration of one. I cannot laugh at this book. I shudder at it and thank the Life Force that my late husband had just this single copy printed and bound. I have burned . . . the original manuscript and would have burned this too, as he suggests . . . but alas! it is almost the only evidence left that the poor fool existed. He also paid a small fortune for it. . . . I do not care what posterity thinks of it, as long as nobody now living connects it with* me.

Michael saw that both book and letter might repay closer attention, so put them with other material to be concentrated on when he had time.

And there they lay. That afternoon he learned that Glasgow University's old theological college was being cleared out for renovation by a firm of property developers. (It is now luxury flats.) Michael found it contained over a dozen large framed oil paintings of eighteenth- and nineteenth-century Scots clergy, and these too would have burned in the municipal incinerator at Dawsholm Park if he had not cut them from their stretchers (they had been screwed to the wall at a prominent height) and taken them to the municipal art gallery in Kelvingrove, where space was found for them in the over-crowded store. Over a decade passed before Michael Donnelly had time to sit down and investigate social history in a leisurely way. He left the People's Palace in 1990 when Glasgow had been declared the official Culture Capital of Europe by Margaret Thatcher's Minister of Arts, and on the way out pocketed again the book and letter which (he was sure) would mean nothing at all to whoever replaced him — if anyone did.

I first met Michael Donnelly in 1977 when Elspeth King had employed me in the People's Palace as an artist-recorder, but when he contacted me in the autumn of 1990 I had become a self-employed writer who dealt with several publishers. He lent me this book, saying he thought it a lost masterpiece which ought to be printed. I agreed with him, and said I would arrange it if he gave me complete control of the editing. He agreed, a little reluctantly, when I promised to make no changes to Archibald McCandless's actual text. Indeed, the main part of this book is as near to a facsimile of the McCandless original as possible, with the Strang etchings and other illustrative devices reproduced photographically. However, I have replaced the lengthy chapter headings with snappier titles of my own. Chapter 3, originally headed: *Sir Colin's discovery—arresting a life—"What use is it?"—the queer rabbits—"How did you do it?"—useless cleverness and what the Greeks knew—"Good-bye"—Baxter's bulldog—a horrible hand*: is now simply called "The Quarrel". I have also insisted on renaming the whole book POOR THINGS. *Things* are often mentioned in the story and every single character (apart from Mrs. Dinwiddie and two of the General's parasites) is called *poor* or call themselves that sometime or other. I print the letter by the lady who calls herself "Victoria" McCandless as an epilogue to the book. Michael would prefer it as an introduction, but if read before the main text it will prejudice readers against that. If read afterward we easily see it is the letter of a disturbed woman who wants to hide the truth about her start in life. Furthermore, no book needs two introductions and I am writing this one.

I fear Michael Donnelly and I disagree about this book. He thinks it a blackly humorous fiction into which some real experiences and historical facts have been cunningly woven, a book like Scott's *Old Mortality* and Hogg's *Confessions of a Justified Sinner*. I think it like Boswell's *Life of Samuel Johnson*; a loving portrait of an astonishingly good, stout, intelligent, eccentric man recorded by a friend with a memory for dialogue. Like Boswell, the self-effacing McCandless makes his narrative a host to letters by others who show his subject from a different angle, and ends by revealing a whole society. I also told Donnelly that I had written enough fiction to know history when I read it. He said he had written enough history to recognize fiction. To this there was only one reply—I had to become a historian.

I did so. I am one. After six months of research among the archives of Glasgow University, the Mitchell Library's Old Glasgow Room, the Scottish National Library, Register House in Edinburgh, Somerset House in London and the National Newspaper Archive of the British Library at Colindale I have collected enough material evidence to prove the McCandless story a complete tissue of facts. I give some of this evidence at the end of the book but most of it here and now. Readers who want nothing but a good story plainly told should go at once to the main part of the book. Professional doubters may enjoy it more after first scanning this table of events.

29 AUGUST, 1879: Archibald McCandless enrols as a medical student in Glasgow University, where Godwin Baxter (son of the famous surgeon and himself a practising surgeon) is an assistant in the anatomy department.

18 FEBRUARY, 1881: The body of a pregnant woman is recovered from the Clyde. The police surgeon, Godwin Baxter (whose home is 18 Park Circus) certifies death by drowning, and describes her as "about 25 years old, 5 feet 10¾ inches tall, dark brown curling hair, blue eyes, fair complexion and hands unused to rough work; well dressed." The body is advertised but not claimed.

29 JUNE, 1882: At sunset an extraordinary noise was heard throughout most of the Clyde basin, and though widely discussed in the local press during the following fortnight, no satisfactory explanation was ever found for it.

13 DECEMBER, 1883: Duncan Wedderburn, solicitor, normally resident in his mother's home at 41 Aytoun Street, Pollokshields, is committed to the Glasgow Royal Lunatic Asylum as incurably insane. Here follows a report from *The Glasgow Herald*, two days later: "Last Saturday afternoon members of the public complained to the police that one of the orators in the open forum on Glasgow Green was using indecent language. The constable investigating found the speaker, a respectably dressed man in his late twenties, was making slanderous statements about a respected and philanthropic member of the Glasgow medical profession, mingling them with obscen-

ities and quotations from the Bible. When warned to desist the orator redoubled his obscenities and was taken with great difficulty to Albion Street police office, where a doctor pronounced him fit to be detained, but not to plead. Our correspondent tells us he is a civil lawyer of good family. No charges are being pressed."

27 DECEMBER, 1883: General Sir Aubrey de la Pole Blessington, once nicknamed "Thunderbolt" Blessington but now Liberal M.P. for Manchester North, dies by his own hand in the gun-room of Hogsnorton, his country house at Loamshire Downs. Neither obituaries nor accounts of the funeral mention his widow, though he had married twenty-four-year-old Victoria Hattersley three years earlier, and neither her legal separation from him nor her death were ever recorded.

10 JANUARY, 1884: By special licence a civil marriage contract is signed between Archibald McCandless, house doctor in Glasgow Royal Infirmary, and Bella Baxter, spinster, of the Barony Parish. The witnesses are Godwin Baxter, Fellow of the Royal College of Surgeons, and Ishbel Dinwiddie, housekeeper. The bride, the groom and both witnesses are all residents of 18 Park Circus, where the marriage takes place.

16 APRIL 1884: Godwin Baxter dies at 18 Park Circus of what Archibald McCandless M.D. (who signs the death certificate) describes as "a cerebral and cardiac seizure provoked by hereditary neural, respiratory and alimentary dysfunction". *The Glasgow Herald*, reporting on the burial service in the Necropolis, mentions "the uniquely shaped coffin", and that the deceased has left his entire estate to Dr. and Mrs. McCandless.

2 SEPTEMBER, 1886: The woman who married Archibald McCandless M.D. under the name Bella Baxter, enrols in the Sophia Jex-Blake School of Medicine for Women under the name *Victoria* McCandless.

Michael Donnelly has told me he would find the above evidence more convincing if I had obtained official copies of the marriage and death certificates and photocopies of the newspaper reports, but if my readers trust me I do not care what an "expert" thinks. Mr. Donnelly is no longer as friendly as formerly. He blames me for the loss of the original volume, which is unfair. I would gladly have sent a photocopy to the publisher and returned the original, but that would have added at least £300 to the production costs. Modern typesetters can "scan" a book into their machine from a typed page, but from a photocopy must type it in all over again; moreover the book was needed by a photographic specialist, to make plates from which the Strang etchings and facsimiles of Bella's letter could be reproduced. Somewhere between editor, publisher, typesetter and photographer the unique first edition was mislaid. These mistakes are continually happening in book production, and nobody regrets them more than I do.

I will end this introduction with a brief contents list in which the slightly edited reprint of the McCandless volume is given pride of place.



I have illustrated the chapter notes with some nineteenth-century engravings, but it was McCandless who filled spaces in his book with illustrations from the first edition of *Gray's Anatomy*: probably because he and his friend Baxter learned the kindly art of healing from it. The grotesque design opposite is by Strang, and was stamped in silver upon the batters of the original volume.

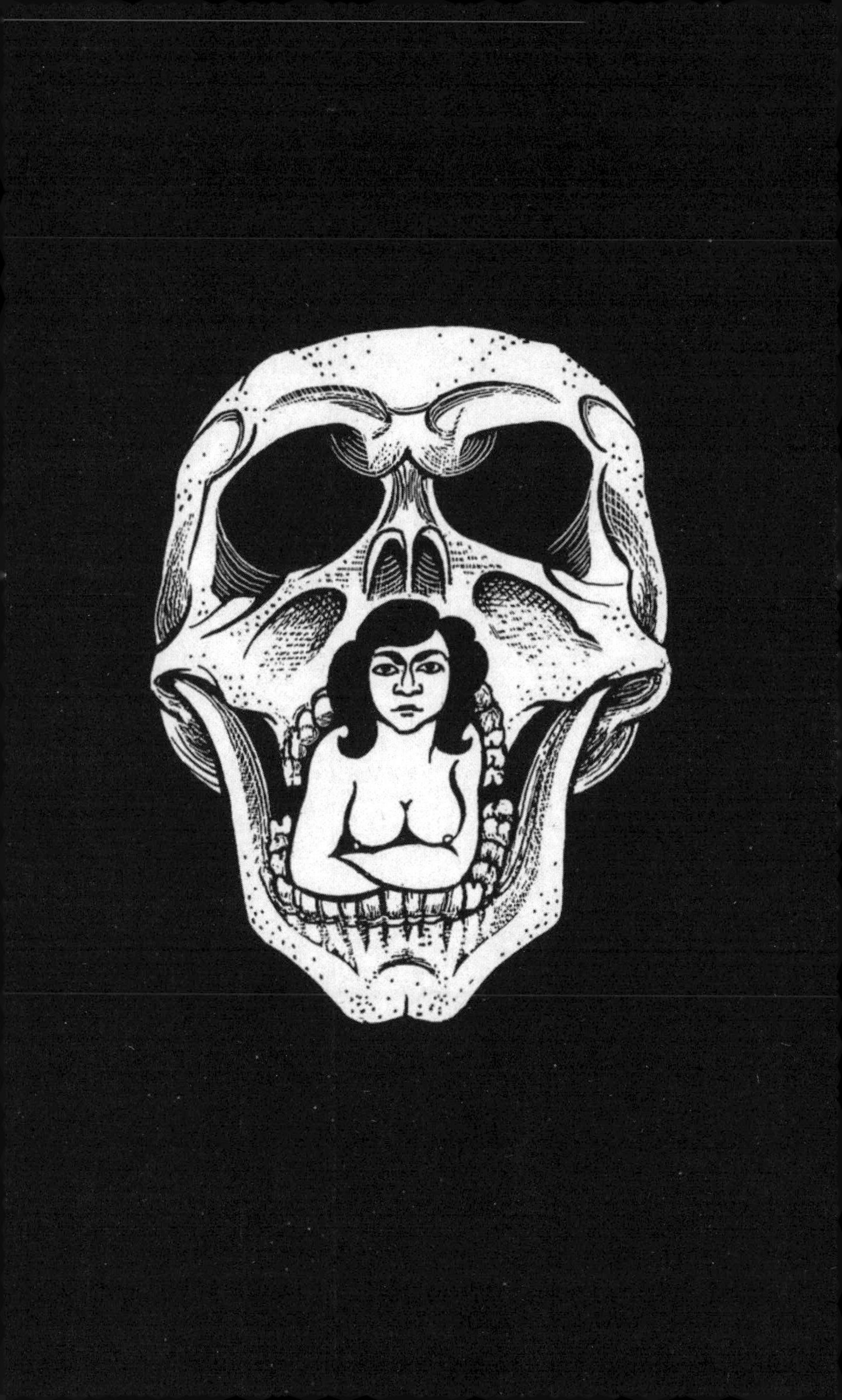

My own dear sweet kind famous doctor, do
Smile on this tribute from a lover who
Was patient—daft old husband—doctor too.
Kiss my last book and (since you can't
return it)
Read it just once, then, if you hate it—
burn it!

Your faithful
Archie, June 1911

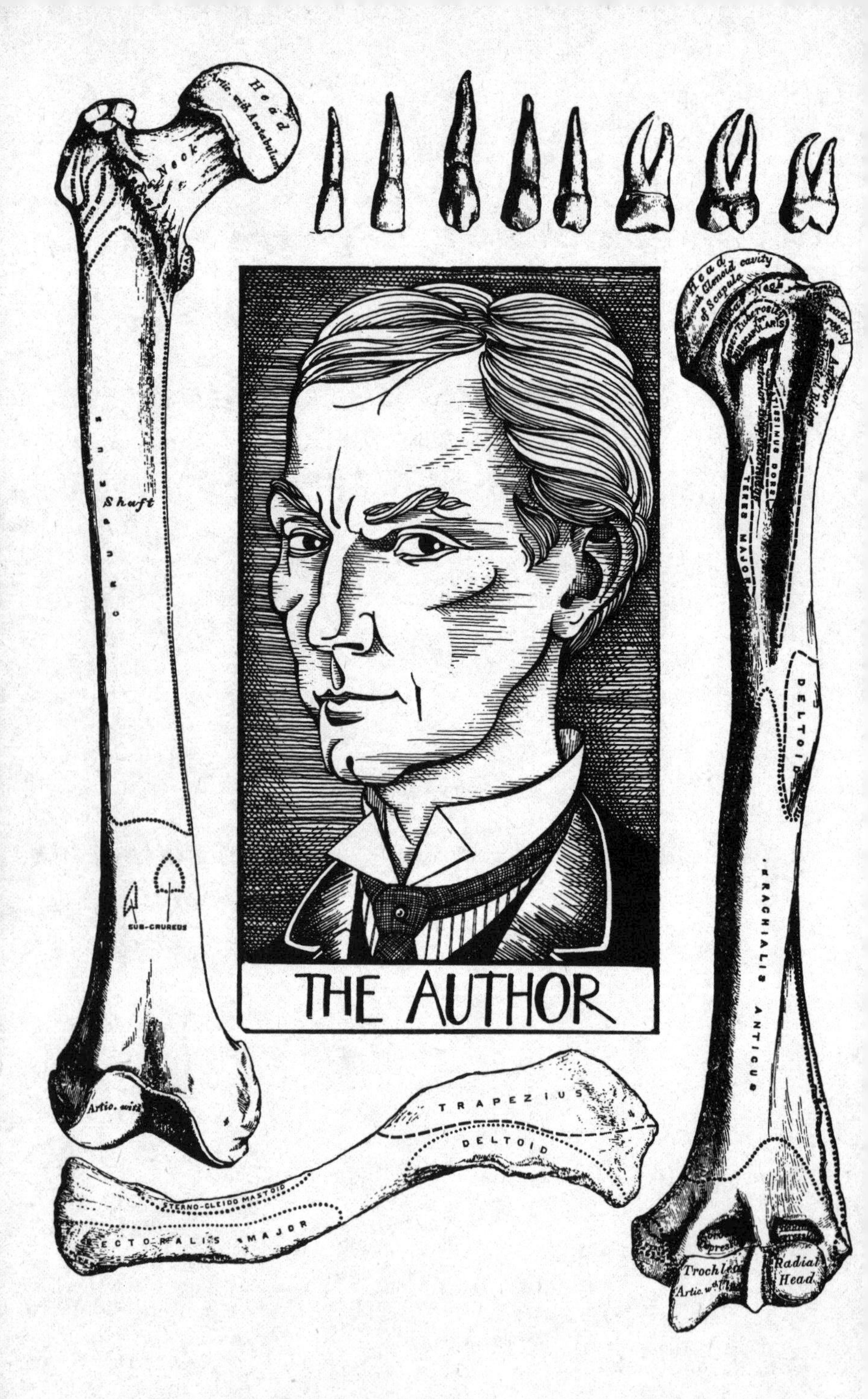
THE AUTHOR
Head
Artic. with Acetabulum
Neck
Shaft
SUB-CRUREUS
TRAPEZIUS
DELTOID
STERNO-CLEIDO MASTOID
Head
Glenoid cavity
of Scapula
Neck
TERES MAJOR
DELTOID
ANTICUS
Trochlea
Radial
Head

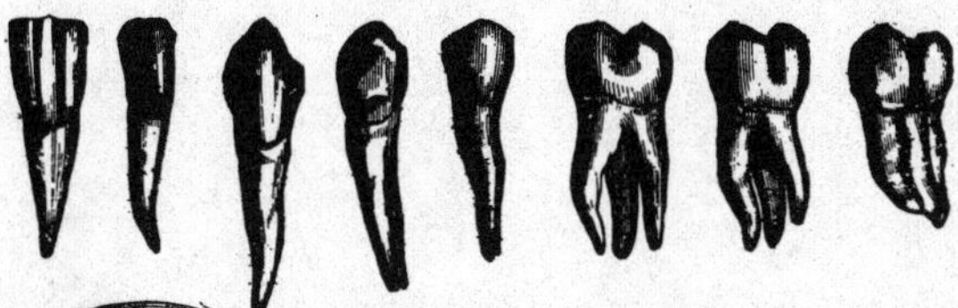

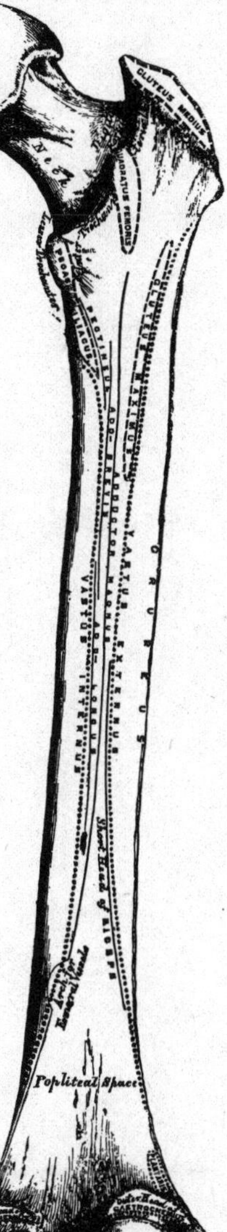

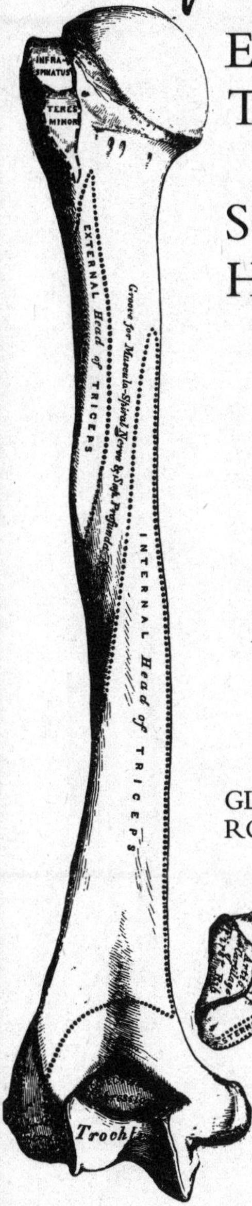

# EPISODES FROM THE EARLY LIFE of a SCOTTISH PUBLIC HEALTH OFFICER

---

ARCHIBALD McCANDLESS M.D.

---

*ETCHINGS by WILLIAM STRANG*

---

GLASGOW: Published for the Author by
ROBERT MACLEHOSE & COMPANY
Printers to the University 1909

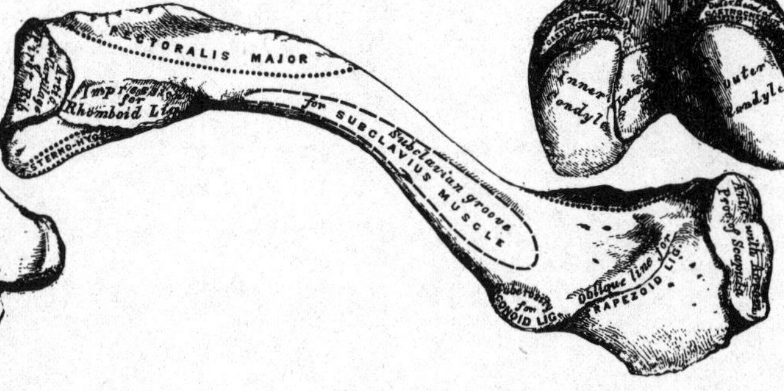

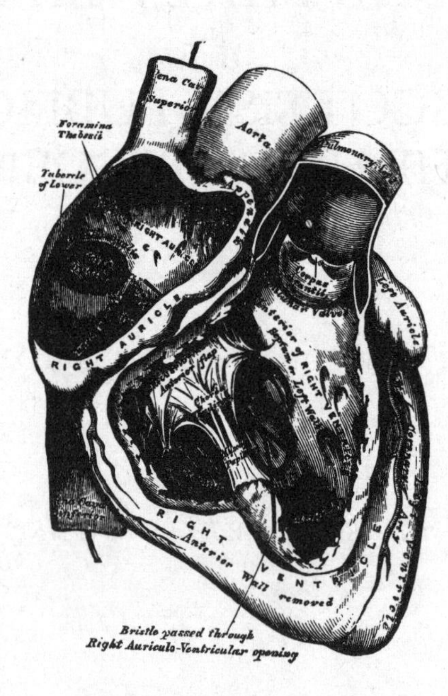
ena Ca
Superio
Foramina
Thebesii
Tubercle
of Lower
Aorta
Appendix
Corpus
Left Auricle
RIGHT AURICLE
Anterior
Wall
removed
RIGHT
VENTRICLE
Bristle passed through
Right Auriculo-Ventricular opening

TO SHE
WHO MAKES MY LIFE
WORTH LIVING

# T A B L E   O F

# CONTENTS

## ILLUSTRATIONS

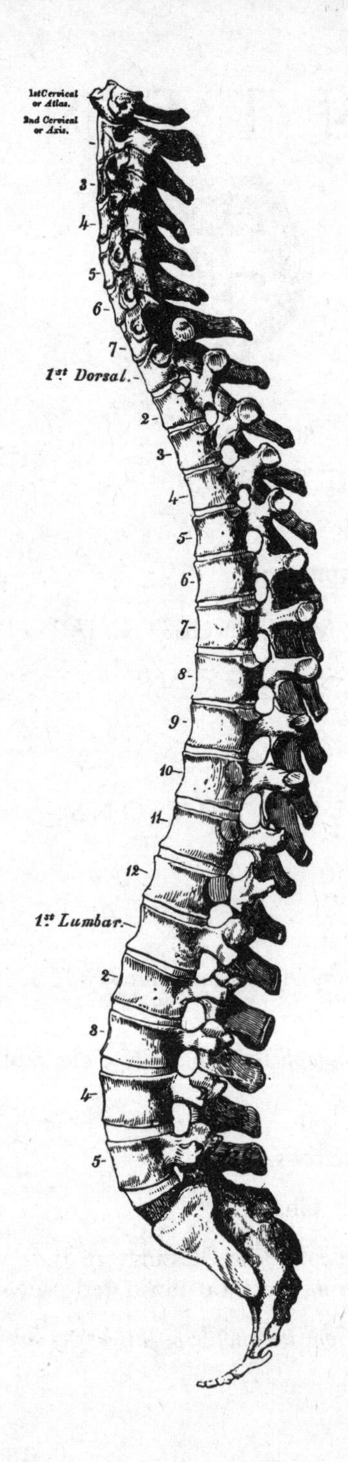
1st Cervical or Atlas.
2nd Cervical or Axis.
3
4
5
6
7
1st Dorsal.
2
3
4
5
6
7
8
9
10
11
12
1st Lumbar.
2
3
4
5

# 1

# Making Me

LIKE MOST FARM WORKERS IN THOSE DAYS my mother distrusted banks. When death drew near she told me her life-savings were in a tin trunk under the bed and muttered, "Take it and count it."

I did, and the sum was more than I had expected. She said, "Make something of yourself with it."

I told her I would make myself a doctor, and her mouth twisted in the sceptical grimace she made at all queer suggestions. A moment later she whispered fiercely, "Don't pay a penny toward the burial. If Scraffles puts me in a pauper's grave then Hell mend him! Promise you'll keep all my money to yourself."

*Scraffles* was the local nickname for my father and for a disease that afflicts badly fed poultry. Scraffles did pay for her burial but told me, "I leave the stone to you."

Twelve years passed before I could afford a proper monument, and by then nobody remembered the position of the grave.

At university my clothes and manners announced my farm-servant origins, and as I would let nobody sneer at me on that account I was usually alone outside the lecture theatres and examination hall. At the end of the first term a professor called me to his room and said, "Mr. McCandless, in a just world I could predict a brilliant future for you, but not in this one, unless you make some changes. You may become a greater surgeon than Hunter, a finer obstetrician than Simpson, a better healer than Lister, but unless you acquire a touch of smooth lordliness or easy-going humour no patient will trust you, other doctors will shun you. Don't scorn a polite appearance because many fools, snobs and scoundrels have that. If you cannot afford a good coat from a good tailor, search for one that fits you among forfeited pledges in the better pawnshops. Sleep with your trousers neatly folded between two boards under your mattress. If you cannot change your linen every day at least contrive to attach a freshly starched collar to your shirt. Attend conversaziones and smoking-concerts arranged by the class you are studying to join—you will not find us a bad set of people, and will gradually fit in by a process of instinctive imitation."

I told him my money could pay for no more than my fees, books, instruments and keep.

"I *knew* that was your trouble!" cried he triumphantly. "But our senate handles bequests for deserving cases like yours. Most of the grants go to divinity students but why should science be excluded? I think we can arrange to give you at least the price of a new suit, if you approach us in the right way and I put in a word. What do you say? Shall we attempt it?"

Had he said—"I think you are entitled to a bursary, this is how to apply, and I will be your referee"—had he said that I could have thanked him; but he lolled back in his chair, hands clasped on bulging waistcoat, simpering up at me (for I had not been invited to sit) with such a sweet coy smug smile that I pocketed my fists to avoid punching his teeth. Instead I told him I came from a part of Galloway where folk disliked begging for charity, but since he had a high opinion of my talents we could arrange to profit us both. I suggested he lend me a hundred pounds, for which I would repay seven and a half per cent on the anniversary of the loan until my fifth year as general practitioner or third as professional consultant, when I would refund the original lump and add a twenty pound bonus. He gaped, so I added swiftly, "Of course I will be bankrupt if I fail to graduate, or get struck early off the Register, but I think I am a safe investment. What do you think? Shall we try it?"

"You are joking?" he murmured, staring at me hard, his lips twitching with the beginnings of a smile he wanted me to imitate. Being too angry to grin at the joke I shrugged, said good-bye and left.

There was perhaps a connection between this interview and an envelope addressed in an unknown hand which came through the post a week later. It contained a five-pound banknote, most of which I spent on a second-hand microscope, the rest on shirts and collars. I could now dress less like a ploughman and more like an indigent bookseller. My fellow students thought this an improvement, for they started greeting me cheerily and telling me the current gossip, though I had no news for them. Godwin Baxter was the only one I talked with as an equal because (I still believe) we were the two most intelligent and least social people attached to the Glasgow medical faculty.

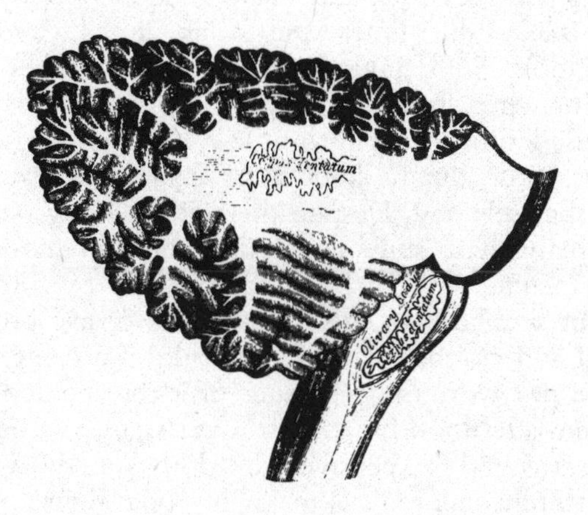

# 2

# Making Godwin Baxter

I KNEW HIM BY SIGHT FOR THREE TERMS before we exchanged a word.

A private workspace had been made in a corner of the dissecting-room by taking a door off a cupboard and installing a bench. Baxter usually sat there, preparing and examining slide sections and making rapid notes, and here his big face, stout body and thick limbs gave him a dwarfish look. Sometimes he ran out to raid the tank of disinfectant where brains were heaped like cauliflowers, and as he passed other people you saw he was a whole head taller than most, but he kept as far from others as possible, being desperately shy. Despite the ogreish body he had the wide hopeful eyes, snub nose and mournful mouth of an anxious infant, with a brow corrugated by three deep permanent wrinkles. In the morning his coarse brown hair was oiled and combed flat on each side of a centre parting, but as the day wore on spiky tufts of it rose behind his ears, and by mid afternoon his scalp was as shaggy as a bear's pelt. His clothes were of expensive grey cloth, quietly fashionable and beautifully tailored to make his odd figure appear as conventional as possible, yet I felt he would look more natural in the baggy pants and turban of a pantomime Turk.

W.S.
GODWIN BAXTER

This was the only son of Colin Baxter, the first medical man to be knighted by Queen Victoria. Sir Colin's portrait hung beside the portrait of John Hunter in our examination hall: a clean-shaven, sharp-faced, thin-lipped man who looked nothing like his son. "Sir Colin's lack of interest in female beauty was legendary," one of the gossips told me, "but his offspring proves he had a peculiar appetite for female ugliness." It was said that Godwin's father got him late in life by a domestic servant, but (unlike my father) gave his son his own surname, a private education and a small fortune. Nothing definite was known of Godwin's mother. Some said she was in a lunatic asylum, others that Sir Colin kept her as his maidservant in black dress, white cap and apron, silently passing plates round the dining-table when he entertained colleagues and the wives of colleagues. The great surgeon died a year before Godwin enrolled as a student. He was a brilliant student apart from hospital work, where his strange appearance and voice frightened patients and offended the staff, so he did not graduate but continued as a research assistant. Nobody knew or was much interested in his line of research. He was allowed to come and go as he pleased because he paid his fees regularly, inconvenienced nobody, and had a famous father. Most thought him a scientific dabbler, but I also heard that he gave unpaid help to a clinic attached to an east-end iron foundry, and treated scorched limbs and fractured spines uncommonly well.

In my second year I attended a public debate on a theme that interested me, though not by its novelty: does life mainly evolve through small gradual changes, or through big catastrophic ones? In those days that theme was supposed to be religious as well as scientific, so the principal speakers swerved from fanatical solemnity to facetious jocularity, and changed the ground of their argument whenever it gave them the slightest advantage over their opponents. From the floor of the hall I stated factual grounds on which we could all agree, and on which we could build a structure of new ideas. I chose my words carefully and was heard at first in silence, then a widespread

murmuring began that swelled into bursts of laughter. Next day an acquaintance told me, "I'm sorry we laughed McCandless, but to hear you steadily quoting Comte and Huxley and Haeckel in your broad Border dialect was like hearing the Queen opening Parliament in the voice of a Cockney costermonger."
While speaking I did not know what so greatly amused folk and glanced curiously over my clothing to see if it was unfastened. The laughter grew deafening. However, I finished what I had to say then walked out through an audience that not only guffawed but started to clap and stamp. As I reached the door a piercing sound brought me to a stop and struck silence into everyone else. Godwin Baxter was speaking from the gallery. In a shrill drawl (yet every word was distinct) he demonstrated how each of the platform speakers had used arguments that undermined all they aimed to prove. He ended by saying "—And those on the platform are the chosen few! The response to the last speaker's sensible argument shows the mental quality of the mass."
I said, "Thank you, Baxter," and left.

A fortnight later I was taking a Sunday stroll along the Cathkin Braes when I saw what seemed a two-year-old child with a tiny puppy approaching from the Cambuslang side. As it neared I recognized Baxter accompanied by a huge Newfoundland dog. We stopped to exchange a few words, found we enjoyed long tramps, and without discussing the matter turned sideways and descended to the river, returning to Glasgow by the quiet path on the Rutherglen bank. A day earlier we had been the only members of the medical faculty to attend a lecture by Clerk Maxwell, and both thought it odd that students who must one day diagnose diseases of the eye cared nothing for the physical nature of light. Godwin said, "Medicine is as much an art as a science, but our science should be as broadly based as possible. Clerk Maxwell and Sir William Thomson are discovering the living quick of what illuminates our brains and thrills along our nerves. The medical faculty overestimate morbid anatomy."

"But you spend days in the dissecting-room."
"I am refining on some of Sir Colin's techniques."
"Sir Colin?"
"My famous progenitor."
"Did you never call him father?"
"I never heard him called anything but Sir Colin. Morbid anatomy is essential to training and research, but leads many doctors into thinking that life is an agitation in something essentially dead. They treat patients' bodies as if the minds, the *lives* were of no account. The smooth bedside manner we cultivate is seldom more than a cheap anaesthetic to make our patients as passive as the corpses we train upon. But a portrait painter does not learn his art by scraping layers of varnish from a Rembrandt, then slicing off the impasto, dissolving the ground and finally separating the fibres of the canvas."
"I agree," said I, "that medicine is as much an art as a science. But surely we come to the art in our fourth year when we enter the hospitals?"
"Nonsense!" said Baxter abruptly. "The public hospitals are places where doctors learn how to get money off the rich by practising on the poor. That is why poor people dread and hate them, and why those with a good income are operated upon privately, or in their own homes. Sir Colin had nothing to do with hospitals. He operated in our town house in winter, our country house in summer. I often assisted him. He was a true artist—he boiled his instruments and sterilized his theatre when hospital boards were ignoring aseptic medicine or denouncing it as a fraud. No surgeons in the public eye dared admit that their filthy scalpels and blood-caked frock-coats had killed scores of patients a year, so went on using them. They drove poor Semmelweis mad, he committed suicide through trying to broadcast the truth. Sir Colin was more discreet than Semmelweis. He kept unorthodox discoveries to himself."
"Please remember," I told him, "that our hospitals have been improved since then."
"They have indeed—thanks to good nursing. Our nurses are now the truest practitioners of the healing art. If every

Scottish, Welsh and English doctor and surgeon dropped suddenly dead, eighty per cent of those admitted to our hospitals would recover if the nursing continued."
I remembered that Baxter was barred from hospital practice outside the poorest sort of charity clinic, which explained his bitterness toward the profession. However, before parting we arranged to go a walk on the following Sunday.

Our Sunday walks became a habit, though we still ignored each other in the dissecting-room, and avoided strolls through busy places. We both shrank from being stared at by others, and any companion of Baxter also became an object of curiosity. We were often quiet together as I could not help wincing sometimes at the sound of his voice. When this happened he would smile and fall silent. Half an hour might pass before I could prod him into saying more but I always did prod him. His voice was repulsive but his words highly interesting. One day I put plugs of cotton-wool in my ears before meeting him and found this let me listen with hardly any pain at all. I heard of his queer education on an autumn afternoon when we nearly lost our way in a network of small paths through the woods between Campsie and Torrance.

I had introduced the topic by speaking of my own childhood. Said he with a sigh, "I entered the world through Sir Colin's dealings with a nurse many years before Miss Nightingale made nursing the good part of British medicine. At that time a conscientious surgeon had to train his own nursing staff. Sir Colin trained one to be his anaesthetist, and worked so closely with her that they managed to produce me, before she died. I have no memory of her. There is nothing she owned in our houses. Sir Colin never spoke of her except once in my teens, when he said she was the cleverest, most teachable woman he knew. That must have attracted him, for he had no interest in female beauty. He had very little interest in *people*, except as surgical cases. As I was educated at home, and saw no other families, and never played with other children, I was twelve before I learned exactly what mothers do. I knew the difference between doctors and nurses, and thought mothers an inferior kind of nurse who specialized in small people. I thought I had never needed one because I was big from the start."

"But surely you read the *begat* chapter in Genesis?"

"No. Sir Colin taught me himself, you see, and only taught what interested him. He was a severe rationalist. Poetry, fiction, history, philosophy and the Bible struck him as nonsense—'unprovable blethers', he called them."

"What did he teach you?"

"Mathematics, anatomy and chemistry. Each morning and evening he recorded my temperature and pulse, took samples of my blood and urine, then analysed them. By the age of six I was doing these things for myself. Because of a chemical imbalance my system needs alternating doses of iodine and sugar. I have to monitor their effect with great exactness."

"But did you never ask him where you originally came from?"

"Yes, and he answered by bringing out diagrams, models, morbid specimens and giving me another lesson on how I was made. I enjoyed these lessons. They taught me to admire my internal organization. This preserved my self-respect when I learned how most people feel about my appearance."

"A sad childhood—worse than mine."

"I disagree. Nobody was cruel to me and I got all the animal warmth and affection I needed from Sir Colin's dogs. He always had several of them."

"I discovered procreation by watching cocks and hens. Did your father's dogs never pup?"

"They were dogs—not bitches. Sir Colin waited till my early teens before teaching me exactly how and why the female body differs from the male. As usual he taught me through diagrams, models and morbid specimens, but said he would arrange a practical experiment with a healthy, living specimen if curiosity inclined me that way. It did not."

"Forgive me asking, but—your father's dogs. Was he a vivisectionist?"

"Yes," said Baxter, and his cheek paled a little. I said, "Are you?"

He halted and confronted me with his mournful, huge, childish face which somehow made me feel like an even smaller child. His voice became so tiny and piercing that despite the cotton-wool plugs I feared damage to my eardrums. He said, "*I have never killed or hurt a living creature in my life, and neither did Sir Colin.*"

I told him, "I wish I could say that."

He stayed silent for the rest of the walk.

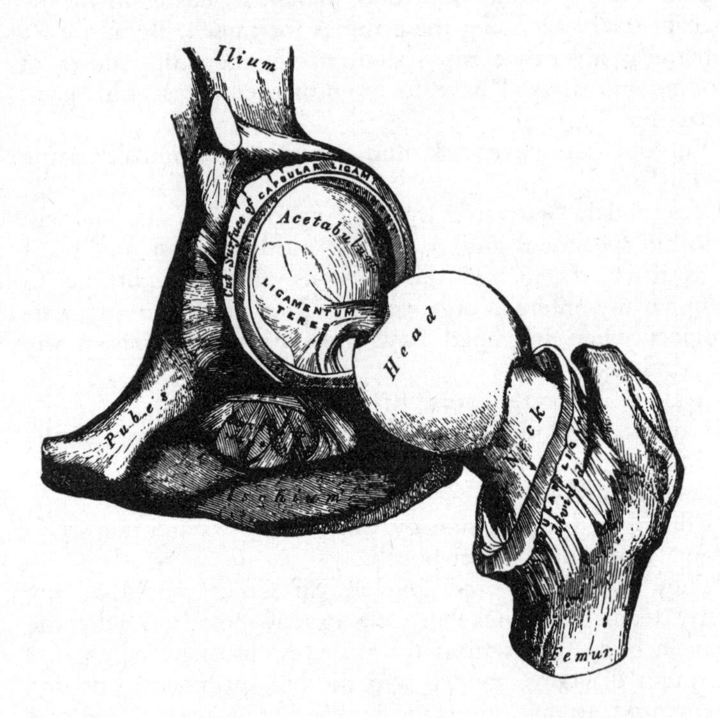

# 3

# The Quarrel

ONE DAY I ASKED HIM THE EXACT NATURE of his researches.

"I am refining Sir Colin's techniques."

"You told me that once before, Baxter, but it is not a satisfying answer. Why refine on out-of-date techniques? Your famous father was a great surgeon but medicine has advanced hugely since his death. In the past ten years we have discovered things he would have thought incredible — microbes and phagocytes, how to diagnose and remove brain tumours and repair ulcerous perforation."

"Sir Colin discovered something better than those."

"What?"

"Well," said Baxter, speaking slowly, as if against his will, "he discovered how to arrest a body's life without ending it, so that no messages passed along the nerves, the respiration, circulation and digestion were completely suspended, the cellular vitality was not impaired."

"Very interesting, Baxter. What use is it, medically speaking?"

"O, it has its uses!" he said, with a smile that greatly annoyed me.

"I hate mysteries Baxter!" I told him, "especially the man-made sort which are always a fraud. Do you know what most students in my year think of you? They think you a harmless insignificant madman, who dabbles with brains and microscopes in an effort to look important."

My poor friend stood still and gazed at me, obviously aghast. I stared stonily back. In a faltering voice he asked if I, too, thought he was that. I said, "If you don't answer my questions frankly, what else can I think?"
"Well," he said, sighing, "come home and I will show you something."
This pleased me. He had never invited me to his home before.

It was a tall, gloomy terrace house in Park Circus, and in the lobby he and his Newfoundland dog were noisily welcomed by two Saint Bernards, an Alsatian and an Afghan hound. He led me straight past them, down a stair to the basement and out into a narrow garden between high walls. Near the house was a paved part with a wooden doocot and pigeons, then came vegetable plots and a small lawn surrounded by a low fence. There were hutches on the lawn and some rabbits grazing. Baxter stepped over the fence and bade me do so too. The rabbits were perfectly tame. Baxter said, "Examine these two and tell me what you think."
He lifted and handed me one, cradling and gently stroking another on his sleeve until I examined it too.

The most obvious oddity in the first was the colour of the fur: pure black from nose to waist, pure white from waist to tail. Had a thread been tied round the body at the narrowest part all hairs on one side would have been black, all on the other side white. Now, in nature such straight separations only occur in crystals and basalt—the horizon of the sea on a clear day may look perfectly straight, but is actually curved. Yet by itself I would have assumed this rabbit was what any one else would assume—a natural freak. If so, the other rabbit was a freak of an exactly opposite sort: white to a waistline *as clean and distinct as if cut by the surgeon's knife*, after which it was black to the tail. No process of selective breeding could produce two such exactly equal and opposite colorations, so I examined them again with my fingertip, noticing that Baxter was watching me with the same cool, close, curious look I was giving his rabbits. One had male genitals with female nipples, one had female genitals with almost imperceptible nipples. Beneath the fur where it changed colour I felt on one body a barely perceptible ridge where the whole body shrank minutely but suddenly toward the tail, in the other was an equally minute ridge where it expanded. The little beasts were works of art, not nature. The one in my hands suddenly felt terribly precious. I set it carefully down on the grass and gazed at Baxter with awe, admiration and a kind of pity. It is hard not to pity those whose powers separate them from all the rest of us, unless (of course) they are rulers doing the usual sort of damage. I think there were tears in my eyes as I said, "How did you do it, Baxter?"

"I have done nothing wonderful," he said gloomily, putting the other rabbit down. "In fact I've done something rather shabby. Mopsy and Flopsy were two ordinary, happy little rabbits before I put them to sleep one day and they woke up like this. They are no longer interested in procreation, an activity they once greatly enjoyed. But tomorrow I will put them back together in exactly the way they were before."

"But Baxter, what can your hands *not* do if they can do this?"

"O, I could replace the diseased hearts of the rich with the healthy hearts of poorer folk, and make a lot of money. But I have all the money I need and it would be unkind to lead millionaires into such temptation."

"You make that sound like murder, Baxter, but the bodies in our dissecting-rooms have died by accident or natural disease. If you can use their undamaged organs and limbs to mend the bodies of others you will be a greater saviour than Pasteur and Lister—surgeons everywhere will turn a morbid science into immediate, living art!"

"If medical practitioners wanted to save lives," said Baxter, "instead of making money out of them, they would unite to prevent diseases, not work separately to cure them. The cause of most illness has been known since at least the sixth century before Christ, when the Greeks made a goddess of Hygiene. Sunlight, cleanliness and exercise, McCandless! Fresh air, pure water, a good diet and clean roomy houses for everyone, and a total government ban on all work which poisons and prevents these things."

"Impossible, Baxter. Britain has become the industrial workshop of the world. If social legislation arrests the profits of British industry our worldwide market will be collared by Germany and America and thousands would starve to death. Nearly a third of Britain's food is imported from abroad."

"Exactly! So until we lose our worldwide market British medicine will be employed to keep a charitable mask on the face of a heartless plutocracy. I keep that mask in place by voluntary work in my east-end clinic. It soothes my conscience. To transplant a simple abdomen would need an operation lasting thirty-three hours. Before I started I would spend at least a fortnight discovering and preparing a body compatible with my patient's. In that period several of my poor patients would die or suffer great pain through lack of conventional surgery."

"Then why spend time refining your father's techniques?"

"For a private reason I refuse to disclose to you, McCandless. I know this is not the frank answer of a friend, but I now see you were never my friend, but tolerated the company of a harmless, insignificant madman because other well-dressed students would not tolerate yours. But have no fear for the future, McCandless, you are a clever man! Not brilliant, perhaps, but steady and predictable, which people prefer. In a few years you will be an efficient house-surgeon. All you hunger for will be obtained: wealth, respect, companions and a fashionable wife. I will continue to seek affection by following a lonelier road."

While speaking we had re-entered the house and climbed again to the dim lobby where the five dogs sprawled upon Persian rugs. Sensing their master's hostility they erected their necks and ears and pointed their noses at me, then

grew as still as dog-faced sphinxes. In the stairwell above I sensed rather than glimpsed a head in a white cap staring down over the banisters of a landing, perhaps an ancient housekeeper or maidservant.
"Baxter!" I whispered urgently, "I was daft to say these things. I promise I did not mean to hurt you."
"I disagree. You did mean to hurt me, and have done so more than you intended. Good-bye."
He opened the front door for me. I grew desperate. I said, "Godwin, since you have no time to publicize your father's discoveries and your refinements on them, lend the notes to me! I'll make it my life's work to publicize them. I'll attribute *everything* to you — *everything*, without ever trespassing on your valuable time. And when the public outcry comes — for there will be huge controversy — I will defend you, I will be your bulldog just as Huxley was Darwin's bulldog! McCandless will be Baxter's bulldog!"
"Good-bye, McCandless," he said inflexibly, and the dogs were growling, so I let him usher me onto the doorstep where I pled, "At *least* let me shake your hand, Godwin!"
"Why not?" he said, and held one out.

We had never shaken hands before nor had I looked closely at his, perhaps because in company he kept them half-hidden by his cuffs. The hand I intended to grasp was not so much square as cubical, nearly as thick as broad, with huge thick first knuckles from which the fingers tapered so steeply to babyish tips with rosy wee nails that they seemed conical. A cold grue went through me — I was unable to touch such a hand. I shook my head wordlessly at him, and he suddenly smiled as he had done in earlier days when I winced at the sound of his voice.

He also shrugged his shoulders
and shut me out.

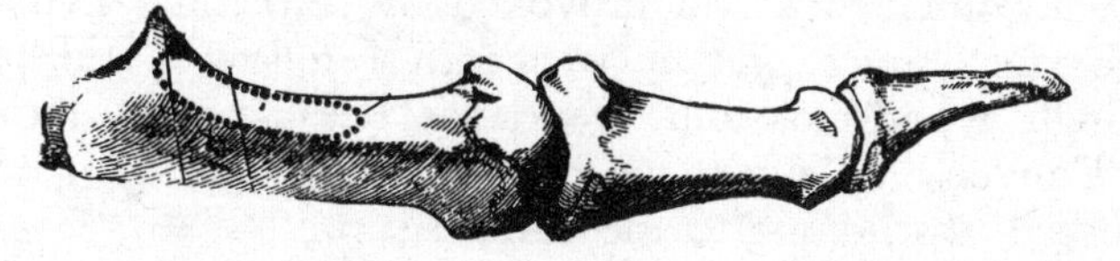

# 4

# A Fascinating Stranger

THEN CAME THE LONELIEST MONTHS I have known. Baxter no longer came to the University. The bench was removed from his old workspace, which became a cupboard again. I strolled round Park Circus at least once a fortnight, but saw nobody enter or leave his front door, and I lacked courage to climb the steps and knock. Yet clean unshuttered windows showed the house was occupied, and I should have realized that when not with a visitor he would prefer to use the servants' entrance through the back garden. My longing for his company was not mercenary, for I no longer thought him a scientific miracle-worker. My studies showed we could not even graft the forepart of a worm or caterpillar to the hindpart of another. This was twenty years before Jannsky identified the main blood groups, so we could not even transfuse blood. I classified my experience of the rabbits as a hallucination based on a natural coincidence and provoked by something hypnotic in Baxter's voice, yet at weekends I followed old paths through woodlands and moorlands because they recalled our conversation when we walked them together. And of course, I was hoping to meet him again.

One cold bright Saturday when winter was becoming spring I walked up Sauchiehall Street and heard what at first seemed an iron-shod carriage wheel scraping a kerbstone. A moment later I recognized a familiar voice saying, "Bulldog McCandless! How is my bulldog this weather?"

"A lot better for hearing the sound of your ugly voice, Baxter," said I. "Have you never thought of getting a new larynx? The vocal chords of a sheep would twang more melodiously than yours."

He walked beside me at the usual stumping trudge which carried him as fast as my own swift stride. A walking-stick was clenched under his arm like an officer's baton, he wore a curly-brimmed topper on the back of his head, his chin was held high and an exuberant smile showed he now cared nothing for the glances of other pedestrians. With a pang of envy I said, "You look happy, Baxter."

"Yes, McCandless! I now enjoy more flattering company than you ever provided—a fine, fine woman, McCandless, who owes her life to these fingers of mine—these skeely, skeely fingers!"

He wagged them in the air before him as if playing a keyboard. I was jealous. I said, "What did you cure her of?"

"Death."

"You mean that you *saved* her from death."

"Partly, yes, but the greatest part is a skilfully manipulated resurrection."

"You don't make sense, Baxter."

"Then come and meet her—I would welcome a second opinion. Physically she is perfect but her mind is still forming, yes, her mind has wonderful discoveries to make. She knows only what she learned in the last ten weeks, but you will find her more interesting than Mopsy and Flopsy put together."

"So your patient is amnesic?"

"That is what I tell people but don't you believe me! Judge for yourself."

And the only other words he said before we reached Park

Circus were, that his patient was called Bell, short for Bella, and lived in a great clutter because he wanted her to enjoy seeing, hearing and handling as many things as possible.

As Baxter unlocked his front door I thought I heard a piano playing *The Bonnie Banks o' Loch Lomond* so loud and fast that the tune was wildly cheerful. He led me into a drawing-room where I saw the music being made by a woman seated at a pianola. Her back was toward us. Curly black hair hid her body to the waist, her legs pumped the treadles turning the cylinder with a vigour that showed she enjoyed exercise as much as music. She flapped her arms sideways like a seagull's wings, regardless of the beat. She was so engrossed that she did not notice us. I had time to study the room.

It had tall windows overlooking the Circus, a bright fire under a marble mantelpiece. The big dogs lay somnolent on a hearth-rug, their chins cushioned on each other's flanks. Three cats sat as far apart as possible on the backs of the highest chairs, each pretending not to see the rest but all twitching if one of them moved. Through an open double door I saw a room overlooking the back garden, and by the fire in this room a placid elderly lady sat knitting, a small boy played with toy bricks at her feet, two rabbits sipped milk from a saucer. Baxter murmured that the lady was his housekeeper, the boy her grandson. One rabbit was pure black, the other pure white, but I decided to draw no fantastic conclusion from this. What made the place strange was a multitude of things on the carpets, tables, sideboards and seats: a tripod upholding a telescope, a lantern-slide projector aimed at a standing screen, celestial and terrestrial globes each a yard in diameter, a half-put-together jigsaw puzzle showing the British Islands, a fully furnished doll's house with the front open exposing everybody from a thin maidservant in the attic bedroom to a fat cook rolling pastry in the basement kitchen, a toy farm with hundreds of accurately carved and painted animals, a brilliant flock of real stuffed humming-birds wired to a silver stand shaped like a bush with leaves and fruit of coloured glass, a xylophone, harp, kettledrums, an erect human skeleton and glass jars holding pickled limbs and bodily organs. These specimens probably came from old Sir Colin's collection, but their brown morbidity was contradicted by surrounding vases of daffodils, pots of hyacinths and a great crystal bowl in which tiny, jewel-like tropical fish darted and large golden ones glided. Many books were propped open at vivid illustrations. I noticed a Madonna and Child, Burns Stooping to a Field Mouse, The *Fighting Téméraire* Towed to Her Last Berth and Kobolds Discovering the Skeleton of Ichthyosaurus in a Cavern under the Harz Mountains.

The music stopped. The woman stood and faced us, stepping unsteadily forward then pausing as if to keep balance. Her tall, beautiful, full-bodied figure seemed between twenty and thirty years, her facial expression looked far, far less. She gazed with the wide-open eyes and mouth which suggest alarm in an adult but in her suggested pure alert delight with an expectation of more. She wore a black velvet gown with narrow lace collar and cuffs. She spoke carefully, with a north of England accent, and each syllable was as sweet and distinct as if piped on a flute: "Hell low God win, hell low new man."
Then she flung both arms out straight toward me and kept them there.
"Give only one hand to new men, Bell," said Baxter kindly. She dropped her left hand to her side without otherwise moving or altering her bright expectant smile. Nobody had looked at me like that before. I grew confused as the offered hand was too high for me to shake in the conventional way. I surprised myself by stepping forward, rising on tiptoe, taking Bell's fingers in mine and kissing them. She gasped and a moment later slowly withdrew her hand and looked at it, rubbing the fingers gently with her thumb as if testing something my lips had left there. She also cast several astonished but happy little glances at my fascinated face, while Baxter beamed proudly on both of us

like a clergyman introducing two children at a Sunday-school picnic. He said, "This is Mr. McCandless, Bell."
"Hell low Miss terr Candle," she said, "new wee man with carrot tea red hair, inter *rested* face, blue neck tie, crump pled coat waist coat trou sirs made of brown. Cord. Dew. Ray?"
"Corduroy my dear," said Baxter, smiling as joyfully on her as she on me.
"Cord dew roy, a *ribbed* fab brick wove ven from cot ton Miss terr Make Candle."
"Mac Cand *less*, dear Bell."
"But dear Bell has no candle so dear Bell is candle-less too, God win. Please be Bell's new Candle you new wee candle maker."
"You reason *beautifully*, Bell," said Baxter, "but have still to learn that most names are not reasonable. O Mrs. Dinwiddie! Take Bell and your grandson down to the kitchen and give them lemonade and a doughnut sprinkled with sugar. McCandless and I will be in the study."

As we climbed the stairs Baxter said eagerly, "So what do you think of our Bella?"
"A bad case of brain damage, Baxter. Only idiots and infants talk like that, are capable of such radiant happiness, such frank glee and friendship on meeting someone new. It is dreadful to see these things in a lovely young woman. She only looked thoughtful once, when your housekeeper led her away from me—from us, I meant to say."
"You noticed that? But it is a sign of maturity. You are wrong about the brain damage. Her mental powers are growing at enormous speed. Six months ago she had the brain of a baby."
"What reduced her to that state?"
"Nothing reduced her to it, she has risen from it. It was a perfectly healthy little brain."
His voice must have had hypnotic qualities for I suddenly knew what he meant and believed him. I stood still and clutched the banister feeling very sick. I heard my voice stammer a question about where he got the other bits.

"That is what I want to tell you, McCandless!" he cried, putting an arm round my shoulder and lifting me easily up the stairs with him. "You are the only one in the world I can talk to about this."

As my feet left the carpet I thought I was in the grip of a monster and started kicking. I also tried to yell but he put a hand over my mouth, carried me to a bathroom, held my head under a cold shower, carried me to his study, placed me on a sofa and gave me a towel. I grew calmer while using it, but nearly panicked again when he handed me a tumbler of grey slime. He said it was concocted from fruit and vegetables, that it strengthened the nerves, muscles and blood without over-stimulating them, that he drank nothing else. I refused it, so he hunted in cupboards under a lot of glass-fronted bookcases until he found a decanter of port nobody had tasted since his father died. As I sipped the dark ruby syrup I suddenly felt that Baxter, his household, Miss Bell, yes and me, and Glasgow, and rural Galloway, and all Scotland were equally unlikely and absurd. I started laughing. Mistaking my hysteria for a return to common sense he gave a sigh of relief that sounded like a steam whistle in the room next door. I winced. He produced cotton wool from a drawer. I plugged my ears with it.

He told me the following story.

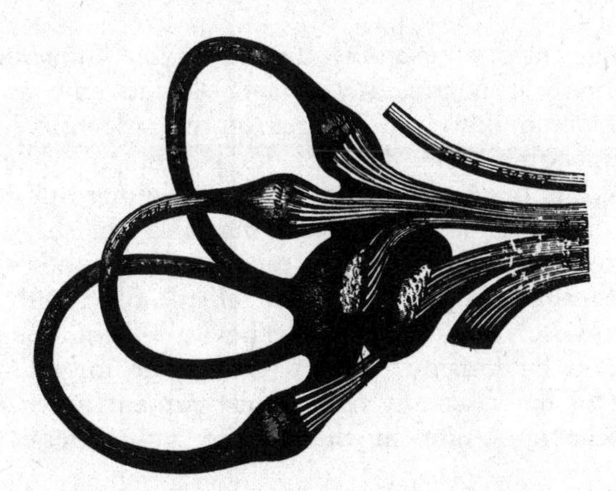

# 5

# Making Bella Baxter

"GEORDIE GEDDES WORKS FOR GLASGOW Humane Society, who give him a rent-free house on Glasgow Green. His job is to fish human bodies out of the Clyde and save their lives, if possible. When not possible he puts them in a small morgue attached to his dwelling, where a police surgeon performs autopsies. If this official is not available they send for me. Most of the bodies are suicides, of course, and if no one claims them they are transferred to dissecting-rooms and laboratories. I have arranged such transfers.

"I was called to examine the body you know as Bella soon after our quarrel a year ago. Geddes saw a young woman climb onto the parapet of the suspension bridge near his home. She did not jump feet first like most suicides. She dived clean under like a swimmer but *expelling* the air from her lungs, not drawing it in, for she did not return to the surface alive. On recovering the body Geddes found she had tied the strap of a reticule filled with stones to her wrist. An unusually deliberate suicide then, and committed by someone who wished to be forgotten. The pockets of her discreetly fashionable garments were empty, with neat holes cut in the linings and lingerie where women of the wealthier class have their names or initials stitched. Rigor had not set in, the body had hardly cooled before I arrived. I found she was pregnant, with pressure grooves round the finger where wedding and engagement rings had been removed. What does that suggest to you, McCandless?"

"Either she was carrying the child of a husband she hated or the child of a lover she had preferred to her husband, a lover who abandoned her."

"I thought so too. I cleared her lungs of water, her womb of the foetus, and by a subtle use of electrical stimulus could have brought her back to self-conscious life. I dared not. You will know why if you see Bella asleep. Bella's face in repose is that of the ardent, wise, sorrowful woman who lay before me on the mortuary slab. I knew nothing about the life she had abandoned, except that she hated it so much that she had chosen *not to be*, and forever! What would she feel on being dragged from her carefully chosen blank eternity and forced *to be* in one of our thick-walled, understaffed, poorly equipped madhouses, reformatories or jails? For in this Christian nation suicide is treated as lunacy or crime. So I kept the body alive at a purely cellular level. It was advertised. Nobody claimed it. I brought it here to my father's laboratory. My childhood hopes, and boyhood dreams, my education and adult researches had prepared me for this moment.

"Every year hundreds of young women drown themselves because of the poverty and prejudices of our damnably unfair society. And nature too can be ungenerous. You know how often it produces births we call *unnatural* because they cannot live without artificial help or cannot live at all: anacephalids, bicephalids, cyclops, and some so unique science does not name them. Good doctoring ensures the mothers never see these. Some malformations are less grotesque but equally dreadful—babies without digestive tracts who must starve to death as soon as the umbilical cord is cut if a kind hand does not first smother them. No doctor dare do such a thing, or order a nurse to do it, but the thing gets done, and in modern Glasgow—second city of Britain for size and foremost for infant mortality—few parents can afford a coffin, a funeral and a grave for every dead wee body they own. Even Catholics consign their unchristened to limbo. In the Workshop of the World limbo is usually the medical profession. For years I had been planning to take a discarded body and discarded brain from our social midden heap and unite them in a new life. I now did so, hence Bella."

Like most who listen closely to a tale told in a calm manner I too had grown calm, which helped me think sensibly again.

"Bravo, Baxter!" I cried, raising my glass as if toasting him. "How do you explain her dialect? Is there Yorkshire blood in her veins or do the parents of *her brain* come from northern England?"

"Only one explanation is possible," said Baxter broodingly. "The earliest habits we learn (and speech is one of them) must become instinct through the nerves and muscles of the whole body. We know instincts are not wholly seated in the brain, since a headless chicken can run for yards before it drops. The muscles of Bella's throat, tongue and lips still move as they did in the first twenty-five years of their existence, which I think was nearer Manchester than Leeds. But all the words she uses have been learned from me, or from the elderly Scotswomen who run my household, or from children who play with her here."

"How do you explain Bella's presence to them, Baxter? Or are you such a domestic tyrant that your underlings dare not ask for explanations?"

Baxter hesitated, then muttered that his servants were all former nurses trained by Sir Colin, and not surprised by the presence of strange people recovering from intricate operations.

"But how do you explain her to *society*, Baxter? Are your neighbours in the Circus—the parents of those who play with her—the policeman on the beat—are *they* told she is a surgical fabrication? How will you account for her on the next government census?"

"They are told she is Bella Baxter, a distant niece whose parents died in a South American railway accident, a disaster where she sustained a concussion causing total amnesia. I have dressed in mourning to support this story. It is a good one. Sir Colin had a cousin he quarrelled with many years ago, who went out to the Argentine before the potato famine and was never heard of again. He could easily have married the daughter of English emigrés in a racial hodge-podge like the Argentine. And luckily Bella's complexion (though different before I arrested her cellular decay) is now as sallow as my own, which can pass as a family trait. This is the story Bella will be told when she learns that most people have parents and wants a couple of them for herself. An extinct, respectable couple will be better than none. It would cast a shadow upon her life to learn she is a surgical fabrication. Only you and I know the truth, and I doubt if you believe it."

"Frankly, Baxter, the story of the railway accident is more convincing."

"Believe what you like, McCandless, but please go easy on the port."

I refused to go easy on the port. I deliberately filled the glass a second time while saying with equal deliberation, "So you think Miss Baxter's brain will one day be as adult as her body."

"Yes, and quickly. Judging by her speech how old would you say she is?"

"She blethered like a five-year-old."

"I judge her mental age by the age of children she can play with. Robbie Murdoch, my housekeeper's grandchild, is not quite two. They crawled around the floor very happily till five weeks ago, then she began to find him boring and developed a passionate admiration for a niece of my cook. This niece is a bright six-year-old who, after Bella's novelty wore off, finds *her* very boring. I think Bella's mental age is nearly four, and if I am right then her body has stimulated the growth of her brain at a wonderful rate. This will cause problems. You did not notice it, McCandless, but you attracted Bella. You are the first adult male she has met apart from me, and I saw her sense it through the finger tips. Her response showed that her body was recalling carnal sensations from its earlier life, and the sensations excited her brain into new thoughts and word forms. She asked you to be her candle and candle maker. A bawdy construction could be put on that."

"Havers!" I cried, appalled. "How dare you talk of your lovely niece in that monstrous way. Had you played with other bairns when you were young you would know such talk is commonplace childhood prattle. Come-a-riddle come-a-riddle come-a-rote-tote-tote, a wee wee man in a wee wee boat. Willie Winkie runs through the toon in his night goon. I had a little husband no bigger than my thumb. Little Jack Horner stuck his in a plum. But how will you educate Miss Baxter if she outgrows this pleasant state?"

"Not by sending her to school," he said firmly. "I will not let people treat her as an oddity. I will shortly take her on a carefully planned journey round the world, staying longest in the places she enjoys. In this way she will see and learn many things by talking to folk who will not find her much queerer than most British travellers, and charmingly natural when compared with her gross companion. It will also let me remove her quickly from attachments which look like becoming romantic in an unhygienic way."

"And of course, Baxter," I told him recklessly, "she will be wholly at your mercy with no public opinion to protect her, not even through the frail agency of your domestic servants. When we last met, Baxter, you boasted in the heat of a quarrel that you were devising a secret method of getting a woman all to yourself, and now I know what your secret is—abduction! You think you are about to possess what men have hopelessly yearned for throughout the ages: the soul of an innocent, trusting, dependent child inside the opulent body of a radiantly lovely woman. I will not allow it, Baxter. You are the rich heir of a mighty nobleman, I am the bastard bairn of a poor peasant, but between the wretched of the earth there is a stronger bond than the rich realize. Whether Bella Baxter be your orphaned niece or twice orphaned fabrication, *I* am more truly akin to her than you can ever be, and I will preserve her honour to the last drop of blood in my veins as sure as there is a God in Heaven, Baxter!—a God of Eternal Pity and Vengeance before whom the mightiest emperor on earth is feebler than a falling sparrow."

Baxter replied by carrying the decanter back to the cupboard where he had found it and locking the door.

I cooled down while he did this, remembering I had stopped believing in God, Heaven, Eternal Pity et cetera after reading *The Origin of Species*. It still seems weird to recall that after unexpectedly meeting my only friend, future wife and first decanter of port I raved in the language of novels I knew to be trash, and only read to relax my brain before sleeping.

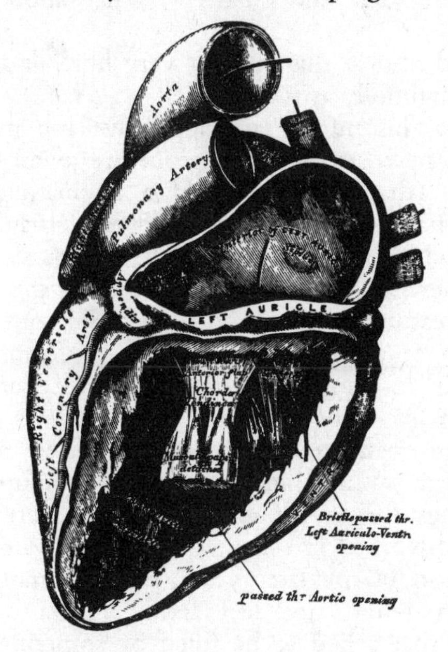

# 6

# Baxter's Dream

BAXTER RETURNED, SAT DOWN AND LOOKED at me with his lips compressed and his eyebrows raised. Maybe I blushed. Certainly my face felt hot. He said patiently, "Use your memory, McCandless. I am an ugly fellow but have you known me do an ugly thing?"

I pondered then said sulkily, "What about Mopsy and Flopsy?"

He looked hurt at this but not very hurt, and after a while spoke thoughtfully as if to himself.

"Sir Colin, his nurses and dogs gave me more attention than most newcomers to this globe are given, but I wanted more than that. I dreamed of a fascinating stranger—a woman I had not yet met so could only imagine—a friend who would need and admire me as much as I needed and admired her. No doubt a mother supplies this want in most young creatures, though rich families often employ a servant to take the mother's place. I formed no special attachment to those who fostered me, perhaps because there were so many of them. I was always a mighty big fellow and seem to recall at least three mature nurses feeding and washing and clothing me before I could do these things for myself. Perhaps there were more, for I think they worked in relays. I may be imposing on infancy an obsession of my later years, but I cannot remember a day when I did not feel inside me a woman-shaped emptiness that ached to be filled by someone stranger and bonnier than I ever met at home. This ache grew stronger with puberty, which happened with catastrophic suddenness. My voice, alas, did not break, and remains mezzo-soprano to the present day, but I woke one morning with the enlarged penis and heavy testes which afflict most of our sex."

"And then, as you told me before, your father explained how female anatomies differed from yours and offered to provide you with a healthy specimen in full working order. You should have jumped at the chance."

"Did you not hear me, McCandless? Must I say everything twice? *I needed to admire a woman who needed and admired me.* Will I say it anatomically? Spermatic ejaculation can only induce homoeostasis in me if accompanied by prolonged stimulation of higher nerve centres whose pressure upon the ductless glands changes the chemistry of my blood not for a few spasmodic minutes but for many tingling days. The woman I imagined stimulated me like that. I found her picture in Lamb's *Tales from Shakespeare*: a book that must have been left here by one of Sir Colin's patients—it was the only work of fiction in the house. Ophelia was listening to her brother, an insipid looking lad despite his fierce little beard. He was saying something she was only pretending to take seriously, for her eager face looked toward something wonderful outside the picture, and I wanted it to be me. Her expression excited me more than her lovely body in a flowing violet gown, because I thought I knew all about bodies. Her expression excited me more than her lovely face, for I had seen women with such faces in the park—when they walked toward me their faces froze, grew pale or bright pink and tried not to see me at all. Ophelia could look at me with loving wonder because she saw the inner man I would become—the kindest, greatest doctor in the world who would save her life and the life of millions. I read the miserable story of the play in which she was the one true loving soul. It obviously described the spread of an epidemic brain fever which, like typhoid, was perhaps caused by seepings from the palace graveyard into the Elsinore water supply. From an inconspicuous start among sentries on the battlements the infection spread through prince, king, prime minister and courtiers causing hallucinations, logomania and paranoia resulting in insane suspicions and murderous impulses. I imagined myself entering the palace quite early in the drama with all the executive powers of an efficient public health officer. The main carriers of the disease (Claudius, Polonius and the obviously incurable Hamlet) would be quarantined in separate wards. A fresh water supply and efficient modern plumbing would soon set the Danish state right and Ophelia, seeing this gruff Scottish doctor pointing her people toward a clean and healthy future, would be powerless to withhold her love.

"Daydreams like these, McCandless, accelerated my heart and changed the texture of my skin for hours on end when I was not busy with my studies. A prostitute procured for me by Sir Colin would have been a contrivance of his, a clockwork doll driven by money instead of a spring."

"But a warm living body, Baxter."

"I needed to see that expression."

"In the dark—" I began to say, but he bade me shut up. I sat feeling more of a monster than he was.

After a while he sighed and said, "My daydream of becoming a kindly popular beloved healer proved impossible. I was the most brilliant medical student the University has known—how could I not be? As Sir Colin's most trusted helper I knew by practice what many lecturers taught as theory. But in Sir Colin's operating-theatre the only patients I touched were anaesthetized. Look at this hand, although of course the sight pains you, this cube with five cones protruding from the top, instead of a kipper with five sausages stuck to the edge. The only patients I am allowed to touch are too poor or unconscious to have a choice in the matter. Several well-known surgeons like my assistance when operating on celebrities whose deaths would damage their reputations, for my ugly digits and (to tell the truth) my ugly head are better than theirs in an emergency. But the patients never see me, so that was no way to win the admiring smile of an Ophelia. But I have nothing to complain about now. Bella's smile is happier than Ophelia's was, and makes me happy too."

"So Miss Baxter does not dread your hand?"

"No. From the moment she opened her eyes here these hands have served her food, drink and sweetmeats, placed flowers before her, offered toys, shown how to use them, displayed the bright pages of her picture-books. At first I made the servants who washed and dressed her wear black woollen mittens in her presence, but I soon saw this was pointless. The fact that others have different hands does not stop her thinking me and my hands as normal and necessary as this house and our daily meals and the morning sunlight. But you are a stranger, McCandless, so your hands thrill her. Mine do not."

"You hope this will change, of course."

"Yes. O yes. But I am not impatient. Only bad guardians and parents expect admiration from young brains. I am glad Bella takes me as much for granted as the floor under her: that floor on which she enjoys the music of the pianola, yearns for the company of the cook's grand-niece, and thrills to the touch of your hand, McCandless."

"May I see her again soon?"

"How soon?"

"Now . . . or this evening . . . at any rate, before you leave on your trip round the world."

"No, McCandless, you must wait till we return. Your effect on Bella does not worry me. Her effect on you does, at present."

He ushered me to the front door as firmly as the last time I visited him, but before shutting me out he patted me kindly on the shoulder. I did not flinch from the contact but said suddenly, "One moment, Baxter! That lady you spoke of who drowned herself—how advanced was her pregnancy?"

"At least nine months."

"Could you not have saved the child?"

"Of course I saved it—the thinking part of it. Did I not explain that? Why should I seek elsewhere for a compatible brain when her body already housed one?
But you need not believe this
if it disturbs you."

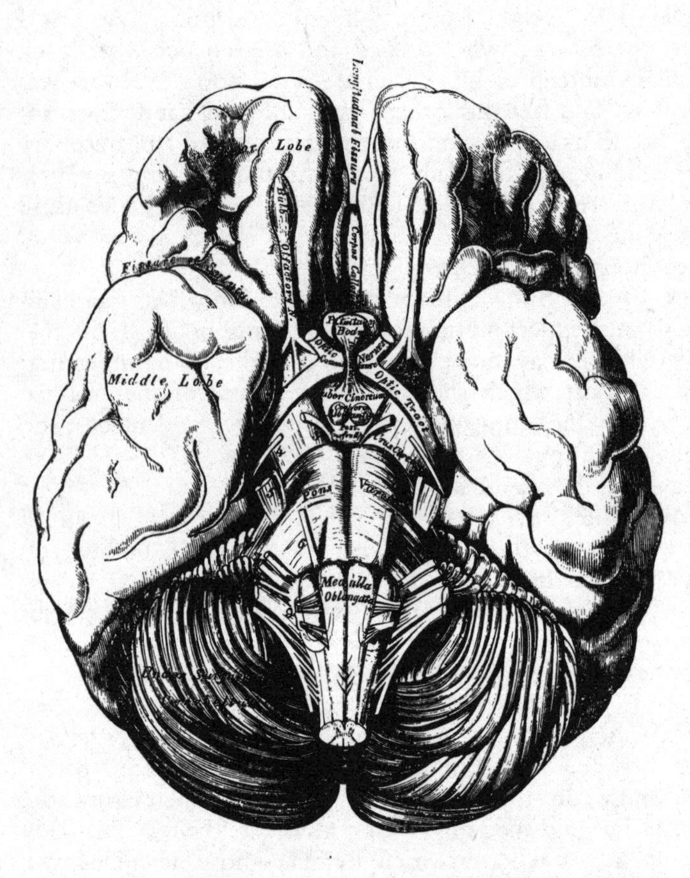

# 7

# By the Fountain

FIFTEEN MONTHS PASSED BEFORE I MET HER again and they were unexpectedly happy. Scraffles died and astonished me by leaving me a quarter of his money—his widow and legitimate son divided the rest. I became a house-doctor in the Royal Infirmary with a wardful of patients who seemed to need me and some who pretended to admire. I hid how much I needed them under a smooth, lordly surface broken by unexpected flashes of genial humour. I flirted with the nurses under me to the usual extent—that is, with all of them equally. I was invited to smoking-concerts where everyone had to sing something. My songs in the Galloway dialect were laughed at when comic and applauded when pathetic. I mostly thought of Bella during unoccupied moments, especially in the half hour before going to bed and falling asleep. I was trying to read through the novels of Bulwer-Lytton at the time, but his characters seemed conventional puppets when I recalled her arms flapping above the pianola like ravens' wings, her smile of continual delight, her jerky walk and swaying stance and arms outstretched as if to embrace me as nobody else had done. I did not dream of her because I never dream at all, but when we next met I believed for almost a minute that I was in bed dreaming although I was wide awake in a public park.

A fortnight of hot calm cloudless summer weather had

made Glasgow detestable. With no rain to wash it down or breeze to blow it away the industrial smoke and gases hung in a haze filling the valley to the height of the surrounding hills, a gritty haze that put a grey film on everything, even the sky, and prickled under the eyelids, and made crusts in the nostrils. The air seemed cleaner indoors, but one evening a need of exercise took me walking beside a dull stretch of the Kelvin. At one point it fell over a weir which churned effluent from the upstream paper-mill into heaps of filthy green froth, each the size and shape of a lady's bonnet and divided from its neighbour by a crevice floored with opaque scum. This substance (which looked and stank like the contents of a chemical retort) flowed through the West End Park completely hiding the river under it. I imagined the mixture when it entered the oil-fouled Clyde between Partick and Govan, and wondered if men were the only land beasts who excreted into water. Wishing to think pleasanter thoughts I strolled to the Loch Katrine memorial fountain whose up-flung and downward trickling jets gave some freshness to the air. Well-dressed people and their children paraded round it and I moved among them staring at the ground as I usually do in crowds. I tried to remember the colour of Bella's eyes but was remembering how her syllables sounded like pearls dropping one by one into a dish when she said, "Candle, where are your cord dew *roys*?"

She shone before me like a rainbow's end but solid, tall, elegant, leaning on Baxter's arm and wistfully smiling. Her eyes were golden brown, her dress crimson silk with a jacket of sky-blue velvet. She wore a purple toque, snow-white gloves and the fingers of her left hand twirled the amber knob of a parasol whose slim shaft, slanting over her shoulders, spun a buttercup-yellow silk dome with a grass-green fringe behind her head. With these colours her black hair and eyebrows, sallow skin and bright golden-brown eyes seemed dazzlingly foreign and right, but if she seemed a glorious dream Baxter loomed beside her like a nightmare. When apart from Baxter my memory always reduced his monstrous bulk and shaggy boyish head to something

W.S.
BELLA CALEDONIA

more probable, so even after a week the unexpected sight of him was shocking. I had not seen him for seventy weeks. He was muffled in the thick cape and overcoat he wore outdoors in every sort of weather, because his body lost heat faster than most people's, but his face shocked me most. It usually looked unhappy, but now his aghast eyes seemed to reflect an absence of something as essential as sanity or oxygen, an absence that was slowly killing him. There was nothing hostile in this settled gloom—he gave me a nod of dreary recognition—yet it menaced me because for a moment I feared that what he ached for and needed could not be mine either, though Bella was now smiling at me as eagerly and expectantly as in her younger days. She had taken her right hand from under Baxter's arm and was holding it straight out to me. Again I rose on tiptoe to take her fingers and touch them with my lips.

"Haha!" she laughed, thrusting the hand above her head as if grasping a butterfly. "He is still my little Candle, God! You were the first man I ever loved after wee Robbie Murdoch, Candle, and now I me Bell Miss Baxter citizen of Glasgow native of Scotland subject of the British Empire have been made a woman of the world! French German Italian Spanish African Asian American men and some women of the north *and* the south kinds have kissed this hand and other parts but I still dream of the first time though oceans deep between have roared since auld lang syne. Sit on that bench, God. I am taking Candle for a walk saunter stroll dawdle trot canter short gallop and circum-ambu-*lation*. Poor old God. Without Bella you will grow glum glummer glummest until just when you think I am for ever lost crash bang wallop, out I pop from behind that holly bush. Guard him, lads."

She and Baxter were accompanied by five children whose big boots and coarse clothes showed they belonged to the servant or artisan class. If small companions were still a clue to Bella's brain then her mental age was now between twelve and thirteen. Baxter, with no change of expression, slumped obediently into a space on a crowded bench. From one side of him an army officer hurriedly departed, from the other a nursemaid with a baby that had started to scream. Two of the boys took their places. The rest stood in a row before him, facing outward with legs astride and folded arms. "Good!" said Bella approvingly. "If anyone stares at God stare back until they stop. This will keep you going while I am away."

From a poke in her pocket she gave each child a large sweet of the kind called gobstoppers, then drew my hand under her arm and hurried me off past the duck pond.

Bella's firm and talkative manner made me expect a torrent of words, not what happened. She strode forward glancing from side to side until she saw a narrow path through a shrubbery and steered me abruptly up it. At a bend in the path she stopped, snapped shut her parasol, hurled it like a spear into a thick rhododendron bush and dragged me in after it. I was too surprised to resist. When the leaves were higher than our heads she released me and unbuttoned her right hand glove, smiling and licking her lips and muttering "Now then!"

Stripping off the glove she clapped her naked palm over my mouth while flinging her left arm round my neck. The edge of the palm blocked my nostrils and though still too astonished to struggle I was soon gasping for breath. So was she. Her eyes were shut, she wrenched her head from side to side moaning through flushed and pouting lips, "A Candle oh Candle the Candle of Candle to Candle by Candle from Candle I Candle you Candle we Candle . . ."

From feeling as helpless as a doll I suddenly wished to be nothing else, her pressure on my mouth and neck became terribly sweet, I began struggling not against suffocation but against a delight too great to be borne. A moment later I was free again, dazed and watching her pick the glove from the branch where it hung and pull it on again.

"Do you know, Candle," she murmured after some deeply contented sighs, "I haven't had a chance to do that since I got off the ship from America a fortnight ago?

Baxter has not left me alone with anyone except him. Did you enjoy what we did?"
I nodded. She said slyly, "You didn't enjoy it as much as I did. You would not have pulled away so soon and would have acted more daft. But men seem better at acting daft when they're miserable."
She retrieved her parasol and cheerfully waved it to some starers on a terrace of the hillside above. I was depressed to see we had been overlooked, but relieved to realize the watchers must first have thought she was trying to strangle me then decided she was coping with a bleeding nose.

When we regained the path she brushed twigs, leaves and petals off our clothing, drew my hand under her arm again and walked onward saying, "What will we talk about?"
I was too bemused to answer till she had repeated the question.
"Miss Baxter—Bella—oh dear Bell have you done that with many men?"
"Yes, all over the world, but mostly in the Pacific. On the boat out of Nagasaki I met two petty officers—they were devoted to each other—and I sometimes did it six times a day with each of them."
"Did you . . . do anything *more* with other men, Bella, than you and me did together in the shrubbery just now?"
"You rude little Candle! You sound as miserable as God!" said Bella, laughing heartily. "Of course I never do more than we've just done with MEN. More with men makes babies. I want fun, not babies. I only do more with women, if I like the look of them, but a lot of women are shy. Miss MacTavish ran away from me in San Francisco because doing more than kissing hands and faces frightened her. I'm glad we can talk straight about these things, Candle. A lot of men are shy too."
I told her I was not afraid of straight talking because I was a qualified doctor who had grown up on a farm. I also asked about Miss MacTavish.
"She was the main part of our cortège retinue ong-to-rage suite train trail or body of retainers when we left Glasgow.

She was my teacher escort governess companion instructor chaperon pedagogue duenna guide philosopher and friend until San Francisco. She taught me a lot of words and poetry before the final fracture. You grew up on a farm! Was your dad a frugal swain tending his flocks on the Grampian hills or a ploughman homeward plodding his weary way? Tell tell tell your Bell Bell Bell. I am a collector of childhoods since that collision destroyed all memory of my own."

I told her about my parents. When she heard I could not recall where my mother was buried she smiled and nodded though tears started flowing down her cheeks.

"Me too!" she said. "In Buenos Aires we tried to visit my parents' grave, but Baxter found the railway company that paid for the interment had put them in a graveyard on the edge of a bottomless canyon, so when Chimborazo or Cotopaxi or Popocatapetl erupted the whole shebang collapsed in an avalanche to the bottom crushing headstones coffins skeletons to a powder of in-fin-it-es-im-al atoms. Seeing them in that state would have been like visiting a heap of caster sugar, so instead Baxter took me to the house where he said I had lived with them. It had a dusty courtyard with a cracked water tank in a corner and some chickens pecking about and an old caretaker janitor gatekeeper porter concierge (stop tinkling Bell) an old man who called me Bella Señorita so I suppose he remembered me but I could not remember him. I stared and stared and stared and stared and stared at those scrawny chickens and that cracked tank with a vine growing out the side and I STROVE to remember them but could not. God knows every language so he questioned the old man in Spanish and I learned I had not lived there long because my pa and ma had been migrants wandering hither and yonder upon the wastes of the waters like the son of man who hath no space whereon to rest the sole of his foot as Miss MacTavish aptly remarked. My pa Ignatius Baxter marketed rubber copper coffee bauxite beef tar esparto-grass all things whose markets fluctuate so he and mama had to fluctuate too. But what I want to know is, what was I DOING while they fluctuated?

I have eyes and a mirror in my bedroom, Candle, I SEE I am a woman in my middle twenties and but nearer thirty than twenty, most women are married by then—"

"Marry *me*, Bella!" I cried.

"Don't change the subject Candle, why were my parents still carting a lovely thing like Bell Baxter about with them? That is what I want to know."

We walked on in silence, she obviously brooding upon the mysteries of her origin, I fretting over her neglect of my impulsive but sincere proposal. At last I said, "Bell—Bella—Miss Baxter, I accept the fact that you have done what we did in the shrubbery with many men. Do you ever do it with Godwin?"

"No. I can't do it with God, and that's what is making him miserable. He's too ordinary to have fun with in that kind of way. He's as ordinary as I am."

"Nonsense, Miss Baxter! You and your guardian are the most extraordinary couple I have ever—"

"Shut up Candle, you are too impressed by appearances. I have not read *Beauty and the Beast* or Ruskin's *Stones of Venice* or Dumas' *Hunchback of Notre-Dame* or is it Hugo's in the Tauchnitz limp covered English translation costing two shillings and sixpence from start to finish, but I have been told enough about these mighty epics of our race to know most folk think God and me a very gothic couple. They are wrong. At heart we are ordinary farmers like Cathy and Heathcliff in *Wuthering Heights* by one of those Brontës."

"I have not read it."

"You must because it is about us. Heathcliff and Cathy belong to a farming family and he loves her because they've been together and played together almost forever and she likes him a lot but finds Edgar more lovable and marries him because he is outside the family. Then Heathcliff goes daft. I hope Baxter won't. There he is, all alone, how very handy. I'm glad he sent the lads home."

When we reached the fountain the park-keepers were blowing their whistles before locking the gates and a deep-

red sun was sinking behind bars of purple and golden cloud. The solitary bulk of poor Baxter was slumped exactly as we had left him, hands clasped on the knob of a stout stick planted upright between his legs, chin resting on hands, aghast eyes seeming to gaze at nothing. When we stood arm in arm before him our heads were level with his own, yet he still seemed not to see us.
"Boo!" said Bella. "Do you feel better now?"
"A little better," he murmured with an effort at a smile.
"Good," said Bella, "because Candle and I are going to get married and you must be happy about that."

Then came the most terrifying experience of my life. The only part of Baxter which moved was his mouth. It slowly and silently opened into a round hole bigger than the original size of his head then grew larger still until his head vanished behind it. His body seemed to support a black, expanding, tooth-fringed cavity in the scarlet sunset behind him. When the scream came the whole sky seemed screaming. I had clapped my hands to my ears before this happened so did not faint as Bella did, but the single high-pitched note sounded everywhere and pierced the brain like a dental drill piercing a tooth without anaesthetic. I lost most of my senses during that scream. They returned so slowly that I never saw how Baxter came to be kneeling beside Bella's body, beating the sides of his head with his fists and quivering with human-sounding sobs as he moaned in a husky baritone voice, "Forgive me Bella, forgive me for making you like this."
She opened her eyes and said faintly, "What's that supposed to mean? You aren't our father which art in Heaven, God. What a silly fuss to make about nothing. Still, your voice has broken, there's that to be grateful for. Help me up both of you."

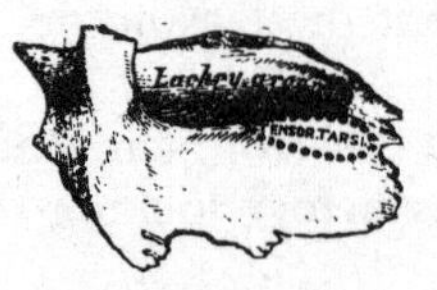

# 8

# The Engagement

As SHE WALKED BRISKLY BETWEEN US from the park, a hand on the arm of each, I knew her instant recovery of health and high spirits must seem callous to Baxter; but though he was the sincerest man I ever met his ordinary new voice made me feel he was putting on an act when he said, "It is agony to find you treating me like a wrecked ship and McCandless like a life-boat, Bell. Your romances on the world tour were bearable because I knew they were transient. For nearly three years I have lived with and for you and wished that never to end."

"I am not deserting you, God," she told him soothingly, "or not right away. Candle is very poor so we'll both find it handy to live with you for a long time. Turn your father's old operating-theatre into a drawing-room for us and you will be a welcome guest whenever you call. And of course we will eat with you. But I am a very romantic woman who needs a lot of sex but not from you because you cannot help treating me like a child, and I cannot CAN NOT treat you like one. I am marrying Candle because I can treat him how I like."

Baxter looked at me enquiringly. In a slightly ashamed voice I told him that though I had always tried to be a dour, independent sort of man Bella was correct: I had worshipped and longed for her from the moment he introduced us—everything about her seemed to me the acme of womanly perfection—I would gladly endure the

most horrible agonies to save her from the smallest inconvenience. I added that Bella would always be able to do whatever she wanted with me.
Said Bella, "And Candle's kisses are almost as strong as your yells, God, and would make me faint too if I was not a grown-up woman."
Baxter nodded his head rapidly for several seconds then said, "I will help you both to do whatever you want but first please grant me one favour, a favour which may save my life. Do not see each other for a fortnight. Give me fourteen days to strengthen myself for the loss of you, Bell. I know you mean to keep me as a friendly convenience but you cannot foresee how marriage may change you, Bell—nobody can. Please grant me this. Please!"
His lips trembled, his mouth seemed shaping for another outcry, so we hurriedly agreed. I doubted if he could have screamed a second time as loudly as the first, but I feared that another sudden enlargement of his oral cavity would disconnect his spine and cranium.

Baxter stood with his back to us as we said good-bye under a street lamp. Bell murmured, "A fortnight for me is years and years and years."
I told her I would write to her every day, and taking a tiny pearl mounted on a pin from the knot of my necktie I told her it was the only pretty thing, and the most expensive thing, I owned, and asked if she would keep it with her for ever and ever and think of me whenever she saw or touched it. She nodded her head violently seven or eight times, so I stuck it into the lapel of her jacket and told her this meant we were engaged to be married. I then begged her to give me her glove or scarf or handkerchief, any token whose texture or scent had been close to her person, making it a sacred relic of the covenant between us. She frowned thoughtfully then gave me the poke of gob-stoppers saying, "Take the lot."
I saw that to her still developing brain this was a noble sacrifice so there were tears in my eyes as I pressed my lips to the kidskin sheaths on her fingertips. I nearly put my lips

to her lips, then remembered that if my mouth on her naked fingers nearly made her faint it would be wiser to wait for total privacy before I grew more ardent. Yet I hurried away enraptured by the wonderful adventure of living. If Baxter's scream had been my most terrifying experience this moment was my sweetest. I was already devising phrases for the love-letter I would write when I got to my lodgings. I knew Baxter hoped that a fortnight apart from me would change her mind, but I had no fear of losing her because I knew he would submit her to no unkind pressure, would do nothing sneaking or dishonest. I also believed he could protect her from other men.

I performed my hospital duties in an absent-minded way for nearly a week. My imagination had awakened. The imagination is, like the appendix, inherited from a primitive epoch when it aided the survival of our species, but in modern scientific industrial nations it is mainly a source of disease. I had prided myself on lacking one, but it had only lain dormant. I now did what people expected of me but without rigour or enthusiasm, because I was composing love-letters in my head when not scribbling them down and running out to post them. I discovered that I possessed a strong poetic faculty. All my memories and hopes of Bella became rhyming sentences so easily that I often felt I was not composing them but remembering them from a previous existence. Here is a specimen:

*O Bella fair, without compare,*
*My memory sweetly lingers*
*By Kelvin's side (my future bride!)*
*Where first I kissed your fingers.*
*I have been blithe with comrades dear,*
*I have been merry drinking,*
*I have been joyful gathering gear,*
*I have been happy thinking,*
*I have known glee by pond and sea,*
*And spate that cleaves the mountain,*
*But known no glee (my bride to be!)*

*No joy so great (my future mate!)*
*As by the Memorial Fountain.*

The many other verses I posted to her were equally spontaneous and equally good, and ended with stronger and stronger requests that she reply to me. I give verbatim the only reply I at last received. I was overjoyed by the bulk of the envelope it came in, which contained nearly a dozen sheets of notepaper. However, her writing was so huge that there was only room for a few words on each, though like the ancient Hebrews and Babylonians she had saved space by dispensing with vowels:

*DR CNDL,*
*Y WNT GT MCH FRM M THS WY. WRDS DNT SM RL 2 M WHN NT SPKN R HRD. YR LTTRS R VRY LK THR MNS LV LTTRS, SPCLLY DNCN WDDRBRNS.*
*YRS FTHFLLY,*
*BLL BXTR.*

By murmuring these consonants aloud I gradually made sense of everything but *SPCLLY DNCN WDDRBRNS*, and what I understood alarmed and disturbed me, because the only words which fed my hopes were the second last two which declared she was mine faithfully. This is a conventional business phrase, but Bella was neither conventional nor in business. Even so, I decided to break my word to Baxter and visit her as soon as possible. On leaving the Royal Infirmary to do so that evening I was hailed by Mrs. Dinwiddie, Baxter's housekeeper, who was waiting for me at the gate in a cab. She handed me the following note, asking me to read it at once:

*Dear McCandless,*
*I was mad to part you and Bella. Come at once. I have accidentally injured all three of us in a terrible way. Only*

*you, perhaps, may save us if you come here quickly, tonight, before sunset, as soon as possible.*

*Your miserable and, believe me,*
*Sincerely repentant friend;*
*Godwin Bysshe Baxter.*

I leapt into the cab, was carried to Park Circus and rushed into the downstairs drawing-room crying, "What is wrong? Where is she?"

"Upstairs in her bedroom," said Baxter, "and not ill, and all too happy. Try to be calm, McCandless. Hear the whole ghastly story from me before attempting to change her mind. If you need a drink I can offer you a glass of vegetable juice. Port is out of the question."

I sat down and stared at him. He said, "She is waiting to elope with Duncan Wedderburn."

"Who?"

"The worst man possible—a smooth, handsome, well-groomed, plausible, unscrupulous, lecherous lawyer who specialized—until last week—in seducing women of the servant class. He is too lazy to live by honest toil. Besides, a legacy from a doting old aunt has made toil unnecessary. He pays for his gambling losses and grimy amours by charging improperly high fees for slightly improper jobs on the shady side of the law. Bella now loves him, not you, McCandless."

"How did they meet?"

"The morning after she got engaged to you I decided to make a will leaving her everything I own. I visited a very respectable elderly lawyer, an old friend of my father. When he asked about Bell's exact relationship to me I answered in a confused manner for I suddenly suspected—without being absolutely certain—that he knew too much about the Baxter family to believe the story I told my servants. I blushed, stammered, then pretending an anger I did not feel declared that since I was paying for his services I saw no reason to answer impertinent questions which cast doubts on my honesty. I wish I had not said that! But I was flustered. He replied very coldly that he had only questioned me to ensure my will could not be contested by some other relative of Sir Colin; that he had served the Baxter family for nearly three generations, and if I could not trust his discretion I should go elsewhere. I longed to tell that good old man the whole truth, McCandless, but he would have thought me a lunatic. I apologized and left.

"I saw that the secretary who showed me out had been listening at his master's keyhole, for he was far less obsequious than when he showed me in. I detained him in the corridor to the front door, taking out a sovereign and absent-mindedly fingering it. I said his master was too busy to do a piece of work for me—could he recommend someone else? He whispered the name and address of a solicitor who worked from a private house on the south side. I tipped the scoundrel and took a cab there. Alas, Wedderburn was in. I explained what I wanted and said I would pay extra to have it as soon as possible. He asked for no more information than I gave him. I was grateful. I admired his good looks and suave manner, and knew nothing then about the black iniquity of his soul.

"He called here the following day with copies of the will for signature. Bella was with me, here, in this room, and welcomed him with her usual effusiveness. His response was so cool, remote and condescending that it obviously hurt her. That annoyed me though I did not show it. I rang for Mrs. Dinwiddie to act as witness and the documents were signed and sealed while Bell sulked in a corner. Wedderburn then handed me his bill. I left the room to fetch the guineas from my strongbox and I promise you, McCandless, I returned in four minutes or less. I was glad to see that, although Mrs. Dinwiddie had now also left the room and Wedderburn seemed as cool as ever, Bella was again chattering as brightly as usual. And that, I thought, was the last of Duncan Wedderburn. This morning over the breakfast table she cheerfully told me that for the last three nights he has visited her bedroom after the servants retire. An imitation owl-hoot is his midnight signal, a lit candle in the window is hers, then up goes a ladder and up goes he! And tonight two hours from now she will elope with him unless you change her mind. Try to be *calm*, McCandless."

I had grasped my hair with both hands and now I wrenched at it crying, "O what have they DONE together?"

"Nothing whose outcome you need dread, McCandless. I noticed her romantic nature quite early on our world tour, and in Vienna paid a highly qualified woman to teach her the arts of contraception. Bell tells me Wedderburn is versed in them too."

"Have you not told her how evil and treacherous he is?"

"No, McCandless. I only discovered that this morning when she told *me* how evil and treacherous he is. The cunning fiend has seduced her with accounts of his debaucheries with all the women he has cheated and betrayed, and not just women, McCandless! He has indulged in an orgy of confession—she says it was as good as a book—and of course he declares that love of her has purified his life and made a new man of him and he will *never* abandon *her*. I asked if she believed this. She said not much but nobody had ever abandoned her before and the change might do her good. She also said that wicked people needed love as much as good people and were much better at it. Go to her McCandless and prove her wrong."

"I am going," I said, standing up, "and when Wedderburn arrives, Baxter, set your dogs on him. He is a burglar with no legal right here."

Baxter stared at me with the distaste and amazement he would have shown had I told him to crucify Wedderburn on the spire of Glasgow Cathedral. He said reproachfully, "I must not thwart Bell, McCandless."

"But Baxter, she has a mental age of ten! She is a child!"

"That is why I must not use force. If I hurt someone she loves her liking for me will turn to fear and distrust and my life will have no purpose. It will still have a purpose if I keep a house for her to return to when she tires of Wedderburn, or he of her. But maybe you can stop either happening. Go to her. Woo her. Tell her it is with my blessing."

# 9

# At the Window

I RAN UPSTAIRS IN A RAGE WHICH MELTED into grief at the sight of Bella, for her thoughts were not on me. Through an open door on the first landing I saw her sitting at an open window, an elbow on the sill and her hand supporting her cheek. She wore a travelling-costume; there was a strapped-up portmanteau at her feet with a broad-brimmed hat and veil resting on top. Though looking into the garden she appeared to me in profile, and in her expression and pose I saw what had never been there before: contentment and serenity tinged with melancholy at some thought of the past or future. She was no longer violently, vividly in the present. I felt like a small boy spying on a mature woman, and coughed to attract her attention. She looked round and gave me a sweetly welcoming smile. She said, "How kind of you to come, Candle, and keep me company during my last few minutes in the old, old home. I wish God could be here but he's so miserable I can't stand him just now."

"I'm miserable too, Bella. I thought you and I were to marry."

"I know. We arranged that years ago."

"Six days — less than a week."

"Anything more than a day seems eternity to me. Duncan Wedderburn suddenly touched me in places you never did and now I'm daft about him. When the gloaming comes so will he, stepping quietly from the lane through that door in the far-away wall and padding the latch with a cloth so it won't click. Then tiptoe tiptoe tiptoe up the path he will come, and stealthily lift the ladder hidden in that bed of curly kail—it is not well hidden, you can easily see it—and O how tenderly how expertly he will raise it upright, how slowly tilt the top toward me till I can grip it and with my own hands place it on the sill of my window. You never did that with me. Then he will hurry us off to life, love and Italy, the coast of Coromandel where Afric's sunny fountains pour down the golden sands. I wonder where we will end? Poor dear Duncan so enjoys being wicked. He probably would not want me if he knew God would let us walk together out of the front door in broad daylight. And Candle, besides our engagement I will always remember how often you visited me in the old days, and listened when I played to you on the pianola, and what a wonderful woman you made me feel by always kissing my hand afterwards."

"Bella, I have met you only three times in my life and this is the third."

"Exactly!" cried Bella with a frightening gust of anger. "I am only half a woman Candle, less than half having had no childhood, the bit of life Miss MacTavish said we dragged clouds of glory into, no sugar-and-spice-and-all-things-nice-little-girlhood, no early-love's-young-dream-womanhood. A whole quarter century of my life has vanished crash bang wallop. So the few wee memories in this hollow Bell tinkle clink clank clatter rattle clang gong ring dong ding sound resound resonate detonate vibrate reverberate echo re-echo around this poor empty skull in words words words words wordswordswordswordswordswordswordswordswordswords that try to make much of little but cannot. I need more past. On our boat up the Nile a fine lady travelled alone and someone told me *she was a woman with a past*, O how I envied her. But Duncan will give me a lot of past fast. Duncan is quick."

"Bell!" I pled, "you will NOT go off and marry this man! You will NOT carry his bairns!"

"I know!" said Bella, looking at me in a startled way. "I am engaged to you."

She pointed to the lapel of her travelling-coat where I saw the tiny pearl of my tie-pin. She said cunningly, "I bet you've eaten all my gobstoppers."
I told her I had placed the gobstoppers in a glass jar with a lid which now stood on a sideboard of my lodgings, because the heat of my body would gradually melt them into a shapeless lump if I carried them in my pocket. I also said that since Baxter refused to protect her from this bad and worthless man, and since she refused to protect herself, I would go down and wait for him in the lane; if my words did not turn him away I would knock him down. She glowered at me—I had never seen her glower before—and her lower lip swelled and stuck out like an angry baby's, and for a moment I feared she would bawl like one.

A lovely thing happened instead. Her face relaxed into a smile as delighted as when we first met, she stood and stretched her arms straight out to me like then, but now I stepped between them and we embraced. I could not remember being so close to another person before, she pulled my face so deep into her bosom that I had less air than when she embraced me in the park. I dared not stay till I lost consciousness so again struggled free. She stood holding my hands and said kindly, "My dear wee Candle, when I try to give you pleasure you cannot take it and break away. So how can you give much pleasure to me?"
"You are the only woman I have loved, Bella, I am not like Duncan Wedderburn who has been practising on servant women all his life, if you count the wet-nurse who was hired to suckle him. My mother served on a farm. Her boss practised on her, making me, and I am lucky that he did not fling us both out afterwards. There was no time for love in our lives—the pay was too poor, the work too hard for it. I learned to survive on small quantities of it, Bell. I cannot suddenly start enjoying whole armfuls."
"But I can and will, Candle. O yes!" said Bella, still smiling but nodding very definitely. "And you once said I could do anything I liked with you."

I smiled and nodded back, being now sure I would win her, and said she could still do what she liked with me, but not what she liked with other men. She frowned and sighed fretfully at that, then laughed aloud and cried, "But Duncan won't be here for hours and hours and hours so come upstairs and let me surprise you!"
Pulling my right hand under her arm she led me to the door. Feeling completely happy I asked about the surprise; she told me not to ask before it happened.

As we climbed to the top landing she said thoughtfully, "Duncan is an amateur boxing champion."
I told her that I too was a fighter; that more than one big boy in the playground of Whauphill school had thought my quiet ways and smaller size made me an easy mark to hit, but without always winning I had always proved them wrong. She squeezed my hand. I then noticed something oddly familiar: the mingled aroma of carbolic and surgical spirit that goes with hospitals. I knew old Sir Colin's operating-theatre, like all such theatres, would have been on the top floor, but had not thought it was still in use. We had climbed up to brightness. There was still an hour before sunset. A breeze had swept the sky clean, and near the summer solstice there is always light in the Scottish skies, however dark the streets and fields. The top landing was directly under a big cupola lighting the stairwell. Bella put her hand on a door-knob and said, "You must wait outside and not peep until I call you, Candle, then you *will* be surprised."
She slipped sideways through the door, closing it so quickly behind her that I had no glimpse of the interior.

While I waited some very queer ideas entered my head. Could Wedderburn have so corrupted her that on being called in I would see her naked? The notion made me tremble with an agony of conflicting feelings, but as the moments passed I was tormented by another and even worse suspicion. Most big houses have narrow back-stairs for servants. Had Bella crept down these, was she even now walking briskly towards Charing Cross where she would take a cab to Wedderburn's rooms? This image of her came so clear to my mind that I was about to open the door when it swung inward and I knew she must be standing behind it, the room before me was so empty of visible life. I heard her say, "Step inside and shut your eyes."

I stepped inside but did not shut my eyes at once.

This was indeed old Sir Colin's operating-theatre, built to his specifications when the Circus had been built in the days of the Crystal Palace. The furnishings were few and gaunt but bathed in warm evening sunlight. This flooded in from tall windows and from a ceiling which seemed to be four skylights sloping up to a reflector in the centre, a reflector casting a pool of greater brightness on the operating-table beneath. I saw benches with what looked like barred hutches and kennels on them and noticed a whiff of animal in the hospital smell. I heard the door click shut behind me, felt Bella breathing on the nape of my neck. Suddenly certain she was naked I half closed my eyes and began trembling. From behind she slid an arm across my chest, and with relief I saw it clothed in the sleeve of her travelling-coat. She pressed me back against her body and I relaxed there, noticing briefly that the chemical odour of the place was unusually strong. I felt as much as heard her murmur in my ear, "Bell will let *nobody* hurt her wee Candle."

She put her hand over my mouth and nose,
and when I tried to breathe
I became unconscious.

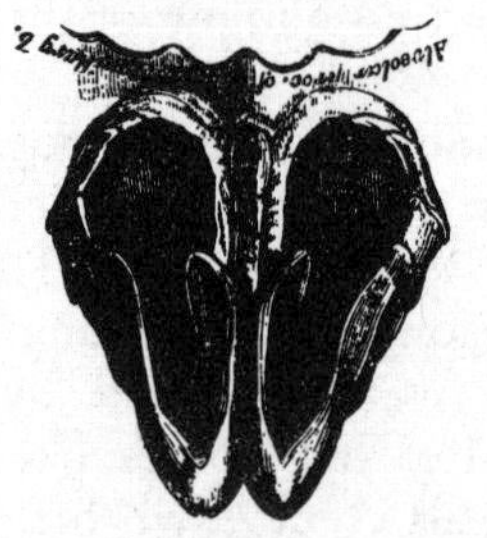

# 10

# Without Bella

I HEARD THE FAINT STEADY HISSING OF A GAS chandelier. I had a headache, but did not open my eyes because light would hurt them. I knew something horrible had happened, that something essential was taken from me, but I did not want to think of it. Nearby someone sighed and whispered, "Evil. I am evil."
Bella came to mind. I sat up and a blanket slipped from me.

I was sitting (had been lying) on the sofa in Baxter's study. I was coatless, my waistcoat unbuttoned, my collar and shoes removed. The sofa was a massive mahogany article upholstered in black horsehair. Baxter sat gloomily watching me at the other end of it. Through the windows (whose curtains were not drawn) I saw a big half moon in a clear night sky, a sky so full of deep blue light that it was starless. I said, "Time?"
"Well after two."
"Bell?"
"Eloped."
After a moment I asked how he had found me. He handed over a sheaf of pages scrawled with Bella's huge shorthand. I gave them back saying my head ached too much to decipher anything. He read them aloud.
"Dear God, I have chloroformed Candle in the operating-theatre. Ask him to live with you when he wakes up, then

you can both talk often about, Yours Faithfully, Dearly Beloved Bell Baxter. P.S. I will telegraph to say where I am when I get there."
I wept. Baxter said, "Come down to the kitchen and eat something."

Downstairs I sat with my elbows on the kitchen table while Baxter foraged in the larder then placed before me a jug of milk, mug, plate, knife, loaf, cheese, pickles and the cold remains of a roast fowl. He handled the last with a distaste he tried and failed to hide, for he was vegetarian and only got in meat for his servants. While I tackled the food he slowly drank nearly a gallon of the grey syrup which was the main part of his diet, ladling it into a tankard from a glass carboy of the sort used to transport industrial acid. Once when he left the room to satisfy a call of nature I sipped a little out of curiosity, and found it as briny as sea-water.

We sat till dawn in a melancholy silence broken by bursts of talk. I asked him where Bella learned to use chloroform. He said, "When we returned from abroad I knew she would need more than toys to keep her occupied, so I started a small veterinary clinic. I put word about that sick animals brought to our backdoor would be treated free of charge. Bella was my receptionist and assistant, and a fine clinician in both capacities. She liked meeting strangers and mending animals. I taught her to stitch wounds and she did so with the deft passionate steadiness working-class women bring to sewing shirts and middle-class women to frivolous embroidery. Many lives and limbs have been lost, McCandless, by excluding women from the more intricate medical arts."
I felt too tired and sick to argue the point.

A while after this I asked why he had suddenly made a will the day after Bella and I got engaged. He said, "To provide for her after my death. You won't get rich for years, McCandless, however hard you work."

I accused him of planning to kill himself after our marriage. He shrugged and said he would have had nothing to live for after it.

"You selfish fool, Baxter!" I cried angrily. "How could Bell and me enjoy your money if we got it by your suicide? We would have kept it, of course, but it would have made us miserable. This elopement has not been a wholly bad thing if it has saved three of us from that."

Baxter swung his back toward me and muttered that his death would not have looked like suicide. I thanked him for the warning, said I would watch him closely in future, and that if he ever died in unhappy circumstances I would take appropriate steps. He stared round at me, astonished, and said, "What steps? Will you have me buried on unholy ground?"

I told him sulkily that I would freeze him on ice till I found how to animate him again. For a moment he seemed about to laugh, but checked himself. I said, "You must not die now. If you do all your property will go to Duncan Wedderburn."

He pointed out that the House of Commons was debating a bill to let married women keep their own property. I told him that bill would never be made law. It would undermine the institution of marriage and most M.P.s were husbands. He sighed and said, "I deserve death as much as any other murderer."

"Nonsense! Why call yourself that?"

"Don't pretend to have forgotten. By a straight question you exposed my guilt the first day I showed you to Bella. Excuse me."

It was then he left to empty his bladder or bowels. Either operation took nearly an hour, and when he returned I said, "Sorry, Baxter, I haven't the faintest idea why you call yourself a murderer."

"That little nearly nine-month-old foetus I took living from the drowned woman's body should have been coddled as my foster child. By recasting its brain in the mother's body I shortened her life as deliberately as if I stabbed her to

death at the age of forty or fifty, but I took the years off the start, not the ending of her life—a much more vicious thing to do. And I did it for the reason that elderly lechers purchase children from bawds. Selfish greed and impatience drove me and THAT!" he shouted, smiting the table so hard with his fist that the heaviest things on it leapt at least an inch in the air, "THAT is why our arts and sciences cannot improve the world, despite what liberal philanthropists say. Our vast new scientific skills are first used by the damnably greedy selfish impatient parts of our nature and nation, the careful kindly social part always comes second. Without Sir Colin's techniques Bell would now be a normal two-and-a-half-year-old infant. I could enjoy her society for another sixteen or eighteen years before she grew independent of me. But my damnable sexual appetites employed my scientific skills to warp her into a titbit for Duncan Wedderburn! *DUNCAN WEDDERBURN!*"
He wept and I brooded.

I brooded hard for a long time, then said, "What you last said is mainly true, apart from your remark about the impossibility of improving things scientifically. As a member of the Liberal Party I am bound to disagree there. As to you shortening Bell's life, remember that the only sure thing we know about ageing is that misery and pain age folk faster than happiness does, so Bella's emphatically happy young brain may prolong her body well past the common span. If you committed a crime by making Bell as she is I am thankful for that crime because I love her as she is, whether she marries Wedderburn or no. I also doubt if the woman who chloroformed me will be anyone's helpless plaything. Maybe we should pity Wedderburn."
Baxter stared at me then reached across the table. He gripped my right hand so that the knuckles cracked, I roared with pain and sustained bruises which took a month to heal. He apologized and said he had been expressing heart-felt gratitude. I begged him to keep his gratitude to himself in future.

After this we grew slightly more cheerful. Baxter began strolling about the kitchen, smiling as he only did when he thought of Bell and forgot himself.

"Yes," he said, "not many two-and-a-half-year-olds are so sure-footed, steady-handed, quick-witted. She remembers everything that happens to her and every word she hears, so even when it makes no sense she picks up the meaning later. And I have saved her from one crushing disadvantage I never had myself: she has never been small so has never known fear. Do you remember all the sizes of midget you were before reaching the height you are now, McCandless? The twenty-four-inch-long gnome? Yard-tall goblin? Four-foot dwarf? Did the giants who owned the world when you were wee let you feel as important as they were?"

I shuddered and said that all childhoods were not like mine.

"Perhaps not, but even in the homes of the rich screaming babies, terrified toddlers, sulky adolescents are commonplace, I hear. Nature gives children great emotional resilience to help them survive the oppressions of being small, but these oppressions still make them into slightly insane adults, either mad to seize all the power they once lacked or (more usually) mad to avoid it. Now Bella (and this is why you may be right about pitying Wedderburn) Bella has all the resilience of infancy with all the stature and strength of fine womanhood. Her menstrual cycle was in full flood from the day she opened her eyes, so she has never been taught to feel her body is disgusting or to dread what she desires. Not having learned cowardice when small and oppressed she only uses speech to say what she thinks and feels, not to disguise these, so she is incapable of every badness done through hypocrisy and lying—nearly every sort of badness. All she lacks is experience, especially the experience of decision making. Wedderburn is her first major decision but she has no delusions about his character. Mrs. Dinwiddie has sewn enough money into the lining of her coat to ensure she will not lack funds if she and Wedderburn suddenly part. My main fear is that someone who interests her more will attract her into an adventure we cannot imagine. Still, she knows how to send a telegram."

"Her worst fault," I said (Baxter at once looked indignant) "is her infantile sense of time and space. She feels short intervals are huge, yet thinks she can grasp all the things she wants at once, no matter how far they are from her and each other. She talked as if her engagement to marry me and her elopement with Wedderburn were simultaneous. I had no heart to tell her time and space forbid this. I did not even explain that the moral law forbids it."
Baxter was halfway through explaining that our ideas of time, space and morality were convenient habits, not natural laws, when I yawned in his face.

There was daylight and bird-song outside the window. Mournful hooters were summoning workers into shipyards and factories. Baxter said a bed was prepared for me in a guest-room. I answered that I would be on duty in a couple of hours and wanted nothing from him but the use of a wash-basin, razor and comb. As he led me upstairs he said, "We have talked about Bella exactly as she foretold in her letter, so you had better live here too. I ask this as a favour, McCandless. The company of elderly women is not enough for me now."
"Park Circus is very far from the Royal Infirmary compared with my digs on the Trongate. What would your terms be?"
"A rent-free room with free gas-light, free coal fire and free bed-linen. Free laundering of your small clothes and shirts, free starching of your collars, polishing of your boots. Free hot baths. Free meals when you choose to eat with me."
"Your food would sicken me, Baxter."
"You would be given the same meals Mrs. Dinwiddie and the cook and housemaid give themselves—plain fare excellently cooked. You would have the free use of a good library which has been greatly enlarged since Sir Colin's time."
"And in return?"
"When you have a spare moment you could help me in the clinic. From dogs, cats, rabbits and parrots you may learn much to help you mend featherless bipedal patients."

"Hm! I will think it over."

He smiled as if he thought my remark an empty show of manly independence. He was right.

That evening I borrowed a big trunk, packed it, paid my Trongate landlord a fortnight's rent for notice of quittal, and came in a cab to Park Circus with all my goods, gear and chattels. Baxter received me without comment, showed me my new room and handed me a telegram wired from London a few hours before. It said M HR (am here) with no name at the end.

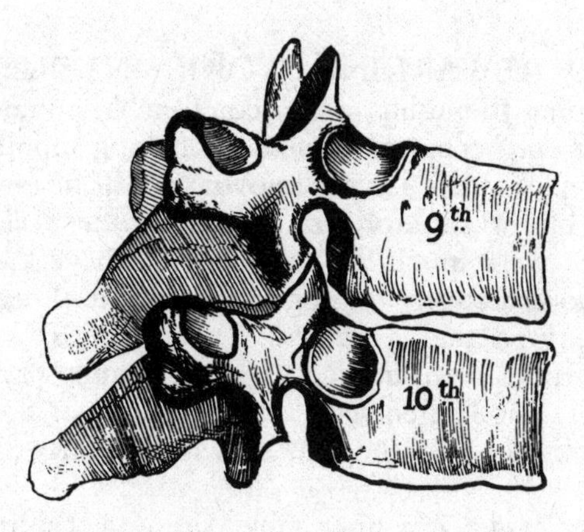

# 11
# Eighteen Park Circus

IF HARD REWARDING WORK, INTERESTING, undemanding friendship, and a comfortable home are the best grounds for happiness then the following months were perhaps the pleasantest I have known. All Baxter's servants had begun life as country girls of my mother's class, and though none were much less than fifty I believe they liked having a comparatively young man in the house who enjoyed the food they prepared. They never saw me eat because my meals were hoisted up to the dining-room on a dumb-waiter, but I often sent a cheap bunch of flowers or note of thanks down to the kitchen with the dirty plates.

I ate with Baxter at a huge table, sitting as far from him as possible. Having little or no pancreas he made his digestive juices by hand, stirring them into his food before chewing and swallowing. When I asked about the ingredients he evaded the question in a shamefaced way which suggested some were extracted from his bodily wastes. The odour at his end of the table confirmed this. Behind his chair was a sideboard loaded with carboys, stoppered vials, graduated glasses, pipettes, syringes, litmus papers, thermometers and a barometer; also the Bunsen burner, retort and tubing of a distillation plant. This last bubbled on a low gas throughout the day. At unpredictable moments in every meal he would stop chewing and stay absolutely still as if listening to something remote, yet inside himself. After seconds like this he would slowly stand, carefully carry his plate to the sideboard and spend minutes concocting messes for addition to it. On the sideboard lay a chart where every four hours he recorded his pulse, respiration and temperature, besides chemical changes in his blood and lymphatic system. One morning before breakfast I studied it and was so disturbed that I never looked at it again. It showed daily fluctuations too irregular, sudden and steep for even the strongest and healthiest body to survive. Times and dates (noted in Baxter's clear, tiny, childish yet firm script) showed that when talking to me the day before his neural network had passed through the equivalent of an epileptic seizure, yet I had noticed no change in his manner. Surely all this apparatus and charting must be pretences, ploys by which an ugly hypochondriac exaggerated his diseases in order to feel superhuman?

Outside the dining-room life at 18 Park Circus was splendidly commonplace. After the evening meal we tended the sick animals in the operating-theatre, then retired to the study where we read or played chess (which Baxter always won) or draughts (which I nearly always won) or cribbage (where the victor was unpredictable). We resumed our long weekend tramps and all the time talked about Bella. She did not let us forget her. Every three or four days a telegram saying "M HR" arrived from Amsterdam, Frankfort-on-Maine, Marienbad, Geneva, Milan, Trieste, Athens, Constantinople, Odessa, Alexandria, Malta, Morocco, Gibraltar and Marseilles.

One foggy November afternoon came a telegram from Paris saying DNT WRRY. Baxter grew frantic. He cried, "There must be something dreadful to worry about if she tells me not to do it. I will go to Paris. I will hire detectives. I will find her."
I said, "Wait till she summons you, Baxter. Trust her

honesty. That message means she is not disturbed by an event which would upset you or me. Rather than thwart her you trusted her to Duncan Wedderburn. Better trust her to herself, now."

This convinced but did not calm him. When the same message came from Paris exactly a week later his resolution collapsed. I went to work one morning feeling sure he would have left for France when I got back, but as I entered the front door he hailed me vigorously from the study landing shouting, "News of Bella, McCandless! Two letters! One from a maniac in Glasgow and one from her residence in Paris!"

"What news?" I cried, casting off my coat and running upstairs. "Good? Bad? How is she? Who wrote these letters?"

"The news is certainly not altogether *bad*," he said cautiously. "In fact, I think she is doing remarkably well, though conventional moralists would disagree. Come into the study and I will read the letters to you, leaving the best till last. The other one has a south Glasgow postmark, and a maniac wrote it."

We composed ourselves on the sofa
He read aloud what follows.

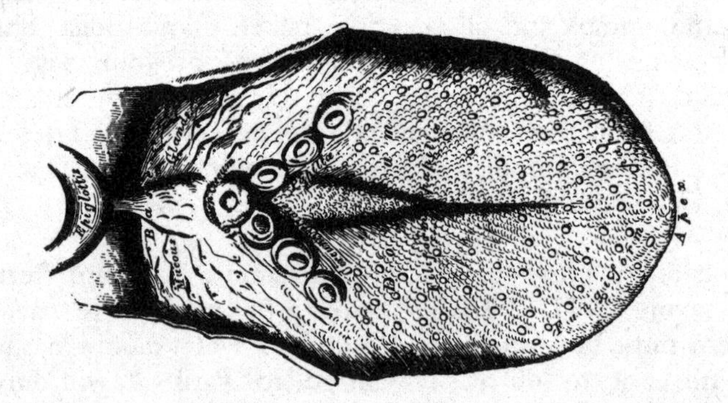

# WEDDERBURN'S LETTER: MAKING A MANIAC

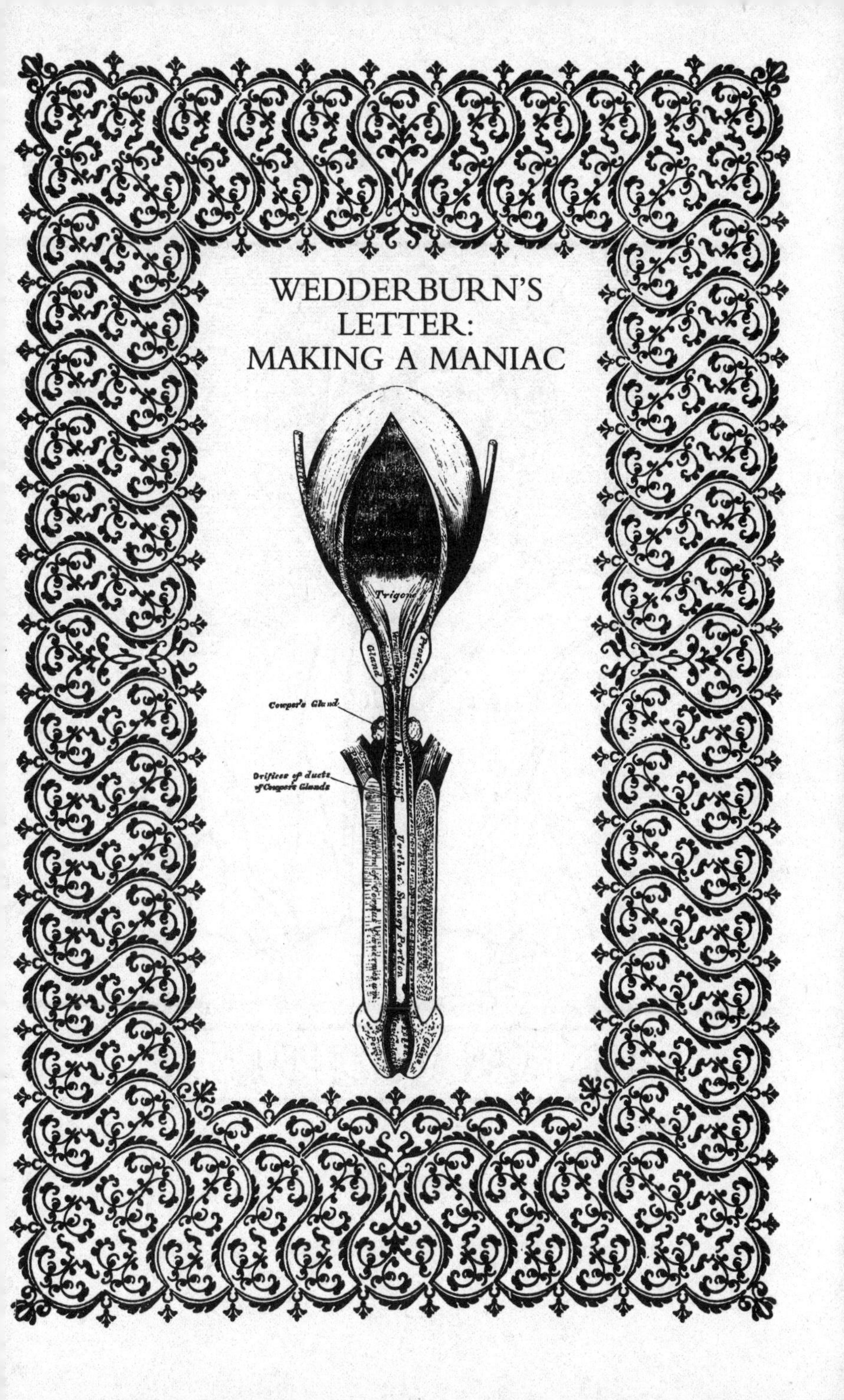

W.S.
DUNCAN WEDDERBURN

*41 Aytoun Street,*
*Pollokshields.*
*November 14th.*

*Mr. Baxter,*

*Until a week ago I would have been ashamed to write to you, sir. I then thought my signature on a letter would convulse you with such loathing that you would burn it unread. You invited me to your home on a matter of business. I saw your "niece", loved her, plotted with her, eloped with her. Though unmarried we toured Europe and circled the Mediterranean in the character of husband and wife. A week ago I left her in Paris and returned alone to my mother's home in Glasgow. Were these facts made public The Public would regard me as a villain of the blackest dye, and that, until a week ago, is how I viewed myself: as a guilty reckless libertine who had ravished a beautiful young woman from her respectable home and loving guardian. I now think much better of Duncan Wedderburn and far, far worse of you, sir. Did you see the great Henry Irving's production of Goethe's* Faust *at the Glasgow Theatre Royal? I did. I was deeply moved. I recognized* myself *in that tormented hero, that respectable member of the professional middle class who enlists the King of Hell to help him seduce a woman of the servant class. Yes, Goethe and Irving knew that Modern Man—that Duncan Wedderburn—is essentially double: a noble soul fully instructed in what is wise and lawful, yet also a fiend who loves beauty only to drag it down and degrade it. That is how I saw myself until a week ago. I was a fool, Mr. Baxter! A blind misguided fool! My affair with Bella was Faustian from the start, the intoxicating incense of Evil was in my nostrils from the moment you foisted me onto your "niece". Little did I know that in THIS melodrama I would play the part of the innocent, trusting Gretchen, that your overwhelming niece was cast as Faust, and that YOU! YES, YOU, Godwin Bysshe Baxter, are Satan Himself!*

"Notice, McCandless," said Baxter at this point, "that the fellow writes as you talk when you are drunk."

*I must try to write calmly. Exactly a week ago I crouched in the corner of a stationary carriage with Bella on the platform outside, chattering to me through the window. She was bright and beautiful as ever, with a fresh expectant youthfulness which seemed wholly new, yet hauntingly familiar. WHY was it familiar? Then I remembered Bella had looked exactly like that when we first became lovers. And now, with every appearance of kindness (for it was I who had said we must part) she was discarding me like a worn shoe or broken toy, having been RENEWED by someone I had never seen, someone she must have glimpsed that very morning, for we had arrived in Paris from Marseilles only six hours before. In those six hours she had met nobody, spoken to nobody but me and the manageress of our hotel—I had been beside her the whole time, apart from my visit to the nearby Cathedral which took thirty minutes or less—yet in that time she had fallen in love anew! All things are possible for a witch. Suddenly she said, "Promise when you get to Glasgow that you tell God I will soon want the candle." I promised, although I thought the message gibberish—or more witchcraft. This letter discharges that promise.*

*Why, having discharged it, am I gripped by an urge to*

*tell you more, tell you all? Whence this hunger to disclose to YOU, Mephisto Baxter, the innermost secrets of my guilty and tortured heart? Is it because I believe you already know them?*

"Catholicism just might restore his sanity," muttered Baxter. "Lacking the rites of the confessional he will seize any excuse to blether out his second-hand, second-rate sentiments to anyone."

*Did you see at the Theatre Royal two years ago Beerbohm-Tree's production of* She Stoops to Conquer *by that greatest of Irishmen, Oliver Goldsmith? The hero is a bright clever handsome gentleman, liked by his companions, favoured by the elderly, attractive to women. He has but one defect. He is only at ease with women of the servant class. Respectable women of his own income group make him feel frigid and formal, and the more beautiful and pleasant they are the more awkward and incapable of loving them he feels. My case entirely! As a child I took it for granted that only women who worked with their hands would not find the natural Duncan Wedderburn a disgusting creature, and the result of this was that working women became the only class of female who attract me. As an adolescent I thought this proved me a kind of monster. Will you believe me when I say, that on entering University I discovered that TWO-THIRDS of the students felt exactly as I did? Most of them conquered this instinct to the extent of marrying respectable women and getting children by them, but I doubt if they are truly happy. My instincts were too strong for that, or perhaps I was too honest to live a lie. Goldsmith's hero is eventually saved by a beautiful heiress of his own class who wins him by dressing up and talking like her maid.*

Alas, no such happy ending is possible for a Glasgow solicitor in the nineteenth century. My love life was below the stairs and behind the scenes of my professional life, and in these cramped surroundings I enjoyed the ecstasies and obeyed the moral code enjoyed, preached and practised by Scotland's National Bard, Rabbie Burns. As I told each panting fair one I would love her for ever I was perfectly sincere, and indeed, I would have married every one of them had the social gulf between us not forbade this. My few poor bastard bairns (excuse the Scotticism, but to my ear the word *bairns* has a truer human warmth than *babies* or *children*) my few poor bastard bairns (fewer than the number of your fingers, Mr. Baxter, for my precautions prevented a great many) my few poor bastard bairns were never uncared for. Every one went into the charitable institution of my friend Quarrier. You know (if you read *The Glasgow Herald*) how that great philanthropist fosters such tender unfortunates, then ships them to Canada where they are put to good domestic agricultural use on the expanding frontier of our Empire in the North. Nor did their mothers suffer. No delicious scullions, tempting laundry manglers, luscious latrine scrubbers ever lost a day's work by dallying with Duncan Wedderburn, though the shortness and irregularity of their free time meant I had to court several at once. Basically innocent despite my wicked ways—fundamentally honest underneath my superficial hypocrisies—such was the man you introduced to your so-called niece, Mr. Baxter.

AT FIRST SIGHT I knew this was a woman to whom class distinctions were meaningless. Though beautifully dressed in the height of fashion she looked at me as gladly and frankly as a housemaid who has been tipped *half a crown and chucked under the chin behind her mistress's back. I knew she was seeing and welcoming the natural Wedderburn inside the solicitor. I hid my confusion under a chilly mask which may have struck you as bad manners, but my heart beat so hard that I feared you might hear the pounding. In matters of the heart it is best to be direct. When left with her I said, "May I see you again, soon, without anyone else knowing?"*

*She looked startled, but nodded. I said, "Is your bedroom at the back of the house?"*

*She smiled and nodded. I said, "Will you put a lit candle on the sill tonight when everyone else here is in bed. I will bring a ladder."*

*She laughed and nodded. I said, "I love you."*

*She said, "I've got another lad who does that," and was prattling about her fiancé when you returned, Mr. Baxter. Her guile astonished and excited me. To this day I can hardly believe it.*

*But though I foolishly believed I had deceived you, I never tried to deceive her. I exposed all my past iniquities more frankly and fully than I have courage and space to do here*

("Thank goodness for that!" muttered Godwin fervently.)

*because (blind fool that I was) I believed we would soon be man and wife! I had never before heard of a man-loving middle-class woman in her twenties who did NOT want marriage, especially to the man she eloped with. I was so sure Bella would soon be my bride that, by a piece of harmless chicanery, I obtained a passport on which we were named as husband and wife. This was to facilitate our honeymoon on the continent which I meant to start as soon as the civil contract was signed. And I swear with hand on heart that monetary gain had no part in my determination to turn Bella Baxter into Bella Wedderburn. I admit that your manner when ordering your will made me feel that you were perhaps not long for this world, but I was sure you would at least live long enough to see us return from our honeymoon. The most I expected from you sir, in the financial line, was a small steady allowance enabling me to support Bella in the style she enjoyed with you. A few thousand per annum would easily have done it, and Bella's way of talking suggested there was no limit to your generosity where she — the woman you pretend to be your niece — is concerned. You must both be laughing heartily at how cunningly you have duped me! For when we boarded the London train on that soft summer evening I had arranged to break our journey at Kilmarnock where I had persuaded a local registrar to wait up for us, receive us in his home and unite us. Imagine my consternation when before we reached Crossmyloof she declared she* COULD NOT MARRY ME BECAUSE SHE WAS ENGAGED TO ANOTHER!!!! *I said, "Surely that is in the past?"*

*She said, "No — in the future."*

*I said, "Where does that leave me?"*

*She said, "Here and now, Wedder," and embraced me. She was a Houri, a Mahomet's paradise. I bribed the guard to give us a complete first-class carriage to ourselves. It was not an express train, so it* MUST *have stopped at Kilmarnock, Dumfries, Carlisle, Leeds and all stations north of Watford Junction, but I knew only the motion and brief pauses in our pilgrimage of passion. I was man enough for her, but the pace was terrific.*

"Is this causing you pain, McCandless?" asked Baxter.
"Go on!" I told him, hiding my face in my hands, "Go on!"
"Then I will, but remember he is exaggerating."

*At last the rattle of points, shriek of whistles and decreasing rhythm of the wheels showed that our coal-fired steed was panting to a halt in the southern terminus of the Midland line. As we adjusted our clothing she said, "I can't wait to do that all over again in a proper bed." Feeling sure our Acts of Union had obliterated all feeling for the other man I again asked her to marry me. She said in a surprised way, "Don't you remember my answer to that one? Let us go to the station hotel and order a huge breakfast. I want porridge and bacon and eggs and sausages and kippers and heaps of buttered toast and pints of sweet hot milky tea. And you must eat a lot too!"*

*I needed the hotel. The previous day had been a strenuous one and I had now not slept for twenty-four hours. Bella seemed as fresh as when we left Glasgow. As we approached the reception desk I stumbled, clung to her arm for support and heard her say, "My poor man is exhausted. We shall need to have breakfast served in our room."*

*And so it befell that while Bella ate her huge breakfast I removed my coat, shoes, collar and lay down for a brief nap on top of the bed. I had many dreams, but the only one I remember is entering a barber's shop to be shaved by Mary Queen of Scots. She coated my face and throat with warm soapy lather and had just begun removing it when I woke to find I was really being shaved by Bella. I lay naked in bed, my shoulders and head supported by pillows with a towel spread over them. Bella, wearing a silk négligé, was stroking my cheeks with the honed edge of my razor. She laughed aloud to see how wide I opened my eyes.*

*She said, "I'm taking your bristles off to make you as smooth and sweet and handsome as you were last night, Wedder, because it is almost night again. Don't look so terrified, I'm not going to slash you! I've shaved off a lot of hair around wounds and suppurations in the carcasses of dogs, cats and an old mongoose. What a sound sleeper you are! You never opened your eyes this morning when I undressed you and slid you between the sheets. Guess where I've been today! Westminster Abbey and Madame Tussaud's and a matinée performance of* Hamlet. *How wonderful to hear ordinary soldiers and princes and grave-diggers talking poetry! I wish that I talked poetry all the time. I also saw a lot of ragged little children and I gave them some of the money I took from your pockets before I went out. Now I'll wipe your face with these soft warm cloths, and help you into your nice quilted dressing-gown, and you can sit up for half an hour before bedtime and eat the tasty supper I have ordered, for we must maintain your strength, Wedder."*

*I arose in that dazed state felt by all who oversleep from exhaustion and waken when they usually retire. The supper was a collation of cold meats, pickles and salad with an apple tart and two bottles of India Export Ale. There was coffee from a pot kept hot on a trivet by the fire. Growing livelier and more alert I glanced at my Fate who had curled herself snakelike in the easy chair across the table from me. She gazed upon me with a smile of such peculiar meaning that I shuddered with awe, dread and intense desire. Her naked shoulders were white against the dishevelled black cloak of her hair, her softly heaving . . .*

"I am going to omit several sentences here, McCandless," said Baxter, "for they are hideously over-written, even by Wedderburn's standards. All they tell us is that he and our Bella spent the night as they had spent it on the train, except that shortly before 7 a.m. he begged her to let him sleep. I will read on from that point."

*"Why?" she asked. "You can sleep all you like after breakfast. I've told the management here that you are an invalid, and they're very sympathetic."*
*"I don't want to spend my whole honeymoon in the Midland railway terminal hotel," I sobbed, forgetting in my anguish that we had never married, "I had meant us to go abroad."*
*"Whoopee!" she said, "I love abroad. Which bit of it first?"*
*In Glasgow (which now seemed years ago) I had planned to enjoy her in some quiet little inn of a lonely Breton fishing village, but now the thought of being in a lonely place with Bella chilled me to the soul. I muttered, "Amsterdam," and fell asleep.*

*She woke me at ten, having gone to the Thomas Cook agency with my wallet, arranged for us to catch an afternoon boat to the Hague, paid our hotel bill, packed our bags and taken them to the foyer. Only my dressing-case and a fresh suit of clothes remained.*
*"I'm hungry and sleepy! I want my breakfast in bed!" I cried.*
*"Don't worry poor lad," she said soothingly. "Breakfast will be downstairs for us in another ten minutes, then you can sleep all you like on the cab, the train, the boat, the other train and the other cab."*

*Now you know the pattern of my existence as we fled across Europe and round the Mediterranean. My strenuous waking hours were all at night in bed with a woman who never slept, so during the day I was either dozing or being guided about in a daze. I foresaw this likelihood before leaving London, and on the boat to the Hague decided to prevent it by* EXHAUSTING *Bella! I can almost hear the yells of fiendish laughter erupting from your hideous throat at the folly of the idea. By an iron exertion of will-power and continual cups of strong black coffee I rushed her daily by train, riverboat and cab to and in and out of the most tumultuous hotels, theatres, museums, racecourses and alas alas gambling casinos on the Continent, covering four nations in a single week. She enjoyed every minute of it, and with bright glances and light caresses promised she would soon show her gratitude in private acts of love. My one hope became this: that though the public transports and giddy whirl of the day did not reduce her to unconsciousness when she got to bed, they might do it for me. Vain hope! Between Bella and the natural Wedderburn—the lowest part of Wedderburn—was a sympathetic bond which my poor tortured brain* COULD NOT *stupefy or resist. Again and again I fell into bed as into the sleep of death and woke soon after to find I was pleasuring her. Like a victim of vertigo flinging himself* FORWARD *over a precipice instead of backward away from it, I* CONSCIOUSLY *embraced the dance of love with groans of ecstasy and despair until gleams of light through the shutters showed I was entering the purgatory of yet another day. In Venice I collapsed, rolled down the steps of San Giorgio Maggiore into the lagoon, thought I was drowning and thanked God for it. I woke up in bed with Bella again. I was seasick. We were in a first-class cabin of a ship cruising the Mediterranean.*

*"Poor Wedder, you have been forcing the pace!" she said. "No more casinos and café dansants for you! I am your doctor now and I order complete rest, except when we are cosy together, like now."*

*From then on until the day I escaped I was a man of straw and her helpless plaything. But by staying prone whenever possible during daytime I at last began to slowly recover some strength.*

*Yet I still thought her kind! GUFFAW! GUFFAW!! GUFFAW!!! Yes, you damnable Baxter, let the violence of your laughter split your damnable sides! I still believed my Angelic Fiend was kind! When she raised my head with her arm to put forkfuls of food into my mouth, tears of gratitude rolled down my cheeks. When she steered me into British banks in the ports we touched, told the clerk that her poor man was not very well and steered my hand to sign a cheque or money order, tears of gratitude rolled down my cheeks. One glittering blue day we two lay side by side and hand in hand on deck-chairs, steaming down the Bosphorus with all Asia to port of us and Europe to starboard, or vice versa.*

*"You are only good for one thing, Wedder," she said thoughtfully, "but you are very good at it indeed, a true grandee monarch magnifico excellency emperor lord-high-paramount president principal provost bobby-dazzler and boss at it."*

*Tears of gratitude rolled down my cheeks. I was so dependent and dilapidated that I still kept begging her hopelessly to marry me. My eyes were not even opened by the events in Gibraltar.*

*We left the ship and stayed there for a time while I arranged to sell my Scottish Widows and Orphans shares, a transaction which could not be hurried. I remember a bank manager saying in an insistent way which made my head ache, "Are you sure you know what you are doing, Mr. Wedderburn?" so I looked at Bella who said simply, "We need money Wedder, and we are not the only ones." I signed a document. She led me out of the bank and through the Alameda Gardens toward the South Bastion, where we had lodgings. Suddenly Bella was confronted by a stout, stately, well-dressed woman who said, "How astonishing to see you Lady Blessington, when did you arrive? Why did you not call on us at once? Do you not remember me? Surely we were introduced four years ago, at Cowes, on board the Prince of Wales' yacht?"*

*"How wonderful!" cried Bella. "But most folk call me Bell Baxter when I'm not with my Wedderburn."*

*"But surely—surely you are the wife of General Blessington who I met at Cowes?"*

*"Oo I hope so! Though God says I was in South America four years ago. What is my husband like? Handsomer than droopy old Wedders here? Taller? Stronger? Richer?"*

*"There is obviously some mistake," said the lady coldly, "though your appearance and voice are remarkably similar."*

*She bowed and walked on.*

*"I saw that woman bowling along in an open carriage yesterday," said Bella broodingly, "and someone said she was the wife of an old admiral who governs this great big Rock. She never answered one of my questions. Can I crash in on her and ask them again? Why should I* not *have a*

*spare military husband somewhere, and more than the few names I already have, and go for sails on royal yachts?''*

*It was thus I learned that my Awful Mistress had no memories of her life before the shock which made that strangely regular crack which circles her skull under the hair—IF CRACK IT BE, Mr. Baxter! But YOU know, and I NOW KNOW what it REALLY is—*

"Baxter," I groaned, "has Wedderburn deduced everything?"

"Wedderburn has deduced nothing sensible, McCandless. His flimsy brain has never recovered from his breakdown in Venice. Listen."

*YOU know, and I NOW KNOW what it REALLY is—a witch mark. Yes! The female equivalent of the mark of Cain, branding its owner as a lemur, vampire, succubus and thing unclean.*

"I will now skip six pages of superstitious drivel and resume on the second last page where he describes Bella bringing him to Paris by overnight train. They are again short of money so do not want to pay for a cab. They stroll through not-yet-crowded streets where the huge returning wagons of the night-soil collectors are the only vehicles. The sky is milky grey, the air fresh, sparrows audible. Bell gazes with eager pleasure at all she sees, though carrying their luggage in two heavy cases, one on each shoulder. Wedderburn carries nothing. He has recovered most of his physical strength but dare not admit it to Bella lest (I quote) *she drain me once more of all manhood.* Listen."

*The Rue Huchette is a very narrow street near the river. Here we found a small rather noisy hotel, considering the hour. The waiter of a nearby café was setting out chairs and tables on the cobbles, so I sat while Bella went to investigate.*

*She soon returned without the luggage and in high spirits. A room would be ready for us in an hour; also the manageress, though the widow of a Frenchman, had been born in London and spoke fluent Cockney. She had invited Bella to wait in her office, and as it was very small would I like to sit where I was? I could wait in a foyer if I preferred, but the foyers too were very small, many overnight customers were about to leave and might tumble over me. In a dolorous voice I said I would wait outside, hiding my delight at the first chance since our elopement to be without Bella in the open air. She smiled so brightly as she whisked back into the hotel that I nearly believed she was as glad to be rid of me.*

*From the waiter I ordered coffee, a croissant and a cognac. These gave me courage. At last I felt strong enough to open and read the letter I had received in Gibraltar along with the money order from the Clydesdale and North of Scotland Bank. I knew that letter, addressed to me in my mother's hand, would be full of bitter and just reproaches: reproaches I could never have faced without brandy in my guts and* NO BELLA *beside me, for Bella would never have left me in peace to stew in the remorse and misery I so richly deserved. Almost luxuriously I tore open the envelope and winced over its contents.*

*The news was more terrible than I had feared. Mother was nearly destitute. She could only afford to keep two servants now, Auld Jessy and the cook. With these two I had first discovered the pleasures of love, but they were now long past their best. Auld Jessy had grown so doddery we had meant to send her to the poor-house after Christmas. Cook was now a dipsomaniac. These served mother without pay because nobody else would give them house-room. Less tragic but more poignant was the fact that my frail lovely mother, a lonely widow of forty-six years, could no longer order clothes from London and Edinburgh, but must shop for them herself, in Glasgow. Guilt and rage brought me panting to my feet—mainly rage against Bella, for* what had she done with all my money? *Without thinking I strode forward down a lane like a corridor, grinding my teeth at the memory of my sufferings in the grip of that gorgeous monster.*

*Was it the Hand of God that steered me over that busy bridge then stopped me short before the open door of the great Cathedral? I think it was. I had never entered a Roman Catholic edifice before. What trembling hope drew me into this one?*

*I saw receding aisles of mighty pillars like avenues of titanic stone trees upholding an overarching dimness; I heard a glorious blast of* Honestly, McCandless, his style is so sickeningly derivative that I will summarize what follows. Duncan Doubleyou has never prayed to God before but decides he'll have a go because others are doing it here. He drops a centime into a box through a slit in the lid; lights a candle; sticks it on a spike before an altar; kneels down with tight shut eyes and tells The First Mover of All Things that Duncan Doubleyou is evil wicked rotten and wrong mainly because of Bad Bell Baxter, so please send help. Suddenly the world feels brighter. Wedderburn, opening eyes, sees sunlight beaming in on him through stained-glass window behind altar; rays through a heart-shaped crimson pane are casting a bright pink shadow on the bosom of Duncan Doubleyou's white silk fashionable waistcoat. A personal telegram to Duncan Doubleyou from The Prime Mover? DW's first reaction is Protestant. He wants to go somewhere private and think it over, a small intimate place with a seat and a lock on the door where he can be safe from interruption. He sees a row of cubicles with ordinary folk going in and out, each door with an indicator saying if vacant or engaged. He bolts himself into a vacancy which of course proves to be a confessional box. If I tell you that the padre behind the grille spoke English, can you guess what happened then, McCandless?"

"Not exactly."

"Wedderburn wants to confess all his sins from the age of five (when Auld Jessy taught him masturbation) to half an hour earlier when Bella booked him into what sounded like a brothel. He also wants professional advice on the value of the Sacred Heart telegram just got from God. Priest says all who pray before that shrine get that telegram when the sun shines from a certain direction, and the message is always good if properly read. Priest says he cannot absolve Monsieur Doubleyou of his sins because Monsieur is a heretic or pagan, but if Monsieur Doubleyou will give a five-minute précis of the sins which now so afflict him, priest will give him a straight opinion. Out pours the story. Priest tells Monsieur Doubleyou to marry Bella and go home to his mother or leave Bella and go home to his mother or rot in Hell. Priest advises Monsieur Doubleyou to take instruction in the Catholic Faith when he returns to Glasgow and now Adieu Monsieur, I will pray for your soul. Wedderburn steps into the street where *the sunlight shone on me like a benediction, for I felt that a hideous burden had fallen from my shoulders* et cetera. In other words, he at last discovers he is sick and tired of Bella. Back to the hotel then! Bella is unpacking in the bedroom. 'Stop!' cries Wedderburn, and tells her he must return to Glasgow and WORK, but he cannot take her with him unless she returns as his wife. She says cheerfully, 'That's all right Wedder, I want to see a bit more of Paris,' packs his things into one of the cases and gives him money for the fare home. He says, 'Is that all?' She says, 'It's all that's left of your money, but if you need more I'll give you what God gave me.' She takes out her sewing-scissors, unstitches the lining of her travelling-coat, removes £500 in Bank of England notes and gives it to him saying, 'That is to pay for all the fun you gave me. You deserve a lot more, but this is all I have. Still, it's quite a lot, and God gave it to me because he said something like this would happen with you.'

"I now return to the letter, McCandless. Wedderburn's description of how he acted on hearing that I knew of his elopement before it happened is of great clinical interest."

*As my brain tried at once to grasp and repel the hideous meaning of her words I came to know what madness is. Writhing my head from shoulder to shoulder and mouthing as if biting the air or silently screaming I retreated into a corner and slowly sank to the floor, frantically punching at the space around my head as if boxing with a loathsome and swarming antagonist like huge wasps or carnivorous bats; yet I knew these vermin were not really outside but* INSIDE *my brain and gnawing, gnawing. They gnaw there still. Bella must have called in her new friend, the manageress, but my madness multiplied these two into a jabbering crowd of dishevelled women of every age and shape, their scanty clothing displaying their sexual charms to the full as they flooded vengefully over me like all the serving-women I have ever seduced. And Bella seemed one of them! With their strong soft limbs they bound my limbs and body as tight as a baby in swaddling bands. They poured brandy down my throat. I grew stupid and passive. Bella took me by cab to the Gare du Nord, bought a ticket, put it in my waistcoat pocket, told me which other pockets held money and passport, placed me and my luggage in a train, and all the time she poured out a maddening stream of soothing chat: "—poor Wedder, poor old lad, I've been bad for you, I've over-tired you, I bet you are glad to be going home to your mother's house and a nice long rest, think of the money you will save, but we had some good times together, I don't regret a moment of it, I'm sure there is not a better athlete and sportsman than Duncan Wedderburn in the whole wide world but do tell God I want the candle soon do you remember our first night in the train?" et cetera, and when the train moved from the station she ran along the platform beside it shouting through the window,* "GIVE MY LOVE TO BONNY SCOTLAND!"

*So I know who your niece is now, Mr. Baxter. The Jews called her Eve and Delilah; the Greeks, Helen of Troy; the Romans, Cleopatra; the Christians, Salome. She is the White Daemon who destroys the honour and manhood of the noblest and most virile men in every age. She came to me in the guise of Bella Baxter. To King Louis she was Madame de Maintenon, to Prince Charlie she was Clementina Walkinshaw, to Robert Burns she was Jean Armour et cetera and to General Blessington she was Victoria Hattersley. Does that name make you tremble, Lucifer Baxter? The General's matrimonial disaster was not noised aloud by the newspapers, but we lawyers have other sources of knowledge, and through these I have penetrated your secret.* FOR THE WHITE DAEMON IS IN EVERY AGE AND NATION THE PUPPET AND TOOL OF A VASTER, DARKER DAEMON!!!!! *Eve was ruled by the Serpent, Delilah by the Philistine Elders, Madame de Maintenon by Cardinal Thingummy and Bella Baxter by* YOU, *Godwin Bysshe Baxter, Arch-Fiend and Manipulator of this Age of Material Science! Only in Modern Glasgow—the* BABYLON *of Material Science—could you have gained wealth, power and respect by carving up human brains, prowling through morgues and haunting the death-beds of the poor. You would have been burned as a warlock for that when Scotland was a Spiritual Nation, GOD-SWINE BOSH BACK-STAIR, BEAST OF THE BOTTOMLESS PIT!!!!!*

*You probably do not know you are Antichrist, for none are as deluded as the damned, so the Father of All Lies is condemned to know himself least of all. But you are a scientist. Examine the proofs I will now present coldly and logically, without using a lot of capital letters, except at the start.*

*THE COMING OF THE BEAST*

| *BIBLE PROPHECIES* | *MODERN FACTS* |
|---|---|
| *1 The number of the Beast is 666.* | *You live at 18 Park Circus, which number is the sum of 6+6+6.* |
| *2 The Beast supports a Woman clothed in scarlet.* | *Bella is very fond of red.* |
| *3 The Beast is called* Babylon, *because that city ruled the biggest* material empire *in the ancient world, and persecuted the children of God, the* spiritual *people of that day. (Note that Protestant fanatics say Rome is the modern Babylon and the headquarters of the Beast, but remember that Roman* | *The British Empire is the largest Empire the world has ever known. It is wholly* material, *being based on industry, trade and military might. It was invented in Glasgow. Here James Watt conceived the steam engines which drive the British rail trains and merchant fleets and battle fleets, and here the best of* |

| BIBLE PROPHECIES | MODERN FACTS |
|---|---|
| Catholicism—with all its flaws—is nowadays a wholly spiritual empire.) | these locomotives and ships are built. Here Adam Smith invented modern capitalism. Here Sir William Thomson devises the telegraph cables binding the empire together over the ocean floors, also the diesel electric engines of the future. |
| 4 The Beast (and the Woman he supports) are also called Mystery. | Chemistry, electricity, anatomy et cetera are Mysteries to nearly everybody—except you! |
| 5 The Beast is worshipped by all the kings of this earth. | Though Queen Victoria prefers Edinburgh to Glasgow, Balmoral to the rest of Scotland, the Grand Duke Alexis, son of the Tsar of Russia, called Glasgow "The centre of intelligence of England" in his speech at the launching of the Livadia last year, built for his father at Elder's shipyard. |
| 6 The Beast has seven heads—seven bits sticking up. (Protestant fanatics say it must therefore be Roman | But Glasgow is built on seven hills! Golf Hill, Balmano Brae, Blythswood Hill, Garnet Hill, Partick |

| *BIBLE PROPHECIES* | *MODERN FACTS* |
|---|---|
| *because Rome is notoriously built upon seven hills.)* | *Hill, Gilmore Hill crowned by the University, Woodlands Hill crowned by Park Circus where you sacrificed me to the Scarlet Whore of Modern Babylon!* |
| *7 The Scarlet Woman on the Beast's back holds a golden cup full of abominations.* | *I do not exactly know what the cup is nowadays because Bella disliked wine and spirits, but if you and I meet and discuss the matter calmly surely we will find something?* |

*I am horribly lonely. Mother keeps telling me to pull myself together. I long to sit close to her but when I do she fidgets and asks why I do not go out to music-hall, sports-club or other "THINGS" I used to be busy with before my trip abroad. I dread such "THINGS" nowadays. When I was little Auld Jessy cared for me when Mother got the fidgets. So now I pretend to go out for a "night on the town" but skulk round by the backdoor tradesman's entrance into the kitchen, where I sit tippling with Auld Jessy and the cook. I never drank alcohol in my Casanova days, for a devotee of Venus must abjure Bacchus. It is cold in the kitchen. I have so wasted the Wedderburn fortune that Mother cannot afford to let servants use our coals. Auld Jessy and the cook sleep together for warmth, so I sleep between them. I cannot sleep alone. Come back please warm me Bella.*

*Tomorrow I will start a new life by doing three things all at once. I will make Mother rich again by undeviating devotion to the science and art of property conveyancing. I will save my Bella from Beastly Baxter by boxing with the Modern Babylon at street corners, in the open forum of Glasgow Green and through letters to the press. I will embrace the only true Catholic faith, make a vow of eternal chastity, and end my days in the peace of a cloister. I need rest. Help me.*

*I am Faithfully and Forever,*

*Bella's Outcast Welter Weight*

*Bleeding Waistcoat Hearted*

*Duncan McNab Wed Wed Wedder*

*(Writer to the Signet and Auld Jessy's Big Tumshie).*

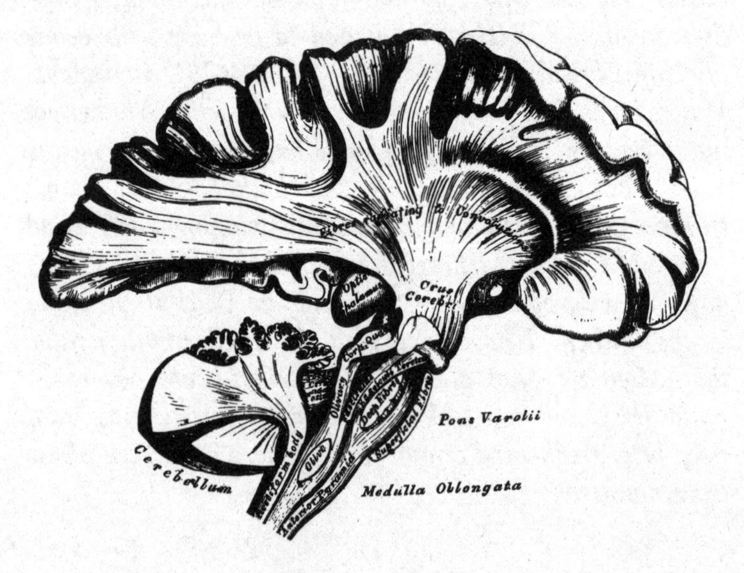

# 13

# Intermission

WE WERE SILENT FOR A WHILE AFTER Baxter stopped reading. At last I said, "Can we do nothing to save that poor fellow's sanity?"
"Nothing," said Baxter crisply. He had put the sheaf of pages back in an envelope and from a brown paper packet drew out a bulkier sheaf. Holding it carefully on his knees he smiled down at it, gently caressing the topmost page with the tiny delicate tips of his conical thumbs.
"A letter from Bell?" I asked. He nodded and said, "Why worry about Wedderburn, McCandless? He is a middle-class male in the prime of life with legal training, a secure home and three supportive females. Think of your fiancée, the attractive woman with the three-year-old brain he has left penniless in Paris. Do you not fear for her?"
"No. With all his advantages Wedderburn is a poor creature. Bell is not."
"True. Right. Correct. Exactly. Yes indeed!" cried he in an ecstasy of agreement. I said grimly, "Bell's use of synonyms seems infectious. Has she many in that letter?"
He smiled at me like a wise old teacher whose favourite pupil has answered a difficult question and said, "Forgive my excitement, McCandless. You cannot share it because you have never been a parent, have never made something new and splendid. It is wonderful for a creator to see the offspring live, feel and act independently. I read Genesis three years ago and could not understand God's displeasure

when Eve and Adam chose to know good and evil—chose to be Godlike. That should have been his proudest hour."

"They deliberately disobeyed him!" I said, forgetting *The Origin of Species* and speaking with the voice of *The Shorter Catechism*. "He had given them life and everything they could enjoy, everything on earth, except two forbidden trees. Those were sacred mysteries whose fruit did harm. Nothing but perverse greed made them eat it."

Baxter shook his head and said, "Only bad religions depend on mysteries, just as bad governments depend on secret police. Truth, beauty and goodness are not mysterious, they are the commonest, most obvious, most essential facts of life, like sunlight, air and bread. Only folk whose heads are muddled by expensive educations think truth, beauty, goodness are rare private properties. Nature is more liberal. The universe keeps nothing essential from us—it is all present, all gift. God is the universe plus mind. Those who say God, or the universe, or nature is mysterious, are like those who call these things jealous or angry. They are announcing the state of their lonely, muddled minds."

"Utter blethers, Baxter!" I cried. "Our whole lives are a struggle with mysteries. Mysteries endanger us, support us, destroy us. Our great scientists have cleared away these mysteries in some directions by deepening them in others. The second law of thermo-dynamics proves the universe will end by turning into cold porridge, but nobody knows how it began, or if it began. Our science stems from Kepler's discovery of gravitation, but though we can describe how the vastest galaxies and flimsiest gases gravitate we don't know what gravity is or how it works. Kepler speculated that it was a form of inorganic intelligence. Modern physicists do not even speculate, but hide their ignorance under formulae. We know how species began but cannot create the smallest living cell. You grafted a baby's brain into a mother's skull. Very clever. It does not make you an all-knowing god."

"I disagree with your language, not your facts, McCandless," said Baxter with another annoyingly generous smile.

"Of course no single mind can know more than a fraction of past, present and future existence. But what you call *mysteries* I call *ignorances*, and nothing we do not know (whatever we call it) is more holy, sacred and wonderful than the things we know—the things we are! The loving kindness of people is what creates and supports us, keeps our society running and lets us move freely in it."

"Lust, fear of hunger and the police also play a part. Read me Bell's letter."

"I will, but let me start by astonishing you. This letter is a diary written over a period of three months. Compare the first page with the last."

He handed me two pages.

They did astonish me, though the first, as I expected, was covered with big capital letters cryptically grouped:

*DR GD I HD N PC T WRT BFR*
*W R FLT PN THS BL BL S*

The last page contained forty lines of closely written words, of which a sentence caught my eye:

*Tell my dear Candle that his wedding Bell no longer thinks he must do all she bids.*

"Good for a three-year-old?" asked Baxter.

"She is still learning," I said, returning the two pages.

"Still learning! Still gaining wisdom and aptitude for life while struggling toward what is good in it. This letter justifies me, McCandless. Imagine I am Shakespeare's old schoolteacher, one who taught him to write. Imagine this letter is a present from my former pupil, the original manuscript of *Hamlet* in his own hand. The soul who wrote this has soared as far beyond my own soul as my soul soars beyond—"

He checked himself, looked away from me then said, "—at least beyond Duncan Wedderburn. My Shakespearean analogy is not far-fetched, McCandless. The close-packed sense within her sentences, her puns, her very cadences are Shakespeare's."

"Then read it to me."

"At once! It is undated, but obviously begun on shipboard soon after Wedderburn knelt snivelling in a Trieste gutter, or (if you prefer his own vainglorious account of the incident) soused himself in the Grand Canal. Apart from that detail Bella's letter confirms the main part of his: even confirms one fact which he reported as a hallucination. But her epistle outshines Wedderburn's as vividly as the Gospel according to Saint Matthew (which contains Christ's sermon on the mount) outshines the Gospel according to Saint John (which does not). Or have I got that wrong, McCandless? You had the Bible drummed into you at school. Was it Saint Mark or Saint Luke who—"

I said I would break into the closet where his father kept the port if he did not start reading. He said, "At once then! But before I read let me give you a *title* for Bell's letter, a title which is not her own but which will prepare you for the breadth, depth and height of what her letter encompasses. I call it MAKING A CONSCIENCE. Listen."
He cleared his throat and read with a distinct tone and grave elation I thought theatrical. Later his delivery was interrupted by a few heartfelt sobs he tried, and failed, to contain. The following letter is given, not as Bella spelled it, but as Baxter recited it.

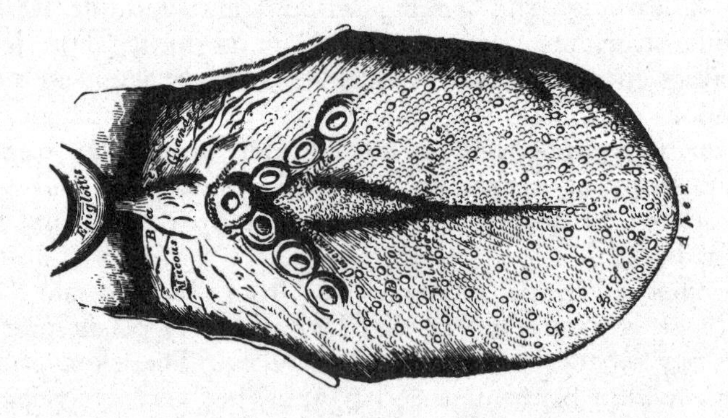

# BELLA BAXTER'S LETTER: MAKING A CONSCIENCE

# 14

# Glasgow to Odessa: The Gamblers

*Dear God,*
*I had no peace to write before*
*we are afloat upon this blue blue sea.*
*Wedder is snug in bunk and glad at last*
*not to be do do doing all the time—*
*the silly chap has done some silly things.*
*How Auld Lang Syne seems that soft warm bright night*
*when I bade you good-bye, chloroformed Candle,*
*then skipped down ladder into Wedder's arms.*
*Swift as the wind we sped in cab to train*
*and curtained carriage where we wed wed wed,*
*went wedding all the way to London town*
*and booked into Saint Pancras's Hotel.*
*And yet poor Duncan wanted marriage too!*
*He did not get it. Please tell Candle so.*
*You never wedded, God, so may not know*
*eight hours of it takes much more out of men*
*than they can give without a lot of rest.*

*Next day was all my own. I saw some sights,*
*then waked my Wedder with a good high tea.*
*"Where have you been?"*
*I told.*
*"Who did you meet?"*
*"No one." "Do you expect me to believe*
*you walked all day and never saw a man?"*
*"No—I saw crowds of men but spoke to none,*
*except a policeman in Regent's Park*
*from whom I asked the way to Drury Lane."*
*"Of course!" he said. "It would be the police!*
*They're very tall and handsome are they not?*
*Guards officers are strong and handsome too.*
*They prowl the parks for girls who won't say no.*
*Perhaps your* policeman *was in the Guards.*
*The uniforms are very similar."*
*"Have you gone daft?" I asked him. "What is wrong?"*
*"I'm not the only man you ever loved—*
*admit you have had hundreds before me!"*
*"Not hundreds—no. I never counted them,*
*but half a hundred might be about right."*
*He gasped, gaped, groaned, writhed, sobbed*
*and tore his hair*
*then asked for details. That is how I learned*
*he did not think that kissing hands is love.*
*Love (Wedder thinks) only deserves the name*
*when men insert their middle footless leg.*
*"If that is so Dear Wedder, rest assured*
*you are the only man I ever loved."*
*"Liar cheat whore!" he screamed. "I am no fool!*
*You are no virgin! Who deflowered you first?"*
*It took a while to find out what he meant.*

*It seems that women who have not been wed*
*by wedders like my Wedder all possess*
*a slip of skin across the loving groove*
*where Wedderburns poke their peninsula.*
*This slip of skin he never found on me.*
*"And how do you explain the scar?" he asked,*
*referring to a thin white line which starts*
*among the curls above my loving groove*
*and, like the Greenwich line of longitude,*
*divides in two the belly Solomon*
*has somewhere likened to a heap of wheat.*
*"Surely all women's stomachs have that line."*
*"No no!" says Wedder. "Only pregnant ones*
*who've been cut open to let babies out."*
*"That must have been B.C.B.K.," I said,*
*"the time Before they Cracked poor Bella's Knob."*
*I let him feel that crack which rings my skull*
*just underneath the hair. He sighed and said,*
*"I told you everything—my inmost thoughts,*
*childhood and darkest deeds. Why did you not*
*speak of* your *past? Or rather, lack of past."*
*"You never gave me time before tonight*
*to tell you anything, you talked so much.*
*I thought you did not want to know my past,*
*my thoughts and hopes and anything of me*
*not obviously useful when we wed."*
*"You're right—I am a fiend! I ought to die!"*
*he yelled, then punched his head, burst into tears,*
*pulled off his trousers, wed me very quick.*
*I soothed him, babied him (he* is *a baby)*
*and got him wedding at a proper speed.*
*Yes, wed he can and does, but little Candle,*

*if you are reading this do not feel sad.*
*Women need Wedderburns but love much more*
*their faithful kindly man who waits at home.*

*I had a baby once. God, is that true?*
*If it is true what has become of her?*
*For I am somehow sure she is a girl.*
*This is a thought too big for Bell to think.*
*I must grow into it by slow degrees.*

*God, do you read the change there is in me?*
*I am not quite as selfish as I was.*
*I felt for Candle though he is not here*
*and tried to comfort him. I start to fear*
*the feeling that will grow if I think much*
*about the little daughter I have lost.*
*Strange how the baby-minded Wedderburn*
*has taught this cracked and empty-headed Bell*
*to be more feelingful for other folk.*
*He managed it by making me his nurse*
*when we reached Switzerland. I'll tell you how.*

*The jealousy which he had shown in London*
*did not depart when we reached Amsterdam.*
*The only time we were not arm-in-arm*
*was when he left me in a waiting-room*
*to see a doctor for his* lethargy —
*that's what he called the tiredness that he felt,*
*which was quite natural. We all need rest,*
*and time to sit and look and dream and think.*
*The doctor's pills let him dispense with rest.*
*We rushed through racecourses and boxing-clubs,*

*cathedrals, café-dansants, music-halls.*
*His face was white, his eyes grew huge and shone.*
*"I am no weakling, Bell!" he cried. "On! On!"*

*Thank you, dear God, for teaching me to sleep*
*by simply sitting down and shutting eyes.*
*In omnibuses, trains, cabs, trams and boats*
*this came in handy, but was not enough—*
*I had to find some other way to sleep.*
*The second night abroad we went to see*
*an opera by Wagner. It was long,*
*and Wedder, every time I shut my eyes,*
*nudged me and hissed, "Wake up and concentrate!"*
*This taught me how to sleep with open eyes.*
*Soon I could also do it standing up*
*and rushing arm-in-arm from place to place.*
*I think I answered questions in my sleep—*
*the only answer he required was, "Yes dear."*
*I always wakened up in our hotels,*
*offices where I sent you telegrams*
*(while Wedder telegrammed to his mama)*
*in restaurants, because I like my food,*
*but nowhere else except the Frankfort zoo*
*and German betting-shop I will describe.*

*I think it was the smell which wakened me.*
*This place (just like the zoo) stank of despair,*
*and fearful hope, also of stale obsession*
*which seemed a mixture of the first two stinks.*
*My fancy nose perhaps exaggerated—*
*I opened eyes upon a brilliant room.*
*Do you remember taking me to see*

*the Glasgow Stock Exchange? It looked like that.*
*Around me fluted columns, cream and gold,*
*held up a vaulted ceiling, blue and white,*
*from which hung shining crystal chandeliers*
*which lit up all the business underneath—*
*six tables where smart people played roulette.*
*Against the walls were sofas, scarlet plush,*
*where more smart people sat, and one was me.*
*And Wedderburn was standing by my side,*
*and gazing at the table nearest us,*
*and muttering, "I see. I see. I see."*
*I thought that he was talking in his sleep*
*with open eyes, as I had done. I said,*
*(gentle but firm) "Let's go to our hotel,*
*dear Duncan. I will put you into bed."*
*He stared at me, then slowly shook his head.*
*"Not yet. Not yet. I have a thing to do.*
*I know you inwardly despise my brain—*
*think it a mere appendage to my prick*
*and less efficient than my testicles.*
*I tell you Bella, that this brain now grasps*
*a mighty FACT which other men call CHANCE*
*because they cannot grasp it. Now I see*
*that GOD, FATE, DESTINY, like LUCK and CHANCE*
*are noises glorifying IGNORANCE*
*under the label of a solemn name.*
*Up, woman, and attend me to the game!"*
*The people at the table turned to stare*
*as we approached. One offered him a chair.*
*He murmured thanks, and into it he slid.*
*I stood behind to watch, as he had bid.*

*Dear God I am tired. It is late. Writing like Shakespeare is hard work for a woman with a cracked head who cannot spell properly, though I notice my writing is getting smaller. Tomorrow we stop at Athens. Do you remember taking me there ages ago by way of Zagreb and Sarajevo? I hope they have mended the Parthenon. Now I will creep to Wedder's side and say what led to his collapse another day, ending this entry with a line of stars.*

* * * * * * * * * * * * * *

*At dawn our ship, which is a Russian one,*
*left Constantinetcetera; now we steam*
*out of the Bosphorus toward Odessa.*
*The air is fresh and calm, the sky clear blue.*
*I wrapped my man up warm and made him sit*
*outside upon a deck-chair for an hour.*
*Had I not done it he'd have crouched below,*
*reading the Bible in his bunk all day.*
*Again he begged to be joined onto me*
*in "wholly wedlock". Wholly wedlock! Ugh.*
*The joys of wedding cannot be locked up,*
*not even partly, nor can his nipple-noddle*
*remember I must marry someone else.*

*The mob who clustered round the roulette table*
*did not seem smart when we were part of it.*
*Of course some folk were rich or richly dressed*
*with fine silk waistcoats, officers' tail coats*
*and obvious breasts in low-cut velvet gowns.*
*Others were wealthy in a middling way*
*like merchants, owners of small properties*
*or clergymen, all very neat and sober,*

*and some of them escorted by their wives.*
*At first I did not notice any poor*
*(the obviously poor were not let in)*
*but then I saw some clothes were not quite clean,*
*or fraying at the cuffs, or buttoned high*
*to hide the colour of the underwear.*
*The rich laid gold and notes upon the squares.*
*Middle folk bet with silver more than gold,*
*and thought a lot before they placed their bets.*
*The poorest people staked the smallest coins,*
*or stood and stared with faces white as Wedder's.*
*Folk who moved money fast were rich or poor,*
*or turning quickly into rich or poor:*
*yet rich, poor, middling—frantic, stunned, amused—*
*young, in the prime of strength or elderly—*
*German, French, Spaniard, Russian or Swede—*
*even some English folk who seldom bid*
*but stared about as if superior—*
*had something wrong with them. I worked out what,*
*but not before the damage had been done.*

*The spinning wheel and little rattling ball*
*ground something down in those who bet and watched,*
*and they were pleased to feel it ground away*
*because it was so precious that they loathed it,*
*and loved to see others destroy it too.*
*I've since discussed this with a clever man*
*who says the precious thing has many names.*
*Poor people call it money; priests, the soul;*
*the Germans call it will and poets, love.*
*He called it freedom, for that makes men feel*
*to blame for what they do. Men hate that feeling,*

*so want it crushed and killed. I am no man.*
*To me the place stank like a Roman game*
*where tortured minds, not bodies were the show.*
*This crowd had come to see the human mind*
*whose thoughts can wander through eternity*
*pinned to a little accidental ball.*
*Poor Wedder, meanwhile, had begun to bet.*

*Most of the gamblers shifted bets about*
*from black squares onto red and back again.*
*Wedderburn bet upon a single square*
*marked zero, laying one gold coin on it.*
*He lost, bet two, lost those, then bet and lost*
*four, eight, sixteen, then laid down thirty-two.*
*A wooden-rake-man pushed back twelve of these—*
*twenty was highest bet the shop would take.*
*Wedderburn shrugged and let the twenty lie.*
*The ball was rattled round and Wedder won.*
*He won a lot. The little rolls of gold*
*were given him in small blue envelopes.*
*He turned and faced me with a happy smile,*
*the first I had from him since we eloped.*
*While pocketing the gold he murmured, "Well?*
*You did not know that I could do it, Bell!"*
*I felt such pity for his muddled head*
*I did not notice he was glad to think*
*he had done something to astonish me.*
*I should have said, "O Duncan you were grand!*
*I nearly fainted, I was so impressed—*
*now let us have a meal to celebrate."*
*I should have said that. What I said was this.*
*"O Duncan please take me away from here!*

*Let us play billiards—billiards need some skill.*
*Come, let us set the perfect ivory globes*
*gliding and clicking on the smooth green cloth."*
*His face, from white, went red. He frightened me.*
*"You hate to see me win? You hate roulette?"*
*he hissed. "Then woman, know I hate it too!*
*Hate and despise it! And to prove I do*
*will now* AMAZE, APPAL AND PUT TO SHAME
THE CROUPIERS WHO CONTROL—
THE FOOLS WHO PLAY THIS GAME!"

*He stood, strode past me to another table,*
*sat down and started playing as before.*
*I would have left and gone to our hotel*
*but did not know the way, nor yet the name.*
*That was what came of too much sleep-walking—*
*I'd ended up not knowing where I was.*
*I sat upon a sofa by the wall*
*while Wedder left each table where he won*
*and shifted to the next. Folk followed him.*
*I heard much babble, voices shout "Bravo!"*
*then rumpus, stramash, pandemonium.*
*The other gamblers thought he was a hero.*
*Some praised his courage. Ladies in low-cut gowns*
*gave him glad looks, meaning "Come wed me quick."*
*A Jewish broker, weeping like a fountain,*
*begged him to leave before his luck ran out.*
*He played until they shut shop for the night.*
*It took a while to pack his money up.*

*While this was done poor Wedderburn got wooed,*
*fawned on and flattered all he wished, though not*
*by me. I heard a cough and someone say,*

*"Madame, will you forgive if I intrude?"*
*and looking sideways ding ding whoopee God!*
*The dinner bell! I'm feeling ravenous—*
*hungry parched famished and athirst for bortsch,*
*a splendid beetroot soup, but still have time*
*to finish off this entry with a rhyme.*

* * * * * * * * * * * * * *

*I will not write like Shakespeare any more. It slows me down, especially now I am trying to spell words in the long way most people do. Another warm Odessa day. The sky is a high sheet of perfectly smooth pale-grey cloud which does not even hide the horizon. I sit with my little writing-case open on my knees on the topmost step of a huge flight of steps descending to the harbour front. It is wide enough to march an army down, and very like the steps down to the West End Park near our house, God. All kinds of people promenade here too, but if I sat writing a letter on the Glasgow steps many would give me angry or astonished looks, and if I was poorly dressed the police would move me on. The Russians ignore me completely or smile in a friendly way. Of all the nations I have visited the U.S.A. and Russia suit me best. The people seem more ready to talk to strangers without being formal or disapproving. Is this because, like me, they have very little past? The friend I made in the betting-shop who talked to me about roulette and freedom and the soul is Russian. He said Russia is as young a country as the U.S.A. because a nation is only as old as its literature.*
*"Our literature began with Pushkin, a contemporary of your Walter Scott," he told me. "Before Pushkin Russia*

*was not a true nation, it was an administered region. Our aristocracy spoke French, our bureaucracy was Prussian, and the only true Russians—the peasants—were despised by rulers and bureaucracy alike. Then Pushkin learned the folk-tales from his nursemaid, a woman of the people. His novellas and poems made us proud of our language and aware of our tragic past—our peculiar present—our enigmatic future. He made Russia a state of mind—made it real. Since then we have had Gogol who was as great as your Dickens and Turgénieff who is greater than your George Eliot and Tolstoï who is as great as your Shakespeare. But you had Shakespeare centuries before Walter Scott."*

*Not since Miss MacTavish fled from my embraces in San Francisco had I heard so many writers mentioned in so few sentences, and I had read none of them! To stop him thinking Bell Baxter a total ignoramus I said Burns was a great Scottish poet who lived before Scott, and Shakespeare and Dickens et cetera were all English; but he could not grasp the difference between Scotland and England, though he is wise about other things. I also said most folk thought novels and poetry were idle pastimes—did he not take them too seriously?*

*"People who care nothing for their country's stories and songs," he said, "are like people without a past—without a memory—they are half people."*

*Imagine how that made me feel! But perhaps, like Russia, I am making up for lost time.*

*This was the stranger who spoke to me in the betting-shop while the rabble fussed around Wedder. He was a neat little man like Candle, but (I find this hard to explain) more humble than Candle, and also more proud.*

*I saw by his clothes that he was poor, and by his face that he was clever. I felt he was a lovable man, though maybe not a quick wedder, and I was delighted. Nobody but Wedderburn had spoken to me since the policeman in Regent's Park. I said, "Well, you look interesting! What have you to say to me?"*

*He brightened at that and also seemed surprised. He said, "But surely you are a great lady—the daughter of an English milord or baron?"*

*"Not me. Why think that?"*

*"You talk as great ladies in Russia talk. They too say at once what they feel without regard for convention. Since you are that sort I will talk fast, without introducing myself except to say I am an inveterate gambler—a quite unnecessary person who wants to give advice which will cost me nothing but may save you from a terrible loss."*

*This was exciting. I said, "Go on."*

*"The Englishman who has such success, he is your . . .?" He was looking at the fingers of my left hand for a wedding ring. I said, "He and I are wed."*

*This was fooling him slightly because most people think wedding and marriage are the same, but it was easier than complicated explanations. He said, "And your husband has never played roulette before?"*

*"Not roulette."*

*"That explains why he played so systematically. His system was the most obvious in the world—all thinking gamblers discover it during their first game and abandon it before the end. But tonight your husband had the best luck in the world, or worst, depending on how it takes him. The pattern of play, by sheer accident, conformed to his childish system again and again! Astonishing! This hardly*

*ever happens, but when it does it usually befalls a beginner who (forgive me, I could not say this to a conventional Englishwoman) is very much in love, and therefore more confident or desperate than usual. Yes, Cupid and cupidity once in a lifetime coincide to flatter us. That happened to me. I won a fortune but lost the woman I loved, and then, of course, the fortune, for the gambling fever entered my blood. It made me what I am — a lost soul — an existence manqué. If you cannot persuade your husband to leave this infernal little town tomorrow he will return to this casino, lose all he has won, then throw everything else away in an effort to recover it. The revenues of the municipality depend exclusively on the casinos, so the banks have the most modern facilities for speedily converting property into cash at iniquitous rates of exchange. I have seen a great princess — a woman of eighty but still sharp-witted and sensible — I have seen her fooled by beginners' luck into squandering nearly everything but the lives of her servants before she regained her senses."*

*I wanted to kiss that little stranger for the sense he talked and the good he wished to do. Instead I had to sigh and explain that alas my poor man would take no advice from me because he felt weak when he did, strong when he did not. I said, "But he might take advice from another man. Please tell him what you have told me. Here he comes."*

*Wedder, suddenly seeing me talk to a stranger, broke out of the crowd and strode toward us his hair sticking out all ways like the bristles of an over-used scrubbing-brush. His face seemed more blue than white and his eyes were bloodshot. Beside him hurried a servant in the livery of the betting-shop, carrying the winnings in a bag.*

*"Duncan," I said, "please listen to this gentleman. He*

*has something important to tell you."*

*Wedder folded his arms and stood very stiff, staring down at my new friend. The stranger had spoken only a few sentences when Wedderburn said sharply, "Why are you telling me this?"*

*"If I see two children who know nothing about express trains picnic on a railway line it is natural to tell them of the danger," said the stranger, "but if you need a more personal reason, hear this. An English friend (Mr. Astley, of Lovel and Co., a famous London firm) once did me a favour I have never managed to repay. Since I owe the English something I wish to pay them back a little through you."*

*"I am a Scot," said Wedderburn, looking at me, and I saw something imploring in the look.*

*"That need not deter me," said my new friend. "Mr Astley is a cousin of Lord Pibroch."*

*"We must leave, Bell," said Wedderburn tonelessly, and I realized he had folded his arms tight to stop himself trembling. Sleeplessness and excitement had so exhausted him that he could hardly hear or see a thing; all his strength and concentration were needed just to keep him standing and sounding sensible. Instead of giving him a row for his rudeness I slid my arm through his and he clutched it.*

*"My poor man needs rest now, but I shall remember what you told me. Thanks very much. Good night," I said.*

*As we moved toward the door accompanied by the servant I saw Wedderburn was sleep-walking like I had done.*

*In the entrance hall I pinched him awake to learn the name of our hotel. When he got conscious he said he needed a lavatory first and tottered off to it with the servant carrying his winnings, for he would not let those out of his sight. A second later my new friend was beside me again, speaking so fast and quiet that I must tilt an ear toward him.*

*"Your husband looks too distraught to count his winnings tonight. Take and keep as much of the money as you can without him knowing. That will not be theft. If he gambles again it will be your only means of leaving this town with dignity."*

*I nodded, shook his hands with both of mine and said I wished I could help him in some way. He blushed rosy-red, smiled, said, "Too late!" bowed and left.*

*Soon after Wedder came back looking neater. His face was still the same horrid colour but there was no sign of trembling and tiredness in him now. I knew he had taken one of the anti-lethargy pills and another wedding night was coming up. As he gripped my arm in a masterly way I thought, "How long can the poor soul keep going like this?"*

*At the door a very grand looking man said, "Gute Nacht, mein Herr! Your custom tomorrow we shall receive, I furiously hope?"*

*"Of course," said Wedder with a grim smile, "if your gold-mine is not yet exhausted."*

*"Not from me but from your fellow players you have won," said the man amiably, so I knew he was the head shopkeeper.*

*Outside I found that the shop, our hotel, a bank and the railway station were all on the same square, so we had not far to go. On reaching our room Wedder seized the bag from the servant, slammed the door in his face without saying thanks or tipping, ran to our bed (a huge one with a canopy) and emptied the money onto it with a kind of tinkling crash, for some envelopes split open. He flung these envelopes to the floor and began ripping other envelopes and pouring out coins, mad keen to make one big puddle of his gold on the silk bedcover. I realized that, like little Robbie Murdoch with a mud puddle, he would then splash about in it before counting it. This might go on all night. I had to distract him somehow.*

"At this point I will omit two pages," said Baxter. "They cast strong light into that zone where anatomy and psychology are forms of each other, but your future wife will one day teach you such things in person, so why anticipate them here? In chaste and accurate language Bell tells how, for a few hours, she wooed Wedderburn away from his infantile obsession with gold and restored him to a deep and natural slumber on a bearskin hearth-rug. She tells how she removed and hid four hundred friedrichs d'or from the pile on the bed, and how he did not miss these when he awoke and counted the rest into neat heaps. I will continue from there."

*"Tonight this will be multiplied ten- or a hundredfold," he said with a gloating smile. I told him he was a fool.*
*"Bella!" he cried, "all last night people begged me to stop playing before my luck ran out. I played to the very end and won because I was using REASON—not luck. You, at least, should have faith in me because in the eyes of God you are my lawful wedded wife!"*
*"God will let me leave you whenever I choose," I said, "and I will never set foot in that betting-shop again. I bet you will lose* everything *if you go in again—* everything*."*
*"What will you bet?" he asked, with an odd look. I smiled then, because I had a very bright idea. I said—*

*"Give me five hundred of that money. If you come back richer I will return it and marry you. If you lose the rest we will need it to leave this place."*

*He kissed me and wept, saying this was the happiest moment of his life, for now he knew he would have all he could ever want. I wept out of pity for him—what else could I do? Then he gave me the five hundred, we breakfasted and he left. I asked the hotel folk to serve lunch in my room, went back to it and slept.*

*How lovely, God, to waken all alone, and bath and dress alone, and eat alone. When we get married, Candle, we must spend some time apart to stop us going stale. In the afternoon I went walking round a park in the middle of the square, hoping to see my new friend, and so I did, in the distance. I waved my parasol. From opposite sides we approached an empty bench and sat on it. He asked delicately, "Did you?"*

*I smiled, nodded and said, "How is my man doing?"*

*"O, he began early and lost it all in an hour. He staggered us all by his extraordinary coolness. He has since been twice to the bank and four times to the telegraph office—so the rumour goes. Great Britain has the world's largest and busiest money-market. We expect him to return and lose as much again, or more, in an hour or two."*

*"Let us talk of happier things," I said. "Do you know any?"*

*"Well," he said with a rueful smile, "we could talk of the radiant future of the human race a century hence when science, trade and fraternal democracy will have abolished disease, war and poverty, and everyone will live in a hygienic apartment block with a free clinic in the basement*

*run by a good German dentist. But I would feel lost in such a future. If God consulted my wishes (and maybe he did) he would make me a disgraced outchatel—an unemployed manservant—a lover of Russia who would rather chat to a brave Scotswoman in a German public park than fight for the renovation of his homeland. This may not be much but it satisfies me, and is better than being a bed bug. Though of course, bed bugs too must have their unique visions of the world."*

*So we discussed what people want most, and freedom, the soul, Russian literature, how he hated the Poles because they expected to be treated like gentlemen when they were poorer than he was, and hated the French because they had form without content and sympathized with the Poles, and how he liked the English because of Mr. Astley, and how he had been an outchatel—a tutor to a rich general's children—and the sad adventures which had made him a gambler. He was so frank and open that I told him a little about my troubles with Wedder. After some thought he said the best I could do with Wedder was take him on a Mediterranean cruise till he was fit to go home. The vessel should not be a passenger ship, but a cargo ship with passenger accommodation.*

*"There will be few facilities for gambling on a vessel like that," he said, "and very little social stimulus. If he needs rest as much as you say, a Russian vessel might be better than an English or . . . Scottish ship, for the curiosity of the other passengers will lead to less gossip."*

*I kissed him good-bye for that advice. I think my kiss cheered him up.*

*I shall tell the rest fast. Wedder comes back to hotel penniless, Shakespearean, "To be or not to be", et*

*cetera. I tell him the five hundred he bet me will let us continue our wedding trip next day, and I will return it to him. Next day he pays the hotel, we go to the station, he buys tickets to Switzerland. Since half an hour till train arrives he installs me with luggage in the ladies' waiting-room, saying he will smoke a cigar outside. Of course he dodges straight into the betting-shop for a last quick fling which might just recover everything, and loses everything, then charges back to me raving like Hamlet over Ophelia's coffin. I see that the only way to quieten him down is to act a little too—"pile on the agony", as they say in the theatre. I go very frozen-faced and moan in a hollow monotonous voice, "No money? I will get us money."*
*"How? How?"*
*"Never ask. Wait here. I will be gone for two hours. We will catch the later train."*
*Out I go, find a pleasant little café and enjoy four lovely cups of chocolate and eight Viennese pastries. Then I go back looking tragic just in time for the train. Our carriage is crowded. I ignore his whispered attempts at conversation by sleeping with my eyes open. For the next four days I say nothing but, "Never ask!" even when he begs to know where he is being taken. My doomed expression and hollow voice cause him exquisite pangs of guilt which keep him busy when the poor fellow is not shaking in every limb and wet with hot or cold perspiration, for he has used up the last of his anti-lethargy pills and has a craving for more. That would be fatal! Luckily he is so ill that he can go nowhere unless I lead him by the arm. He is so dependent that I can leave him for hours in a hotel bedroom while I*

*make arrangements. In a Trieste shipping office I book our passage upon exactly the sort of ship the outchatel recommended. I cannot write its name, for the Russian alphabet is Greek to me, but it sounds like cut use off.*

*On our way to the docks down a broad but dismal street (it is raining) he suddenly halts us in front of a tobacconist's shop and says on a desperate note I have never heard before, "O Bella, tell me the truth! Are we going a long voyage on a ship?"*

*"Yes."*

*"Please, Bella!" (and he sinks down on his knees in the streaming gutter) "please give me some money to buy cigars! Please! I am completely out."*

*I see the time has come to drop the tragic mask.*

*"You poor sad Wedder," I say, helping him kindly up, "you shall have all the cigars you want. I can afford them."*

*"Bella," he whispers, bringing his face close to mine, "I know how you got that money. You sold yourself to that filthy little Russian gambler who tried to seduce you on the night of my glorious victory."*

*"Never ask."*

*"Yes, you did that for me. Why? I am a stinking midden, a reeking dungheap, a quintessence of shit. You are Venus, Magdalene, Minerva and Our Lady of Sorrows rolled into one—how can you bear to touch me?"*

*However, four minutes later he looked quite cheerful with a cigar clamped between his gnashers.*

*So now you know how the Russian merchant navy brought us to Odessa. We are spending three days here while the boat takes on a cargo of beetroots, in which the region abounds. Wedder is no longer a jealous man. He does not mind me going ashore by myself, though he begs me to come back to him as soon as possible. Since I have at last brought this letter up to date, perhaps I will, today.*

* * * * * * * * * * * * * *

* * * * * * * * * * * *

* * * * * * * * * *

* * * * * * * *

* * * * * *

* * * *

* *

# 15

# Odessa to Alexandria: The Missionaries

*I used to think this a very big world, but yesterday something made me doubt it. The morning was fine again. The ship was leaving Odessa at noon. I sat with Wedder in the one place outside our cabin I can persuade him to go, a nook between two ventilators. He was reading a French Bible because all other books in the passengers' lounge are Russian. Luckily he knows French so that book and he are now inseparable. He reads some parts again and again, then stares a long time at nothing, frowning and whispering "I see." I was reading* Punch or The London Charivari, *an English magazine of art and comedy. The pictures showed many kinds of people. The ugliest and most comical are Scots, Irish, foreign, poor, servants, rich folk who have been poor until very recently, small men, old unmarried women and Socialists. The Socialists are ugliest, very dirty and hairy with weak chins, and seem to spend their time grumbling to other people at street corners.*

*"What are Socialists, Duncan?" I asked.*

*"Fools who think the world should be improved."*

*"Why? Is something wrong with it?"*

*"The Socialists are wrong with it—and my infernal luck."*

*"You told me once that luck is a solemn name for ignorance."*

*"Do not torture me, Bell."*

*He always says that when he wants me to shut my mouth. I watched the gulls circling in a blue sky full of big slow-moving clouds. I saw the huge harbour full of shipping with bright flags and funnels, masts and sails. I looked at the sunlit quay with its cranes, bales, busy brawny dockers and uniformed officers. I wondered how to improve all this, but it looked all right. Then I studied* Punch *again and wondered why the well-dressed English people in the pictures were handsomer and less comic than anyone else, unless they were newly rich. Noisy shouts and clattering hooves interrupted these thoughts. Three galloping horses brought a peculiar carriage lurching along the quay and were pulled to a halt at the end of our gangway. Out climbed one of the well-dressed, handsome people I had been puzzling over in* Punch. *As he came aboard past the Russian seamen and officers I nearly laughed aloud—his thin stiff figure, stiff face, glossy top-hat and neat frock-coat looked so comically English.*

*Bell Baxter likes meeting new people. Wedder will not eat outside our cabin so last night I tied a clean napkin round my poor man's neck, settled him with his dinner tray and headed for the dining-saloon. I am now a well-known character on this ship, and passengers who speak English are always placed at my table. This time I had only two. Both had boarded at Odessa. One was a stout, brown-faced American doctor called Doctor Hooker; the other was the obvious Englishman—Mr. Astley! I got very excited. I said, "Do you work for a London firm called Lovel and Co?"*

*"I am on the board of directors."*

*"Are you a cousin of Lord Pibroch?"*

*"I am."*

*"How wonderful! I am a friend of a great friend of yours, a lovely little Russian gambler who drifts around the German betting-shops in a very poor way—he has even been to jail, but not for anything very nasty. The odd thing is, I do not know his name, but he thinks of you as his best friend because you have been so very good to him."*

*After a long pause Mr. Astley said slowly, "I cannot say I am a friend of the person you describe."*

*He took up his soup-spoon and so did puzzled Bell Baxter. We would have eaten in silence if Doctor Hooker had not cheered me up with stories of his missionary work in China. Just before the meal ended Mr. Astley, thoughtfully stirring his coffee, said, "However, I know the fellow you spoke about. My wife is Russian, the daughter of a Russian general. I once gave some assistance to a servant in her father's household, a sort of male nurse who looked after the younger children. That was years ago."*

*I said accusingly, "He is a very good wise kind soul! He helped me a lot, and gained nothing by it, and likes all Englishmen because of you!"*

*"Ah."*

*I would not have hated him had he said "O!" or "Eh?" but he said "Ah" as if he knew more than everyone else in the world, knew so much that talking was useless. The outchatel called him shy. I think him stupid and cold. I was glad to hurry back to my warm warm Wedder who can be blown up into giving all the solid heat a woman wants. But do not worry, Candle. Your tie-pin still gleams in the lapel of Bell's travelling-coat.*

* * * * * * * * * * * * * *

*Dr. H. looks glad whenever he sees me, unlike Mr. Astley. He is a doctor of medicine as well as divinity so today I asked him to look in on Wedder who still acts like a sick man, though no longer pale and shivering. I stayed outside the cabin during the consultation, but near enough to hear the kindly, rumbling voice of Dr. H. punctuated by short answers (I suppose) from Wedder, who at last started shouting. When Dr. H. came out he said Wedder's illness was not physical.*

*"We disagreed over the doctrine of the Atonement," he told me, "and the inevitability of Hell—he thinks me too liberal. But religion is not his main problem. He is using it to distract him from a very painful recent memory he refuses to discuss. Do you know what it is?"*

*I told him that the poor man had made a fool of himself in a German betting-shop.*

*"If that is all," said Dr. H., "let him sulk himself better in his own good time. Treat him with affection, but do not spoil your own lovely bloom by refraining from cheerful social exercise. Do you play chequers? No? Allow me to teach you."*

*He is a gorgeous man.*

* * * * * * * * * * * * * *

*Dear God we are passing once again between the Isles of Greece where burning Byron loved and sang and I am very glad that the breasts of the girls here no longer suckle slaves and I have just had a glorious breakfast at which Dr. H. and Mr. A. argued tremendously and Mr. Astley started it! We were astonished. For the last two days he has eaten with us and said nothing but "Good morning," "Good afternoon," "Good evening," so we were used to chatting as though he did not exist. This morning my American friend was telling me how the smaller Chinese skull made it hard for the Chinese to learn English when: "Did you find it easy to learn Chinese, Dr. Hooker?" asked Mr. Astley.*

*"Sir," said Dr. H., facing round to him, "I did not visit China to learn the language of Confucius and Lao-tsze. For fifteen years I have served a federation of American Bible societies which—with some assistance from our chambers of commerce and the United States government—employed me to teach the natives of Peking the language and faith of the Christian Bible. For this purpose I found the simplest jargon of the poorest coolies (you call it pidgin English) more useful than Mandarin complexities."*

*Mr. Astley said softly, "The Spaniards who first colonized your continent think Latin the language of the Christian faith and Bible."*

*"The brand of religion I preach and try to practise," said Dr. H., "was preached by Moses and Jesus long before the Roman Emperors took it up and tricked it out in the superfluous pomps of earthly kingship."*

*"Ah."*

*"Mr. Astley sir!" said Dr. H. sternly, "by a simple*

*question and an oblique comment you have drawn from me a confession of faith. Let me ask the same from you. Have you invited Jesus into your heart as your personal saviour? Or are you a Roman Catholic? Or do you support the English State Church whose pope is Queen Victoria?"*

*"When I am in England," said Mr. Astley slowly, "I support the Church of England. It keeps England stable. For the same reason I support the Church of Scotland in Scotland, Hindooism in India, Mahometanism in Egypt. The British Empire would not be governing a quarter of the globe if we opposed the local religions. Had our government made Catholicism the official religion of Ireland it would now easily control that troublesome colony with the help of the papish priests, though of course the Ulstermen would need a corner to themselves."*

*"Mr. Astley, you are worse than an atheist," said Dr. H. gravely. "An atheist has at least a strong conviction of what he does* not *believe. You believe in nothing firm or fixed. You are a timeserver—a faithless man."*

*"Not quite faithless," murmured Mr. Astley. "I am a Malthusiast—I believe in the gospel according to Malthus."*

*"I thought Malthus was a Church of England clergyman with bats in his belfry about expanding populations. Do you tell me he has founded a new religion?"*

*"No, a new faith. Religions involve congregations, preachers, prayers, hymns, special buildings or codes or rituals. My brand of Malthusiasm does not."*

*"Your brand, Mr. Astley? Are there many?"*

*"Yes. All systems prove their vigour through subdivision: Christianity, for instance."*

*"Touché!" said Dr. H., chuckling. "It is a pleasure to cross swords with you. And now sir, explain your sect of Malthusiasm. Convert me to it!"*

*"You are better as you are, Dr. Hooker. My faith offers no comfort to the poor, the sick, the cruelly used and those on the point of death. I have no wish to spread it."*

*"A faith without hope and charity?" cried Dr. H. loudly. "Then fling it from you, Mr. Astley, for it has obviously frozen the blood in your veins! Ditch it. Tie a weight to it and fling it overboard. Get a faith which warms the heart, binds you to your fellow men and points us all toward a golden future."*

*"I dislike intoxicating fluids. I prefer the bitter truth."*

*"Mr. Astley, I see you are one of those sad modern souls who think the material world a harsh machine which destroys the feeling hearts and seeing minds who enter it. Think ye, by the bowels of Christ, that ye may be wrong! Our gloriously varied universe could not have sprouted brains and hearts like ours if the Maker of All had not designed them for this planet, designed the planet for them, and all for Himself!"*

*"Your vision of the world as a place where God grows human vegetables for his own consumption may appeal to a market gardener, Dr. Hooker," said Mr. Astley, "but not to me. I am a businessman. Have you a faith, Mrs. Wedderburn?"*

*"Is that something to do with God?" I asked, pleased that he had spoken to me.*

*"Indeed it is, Mrs. Wedderburn," cried Doctor H., "for most people, if not for Mr. Astley. Even he is a child of God though he won't admit it—but you are especially so. The faith, hope and charity shining from your clear*

eyes guarantee it. Pray tell us, Mrs. Wedderburn, how you perceive Our Father Which Art in Heaven."

Since my quack with the outchatel in the German park I had not had a chance to talk about the great big ordinary queer things because Wedder finds them a torture. And now these two clever men wanted me to talk about EVERYTHING! Out the words tumbled.

"All I know about that god," I said, "is what I was told by my own God—by my guardian, Godwin Baxter. He said god is a handy name for all and everything: your top-hat and dreams Mr. Astley, sky boots Bonnie Banks o' Loch Lomond bortsch me molten lava time ideas whooping-cough ecstasies of wedded bliss my white rabbit Flopsy AND the hutch she lives in—everything named in every dictionary and book there has ever been and ever could be adds up to god. But the wholly-est bit of god is movement, because it keeps stirring things to make new ones. Movement turns dead dogs into maggots and daisies, and flour butter sugar an egg and a tablespoonful of milk into Abernethy biscuits, and spermatozoa and ovaries into fishy little plants growing babyward if we take no care to stop them. And movement causes pain when solid bodies knock into living ones or living ones knock each other, so to stop us getting knocked dead before life wears us out we have generated developed evolved acquired invented matured gained and grown eyes and brains to let us see knocks coming and dodge them. And how beautifully the whole godly clamjamfrie works! I thought of improving the port of Odessa three days ago and could not see where to start. I know things were not always thus. I have read The Last Days of Pompeii and Uncle Tom's Cabin and Wuthering Heights so know that history is full of nastiness, but history is all past so nowadays nobody is cruel to each other, just stupid sometimes when they get into betting-shops. Punch says only lazy people are out of work so the very poorest must enjoy being poor. They also have the consolation of being comic. I know of course that bad accidents sometimes happen, but life goes on. My parents were killed in a train crash but I cannot remember them so I hardly ever weep. Anyway, they must have been old, so nearly worn out. I have been told I lost a baby somewhere else, but I know my little daughter is being cared for. My guardian looks after sick dogs and cats without being paid so a lost little girl is bound to be safe. What bitter truth were you talking about, Mr. Astley?"

While I spoke a strange thing happened. Both men were staring at my face hard harder hardest, but Mr. Astley leaned closer and closer as he did so while Dr. H. leaned further and further back. Yet when I stopped speaking Mr. Astley did not reply, and Dr. H. said in a low voice, "My child, have you never read God's holy Bible?"

"I am nobody's child!" I told him sharply, but of course I had then to explain about the amnesia. When I had done it Dr. H. said, "But ch!—Mrs. Wedderburn, your husband seems to be a devout Christian. Has he given you no religious instruction?"

I told him I could hardly get a word out of poor Wedder since he went biblical. Dr. H. gazed silently at me until Mr. Astley said in a strange voice, "Dr. Hooker, do you intend to instruct Mrs. Wedderburn in the doctrines of original sin and eternal punishment for worldly transgressions?"

*"No sir," said Dr. Hooker shortly.*
*"Mrs. Wedderburn," said Mr. Astley, "your guardian's account of the universe is one to which neither of us object. The bitter truth I spoke of is a statistical matter—a detail of political economy. I was joking when I called it a faith—I said that to annoy Dr. Hooker. I am a phlegmatic fellow, so his American exuberance annoyed me. But we are both glad you find the world a good and happy place."*
*"Shake," said Dr. H. quietly, and held out his hand, and Mr. Astley shook it.*
*"I like seeing you two gentlemen friendly," I told them, "but I feel you are in a conspiracy to hide something from me, and I am going to find out what it is. Shall we take a walk on deck?"*

*So I strolled on deck with them. A lovely morning. Now I am going to have lunch in our cabin with my Wedder, followed by an afternoon of cuddles. I wonder what Dr. H. and Mr. A. will talk about over dinner this evening?*

* * * * * * * * * * * * * * *

*"What brought you to Odessa, Astley?"*
*"Beetroot, Dr. Hooker. My firm refines and sells cane sugar but German beet sugar may cheapen that unless we compete with the German product. But British farmers refuse to grow sugar-beet—they get more for other root crops. To undercut the Germans we need sugar-beet from farmers who work for Asiatic, not European wages, hence my visit to Russia. We also need a port linked to international shipping lanes, hence my visit to Odessa."*

*"So the British Lion is forging trade links with the Russian Bear?"*

*"Too early to say, Dr. Hooker. The Russians offer us land and labour to build a sugar refinery on very good terms, but the soil and climate may not be best for sugar-beet. What brought you to Odessa? Does your federation of Bible societies plan to convert the followers of the Russian Orthodox Church?"*

*"Nope. Fact is, I have retired from missionary work. I came to China fifteen years ago by the straight Pacific line. I am wending my way home to the Land of the Free by the pleasantest and most roundabout route I can find."*

*"Siam, India, Afghanistan?"*

*"Not quite."*

*"The Outer Mongolian and Turkestan or Siberian routes are not exactly pleasure trips either, Dr. Hooker. You must have needed an armed escort for much of the way. Did the United States government pay for that or the American chambers of commerce?"*

*"You are a deep and dangerous man, Astley!" said Dr. Hooker, chuckling a bit. "I would rather be up against ten wily oriental warlords than a single Englishman of your stamp. Yes, a few far-seeing American citizens asked me to report on some aspects of central Asia, the world's largest sink of unclaimed heathendom. Can you blame us? Britain has carved up the rest of the planet. Less than two years ago you grabbed Egypt from the French—and from the Egyptians."*

*"We needed their canal. We paid them for it."*

*"You also shelled Alexandria, our next port of call."*

*"They were arming it against us and we needed their canal."*

*"And now British regiments are fighting the Dervishes in the Sudan."*
*"We cannot tolerate religions which urge the natives to rule themselves. Home rule would disturb trade and our smooth running of the canal."*
*Up piped Bell Baxter: "What are natives, Mr. Astley?"*
*I had been keeping quiet, hoping to learn things, but "undercut", "report on aspects", "unclaimed heathendom", "carved up the planet", "grabbed Egypt", "home rule", "disturb trade" made no sense to me. However, "natives" sounded like people.*
*"Natives," said Mr. Astley carefully, "are people who live on the soil where they were born, and do not want to leave it. Not many English can be regarded as natives because we have a romantic preference for other people's soils, though we are very loyal to our old schools and school friends, our regiments and businesses. Some even feel loyal to the Queen, who is a very selfish old lady."*
*"Are there no British natives?"*
*"In Wales, Ireland and Scotland perhaps. In England we still have a class of farmers, farm servants, estate workers et cetera, but the landowners and city dwellers regard them as useful animals, like horses and dogs."*
*"But why are British soldiers fighting Egyptian natives? It makes no sense to me."*
*"I am glad it makes no sense to you, Mrs. Wedderburn. Politics, like filling and emptying cesspools, is filthy work and women should be protected from it. Let us talk of cleaner things, Dr. Hooker."*
*"Halt there, Astley!" said Dr. Hooker sternly. "In the States we have a high regard for the intelligence and education of the fairer sex. In a few words I can tell Mrs.*

*Wedderburn the whole political state of the planet earth, and do so without for one moment wounding her womanly instincts and your patriotic ones. May I proceed?"*

*"If Mrs. Wedderburn is interested, and will allow me to smoke a cigar with my coffee, I also am interested."*

*Of course I said "yes" to both of them. Mr. A. then offered his cigar case to Dr. H. who thanked him, selected one, sniffed it, said it was excellent, bit the end off, lit it, then forgot all about it, because his speech was so very interesting.*

*"Over breakfast this morning Mrs. Wedderburn spoke of how much better the world is than in the bad old days. She was right, and why? Because the Anglo-Saxon race to which she and I and Mr. Astley belong have begun to control the world, and we are the cleverest and kindliest and most adventurous and most truly Christian and hardest working and most free and democratic people who have ever existed. We should not feel proud of our superior virtues. God arranged it by giving us bigger brains than anyone else, so we find it easier to control our evil animal instincts. This means that compared with the Chinese, Hindoos, Negroes and Amerindians—yes, even compared with the Latins and Semites—we are like teachers in a playground of children who do not want to know that the school exists. Why is it our duty to teach them? I will tell you.*

*"When children or childish people are left to themselves the strongest overcome the rest and treat them unkindly. In China judicial torture is a roadside entertainment. Hindoo widows are burned alive beside their husbands' corpses. Black people eat each other. Arabs and Jews do*

*unmentionable things to the private parts of their infants. The talkative French go in for bloody revolutions, the carefree Italians join murderous secret societies, we all know about the Spanish Inquisition. Even the Germans, who are racially closest to us, have a taste for brutally violent orchestral music and sabre duels. God created the Anglo-Saxon race to stop all that, and we will.*

*"But we cannot improve people suddenly, everywhere. The bullying rulers of the inferior races hate to see us replace them, so to teach them sense we have first of all to thrash them. Our rifles and machine-guns and iron-clad warships and superior military discipline ensure that we always do thrash them, but the process takes time. From their headquarters in the tiny island of Britain the Anglo-Saxons have conquered over a quarter of the planet in a little more than two centuries. But west of the Atlantic another, vaster Anglo-Saxon nation is starting to feel its strength and stretch its limbs—the United States! Who can doubt that, before the end of the twentieth century, the United States will dominate the rest of the planet? Do you doubt it, Astley?"*

*"What you predict is possible," said Mr. A. deliberately, "if the subject races learn nothing from us. But the Japanese seem clever little pupils, and Germany's industrial strength has almost overtaken Britain's."*

*"You sort out the Prussians and leave the Nippons to us, for in our school the pupils can never become masters—their smaller skulls prevent it. I admit the German cranium is on a par with yours and mine, but it lacks flexibility. The point I want to make, Mrs. Wedderburn, is this. Another century of fighting will elapse before the world is finally civilized, but the fighting should not be*

*regarded as warfare. When the British invade Egypt—when the States go into Mexico or Cuba—they are policing and civilizing the natives, not hurting them. Yes, the Anglo-Saxon police-force may take a century to rid the world of bullies, but we will do it. By the year 2000 the Chinese teacup-maker, Indian pearl-diver, Persian carpet-weaver, Jewish tailor, Italian opera-singer et cetera will at last pursue their occupations in peace and prosperity, for Anglo-Saxon law will have at last allowed the meek to inherit the earth."*

*There was a long pause while Dr. H. looked eagerly from me to Mr. Astley and back, but chiefly at Mr. Astley, who at last said, "Ah."*

*Dr. H. said sharply, "Sir, do you disagree with my prediction?"*

*"Not if it pleases Mrs. Wedderburn."*

*Both of these clever men looked hard at me. I suddenly felt very warm and saw from my hands that I was blushing. I said awkwardly, "You said a thing that surprised me, Dr. Hooker. You said brainy people find it easier to control their evil animal instincts. I have seen and played with a lot of animals, and none of them were evil to me. A bitch with a broken leg growled and snapped while I fixed the splint, but only because I was hurting her. When she felt better she treated me like a pal. Are there many evil animals?"*

*"There are NO evil animals," said Dr. Hooker warmly, "and you are right to correct me on that point. Let me explain it another way. Human beings contain two natures, a higher and a lower. The higher nature loves clean, beautiful things: the lower one loves dirty, ugly ones. You are a well-bred young lady so have no lower*

*impulses. You have received an Anglo-Saxon education suited to your sex and class, which has protected you from the degrading spectacle of human filth and misery. You come from Britain, where a fine police-force keeps criminals, the unemployed and other incurably dirty creatures away from places where the nobler natures, the Anglo-Saxon natures live. I hear that in Britain the lower class is predominantly Irish."*

*I said indignantly, "I am a woman of the world, Dr. Hooker. My guardian took me all round it while I was recovering from my accident. I saw all sort of people, and some wore cracked boots and patched coats and grubby underwear, just like the poor people we laugh at in* Punch. *But none were ever as horrid as you suggest."*

*"You have been to China and Africa?"*

*"Parts of them. I have been to Cairo, in Egypt."*

*"And you have seen the fellahin whining for Baksheesh?"*

*"Change the subject, Hooker!" said Mr. Astley sharply, but I would not allow that. I said, "When God took me to see the pyramids we left the hotel in the middle of a crowd. Some people were shouting words like aaa-ee, aaa-ee at the edge of the crowd, but I did not see them. What does Baksheesh mean, Dr. Hooker? I never asked at the time."*

*"If you disembark with me in Alexandria tomorrow I will show you what it means in fifteen minutes or less. The sight will shock but educate you. When you have seen it you will understand three things: the innate depravity of the unredeemed human animal; why Christ died for our sins; why God has sent the Anglo-Saxon race to purify the globe with fire and sword."*

*"You have broken your word, Hooker," said Mr. Astley coldly. "You have not kept our bargain."*
*"I am sorry for it yet glad of it, Astley!" cried Dr. H. (and I had not seen a man so excited since Candle proposed to me and Wedder won at roulette). "Mrs. Wedderburn's speech shows she has recovered from the worst effects of her railway accident. Though she has not regained her earliest memories her speech displays a mind as clear and logical as yours and mine, but if we do not provide the information she craves it will remain the mind of a precocious infant. You English may prefer to keep your women in that state, but in the American West we want our women to be equal partners. Do you accept my invitation to see the seamy side of Alexandria, Mrs. Wedderburn? Perhaps you could persuade your husband to come."*
*"I will accept whether my poor man comes or not," I told him, feeling fearfully excited.*
*"You come too, Astley," said Dr. H. "Let us give our fair companion a joint Anglo-American escort."*
*Mr. A. blew out a thoughtful-looking stream of smoke, shrugged and said, "So be it."*

*I left the table at once. I needed quietness to think of all the new strange things I had heard. Maybe my cracked knob is to blame but I feel less happy since Dr. H. explained there is nothing wrong with the world which the Anglo-Saxons are not curing with fire and sword. Before now I thought everyone I met was part of the same friendly family, even when a hurt one acted like our snappish bitch. Why did you not teach me politics, God?*

* * * * * * * * * * * * * *

At this point Baxter's voice faltered into silence and I saw him struggling to overcome a very deep emotion.

"Read the next six pages for yourself," he said suddenly, and passed them over. I give the pages here as they were given to me: ☛

They are printed by a photogravure process which exactly reproduces the blurring caused by tear stains, but does not show the pressure of pen strokes which often ripped right through the paper.

cyooring with fir and sord. Bee4 now I thot evray wun I met woz part ov the saym frendlay family, eeven when a Hurt wun acted lic owr snapish bitch. Whi did yoo not teech mee politics God?

* * * * * * *

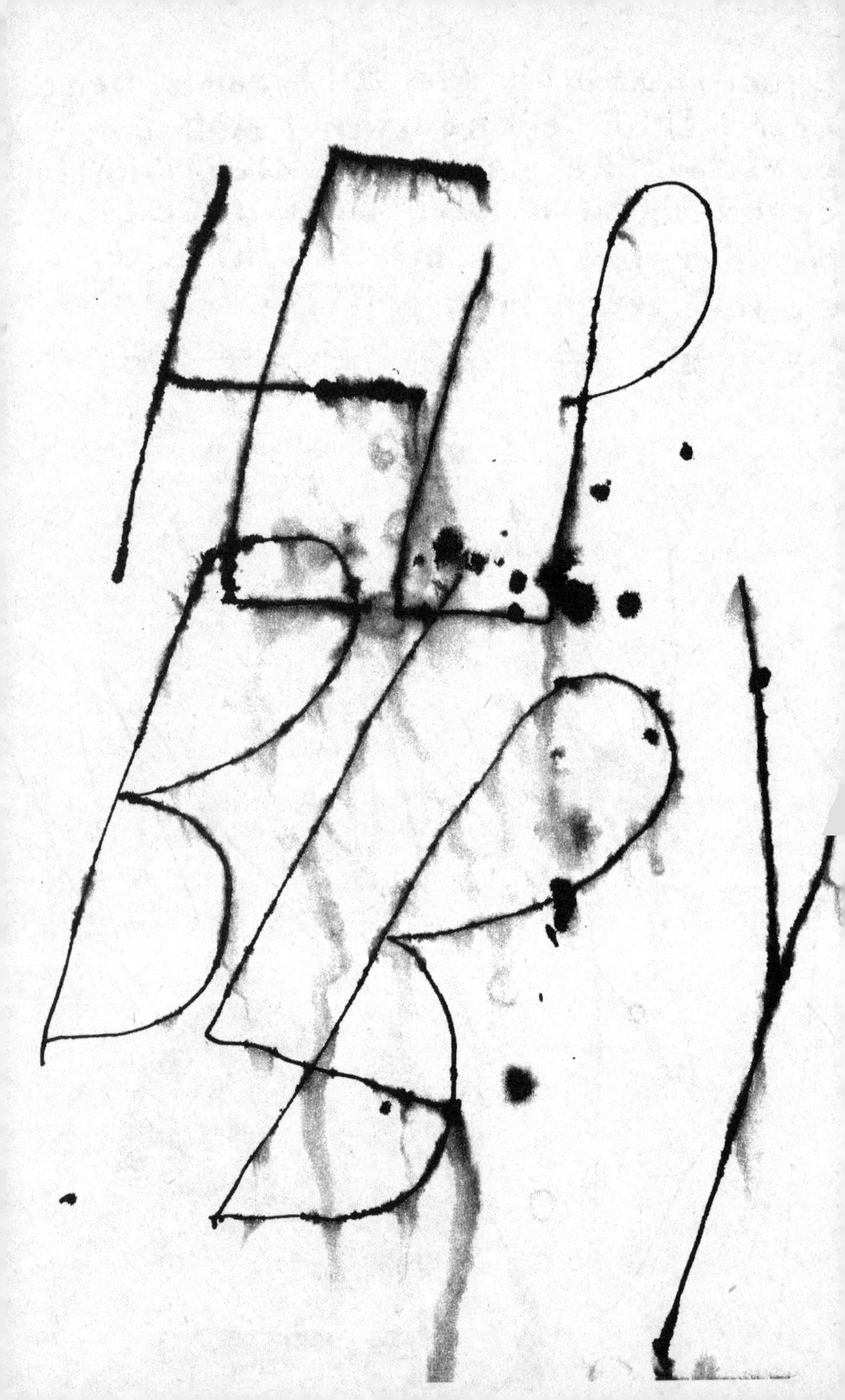

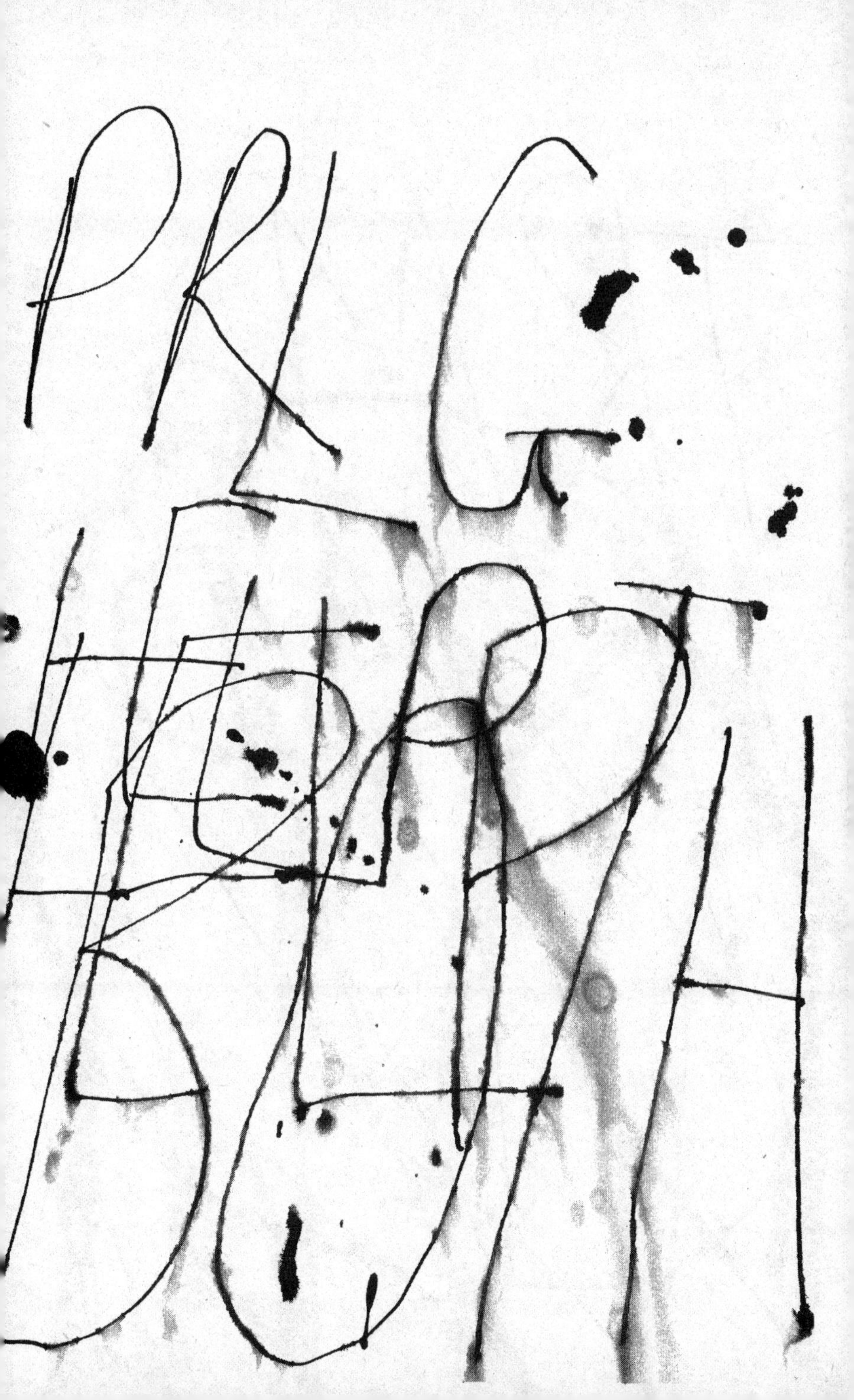

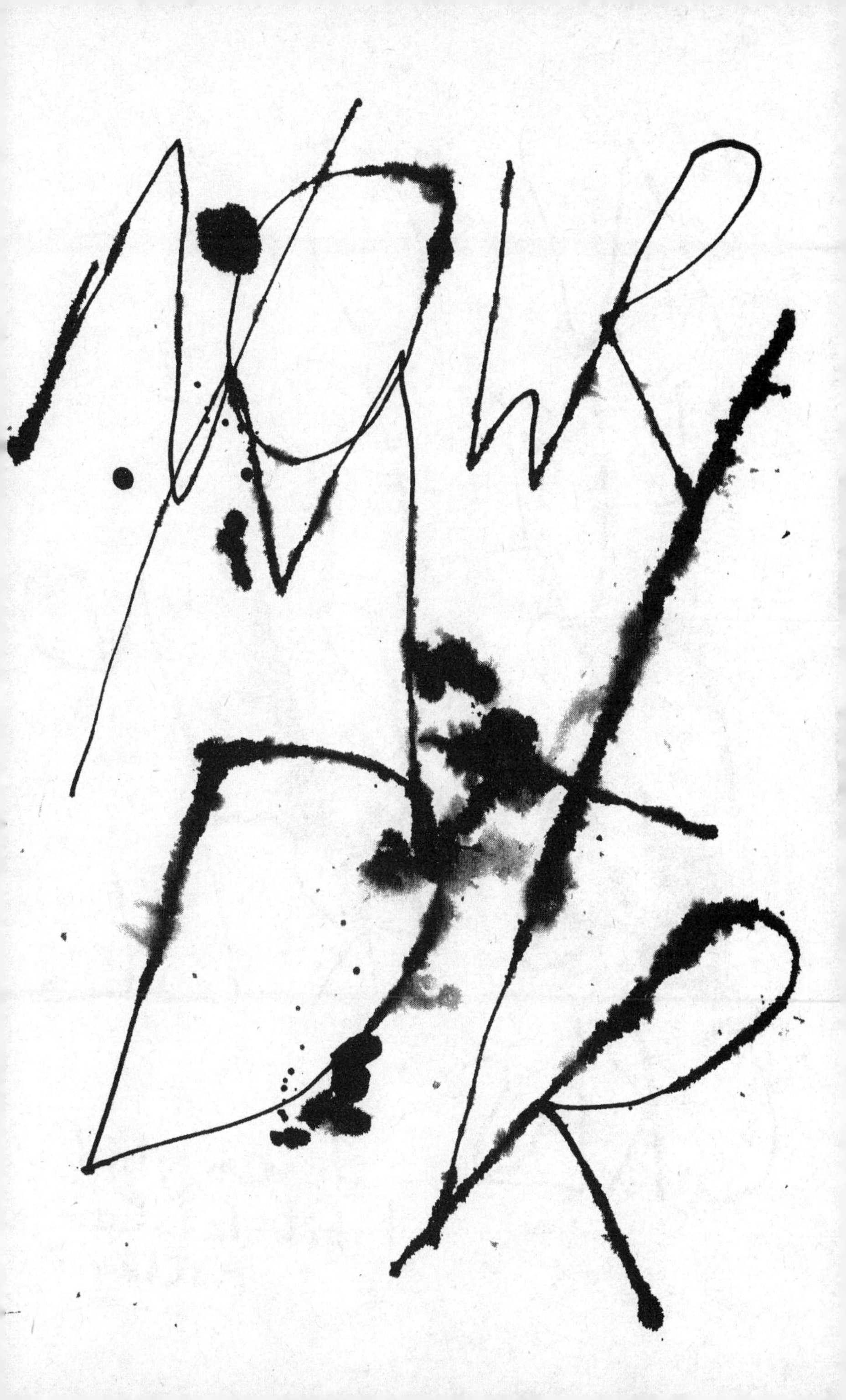

NO
HLP
FR BLND
BAS PRLL
GRLS
I am glad
I bit mister
Astlay

"A catastrophic reversion to an earlier phase with a brisk recovery at the end," I said. "What do the scrawls mean, Baxter? Here—take them back. Only you can decipher them."

Baxter sighed and in a steady, uninflected voice told me, "They say, no no no no no no no no no, help blind baby, poor little girl help help both, trampled no no no no no no no no no no no no no no no no no no no, no where my daughter, no help for blind babies poor little girls I am glad I bit Mr. Astley."

Baxter then laid the letter down, pulled out a handkerchief, folded it into a cushion (his handkerchiefs were a quarter the size of a bed-sheet) and pushed his face into it. For a moment I feared he was trying to smother himself, then muffled eruptions showed he was using it to absorb glandular evacuations. When he removed it his eyes were extra bright.

"What then?" I asked impatiently. "What then? Does the next entry explain all that?"

"No, but what happened emerges eventually. The remaining entries are written weeks or months after her romance with Harry Astley—"

"ROMANCE!" I screamed—

"Calm yourself, McCandless. On her side it was a Platonic affair. That it helped her mental growth is shown in the writing which suddenly becomes small, regular and upright; in her spelling which rapidly conforms to the standard dictionaries; in the separation between her entries, where a straight horizontal line replaces the playful row of stars. But her growth appears most clearly in the quality of her reflections. From now onward these blend the spiritual insights of an oriental sage with the analytical acuteness of David Hume and Adam Smith.

Attend!"

# 16

# Alexandria to Gibraltar: Astley's Bitter Wisdom

*Thinking has maddened me for weeks. My one relief has been argument with Harry Astley. He says I will only find peace by embracing his bitter wisdom—and him. I want neither—except as enemies. He says cruelty to the helpless will never end because the healthy live by trampling these down. I say if this is true we must stop living so. He has given me books which he says prove this is impossible: Malthus'* Essay on Population, *Darwin's* Origin of Species *and Winwood Reade's* Martyrdom of Man. *They make my head ache. I was changing the dressing on his hand today when he told me his wife had died a year ago, then said, "You are not legally married to Wedderburn, are you?"*

*"How clever of you to guess, Mr. Astley."*

*"Please call me Harry."*

*His hand is almost healed though the thumb is very stiff—my teeth have left a circular scar where they nearly met in the ball of it. He said thoughtfully, "That mark will be with me for ever."*

*"I am afraid so, Harry."*
*"May I regard it as an engagement ring? Will you marry me?"*
*"No, Harry. I am engaged to another."*
*He asked about my fiancé so I told him of Candle. When I had finished fixing the new bandage he said he knew many women of rank and title, the Duchess of Sutherland and Princess Louise of Connaught among them, but I was the purest aristocrat he had met.*

---

*Dr. Hooker has left the boat in Morocco without saying good-bye or asking for his New Testament. He lent it to me so I could find peace in Jesus, but there is none. Jesus was as maddened by all-over cruelty and coldness as I am. He too must have hated discovering he had to make people better all by himself. He had one advantage over me—he could do miracles. I asked Dr. Hooker how Jesus would have treated my starving little daughter with the blind baby.*
*"Jesus made the blind to see," said poor Dr. Hooker, looking uncomfortable.*
*"What would Jesus have done for them if he could NOT have made them see?" I asked. "Would he have hurried past like a bad Samaritan?"*
*I think that was why he left the Cut-use-off this afternoon. He does not want to live like Jesus, but unlike Harry Astley dare not say so.*

---

*Astley, Hooker, Wedder, all made miserable by one cracked Bell. The damage to Wedder was done after I returned from Alexandria. I rushed into our cabin and wed wed wed wed him, wedding and wedding and wedding until he begged me not to, said he could give no more but he could and did—it was the only thing which stopped me thinking about what I had seen. I sickened him of weddings, sickened myself too and in the end the thoughts still came back. I brooded for days without saying a word to him. Last night my silly man burst into tears, begged to be forgiven.*

*"For what?" says I. It seems he did not believe my tears and brooding were caused by the sight of beggars in Alexandria—he thought I was sulking because he had driven me to prostitution in Germany. I laughed out loud and told him I had done no such thing; that the money I had got for us was his own, taken when he fell asleep on the night when he won so much. At first he could not believe me, then he scowled straight ahead for a long time muttering "MY money! MY money!" I tried to cheer him up by starting to wed us again but he yelled "I SHALL NOT SERVE" and turned upside-down and the wrong way round with his back toward me and feet on the pillow. And all night long I heard the little whisper, 'My money. My money," coming from the bottom of the bunk.*

---

*Harry is bad because he enjoys how cruelly folk act and suffer, wants to persuade me bad is needed. If he succeeds he will have made me bad too. I listen to him because I need to know all he knows. He is as honest as God and teaches facts God never taught—all the things I must change, so had better note down.*

*WOMEN OF LEISURE— "Napoleon regarded women as the relaxation of the warrior. In England wives are treated as the public ornaments and private pleasure parks of wealthy landowners, industrialists and professional men. The joys of motherhood are closed to them, for after the pains of childbirth their offspring are caressed and cared for by servants. They are supposed to be superior to the animal pleasure of breast-feeding—supposed to be superior to the sexual act itself—yet all the time they are as much parasites, prisoners and playthings as odalisques in a Turkish harem. If an intelligent woman of this class does not find an unconventionally sensitive husband her life can be as painful as that of the women who spend years dying of slow suffocation while drudging in the Lancashire weaving-sheds. And that is why you should marry me, Bella. You will be my slave in law, but not in fact."*

*EDUCATION— "Very poor children learn to beg, lie and steal from their parents—they would hardly survive otherwise. Prosperous parents tell their children that nobody should lie, steal or kill, and that idleness and gambling are vices. They then send them to schools where they suffer if they do not disguise their thoughts and feelings and are taught to admire killers and stealers like Achilles and Ulysses, William the Conqueror and Henry the Eighth. This prepares them for life in a land where rich people use acts of parliament to deprive the poor of homes and livelihoods, where unearned incomes are increased by stock-exchange gambling, where those who own most property work least and amuse themselves by hunting, horse-racing and leading their country into battle.*

*You find the world horrifying, Bell, because you have not been warped to fit it by a proper education."*

*KINDS OF PEOPLE—"There are three kinds of people. The happiest are the innocent who think everyone and everything basically good. Many children are like that and so were you until Hooker (very much against my will) showed you otherwise. The second and biggest kind are half-baked optimists: people with a mental conjuring trick which lets them look at hunger or mutilation without discomfort. They think the wretched deserve to suffer, or that their nation is curing—not causing—these miseries, or that God, Nature, History will make everything right one day. Doctor Hooker is one of that sort and I am glad his rhetoric did not blind you to the facts. The third and rarest sort know human life is an essentially painful disease which only death can cure. We have the strength to live consciously among those who live blindly. We are the cynics."*

*"There must be a fourth kind," I said, "because I am no longer innocent and hate what Dr. Hooker and what you think equally."*

*"That is because you are searching for a way which does not exist."*

*"I will search as long as I live rather than be a childish fool or selfish optimist or equally selfish cynic," I told him, "and I will make my husband a searcher too."*

*"You will be a tiresome couple."*

*HISTORY—"Big nations are created by successful plundering raids, and since most history is written by friends of the conquerors history usually suggests that the plundered were improved by their loss and should be grateful for it. Plundering happens inside countries too. King Henry the Eighth plundered the English monasteries, the only institutions in those days which provided hospitals, schools and shelter for the poor. English historians agree King Henry was greedy, hasty and violent, but did a lot of good. They belong to a class which was enriched by the church lands."*

*THE BENEFITS OF WAR—"Napoleon gave Britain our advantage as an industrial nation. To fight him all around Europe the government introduced heavier taxes which chiefly oppressed the poor, and used much of this money to buy continual supplies of uniforms, boots, guns and shipping. All kinds of factories were built. Many able-bodied men were abroad with the army, but new machines made it possible to run factories with the cheap labour of women and children. This enhanced the profits so much that we could invest in trains, iron-clads and a big new empire. We owe a lot to Boney."*

*UNEMPLOYMENT—"When the Napoleonic war ended it left so many people unemployed and hungry that a parliamentary committee met to discuss the matter—the government feared a revolution. A socialist factory owner called Robert Owen suggested that every firm or business whose profits exceeded five per cent should spend the extra money on the better feeding, housing and schooling of their workers, instead of using it to undercut competitors. However, the Malthusians proved that the better you feed the poor the more they breed. Poverty, hunger and disease may drive some people to steal loaves from bakeries and dream of revolutions, but make revolutions less likely by weakening the bodies of the desperately poor and keeping down their number through infant mortalities. Do not shudder, Bell. What Britain needed—and got!—were military barracks beside every industrial city, a strong police-force, huge new jails; also poor-houses where children are divided from parents and husbands from wives—places so deliberately grim that people with a spark of self-respect spend their last few pennies on cheap gin and die of exposure in ditches rather than enter them. That is how we have organized the world's richest industrial nation and it works very well."*

*FREEDOM—"I am sure there was no word for freedom before slavery was invented. The old Greeks had every sort of government—monarchies, aristocracies, plutocracies, democracies—and argued fiercely about which system gave people most freedom, but all of them kept slaves. So did the ancient Roman republic. So did the stout squires who founded the U.S.A. Yes, the only sure definition of freedom is non-slavery. You may have heard it in a popular song:*

Rule, Britannia! Britannia rule the waves!
Britons never never never will be slaves!

*In the days of Good Queen Bess we English were so disgusted by the cruel way the Spaniards enslaved the American Indians that we plundered their treasure ships whether at war with them or not. In 1562 Sir John Hawkyns (who became paymaster of the navy and hero of the Armada fight) started the British slave trade by stealing black slaves from the Portuguese in Africa and selling them to the Spaniards in the New World. Parliament made that trade a criminal offence in 1811."*

*"Good!" I said, "and now the Americans have abolished it too."*

*"Yes. It only profited their southern farmers. Modern industry finds it cheaper to hire hands for days or weeks—when not needed they are free to beg work from other masters. When many free men are begging for work the masters are free to lower wages."*

*FREE TRADE—"Yes, our parliament has defined freedom as our ability to buy as cheap as possible and sell as dear as possible anywhere, with the help of our army and navy. This enables us to cut up countries with famines as readily as a carpenter cuts wood with a saw. Listen carefully, Bell.*

*"Indian weavers used to make the finest cotton cloth and muslin in the world, and only British merchants were free to sell it—the French had tried to do that, so we drove them out of India. Then we British learned how to make cloth more cheaply with machinery in our own factories, so we needed raw Indian cotton and Angora wool and could stop anyone else buying Indian cloth. Soon after one of the governors we had given to India reported that the plains of Dacca were littered with the bones of the weavers.*

*"Did you know that eight out of ten Irish lived on potatoes? They were peasants whose poor soil grew little else, and money they made by other means went to pay the landlords rent. The landlords were descended from English invaders and conquerors, so they owned the rich soil where corn was grown. Thirty-five years ago a sudden disease killed the potatoes and the peasants started starving. Now, in times of famine people who own big*

*food stocks move it out of the land, because starving people are too poor to pay a good price. The British parliament debated a proposal that we shut the Irish ports until the Irish grain had been eaten by the Irish people. This was voted down because it would interfere with free trade. Instead we sent soldiers to make sure the grain reached the ships. Nearly a million starved to death: a million and a half left the country. Those who reached Britain worked for such low wages that the wages of British workers could be beaten down and our industries make more money than ever. Now go to the stern for a while.''*

*He knows that when I can bear no more I run to the end of the ship and lean over the rail so that the wind blows my screams and wails out to sea. This time I looked hard at him and asked if he would have voted against closing the ports if he had been in parliament. I was not going to bite him if he said yes—I would have spat in his face. He said quietly, "I would not have dared vote against the proposal had I known I must face you afterwards, Bell.''*
*I nearly called him a cunning fiend, but that is how Wedder talks. I swallowed my spit and walked away.*

*EMPIRE—"No thickly peopled place has lacked an empire—Persia, Greece, Italy, Mongolia, Arabia, Denmark, Spain and France have had turns. The least warlike and biggest and longest-lasting empire was Chinese. We destroyed it twenty-five years ago because its government would not let us sell opium there. The British empire has grown rapidly, but in another two or three centuries the half-naked descendants of Disraeli and Gladstone may be diving off a broken pier of London Bridge, retrieving coins flung into the Thames by Tibetan tourists who find the sight amusing."*

*SELF GOVERNMENT—I asked if there are any lands of cheerful, prosperous people who govern only themselves.*

*"Yes. In Switzerland several small republics with different languages and religions have lived peacefully side by side for centuries, but high mountains divide them from each other and the surrounding nations. To improve the world, Bella, you need only build a high mountain between every town and its nearest neighbour, or chop the continents into many islands of equal size."*

*WORLD IMPROVERS— "Yes, I foresee that despite my teaching, Bell, you are going to become the most modern kind of half-baked optimist, the sort who wants to abolish riches and poverty by sharing out the world's goods equally."*

*"That is only common sense!" I cried.*

*"There are four sects who agree with you, but have different plans to bring it about.*

*"The SOCIALISTS want the poor to elect them into parliament, where they plan to tax the surplus of the rich and make laws to give everyone productive work in good conditions, along with good food, housing, education and health care."*

*"A lovely idea!" I cried.*

*"Yes. Beautiful. The other world-improvers point out that parliament is an alliance of monarchs, lords, bishops, lawyers, merchants, bankers, brokers, industrialists, mili-*

*tary men, landlords and civil servants who run it to protect their wealth* AND FOR NO OTHER REASON. *Socialists elected into it will therefore be outwitted by these, or bribed, or compromised into nonentity. I agree with this prediction.*

*"So the* COMMUNISTS *are forming a party of folk from every class of society who will patiently work and wait for a day when their country gets into serious financial trouble, then they will overturn it and become the government—for a short time. Having ruled the land until everybody has what they need and are able to keep it, the Communists say they will disband because neither they nor any further government will be needed."*

*"Hooray!" I cried.*

*"Yes, hooray. The other world-improvers say that groups who come to power by violence always perpetuate themselves by more of it and become a new tyranny. I agree.*

*"The* VIOLENT ANARCHISTS *or* TERRORISTS *dislike those who want power as much as those who have it. Since every other class depends on those who work the land, the mines, the factories and transport, they say such workers should keep what they make to themselves—should ignore money and exchange things by barter—should use explosives to frighten off folk who will not join them yet try to boss them."*

*"So they should!" I shouted.*

*"I agree. I also agree with those who say the police and army are better terrorists than anyone else. Besides, the middle classes hold the keys to the warehouses of food and fuel, no matter who produces it.*

*"So your only hope is among the* PACIFISTS *or*

*PEACEFUL ANARCHISTS. They say we can only improve the world by improving ourselves and hoping others copy us. This means not fighting anyone, giving away money and either living on the free gifts of others or on the work of our own hands. Buddha, Jesus, and Saint Francis took this path and in this century Prince Kropotkin, Count Leo Tolstoï and an American bachelor farmer-author called Thoreau. The movement attracts a lot of harmless aristocrats and writers. They annoy governments by refusing to pay taxes they think evil—which is most of them, since armies and weapons are what taxes mainly pay for. However, the police only imprison and flog ordinary Pacifists. The admirers of the famous ones keep them out of serious trouble. When you go into politics, Bell, be sure to become a Pacifist Anarchist. People will love you."*
*I wept and cried, "O what can I do?"*
*He said, "Let us go to the stern, Bell, and I will tell you."*

*ASTLEY'S SOLUTION—So we leaned over a rail watching the wake of the ship slide foaming backward and out over the slow glossy moonlit waves and he said, "The tearful motherlinesss you feel toward the wretched of this earth is an animal instinct which lacks its proper object. Marry and have children. Marry me. My country estate has a farm on it and a while village—think of the power you will have. Besides caring for my children (who we will not send to public schools) you can bully me into improving the drains and lowering the rents of a whole community. I am offering you the chance to be as happy and good as an intelligent woman can be on this filthy planet."*

*I said, "Your offer does not tempt me, Harry Astley, because I do not love you; but it is the most cunning inducement to lead a totally selfish life you could offer a woman. Thank you, but no."*
*"Then please hold my hand for a moment."*
*So I did and I felt for the first time who he really is—a tortured little boy who hates cruelty as much as I do but thinks himself a strong man because he can pretend to like it. He is as poor and desperate as my lost daughter, but only inside. Outside he is perfectly comfortable. Everyone should have a cosy shell round them, a good coat with money in the pockets. I must be a Socialist.*

---

*Misery stopped me thinking about good things, God, so I did not remember you until this morning. I was awakened by a noise like heavy rain and lay imagining how it would freshen the lettuces for Mopsy and Flopsy—how I would soon breakfast on poached eggs and kidneys and kippers while you ate your mash and bubbles—how we would then visit and mend the sick animals in our hospital. Having basked for many minutes in gladness and peace I opened my eyes and saw Wedderburn's feet beside me and sunlight between the slats of the shuttered window. I remembered that the rainy noise came from a eucalyptus tree outside the hotel, a tree whose hard glossy leaves rattle and hiss against each other in the wind. But the peaceful gladness did not go away. The memory of you kept horror and weeping out because you are wiser and better than Dr. Hooker and Harry Astley put together. You never said that cruelty to the helpless is good or inevitable or unimportant. One day you will tell me how to change what I cannot yet describe without my words swelling HUGE, vowels vanishing, tears washing ink away.*

*Someone rapped on the bedroom door to say they had put a steaming canister of hot water on the floor outside. I had not shaved Wedder since the day we docked in Alexandria, and decided to do it now. Leaping up I swiftly washed and dressed, slipped a towel between his head and pillow and lathered his face all over. This was much easier to do with his head at the bottom of the bed. He neither spoke nor opened his eyes but I knew he was pleased, because he hates shaving himself. As I removed the bristles I reminded him that a ship bound for Glasgow by way of Lisbon and Liverpool was leaving today—— that Mr. Astley was travelling on it, and had offered to book a passage for us. Still without opening his eyes Wedder said, "We are going to Paris by way of Marseilles."*

*"But why, Duncan?"*

*"Since even a thieving trollop like you refuses to marry me only Paris remains. Take me there. Hand me over to the midinettes and the little green fairy then marry who you like—English, American or filthy Russian ha ha ha ha ha."*

*Wedder is a lot cheerier since he decided he is not a fiend and that I probably am. I said, "But Duncan, we cannot afford to stay in Paris. I have only enough money to take us home."*

*This was not true. Your money is still in the lining of my travelling-coat, God, but I felt the kindest way to get rid of Wedder (who hardly ever wants to wed me now) was by returning him to his mother. He said, "Then I must stay in Gibraltar till I have managed to cash the last Consolidated Annuities in my inheritance; and know, woman, you will never again rob or cheat me of a single penny—I shall hold on to the whole amount. Since you care about money you had better abandon me today and return to Britain with your precious Astley."*

*I liked that idea but could not abandon Wedder so far from home. I know nothing about the midinettes and little green fairy, but if they are kind to him he may stop with them in Paris and I will return to Glasgow alone.*

*As usual he wanted tea and toast in bed. I went to the dining-room, asked for these to be sent up and breakfasted for the last time with Harry Astley. Did I tell you he is a widower who guessed long ago that I am not married? Over the ham and eggs (this is a British hotel though the staff are Spanish) I saw he was going to propose again, and prevented it by saying I would only marry a world-improver. He sighed, drummed his fingers on the table-cloth then said I should beware of men who talked about improving the world—many used such talk to entrap women of my sort.*

*"What sort is that?" I asked, interested. He looked away from me and said coldly, "The brave and kind sort who feel generous to the miserable of every class and country—generous also to the cold, rich and selfish."*

*I nearly melted. I said, "Stand up, Harry."*

*He must have been taught young to obey people because although he looked startled and the dining-room was very busy he stood up at once, straight, like a soldier. I sprang to him, tied his arms to his sides with my own and kissed him until he trembled. Then I whispered, "Good-bye Harry," and hurried upstairs to my weary old Wedder.*

*He and Harry are much alike, though Harry has stronger nerves. In the passage from the dining-room I looked back at the last possible moment. The foreign guests were staring at me, the British were pretending nothing odd had happened. Harry Astley, obviously British, was concentrating on his breakfast.*

*Candle must not be jealous. That was the only kiss Harry got from me, and no talkers will trap Bell Baxter. When I come home, God, you will tell us how to improve the world, then you and me, Candle, will marry and do it.*

---

# 17

# Gibraltar to Paris: Wedderburn's Last Flight

*At last, no Wedder! And my own little room in a narrow street in the heart of beautiful sane Paris! Do you remember bringing me here a long time ago? How we gaped at huge pictures in the Louvre? And ate at little tables under trees in the Tuileries Gardens? And visited Professor Charcot at the Salpêtrière, and how hard he tried to hypnotize me? At last I pretended he had done it, because I did not want him to feel silly in front of his huge audience of adoring students. I believe he saw I was pretending—which is why he smiled so wisely and announced that I was the sanest English woman he had ever professionally examined. Let me tell you how I got back here.*

*In Gibraltar Wedder made me wait outside the bank while he collected his money. He emerged with the careless swagger I so admired, though I now knew there was not much underneath. On the boat to Marseilles he ordered bottles of wine with our meals. This was new. I drank none because one sip of it makes me giddy, but he said a meal without wine was no meal at all, and pointed out that the French were all drinking it. This ship, unlike the Cut-use-off, was mainly for passengers. In the afternoons and evenings Wedder played cards with men in a corner of the main saloon, and kept at it long after I went to bed. The night before we docked in Marseilles he came back to the cabin whistling and chirping, "My hinny my hen my humming-bird my pretty partridge my Scots blue Bell, you were right in what you once said! Games of skill not games of chance are this man's métier."*

*He counted his winnings then got into bed the right way round for the first time in weeks. I was starting to enjoy what he called "our second honeymoon" when he suddenly fell asleep. Not me. I knew what was going to happen and that I could not stop it.*

*Instead of going straight to Paris from Marseilles we put up in a hotel recommended by one of the card players on the boat. The same friend introduced him to a café or club or card-school where he played every afternoon and evening while I waited in the hotel drinking cup after cup of chocolate and brooding over Malthus'* On Population. *It took Wedder five days to lose all he had. He behaved better over it than I expected, coming to our room in the afternoon and saying, "Here I am at your mercy again, Bell. I hope you have enough to pay the hotel—I'm totally cleaned out. But you prefer me this way."*

*I had no intention of using your money until the last possible moment, God. I packed some essentials into a handbag, smartened myself up, smartened up Wedder, then took him for a stroll to a railway station where we caught an overnight train to Paris. While waiting for it he tried to break away once or twice, begging to return to the*

*hotel to collect a dressing-case with silver-mounted brushes which had belonged to his father. I said, "No, Wedder, you booked that room for us. Be glad the hotel is getting something valuable in return."*
*I was so relieved to get clean away from Marseilles that I slept sound though sitting upright on the wooden bench of a French third-class carriage.*

*On reaching Paris I saw Wedder had not slept a wink and was on the verge of collapsing. I dragged him into the crooked streets on the less posh side of the river where hotels were likely to be cheap, but they were not yet open. In a cobbled space where three narrow lanes met I plonked us both down at a café table and said, "Rest here Wedder. I will go to the station where trains leave for Calais and buy tickets. We could be in Glasgow three days from now."*
*"Impossible—it would mean social ruin. We are not man and wife."*
*"Then dear Duncan let us return to Glasgow separately."*
*"Fiend-woman! Demon! Have I not proved that I love and need you? That parting with you would be tearing my heart out by the roots?" et cetera.*
*"But you said there were people you wanted to stay with in Paris. Maybe I can arrange that."*
*"What people?"*
*"The midinettes and little green fairy."*
*"Hoist with my own petard ha ha ha ha ha."*
*When Wedder does not want to explain his funny words he gets out of it by using others. At that moment a waiter making the café ready for customers asked if we wanted anything and Wedder said, "Oon absongth."*

*The waiter went away and brought back a little stemmed glass of what seemed water and a tumbler of more water. Wedder added drops from the tumbler to the small glass then held this up. The liquid in it turned a pretty milky green. "Meet the little green fairy!" he said and swallowed it in a gulp. Then he cried, "Oon otray!" to the waiter, folded his arms on the table top and hid his face in them. At this moment I saw a well-dressed man come out of a nearby doorway with "Hôtel de Notre-Dame" painted on the wall above it.*

*"Excuse me, Duncan," I said and went inside.*

*The foyer was so small that a heavy mahogany desk in the middle nearly cut it in two. Folk going in or out had to squeeze round the sides. Behind the desk sat a woman who looked like Queen Victoria but younger and friendlier, a neat plump alert little woman in the black silk gown of a widow.*

*"Do you speak English, Madame?" I asked and, "It is me muver tongue, dear," she answered in a London voice, "and what can I do for you?"*

*I told her I had a poor man outside who badly needed rest; that we had not much money and hardly any baggage, so wanted her smallest and cheapest room. She said I had come to the right shop—a cubicle here would cost only twenty francs for the first hour, to be paid in advance, with twenty for each additional hour or fraction of an hour to be paid before either party left. A cubicle had just been vacated and would be ready for use in ten or fifteen minutes—where was my gentleman friend? I said he was drinking green fairies at the café next door. She asked if he was likely to run away. I laughed and said, "No, I only wish he was!"*

*She laughed too and invited me to drink a cup of coffee with her while waiting. She said, "Judging by your voice you come from Manchester, and it is years since I had a heart-to-heart talk with a sensible down-to-earth English woman."*

*I popped out and told Wedder this. He stared at me blearily then swallowed the second green fairy. I went back in.*

*She began by telling me she had once been Millicent Moon of Seven Dials and keen on the hotel trade, but London hotel regulations made life hard for beginners so she had come to Paris where new hôteliers were encouraged. In the Notre-Dame she had first occupied a very subordinate position, but became so indispensable to the manager that he married her—she was now known as Madame Cronquebil, but I should call her Millie. She had become manager herself after the Franco-Prussian war, when the Communards had suspended Cronquebil from a lamp bracket because of his international sympathies. She said she regretted his demise, but pursued her avocation with a facility and acumen which were appreciated in the correct quarters. French men were a lot easier to manage than British. The British pretended to be honest and practical but were at bottom a race of eccentrics. Only the French were sensible about the important things—did I not agree? I said, "I cannot say, Millie. What are the important things?"*

*"Money and love. What else is there?"*

*"Cruelty."*

*She laughed and said that was a very English idea, but people who loved cruelty had to pay for it, which proved love and money came first. I asked what she meant? She stared and asked what I meant. I said I was afraid to tell her. At this she stopped being motherly and jolly, and asked in a low voice if a man had hurt me?*

*"O no Millie—nobody ever hurt me. I'm talking about worse things than that."*

*I was trembling and starting to weep but she held my hands. This strengthened me so much that I told her what happened in Alexandria. And now I have the strength to tell you about it too, God, but it is so important that I will divide it from the rest of my letter with another line.*

---

*Mr. Astley and Dr. Hooker took me to a hotel where we sat among well-dressed people like ourselves at tables on a veranda chatting eating drinking and a crowd of nearly naked folk mostly children watched us all across a space where two men with whips walked up and down and at first I thought a jolly game was happening for many in the crowd were amusing folk on the veranda by bowing and praying to them and wriggling their bodies and grinning comically until someone on the veranda flung a coin or handful of coins onto the dusty ground before the veranda then one or two or a horde raced out and flung themselves down on the coins scrabbling and screaming while the audience at the tables laughed or looked disgusted or turned away then the men with whips who had stood with folded arms pretending not to see suddenly saw and rushed into the crowd flogging it apart and back which caused laughter too and Mr. Astley said remnants of the race that carved the sphinx and Dr. Hooker said that looks like a deserving case and pointed to a thin little girl blind in one eye carrying a baby with a big head who was blind in both she held it tight in one arm held the other straight out swaying the empty clutching hand from side to side mechanically as if in a trance in a trance I stood and walked to her I think the men shouted and followed I crossed the space and entered the crowd of beggars taking the purse out of my handbag to put into her hand but before I could do that someone snatched it anyway the money could never be enough she was my daughter perhaps I knelt on the ground embraced her and the baby lifted them up waded stumbled back through crippled blind children old men with running sores scrambling screaming stamping each other's fingers to get coins from split purse I climbed onto the veranda a hotel man said you cannot bring these here and I said they are coming home with me and Mr. Astley said Mrs. Wedderburn neither the port authorities nor the captain will let you bring them onto the ship and the baby was wailing and peeing but the little girl clutched me with her other arm I am sure she knew she had found her mother but they dragged us apart* YOU CAN DO NO GOOD *bellowed Dr. Hooker nobody had ever cursed me insulted me like that before how could he say that to me who like all of us is good right through to the backbone* I CAN DO NO GOOD? *I cried hardly believing I had heard such a vile suggestion but Mr. Astley said distinctly none at all so I tried to scream like you once screamed God since I wanted to make the whole world faint but Harry Astley clapped his hand over my mouth O the sheer joy of feeling my teeth sink in.*

*The taste of blood sobered me. I was also surprised, because Mr. Astley did not wince or groan. He only frowned slightly, but two seconds later his face lost colour and he would have collapsed if Dr. Hooker and I had not helped him indoors and placed him on a sofa in the alcove of a lounge. Dr. Hooker ordered hot water, iodine and clean bandages, but though he has a medical certificate it was I who bathed and dressed the wound and bound it with a tourniquet bandage. I also told him I was sorry. In a sleepy voice he told me that a clean, unexpected flesh wound, however painful, was a flea bite to one who had been educated at Eton.*

*On the way back to the ship in a cab I sat silent and rigid, staring straight ahead while they talked. Dr. Hooker said now I knew the great task which lay ahead of the Anglo-Saxon races, and also why Our Father in Heaven had created an afterlife to counteract the evils of life on earth. At the same time (he said) I should not exaggerate the evil of what we had seen. The open sores et cetera were a source of income to those who flaunted them, and most beggars were happier than folk who lived by honest toil. The girl and baby were accustomed to their state, it was not misery in our sense of the word—they were certainly happier and freer in Egypt than they would be in a civilized country. He admired how completely I had recovered from my first reaction to a terrible surprise, but was not sorry to have administered that surprise—from now on I would think like a woman, not like a child. Mr. Astley said my pity was natural and good if confined to the unfortunate of my own class, but if acted on promiscuously it would prolong the misery of many who would be better dead. I had just seen a working model of nearly every civilized nation. The people on the veranda were the owners and rulers—their inherited intelligence and wealth set them above everyone else. The crowd of beggars represented the jealous and incompetent majority, who were kept in their place by the whips of those on the ground between: the latter represented policemen and functionaries who keep society as it is. And while they spoke I clenched my teeth and fists to stop them biting and scratching these clever men who want no care for the helpless sick small, who use religions and politics to stay comfortably superior to all that pain: who make religions and politics, excuses to spread misery with fire and sword and how could I stop all this? I did not know what to do.*

---

*"I still do not know," I told Millie, smiling through my tears. "I had better return to God for advice. But I cannot do that until I am rid of the poor fellow who waits outside."*

*"Bring him in," said Millie firmly. "Your apartment is ready so take him up to it, knock him off quick and we will have another talk. Your heart is too good for this wicked world, my dear. You need advice from a friendly, experienced woman you can trust."*

*I thought "knock him off" a queer way to say "put him to bed", but out I went and saw—no Duncan! Four empty little green fairy glasses stood on the table top, a waiter who wanted paid sprang forward, but my Wedder had vanished.*

*I went back inside. Millie made us more coffee then asked how I had met such a man and why I was wandering in Paris with so little luggage. I told her.*

*She said, "I greatly admire your sense, my dear, in taking a nice long honeymoon with your lover before marrying a respectable husband. Too many women enter marriage completely ignorant of what they ought to give and take. But this Wedderburn is obviously an over-sucked orange. You will be a far better wife to your husband if you now enjoy some variety.''*

*She explained that the hotel was the sort Londoners call a knocking-shop—her customers were men who paid to wed a total stranger for periods of an hour or less. Knocking was illegal in Britain, but any clean intelligent girl could get a licence to do it in France, or find work in a licensed establishment like her own.*

*''Is it possible for strangers to wed so quickly?'' I asked, astonished, and she said many men preferred strangers because they could not wed those they knew best. Most of her customers were married men, and some of them had mistresses too. It seemed a mistress was what I had been to Wedder, though a Parisian kind are called midinettes.*

*''He obviously found one while waiting for you,'' she said. ''Hotels constantly lose business to amateurs—if I did not love my métier I would have retired years ago. I don't suppose you will want to stay here forever, but many deserted women earn enough to return to God while working for me.''*

*''Not to my God,'' I said.*

*''Of course not, dear. I'm talking about Catholics.''*

*Then Wedder strode in. He was in one of his wild states, and demanded a talk with me in private.*

*''Do you want that, dear?'' said Millie.*

*''Of course!'' said I.*

*She led us very stiffly upstairs to this nice little room then said (to Wedder) ''Out of respect for the person of your companion I am forgoing the tariff which is customarily paid in advance, but if in any way she suffers you will be made to pay to an extent you will find astonishing."*

*She said this in a very French voice.*

*"Eh?" said Wedder, looking confused as well as wild.*

*In a more London voice she said, "Remember, walls have ears," and left, shutting the door.*

*He then strode up and down making a speech which sounded more like the Bible than Shakespeare. He spoke about God, his mother, the lost paradise of home, hell-fire, damnation and money. He said that by stealing the five hundred friedrichs d'or I had broken his run of luck, stopped him breaking the casino's bank and cheated him out of marriage. My theft had robbed the poor of vast sums he would have donated to charity and to the church, and deprived us of a town house in London, a yacht in the Mediterranean, a grouse moor in Scotland and a mansion in the Kingdom of Heaven. And now that he no longer wished to marry—now that he wished he were separated from me by a gulf deeper than Hell itself—he was chained by his abject poverty to the fiend who had damned him to Hell—was chained to a woman for whom he now felt nothing but hate hate hate hate hate—loathing, detestation and hate.*

*"But Duncan," I cried happily cutting open the lining of my coat, "luck has returned to you again! Here are Clydesdale and North of Scotland banknotes to the value of five hundred pounds sterling—they are just as valuable as friedrichs d'or. God gave them to me because he knew something like this would happen, and I have kept them for our last moment which has now arrived. Take it all! Return to Glasgow, to your mother, to maidservants who will love your manliness more than I can, to any church*

*of God which catches your fancy. Be free as a bird once more—fly from me!"*

*Instead of cheering up he tried to swallow the notes while flinging himself out of the window, but being unable to get it open he rushed through the door and tried to dive downstairs head first.*

*Luckily Millie had been listening from the room next door (this hotel is full of apertures) and had called out her staff. They swarmed over him and filled him with exactly the right amount of brandy. It was not easy getting him off on the train to Calais. He did not really want to leave me, but many hands make light work and off he went. Millie wanted me to keep most of the five hundred pounds but I said no: Wedder loved money more than I did and it was his reward for the weddings we had enjoyed. I would now earn what I needed by working for a living: a thing I had not done before. She said, "If that's what you really want, dear."*

*So here I am.*

---

# 18

# Paris to Glasgow: The Return

*I am no longer a parasite. For three days I have earned a wage by doing a job as well and fast as possible, not for pleasure but cash like most people do. Each morning I sink into slumber, glad to have knocked off forty and earned four hundred and eighty francs. I am surprised at my popularity. Bell Baxter is certainly a splendid looking woman, but if I was a man there are at least a dozen here I would want more than me: soft little cuddlies, tall supple elegants, wild brown exotics. Millie describes me in our brochure as "The beautiful Englishwoman* (la belle Anglaise) *who will fully compensate you for the pains* (travail) *of Agincourt and Waterloo." She is careful that I only deal with Frenchmen, because (she says) it might embarrass me to meet some of her English clients in later life. Perhaps she also thinks it might embarrass them! She has a lot of these at the weekends who require special services from some of our girls who are between employments at the* Comédie Française. *I watched one of the performances through an aperture last night. Our client was Monsieur Spankybot who arrives in a cab wearing a black mask which he never removes, though he takes off everything else. He has very elaborate requirements for which he pays a great deal, being first treated as a baby, then as a little lad on his first night in a new boarding-school, then as a young soldier captured by a savage tribe. His screams were out of all proportion to what was actually done to him.*

*My best friend here, Toinette, is a Socialist, and we often talk about improving the world, especially for the miserable ones, as Victor Hugo calls them, though Toinette says Hugo's special insights are* très sentimental *and I should apply myself to the novels of Zola. We discuss these things at the café next door because Millie Cronquebil says politics should be detached from the hotel trade. The intellectual life of Paris is in its cafés, and our quarter (which contains the University) has cafés whose customers are writers or painters or savants of other kinds, and the academics have different cafés from the revolutionaries. Our café is mostly frequented by revolutionary hôteliers who say the rich will only disgorge through a* bouleversement *of the* structure totale.

*No time to write more. Someone's coming.*

---

*I am writing the end of this letter in a splendid office which smells of disinfectant and leather upholstery, just like home. I left the Notre-Dame suddenly today after two hours of terrible confusion. The cause was my own ignorance. Will I ever reach the end of it?*

*For obvious reasons we usually rose late in the mornings, but today Millie knocked on my door soon after eight and said I should hurry downstairs at once to the Salon*

*International because the doctor was looking at the girls there.*

*"An early start indeed!" thinks Bell but says aloud, "Certainly, Millie. What doctor is this?"*

*"He is employed by the municipality to enforce public health regulations. Just wear your dressing-gown, dearie, and it will be over in a jiffy."*

*So I joined the queue, noticing many of the girls wore nothing but their chemise and stockings. All the ones outside the alcove seemed quieter and glummer than usual so to cheer them up I said it was good for the municipality to care about our health, and I hoped Toinette (who was ahead of me) would get the doctor to prescribe something which would ease her migraine headaches. This did cheer them up—they giggled and said I had esprit, which puzzled me. But when I reached the alcove I saw an ugly little man with a ferocious scowl who was barking "Wider! Wider!" at poor Toinette like a bad-tempered drill-sergeant. She lay with her legs apart on a padded table while he pressed a thing like a spoon into her loving groove or vagina (as the Latins call it) while nearly sticking his nose and heavy moustache in after it. That was the only part of women he cared about because a moment later he said, "Pah! You may go."*

*"I am not going near him!" I said firmly. "He is no doctor—doctors are kind and gentle and care for every part of their patient."*

*Uproar. More than half the queue fell about laughing.*

*"Do you think you are better than the rest of us?" screamed others.*

*"Do you want him to remove our licence?" screamed Millie, rushing in.*

*"Insanity!" roared the doctor. "She willingly accommodates any quantity of verminous male appendages, but recoils from a clinical spatula in the hands of an impersonal scientist. But no, she is not insane—she is English, and has something to hide."*

*That was how I learned about venereal diseases.*

*"I am sorry Millie, I can no longer work here. As you know, I am engaged to be married. And this medical inspection is unfair and inefficient. Your girls are healthy when they start working here so it is the clients, not the staff who spread the diseases. It is the clients who should be medically examined before we let them into us."*

*"The clients would never allow it and there are insufficient doctors in France."*

*By this time we were tête à tête in her office. I said, "Then train the girls to examine each client before the wedding starts—make it part of the ceremony."*

*"The accomplished ones already do so and the house cannot afford to start classes of instruction for novices. From our earnings I am obliged to pay for rent, rates, gas, furnishings, police bribes, wages and a clear fifteen per cent profit to the lawyer who acts for the company. If my monthly return ever falls below fifteen per cent I will be replaced tout de suite and die a lonely and wretched old woman."*

*Though plump and queenly she began wailing like a little thin child, so I saw that coaxing, kissing and passionate embraces were required. I led her upstairs to her bedroom while Toinette manned the reception-desk.*

*But nothing I did cheered her up. She said she hated Paris and the French and had been trying for years to get back to England. She dreamed of buying a boarding-house in Brighton and ending her life with a decent Church of England funeral, but every time she managed to save a little money an accident like this morning's took it all away so she would never escape from Paris—her cadaver would end on a slab in the public morgue by the Seine, her maquillage smeared by the drippings of water onto it from a rusty tap. She said other lovely, tragic, despairing things which wrung my heart, they were so daft. She said, "It is all so unequal—I have the fifth place in your affections. First comes your mysterious guardian, then your peasant fiancé, then the debauched Wedderburn, then the frigid Astley. Since I was a little tiny girl I have prayed for a pal but God hates me. Every time someone beautiful and friendly enters my life crash bang wallop, out they fly again leaving nuffink behind but a bloody big owl."*

*I said that no god could ever hate her—that she should think of my loving embraces, not imaginary owls—that I would always remember her with love—but how much money had I earned? Surely enough for a third-class fare back to Scotland?*

*"You have earned less than nothing," she said. "I gave the police doctor all you earned and a bit more, to help him forget how you insulted his profession. Frenchmen are very proud. If I had not done that he would have taken my licence away and we would all be out of work."*

*I suddenly felt too cold and tired to say a word. I went to my room, dressed, packed my bags, went downstairs, kissed Toinette wordlessly too (she wept aloud at that) and left the Hôtel de Notre-Dame for ever.*

*I still had some francs left from the money which had brought Wedder and me to Paris. It covered the cost of a cab to the Salpêtrière, and I gave what was left to an attendant with a note to be given directly into the hands of Professor Charcot. The note said Bella Baxter, niece of Mr. Godwin Baxter of Glasgow, was in the vestibule and would like to see him at his earliest convenience. The attendant returned and said the professor's duties would keep him fully occupied for an hour or more, but if I cared to wait in his office his secretary would provide me with coffee. So I was shown into this room which smells like your study in Park Circus.*

*When Charcot at last arrived he was very genial at first: "Bonjour, Mamselle Baxter—the one completely sane English! How is my friend the enormous Godwin? What event must I thank for the unexpected pleasure of your presence here?"*

*I told him. It took a long time because he asked questions which brought out everything and he looked more and more solemn the more I spoke. At last he said abruptly, "You need money."*

*Enough to return to Glasgow, I told him, where my guardian would repay him by a money order. To this he said nothing at all, but sat frowning and drumming his fingers on the desk top until I stood up, thanked him for his attention and said good-bye.*

*"No no. Pardon my abstraction—you need money and shall have it—enough to return in comfort to Scotland whenever you wish after spending tonight in my home as my guest. And do not thank me. You prefer earning money to receiving gifts. I approve. The money will be payment for helping me in a way you have already experienced. Attend!*

*"This evening I am lecturing before a very small, very fashionable audience: the Duc de Germantes (a man of*

*genuine culture) and two or three whose names would not interest you. They are politicians—sensation seekers who like to pose as intellectuals. The lecture will help science indirectly by ensuring my researches are appreciated by those whose hands are on the public purse-strings. Tonight I will question under hypnosis a female farm servant—a religious hysteric but not, alas, as interesting as Jeanne d'Arc or as you Mamselle Baxter. Please enliven the occasion by recounting this evening (under hypnosis, of course, and in response to my questioning) part of what you have just told me."*

*"What part?" asks Bell.*

*"Tell them how you enjoyed life before you saw Alexandria, your rational pleasure in an existence untainted by guilt and the fear of death. Tell them, in your splendidly unpunctuated fashion, how the sight of the poor children affected you, and do not, in the name of God, hold back the tears. Say how you relieved your feelings toward your male companion, and how you were affected by the taste of his blood. Finally, describe your present sense of the human condition. Be as Socialistic, Communistic, Anarchistic as you please—denounce the bourgeoisie, the plutocrats, the aristocrats, even royalty! Do you know anything about royalty?"*

*"I have been told Queen Victoria is a selfish old woman."*

*"Perfect. They will enjoy that. These speeches of yours will be punctuated by my addresses to the audience in rapid French; you need pay no attention. After all, you will be in a hypnotic trance."*

*"I suppose you will tell them that my pity for poor people is caused by a displaced sense of motherhood."*

PROFESSOR JEAN MARTIN CHARCOT

*"You recognize that? Then you are a psychologist!" he cried laughing. "But do not say so tonight! Society is based upon division of labour. I am the lecturer, you are my subject. Our august audience will be disconcerted if anyone but the great Charcot passes opinions. By the way, I will guarantee your anonymity. And you need not mention the names of your friends. After all, you are British. Reserve is instinctive to you, and everyone knows hypnosis cannot influence people against their will. Well?"*

*So tonight I will perform with him again, and tomorrow set off home, but this letter must be posted today, for you must know that the Bell coming back to you is no longer the pleasure-seeking somnambulist who eloped with poor old Wedder. You must answer some difficult questions for me. You must tell me how to do good and not be a parasite. Tell Candle too, for since he and Bell will soon be lifelong partners we must work together. Tell my dear Candle that his wedding Bell no longer thinks he must do all she bids. Tell him also that Millie Cronquebil was wrong in one thing she said: I will* not *be a better wife because of the variety enjoyed in the Notre-Dame, unless it pleases him to see me lying flat murmuring* "formidable!" *in a variety of astonished tones.*

*Meanwhile, all the best, both of you,*
*From she you love most,*
*Ding Dong Bell.*

*P.S. Stroke the pussies, pat the dogs, kiss Mopsy and Flopsy for me.*

"Well, Candle?" said Baxter, laying down the letter and smiling at me, "are you not terrified by the prospect of the return of this truly *formidable* partner? Think of what she did to Duncan Wedderburn!"

I was now too joyful to resent his kindly condescension. My pulse was accelerated. The ductless glands released such vital secretions into my blood-stream (I *felt* them doing it!) that my muscles expanded and I had the strength of several men.

"No, Baxter! I fear nothing from my Bella. She is a kind woman and a perfect judge of character. She knows a man's inmost soul as soon as she shakes his hand. In Wedderburn she sensed the selfish sexual male rampant and served him exactly as he wished. He was fool enough to want a life of unending ecstasy. It was not her fault that no organism can survive through that. I am a virgin. My ecstasies with her will be varied by milder, more comfortable modes of affection. The main strain will fall on you, Baxter. If you do not show her how Mr. and Mrs. McCandless can improve the world you will hideously disappoint her—our marriage may not happen. Are *you* not terrified?"

"No. I will tell you to improve the world along lines clearly indicated by your characters and talents. . . . What is that sound?"

The hour was a little after midnight. As on the night Bella had left us the curtains were wide and I saw the moon through the window, though drifts of hurrying cloud sometimes hid it. The sound was a key turning in a lock downstairs, the front door opening and closing, a light rapid step ascending the stairs. I rose to face her as the study door opened—Baxter stayed seated. She stood before me, her face more gaunt and lined than it had been but her smile as delighted and delightful as ever. She had unfastened her travelling-coat so that I saw both the darned lining and my tiny pearl gleaming in the lapel. She laughed as she saw my eye fix on that, then said, "I am glad you are both still up and the old place is exactly the same—except for this. This is new."

She strode to the fireplace and examined a lidded crystal vase on the overmantel. It contained our gobstoppers.
"The covenant of our plighted troth!" she cried. Removing the lid she took one out, ground it to powder beneath her firm white teeth, swallowed it then, opening her arms to us, cried, "O my God and my Candle, how wonderful to be home but what is there to eat downstairs? Sweets are not enough for a hungry woman. Duncan Wedderburn taught me that, besides what the scar on my stomach meant."
This reminded her of something else. Suddenly she stared hard at Baxter, her face growing thinner, the pupils of her eyes expanding to completely blacken the irises.
"Where is my child, God?" she asked.

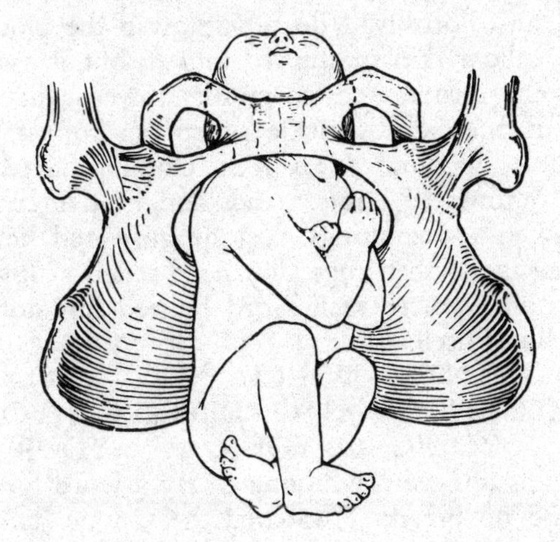

# 19

# My Shortest Chapter

HAD BELLA NOT ARRIVED SO SOON AFTER her letter I think Baxter would have had a reply prepared for that question, but it came now as a shock and changed him horribly. I do not know if the blood drained from his sallow skin or flushed into it, but in two seconds the colour turned greyish-purple. Sweat that suddenly beaded his face did not trickle but sprang from it, for he did not tremble, he vibrated. His loose clothing stayed unmoved but the outlines of boots, hands and head grew indistinct like plucked guitar strings. Yet he answered her. From a woeful cavity in that huge dim head tolled a slow, hollow, iron-sounding voice, each word blurred but not drowned by an echo of itself.

"THE. EVENTS. WHICH. LED. TO. YOUR. CRACKED. HEAD. ALSO. DEPRIVED. YOU. OF. . YOUR. . . YOUR. . . . YOUR. . . . . YOUR . . . . . ."

Silence. His lips were wrestling to say a word for which he could find no breath. I watched the tongue flicker against the back of his upper teeth, saw the word began with L so must be *life*. Half his brain was trying to tell Bella the truth about her origin, the other half was appalled by the attempt and so was I.

"Your *child*, Bella!" I shouted. "The shock that destroyed your memory killed the *child* in you!"

Baxter grew perfectly still, staring at her with aghast eyes and mouth wide open. So did I. She sighed and said softly,

"I feared that," then smiled at Baxter as kindly as if no tears were flowing down her cheeks. Then she sat on his knee, embraced him as far round the waist as her arms could reach, rested her head upon his chest and seemed to fall asleep. He too closed his eyes and his normal colour slowly returned.

Feeling relieved but jealous I watched them a while. Eventually I sat by Bella, embraced her waist and rested my head on her shoulder. She was not completely asleep, for she moved her body to let mine fit it more easily.
The three of us lay a long time
like that.

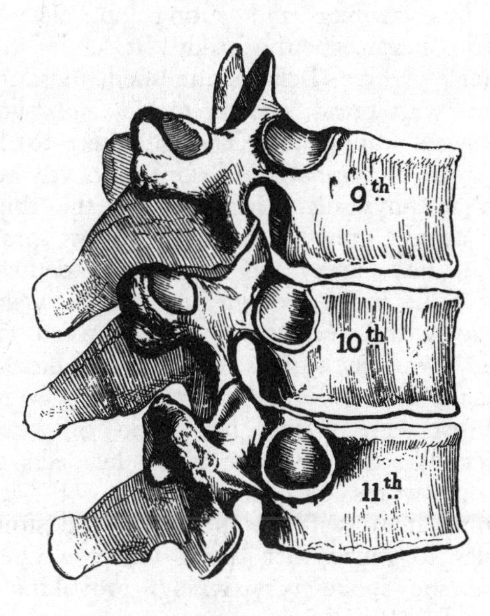

# 20

# God Answers

MAYBE AN HOUR PASSED. SHE ROUSED us by yawning and sitting up. The following conversation began in the study. It ended round the kitchen table where Bella demolished most of a cold boiled ham with bread, cheese, pickles and two or three pints of sweet milky tea. Though used to her quick recovery from emotional shocks I had never before seen it happen so physically. Her face lost the thin haggard look, her cheeks grew rounder, her brow smoother and softer, the tiny lines and wrinkles faded from her freshening skin. From looking any age between twenty-five and forty she became any age between twenty-five and fifteen. Was my strictly scientific eye dazzled by the loving glance she gave me? Surely not, yet more than ham and tea were erasing her marks of weariness and strain. Her eyes fed on our faces, her ears and brain digested our words into the substance of her thought, strengthening it as swiftly as her teeth and stomach used the eatables to renew her body. Between chewing and swallowing she spoke very wisely, provoking a debate which decided her future career, and mine too, and a date for our marriage. But perhaps her radiance did daze me slightly. I talked as much as Baxter and she put together but I remember hardly anything I said. However, I very distinctly recall exactly how the debate began.

Bell said, "Why did you sweat and stammer and tremble when I asked about my child, God? Were you afraid your answer would drive me mad?"

Baxter nodded with a force which made us fear for his neck.

She said, "I suppose that is not surprising. I was a child when I ran away from you—how could *you* have told childish Bell Baxter that she had lost a child of her own? Especially when you did not know who the dad was. You made me strong and sure of myself, God, by teaching me about the fine and mighty things in the world and showing I was one of them. You were too sane to teach a child about craziness and cruelty. I had to learn about those from people who were crazy and cruel themselves. I knew there was something wrong with the world as soon as Wedder told me I had been a mother. I knew my daughter could have been terribly hurt as soon as Dr. Hooker pointed smugly at the little poor girl and blind baby. When Mr. Astley explained how rich nations depend on infant mortalities I knew she might be dead, and I almost wished she were dead when I learned at Millie Cronquebil's how weak and lonely women are used. You are to blame for *nothing*, God, nothing at all where I am concerned. But you know and hate (do you not?) how the weak are made to suffer?"

"Yes."

"Did you never try to stop it?"

"Never," said Baxter drearily, "though I once tried to lessen their pain by treating injured employees of the Blochairn iron foundry and St. Rollox locomotive works."

"Why did you stop?"

"Because I was selfish," said Baxter, starting to sweat and vibrate again, "and had found you. I wanted to win your love far more than I cared for the scorched and broken victims of heavy industry."

Bella calmed him with a smile of tender amused dismay which was also in the tone of her voice.

"Dear God, what a lot of good I have prevented, just by existing! Harry Astley must be right—there *are* too many people in the world, especially pampered pets like me. We must start using your money properly, God. Let us take ship to Alexandria, find the little girl and her baby brother, adopt them and bring them back here."

"No need to go so far Bell," said Baxter, sighing. "Tomorrow I can walk with you up the High Street from Glasgow Cross. To our right you will see railway yards and warehouses on the ground of the old university: the university where Adam Smith devised his world-famous treatise on the Wealth of Nations and his universally neglected one on Social Sympathy. On the other side is a row of ordinary tenements with shops on the ground floor and behind that lie lands of stinking, overcrowded rooms where you will find as much huddled misery as you saw in the sunlight of Alexandria. There are closes where over a hundred people get all their drinking- and washing-water from one communal tap, rooms where a whole family squats in each corner. The commonest diseases are dysentery, rickets and tuberculosis. Here you may pick up any number of wretched little girls. Tell the parents you will train them to be domestic servants and they will bless you for removing them. Bring six of them here. With Mrs. Dinwiddie's help you probably *can,* in three or four years, train most of them to clean a room and launder clothes. You are too ignorant to teach them anything better."

Bella clutched the hair of her head in both hands and cried, "You sound like Harry Astley! Do you want to make me a cynical parasite too, God? Do you too think my hatred of suffering is nothing but displaced motherhood?"

"I will certainly think that if you start mothering children you cannot teach to be independent."

"How can I teach that?"

"By learning to be independent yourself—independent of me and Candle too, whether you marry him or not. Are you willing to work hard?—outside a brothel, I mean."

"You have seen me work hard for hours with the sick animals in our little hospital."

"But now you want to help poor sick people."

"You know I do."
"Would you exhaust your brain and body by toiling in grim places where courage as well as strong judgement is needed?"
"I am ignorant and confused but not a fool or a coward. Give me work which uses me utterly!"
"Then you know what you should become."
"No — tell me!"
"If the answer is not already in your mind," said Baxter gloomily, "nothing I can say is any good."
"Please give me a clue."
"Your work will need hard study as well as practice, but your best friends can help with both."
"I will be a doctor."

Her face was wet with tears and his with sweat, yet they smiled and nodded to each other with such perfect understanding that I nearly envied them, though throughout this talk I had been holding Bell's hand. Perhaps she sensed the envy for she kissed me and said, "Think of all the lectures you will be able to give me, Candle, and how hard I will have to listen!"
"Baxter knows a lot more than I do," I told her.
"Yes," said Baxter, "but I will never tell people all of it."

* * * * * * * * * * * * * *

The stars above divide reported speech from a fast summary.

Baxter told us there were only four women doctors in Britain just now, all with degrees from foreign universities, but the Enabling Bill of 1876 and the work of Sophia Jex-Blake had resulted in Dublin University opening its doors to women medical students and Scottish universities must soon do the same. Meanwhile he would return to work in the charity wards of an east Glasgow infirmary if Bella would enrol as a trainee nurse there. If she did well under the discipline he would contrive to get her assisting him as a theatre nurse. Thus, when she at last went to medical college (whether in Dublin or Glasgow) the lectures would mean more to her than the memory exercises most first-year students found them. He said all doctors and surgeons should be recruited from the nursing profession or begin by working in it. He then argued so fiercely that manual work be the primary training for every British profession that we took a while getting him back to the point.

He then asked Bella if she wished to be a general practitioner or to help particular kinds of people. She said she wanted to help little girls, mothers and prostitutes. He said this was a good idea because at present almost all who worked with these people had different sexual organs from their patients. Bella said she was determined to teach all the women who came to her the most modern and effective contraceptive methods. Baxter and I advised her to keep this intention secret until she was able to practise it. What she then told her patients in the privacy of a consulting-room would be unlikely to cause a public scandal. If she wished to argue publicly for birth control she would do so most effectively after working as a fully qualified clinician for at least five years. She only agreed with us when we admitted that the length of the waiting-period must be her choice and no one else's.

Then Baxter turned to me and said friends of his father had kept him informed of my standing in the Glasgow medical profession. I was a good diagnostic and bacterial pathologist, with wide knowledge of the hygiene which allowed the efficient functioning of the human organism. These were exactly the qualifications needed by a public health officer, and he hoped I would consider that. Prevention of disease was more important than cure. There were no better public benefactors than those who strove to make Glasgow better watered, drained and lit—better *housed*, in short. But his main reason for wanting me in such a position was personal. When Bella eventually got charge of her own clinic (and he would put his fortune into helping her create one) the support of a highly placed local government official would be very useful to her. This argument convinced me.

I now raised the question of my marriage, and suggested it be as soon as possible. Bella said she must first make sure she had contracted no venereal infection through her work for Madame Cronquebil. Baxter said six weeks of sexual quarantine should be sufficient, then said he was tired, bade an abrupt good-bye and went upstairs. I realized that the thought of Bella marrying me instead of him still caused him pain. I told her so, and she laughed at the idea. She did not deny it, but thought it a piece of daftness he would easily recover from. This is the only area in which I found my dear Bella unfeeling toward the pain of another. But when we got children of our own I discovered most younger people are happily unfeeling toward parents and guardians they feel confident with.

So we kissed good night, and went upstairs to the landing from which her bedroom opened, and kissed good night again. She murmured, "You are a lot stronger, Candle. You nearly fainted when we did this in the old days."

I said I feared I was less sensitive now—my body had missed her for so long that it did not yet truly believe she was with me. She laughed quietly and said she was less passionate too.

"I need cuddles more than weddings, nowadays," she said, "and I haven't had a decent all-night-long cuddle since Wedder started sleeping upside-down after Alexandria. Let us sleep together tonight, you necessary Candle. With a sheet between us I can feel your arms all round me yet do you no harm. Would you mind cuddling me just like that?"

I said I would love to do it and that exactly this preliminary marriage rite was very frequent in rural Scotland, where it was called "bundling".

So we went to bed and bundled, and have not slept apart since, except when she has to attend London meetings of the Fabian Society.

# 21

# An Interruption

THOUGH AN ATHEIST I AM NO BIGOT. When we knew Bella was free from disease I arranged a simple presbyterian wedding service, for I thought this a harmless and traditional way to solemnize our vows. The Park church was nearest but I did not want the neighbours' children scrambling at the door, so chose Lansdowne United Presbyterian, less than ten minutes' walk away beside Great Western Road. English readers may blink when I say the service was to be at 9 a.m. on December the 25th. It was the earliest date possible, and the Scottish Church does not think Christmas day holier than other unless it falls on the Sabbath. As I stepped out arm-in-arm with Bella, Baxter and Mrs. Dinwiddie arm-in-arm at our heels, I felt a kind of glee that on my wedding-day people were having holidays all round the world, though the Glasgow shops and offices and factories were as throng with business as ever.

It was a frosty morning. Roof tops, gardens and the quieter streets were coated with snow, but we walked with a steady stride for Baxter had paid a gang of little boys to sweep a track clean from our doorstep to the church. The track descended the hillside through the park, but had been well salted so was not slippy. A thin haze of fog, smoky to the nose, did not hide the nearer distances, and I thought I saw figures enter the building ahead of us. This puzzled me. I had assumed Baxter and Mrs. Dinwiddie would be our only witnesses and congregation. Bella had wished to ask Miss MacTavish, Wedderburn, Astley and Madame Cronquebil in order to show them (she said) "that all's well that ends well". We had persuaded her that, if they came, these guests would embarrass each other, and had finally invited no one and not advertised the occasion at all. But of course the minister must have called the banns as usual.

We entered the church punctually at one minute to nine and saw the nave was empty but for a row of five men in the front pews. Bella said, "Who are they?" and I did not know, though I saw that one looked unusually tall, thin and military. This set me trembling. I felt a disaster was about to happen, and that Bella and I had walked arm-in-arm up this aisle into the same disaster many times before. I felt I was in a bad dream from which I must struggle awake. Baxter murmured, "Steady McCandless!" in a voice so quietly commanding that I stared at him. He nodded back and I realized he had foreseen everything which might happen and was ready for it. I gripped Bella's arm more tightly and went forward with the courage of a Christian who knows God is on his side.

We passed the strangers and stood with our backs to them, facing the communion-table. The minister came round the foot of the pulpit and, after some words of introduction, formally asked if I was Archibald McCandless, only son of Jessica McCandless, spinster of the parish of Whauphill in Galloway. I said I was. He then asked my fiancée if she was Bella Baxter, daughter of Ignatius MacGregor Baxter, commercial agent in Buenos Aires, and of his wife Seraphina Rhinegold Cumberpatch? Bella said she was. I wondered why Baxter had invented for the mother such a long improbable name and reckoned he had calculated that in a world full of oddities a list of names which did not contain a long improbable one was unlikely. By the time I had worked this out the minister was saying that if anyone present knew why these two should not be joined in holy wedlock, let them speak out. Then a high, clear grating voice behind me said, "*This marriage cannot take place!*"

We turned. The words had been spoken by the very tall thin man who stood erect, glaring steadily at us like a neatly carved, life-size wooden puppet. He looked wooden because his thick steel-grey moustache (which covered his mouth) and sharply pointed beard were nearly the same tone as his pinkish-brown skin. A swarthy, thickly built, wild-looking old man was struggling to his feet beside him.

"Who are you?" demanded the minister, his voice suddenly petty and squeaky.

"I am General Sir Aubrey de la Pole Blessinton. The woman who claims to be Bella Baxter is me lawful wedded wife, Victoria Blessinton, whose maiden name was Victoria Hattersley. Here is her father, Blaydon Hattersley, managin director of the Union Jack Steam Traction Company of Manchester and Birmingham."

"Vicky!" cried the old man, stretching his arms toward Bella while tears spilled down his cheeks. "O my little Vicky! Do you not recognize your old dad?"

Bella looked at him with great interest, then looked again with equal interest at her first husband. The General stared fixedly back. The manufacturer sobbed. My own feelings were too strange to describe. I knew Bella was unknowingly seeing the father of her brain in the first husband of her body, the grandfather of her brain in the father of her body. At last she said, "Well you seem a fascinating pair, but I cannot remember seeing either of you before."

The General said, "Speak, Prickett."

A third man stood up and said he was the General's medical adviser and had treated Lady Blessington for a serious illness for at least eight months before her disappearance. He said that the lady who had answered to the name Bella Baxter had a voice and appearance so similar to those of Lady Blessington that he had no doubt they were identical. At this the minister said the wedding could not take place.

I do not know what I would have done if Bella had not kept her arm linked with mine and if Baxter had not taken charge. The gravity of his bulk and manner filled me with childish hope as he said, "General Blessington. Mr. Hattersley. Someone told you when and where this marriage was to take place. The same person may have told you I am a rich man and a practising surgeon who has operated on royalty. Miss Baxter came to me three years ago with no memories of her earlier life. She has since lived with me as my ward, and I have made a will leaving her my entire estate. A year ago she freely engaged to marry my friend Dr. McCandless of Glasgow Royal Infirmary. General Blessington! Mr. Hattersley! Do you want the question of Miss Baxter's identity settled by a judge and jury in a court of law? Or shall we first try to settle it by rational discussion? My home is a short walk from here. I invite you to it."

The General said, "Tell him, Harker."

A fourth man stood up and said he was General Blessington's solicitor, and knew that Sir Aubrey wished to avoid damaging his wife's reputation by a public investigation of private matters. For that reason only the General was prepared to tolerate a private discussion involving the following individuals. On one side himself, his solicitor, his medical adviser, his wife's father, and Mr. Seymour Grimes of the Seymour Grimes Private Detective Agency. (As the last name was mentioned the fifth man stood up.) The solicitor went on to say that the General would allow, on the other side, Mr. Baxter and his friend Dr. McCandless. However, Sir Aubrey insisted that his wife Victoria Blessington await the issue of the discussion in an adjacent room. He had the best possible reasons for excluding her from it. He also insisted that the discussion be held in a suite of rooms he had engaged at St. Enoch's Station Hotel.

"You want to tell God and Candle who I am without me hearing?" cried Bella. "What do you say to that, God?"

"I say I will have nothing to do with it," said Baxter calmly, "unless I am given a good reason."

"Tell him, Prickett," said the General. His medical adviser

edged out of the pew then greatly annoyed Bella by leading Baxter aside and whispering in his ear. Baxter's reply could be heard by everyone: "That is not a reason, it is a lie. I can prove it is a lie. This discussion will not take place unless Miss Baxter is a party to it, and unless it is held in my home. General Blessington and his entourage risk nothing by entering my home; but women have been abducted from British hotels by men who claim to be their husbands, and the police have not intervened."

"Rightly!" barked the General. His solicitor looked hard at him. The General looked impassively back and for a while nobody seemed to move. Then some signal must have been given for in a low voice the solicitor told Baxter, "We will go to your home. Three hired cabs are waiting in the lane beside this building."

"Three cabs can carry six people," said Baxter. "Mrs. Dinwiddie, please return with these five gentlemen to 18 Park Circus. Show them into my study, light the fire and offer them refreshment. I and Miss Baxter and Dr. McCandless insist on returning by foot, but will arrive soon after you. Mr. Harker, please explain these arrangements to your employer."

Baxter then turned his back on the solicitor and told the minister he would be paid for his inconvenience tomorrow and contacted again when the present misunderstanding had been settled. Then he took Bella's free hand under his arm and the three of us went back along the aisle to the door. As we went though I felt I had been ten weeks inside that church, though it had been less than ten minutes.

How fresh, bright and healthy the foggy street and snowy roofs outside looked! Bella felt this too. She said, "I never thought our marriage would be such fun. Is that poor old man really my dad? We must try to cheer him up. Did I really marry that long thin stick with a mask on top? Ee, I am well away from him. Did all these men mean to kidnap me? For a moment they looked as if they would. I am glad you were with us, God. Candle would have died fighting for me but what use is a dead Candle to a kidnapped Bell?

One blast of your lungs would have knocked flat the whole clamjamfrie, God, and they knew it. So at last it looks as if the mystery of the Origin of Bell Baxter's Species is going to be solved. What did that medico whisper to you, God?"

"A lie. He will probably repeat it aloud and you will hear me contradict him."

"Why are you looking so miserable, God? Why are you not as excited as I am?"

"Because you are going to learn that I too have told lies."

"You? A liar?"

"Yes."

"If you have lied to me how can there be any truth? Who can be any good?" said Bella, looking frightened.

"Truth and goodness do not depend on me, Bell. I am too weak. I am as poor a thing as General Blessington. Prepare to despise both of us."

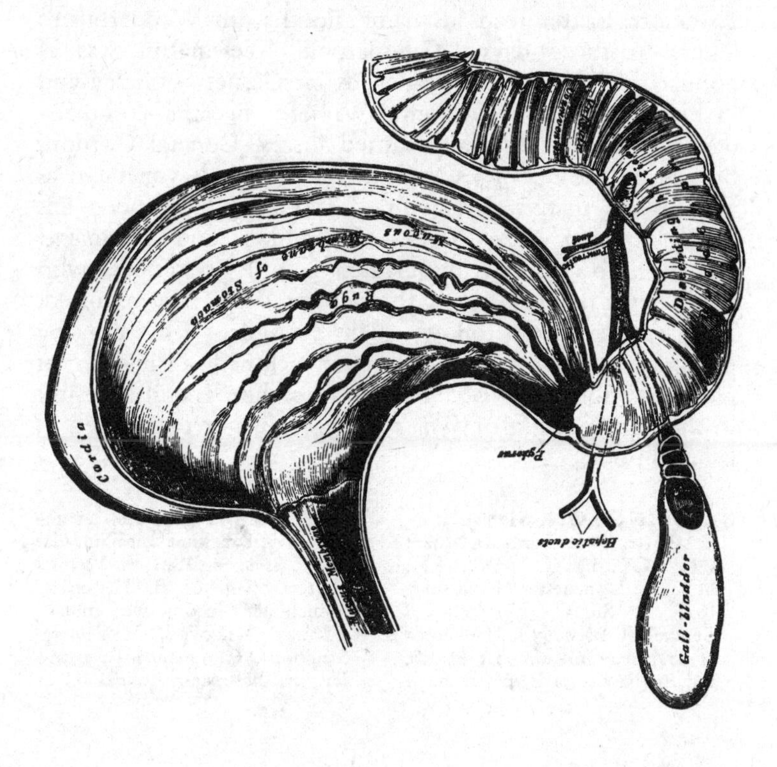

# 22

# The Truth: My Longest Chapter

I KNEW OF GENERAL BLESSINGTON LONG before Baxter read his name aloud from Wedderburn's letter. In those days "Thunderbolt" Blessington was as popular with newspaper readers as Sir Garnet Wolseley and "Chinese" Gordon. Viscount Wolseley became commander-in-chief of the British armed forces. General Gordon, by getting the dervishes to dismember him, is venerated as an imperial martyr. My wife's first husband has been less kindly treated. *The Times* of London and *Manchester Guardian* now ascribe his greatest actions to officers who were never named when the actions were first reported. The popular press follows their example. Why has the unhappy end of a brave warrior eclipsed a lifetime of patriotic effort? The best biography of him is still an entry in the 1883 edition of *Who's Who*. He is not mentioned in later editions.

**BLESSINGTON, Sir Aubrey la Pole**, 13th Bart.; *cr.* 1623; V.C., G.C.B., G.C.M.G., J.P.; M.P. (L.) Manchester North since 1878; *b.* Simla, 1827; *e.s.* of General Q. Blessington, Governor of Andaman and Nicobar Islands, and Emilia *e.d.* of Bamforth de la Pole, Bart., Hogsnorton, Loamshire, and Ballyknockmeallup, Co. Cork; *S. cousin* 1861; *m.* Victoria Hattersley, *d.* of B. Hattersley, Manchester locomotive mnfctr. *Educ.:* Rugby, Heidelberg, Sandhurst. Commanded a native levy on the eastern frontier, Cape of Good Hope, 1849; expedition against the Swazanji, 1850–51 (severely wounded, mentioned in despatches, Brevet of Lieut. Colonel); volunteered for Crimea and served before Sebastopol 1854–56 (twice wounded and mentioned in despatches for repulse of five Russian sorties with very small detachment of the 4th Queen's Own, Crimean War medal and three clasps, Order of Medjidie and Turkish War Medal); Brigade Major in charge of pursuing column in central India during the Mutiny 1857–58 (wounded, present at taking of the forts of Fumuckenugger, Bullubghur, storming of the Cashmere bastion and heights of Delhi, medal for India, bar for Delhi, Order of the Golden Fleece from Portuguese Crown for defence of Goa); Assistant Adjut. General, British Expeditionary Force to China, 1860 (wounded during the destruction of Yangtse shore batteries but present at the entry into Pekin and storming of the Summer Palace); Governor of Norfolk Island Penal Colony, 1862–64; Governor of Patagonia, 1865–68 (crushed the Tehuelches and Gennaken revolts without losing a man); Governor of Jamaica, 1869–72; Commander of Burmese Punitive Expeditionary Force, 1872–73; Lieut. General throughout suppression of first half-breed revolt N.W. Canada, 1874; Adjut. General, Ashanti War, 1875 (wounded, Victoria Cross); Commander-in-Chief of Militia in Canada, 1876 (injured by exploding bombard in tour of Quebec Province, thanked by Parliament with money grant of £25,000, 5th class Legion of Honour); Cons. candidate Loamshire Downs; Grand Warden of G.L. of Freemasons of England, 1877. *Publications:* While England Trembled, account of the government's handling of the 1848 Chartist movement; Purging the Planet, a monodrama; Political Diseases, Imperial Cures, a lecture to the United Service Institute. *Recreations:* hunting, shooting, breeding thoroughbred stock, chairman of Manchester Humane Society Refuge for Waifs and Strays, personal supervision of experimental farm where slum orphans train for resettlement in the Colonies. *Address:* 49 Porchester Terrace, London. *Clubs:* Cavalry, United Service, Pratt's, British Eugenics.

The day after Bella returned to us I read the above entry in Baxter's library, first making sure nobody saw me. Weeks later I learned that Bella and Baxter had separately done the same. We were all too full of plans for Bella's future to investigate or call up the past together—we hoped it would leave us in peace. Only Baxter had used the information to prepare for the past calling unexpectedly on us. As we hurried home from the church that cold Christmas morning only he was in a serious frame of mind. I had been infected by Bella's eager curiosity and a crazy sense of the General's importance. I had no fears that he would take her from me, but thought my love-life might be entering history as the love-lives of Rizzio and Bothwell had done—not enough for me to end disastrously, just enough to make me famous. Even a remark by Baxter did not cure me of that delusion. As we approached number eighteen we saw the General standing within the study window, glaring down on us. Bella shivered. Baxter said gently, "His left eye is glass—he always stares straight forward to make the right eye match it. No great general has been wounded as often as de la Pole Blessington."

"O the poor lad!" said Bella, and waved encouragingly up at him. He gave no sign of seeing this, yet I suddenly feared pity might draw her toward him.

When we entered the study he continued staring out of the window with his back to the room. The old manufacturer was huddled in an arm-chair by the fire. He glanced at us briefly while Bella and I sat down together at the table, then went on gazing into the flames. The General's lawyer and doctor sat primly on the sofa beside the detective. Seymour Grimes was the only visitor who looked comfortable: he held a glass of whisky filled from a decanter Mrs. Dinwiddie had left in easy reach. Baxter went straight to a bureau, unlocked it and brought out a sheaf of papers. He laid them on the table and asked no one in particular, "Does the General prefer to stand?"

"Sir Aubrey *usually* prefers to stand," murmured the General's doctor cautiously.

"Good," said Baxter. He sat where he had a clear view of everyone and began talking at once.

"In a world as thickly peopled as ours nearly everyone must have several others who look and sound like them. Has anyone a better reason for thinking Bella Baxter is Victoria Blessington?"

"Yes," said the old manufacturer. "A week ago I got a letter from a man called Wedderburn. He told me my Vicky was living here, with you. I contacted my son-in-law and was told he had received a similar letter a fortnight before, but had done nothing about it."

GENERAL SIR AUBREY de la POLE
BLESSINGTON BART V.C.

"It was a madman's letter!" said the General's lawyer swiftly. "Wedderburn not only said Lady Blessington had been his mistress, he said she had been the mistress of Robert Burns, Bonnie Prince Charlie and a string of celebrities leading back to the garden of Eden. Are you surprised that the General ignored such an epistle?"
"Yes," said the old man, scowling at the flames. "That letter was the only clue to my Vicky's whereabouts in three whole years. We should have moved heaven and earth to find her when she first disappeared, but Dr. Prickett here said, 'No need to call the police—I am sure it is a temporary derangement—a public scandal will only unhinge her further—if you love your daughter, give her time to return home of her own free will.' Of course Prickett only says what Sir Aubrey wants him to say. I know that now, though I did not know it then. Days passed before Scotland Yard were told, and they handled the whole business very quietly because . . . because . . ." (he made a noise between a chuckle and a sob) ". . . Blessington is the nation's darling—an example to British youth—Lord Palmerston said so! The newspapers never printed the story and nothing was discovered. Or if it was, nobody told me. So as soon as I read Wedderburn's letter I employed Grimes here. Tell them what you found out, Grimes."
The detective nodded, sipped from his glass and spoke in the rapid lingo of a London native. He was an ordinary man of about thirty: so ordinary that I noticed nothing personal in him except his style of speech, which left out first-person pronouns.

"Was called to investigate Lady Blessntn's dispearance seven days ago, three years after event. Lady vanished fromerome sudden being disturbed distressed distraught and in the famly way—eight months and a fortnight pregnant which often drives the fair sex round the twist poor things. Obtained photoportrait of lost lady, a goodun. Came to Glasgow pursuing information in letter from Duncan Wedderburn esquire and find said gentleman incarcerated in locked ward of Glasgow Royal Lunatic Asylum, positively no admittance. Lady B vanished from 49 Pochester Terrace 6 Febry 1880 so examined all police and Humane Society records of distraught or mindless female vagrants apprehended or otherwise detected in Glasgow after that date. Notice female of Lady B type seen diving from bridge into Clyde river on Febry 8 and fished out by Humane Society employee, one George Geddes. Showimphoto. 'Thatser!' sezee. 'Where now?' says I. 'Corpus unclaimed,' sezee, 'so taken to University Medical College by police surgeon on Febry 15,' sezee—wrongly. Godwin Baxter was police surgeon but College ledgers show Mr. Baxter delivered NO corpses there on Febry 15 or anytime after, because on Febry 16 College gets letter fromim saying he is resigning from police work in order to concentrate (sezee) onis private practice. Which he certainly did. By end of Febry coalman, milkman, grocer, butcher deliverin to 18 Park Circus know Mr. Baxter as a resident lady patient. Paralysed. By April she is walkin but childish. Three years later she sits here bloomin like a rose and fit to marry again. Good luck to you, Miss or Lady B!"

Seymour Grimes raised his glass to Bella and swallowed the contents.

"I like that man," whispered Bella so intensely that I did not know if she understood him. Everyone else looked at Baxter.

"Your chain of reasoning has a missing link, Mr. Grimes," he said. "You tell us that George Geddes (a popular and respected person in this city) says he recovered a dead body. How can the corpse he retrieved sit with us here, when you say it lay for seven days in a mortuary?"

"Can't say—not my department," said the detective, shrugging his shoulders.

"I believe I can cast light on this dark business," said the General's doctor, "if Sir Aubrey allows me."

The General gave no sign of having heard him.

"This is my home, Dr. Prickett," said Baxter. "I not only allow, I request you to give your opinion."

"Then I will, Mr. Baxter, though you will not like it. The London medical world is aware that since the start of this century the Glasgow surgeons have been putting electric currents through the nervous systems of dead bodies. It is on record that in the 1820s one of your sort animated the corpse of a hanged criminal, who sat up and spoke. Public scandal was only prevented by one of the demonstrators severing the subject's jugular with a scalpel. Your father was present at that demonstration. I have no doubt he passed on all he learned to you, who were his only assistant, apart from ignorant nurses. Sir Colin was notorious for knowing more than he shared with his colleagues."

"God," said Bella in a dull voice I had not heard from her before, "when we left the church today you said you were going to admit that you lied to me. I think I know now what the lie was. My pa and ma never died in an Argentine train crash. You invented that to hide something worse."

"Yes," said Baxter, and covered his face with his hands.

"So that poor old man really is my father? And that pole of a man who seems afraid to face me is my husband? And I ran away from him and drowned myself? O Candle please hold me tight."

I am glad I did so because the General turned round.

He turned round and spoke in a crisp, thin, high-pitched voice which grew steadily louder.

"Stop shammin, Victoria. You remember perfectly well that Hattersley is your father, that I am your husband and that you ran away from home to escape from your wifely duties. This absurd story about drownins and morgues and loss of memory has been cooked up to hide the plain fact that for three years you have lived with a freak in order to glut your insane appetite for carnal intercourse, first with him, then with a lunatic libertine, and now with a low-bred ruffian. You are doin it now—here—before me eyes. UNHAND ME WIFE, SIR!"

He screamed the last words so loud I nearly obeyed him. One of his icy-blue eyes may have been glass but it matched the other so perfectly that I shuddered at the hatred I read in them. But I suddenly saw Baxter beside us, every inch as tall as the General and five times thicker, and unexpected support came from the old man who still gazed into the fire.

He said, "Do not talk about my Vicky like that, Sir Aubrey. You know whose carnal appetites drove her from home. If she is pretending to have forgotten then we should thank her. If she has truly forgotten it let us thank God."

"I am ashamed of nothing in me treatment of me wife," said the General sharply, but Bella gently untwined her body from mine and went to the old man.

She said, "You are trying to be kind so maybe you are my father. Let me hold your hand."

He looked at her, twisting his mouth in a painful smile that reminded me of my mother's smile, and let her take his right hand between both of hers. She closed her eyes and murmured, "You are strong . . . fierce . . . cunning . . . but can never be kind, because you are afraid."

"Not true!" cried the old man, snatching his hand away. "Strong, fierce and cunning, yes thank God, I am those. Those let me heave myself and your mother and you out of the stinking muck of Manchester, heave us all out by thrusting weaklings under it. I could not haul out your three little brothers—they died of cholera. But I fear nothing in the world except hunger, poverty and the sneers of folk with more money. Only a fool does not fear these, especially when he has suffered them. We all suffered from them until I squeezed your uncle out of his share in the workshop. He squealed like a gashed pig and tried to get his own back by joining Hudson—Hudson! The railway king! But I smashed him and Hudson too. Yes Vicky," said the old man with a sudden roar of laughter; "your old father was the man who smashed King Hudson! But you are a woman and know nothing of business. Ten years later I had an Earl on my board of directors, was putting men into Parliament and employing half the skilled work-force of Manchester and Birmingham. Then one day you turned seventeen, Vicky, and I suddenly saw you were a beauty. I had been too busy to look at you before that or think of getting you groomed for the marriage market. So I dragged you straight to a Swiss convent where the daughters of millionaires are scraped clean and polished along with daughters of marquises and foreign princes. 'Make a lady of her,' I told the mother superior. 'You will not find it easy. She is headstrong, like her ma once was—the sort of donkey who needs more kicks than carrots to drive her in the right direction. I do not care how long you take or how much it costs, but make her fit to marry the highest in the land.' It took them seven years. Your ma was dead (feeble action of the liver) when you got home, and for your sake I was glad. Though a good wife for a poor man she was no use to a wealthy one. Her plain ways would have ruined your chances. Ee the nuns had turned you into a lovely thing—you spoke French like a real Mamselle, though your English still sounded Manchester. But the General did not mind—did you, Sir Aubrey?"

"No. Even her quaint dialect entertained me. She was the purest creature and prettiest thing I had ever met," said the General broodingly. "She had the soul of an innocent child within the form of a Circassian houri—irresistible."

"Did I love you?" said Bella staring at him. He nodded heavily.

"You adored him—worshipped him," cried her father, "you *had* to love him! He was a national hero and cousin of the Earl of Harewood. Besides, you were twenty-four years old and he was the only man apart from me you had been allowed to meet. You were the happiest woman in the world on your wedding-day. I hired and decorated the entire Manchester Free Trade Hall for the reception and banquet, and the Cathedral choir sang the Hallelujah chorus."

"You loved me, Victoria, and I loved you," said the General hoarsely, "so we became husband and wife. I am here to remind you of that, and protect you. Gentlemen forgive me!"—and his right eye flickered disconcertingly toward Baxter and me—"forgive me for shoutin and

insultin you. Perhaps you are honest men despite the circumstances, and me bad temper is notorious. For thirty years I served England (perhaps I should say Britain) by usin meself as harshly as the regiments I commanded and the savages I subdued. Not a muscle in me body is without its separate ache, especially when I sit down. I can only rest when perfectly prone. Will you allow me to rest for a moment?"
"Please do," said Baxter.

Lawyer, doctor and detective sprang from the sofa. The doctor helped the General lie down flat on it.
"Let me put a cushion under your head," said Bella, carrying one over and kneeling beside him.
"No, Victoria. I never use a pillow. Have you truly forgotten that?" said the General, closing his eyes.
"Yes. Truly."
"You remember nothin at all about me?"
"Nothing certain," said Bella uneasily, "yet something in your voice and appearance *does* seem familiar, as if I once dreamed it or heard it or glimpsed it in a play. Let me hold your hand. It might remind me."
He wearily stretched out his hand but when her fingers touched it she gasped and pulled them back as if they had been scorched or stung.
"You are horrible!" she said, not accusingly, but astonished.
"You said so on the day you fled from me," he answered wearily, his eyes still shut, "and you were wrong. Apart from me military honours and social position I am a man like other men. You are still an unstable woman. Prickett should have operated on you after our honeymoon."
"Operated? What for?"
"I cannot tell you. Gentlemen only discuss such things with their physicians."
"Sir Aubrey," said Baxter, "three people in this room are qualified medical men, and the only woman present is training to be a nurse. She has a right to know why you say she is an unstable woman with insane appetites who should have had a surgical operation after her honeymoon."

"Before would have been better," said the General without opening his eyes; "the Mahometans do it to their women soon after birth. It makes em the most docile wives in the world."

"Hints are no use, Sir Aubrey. This morning in church your doctor whispered to me what he thinks—and you think—the name of your wife's illness. If here and now he does not say it aloud it will be discussed in court before a Scottish jury."

"Say it Prickett," said the general wearily. "Bellow it. Deafen us with it."

"Erotomania," muttered his doctor.

"What is that?" asked Bell.

"It means the General thinks you loved him too much," said Baxter.

"It means," said Dr. Prickett hastily, "that you wished to sleep in his bedroom—share his bed—lie with him (I am forced to be blunt) every night of the week. Gentlemen!"—he turned from Bella and appealed to the rest of us—"gentlemen, the General is a kind man who would cut off his right arm rather than disappoint a woman! On the day before his wedding he asked me for an exact description—from the scientific, hygienic standpoint—of a married man's duties. I told him what every doctor knows—that sexual intercourse enfeebles brain and body if over-indulged, but in rational doses does nothing but good. I told him he should allow his lady wife to lie with him half an hour a night during the honeymoon period, and once or twice a week afterwards, though all amorous dalliance should cease as soon as pregnancy was detected. Alas, Lady Blessington was so deranged even in her eighth month she wished to lie with Sir Aubrey all night long. She sobbed and wailed when not allowed to do so."

Tears streamed down Bella's cheeks. She said, "The poor thing needed cuddling."

"You could never face the fact," said the General through clenched teeth, "that the touch of a female body arouses DIABOLICAL LUSTS in potent sensual males—lusts we can hardly restrain. Cuddlin! The word is disgustin and unmanly. It soils your lips, Victoria."

"I know everyone here is telling what they think is the truth," said Bella, drying her eyes, "but it sounds daft. Sir Aubrey talks as if he was liable to tear women apart, but honestly, if he cut up rough with me I think I could break him over my knee like a stick."

"Ha!" cried the General scornfully and his doctor began talking very fast, perhaps annoyed by Bella's words and the equally sceptical glances Baxter and I had exchanged during his account of the case. His voice was almost as shrill as the General's as he said, "No normal healthy woman—no good or sane woman wants or expects to enjoy sexual contact, except as a duty. Even pagan philosophers knew that men are energetic planters and good women are peaceful fields. In *De Rerum Natura* Lucretius tells us that only debauched females wriggle their hips."

"That creed is both false to nature and false to most human experience," said Baxter.

"To *most* human experience? Why certainly!" cried Prickett. "I speak of refined women—respectable women—not those of the vulgar mass."

"This peculiar notion," Baxter told Bella, "was first recorded by Athenian homosexuals who thought women only existed to produce men. It was then adopted by celibate Christian priests who thought sexual delight was the origin of every sin, and women were the source of it. I do not know why the idea is now popular in Britain. Maybe an increase in the size and number of boys' boarding-schools has bred up a professional class who are strangers to female reality. But tell me this, Dr. Prickett. Did Lady Blessington agree to a clitoridectomy?"

"Not only did she agree to one—she begged for it with tears in her eyes. She loathed her hysterical rages, loathed her pathetic desire for contact with her husband, raged against her diseases as much as he did. She eagerly swallowed all the sedatives I administered, but at last I had to tell her they were worse than useless—that I could only cure her by *cutting out* the centre of her nervous excitement. She begged me to do it at once, and was bitterly sorry when I said we must wait until her child was born. Lady Blessington!" said Prickett, turning back to Bella again, "Lady Blessington, I am sorry you remember none of this. You used to consider me a good friend."

Bella shook her head wordlessly from side to side. Baxter said, "So Lady Blessington did not flee from home because she feared your treatment?"

"Certainly not!" cried Prickett indignantly. "Lady Blessington used to say my visits were the pleasantest part of her week."

"Then what was the reason for her flight?"

"She was mad," said the General, "so needed no reason. If she is now sane she will come home with me. If she refuses she is still mad, and it is me duty as her husband to place her in an institution where she will be properly treated. I cannot leave her in a ménage which is turnin me maniac ex-wife into a *nurse*!"

"But she has not been your wife since she drowned herself," said Baxter quickly. "The marriage contract says the marriage lasts *until death do you part*. The only independent witness to the identity of your wife and my ward is the Humane Society official who saw the suicide and retrieved the corpse. Dr. Prickett suggests I gave her a new life. If so I am as much the father and protector of the revived woman as Mr. Hattersley was of the earlier, and as entitled as he once was to present her in marriage to the husband of her choice. Mr. Harker, how does that logic strike you?"

"As piffle, Mr. Baxter: piffle and poppycock," said the lawyer coolly. "I have no doubt Lady Blessington immersed herself in the Clyde, and no doubt the Humane Society official rescued her. He is paid to rescue people. He called you in to resuscitate her, and you plainly succeeded. You then bribed him to let you abduct her and bring her here where, pretending she was an invalid niece, you used drugs to render her childish, and thus enjoyed her physical charms and amorous weaknesses under the façade of being a good uncle and a kind physician. You even took your mistress on a world tour while playing that rôle! By the time you returned to Glasgow you had tired of her, so connived at her elopement with the unfortunate Duncan Wedderburn. Yesterday I visited poor Wedderburn's mother, a terribly distressed lady. She told me her son had been bodily, mentally and financially destroyed by the woman he calls Bella Baxter. Were he not now in a locked ward of Glasgow Royal Lunatic Asylum he would be in jail for defrauding his clients of their funds. Your twice discarded mistress returned to you last month, so you quickly arranged to marry her to McCandless, your weak-minded parasite. If this story is put before a British jury they will believe it, because it is the truth. Look, Sir Aubrey! Look at him! The truth has hit him hard!"

With a groan like underground thunder Baxter had left the chair, pressed his hands to his stomach and bent over them, writhing epileptically. I was surprised he did not fall, but not by his distress. The solicitor had mixed facts and lies so cleverly that for a moment even I believed him. But Bella sprang to Baxter's side, put an arm round his waist and soothed him upright again. This brought me to my senses. If the visitors had never before heard the cold fury of a thoroughly rational Scot, they heard it now.

"Mr. Baxter would be a stone statue if he felt no pain," I told them. "You have used this wise, kind, self-sacrificing man's hospitality to call him a freak and a liar. In the hearing of the patient whose life he saved you have accused him of viciously assaulting her. You know nothing of the terrible crack which rings her cranium—had he not tended her like a mother and educated her like a father it would have caused worse than total amnesia: she would be an imbecile. His tour with her was no amorous excursion, but the best way of reintroducing her to a world she had forgotten. He did not *connive* at her elopement with Wedderburn—he tried to dissuade her, begged me to dissuade her, and when we both failed he gave her means to return to us when she tired of the

escapade. No roué discarding a mistress would have done *that*! You have also had the insolence to call me—his best friend! Archibald McCandless M.D. of Glasgow Royal Infirmary!—you have dared to call me a low-born ruffian and weak-minded parasite. No wonder that vagal nerve discharge has induced reverse peristalsis and that excess pancreatic juice has irritated the oesophagus causing severe heartburn! And you say his pain at such vilification is a sign of *GUILT!!!???* Think black black shame of yourselves, gentlemen. You have almost persuaded me that you are not gentlemen at all."
"Thank you, McCandless," murmured Baxter.

He was sitting now in the arm-chair opposite Mr. Hattersley, Bella standing behind with her hands resting protectively on his shoulders. She watched him with an expression I later saw during our Italian honeymoon on the face of a Botticelli Madonna. Baxter now spoke to the lawyer as if nothing had happened.
"So you think the lady behind me is the same person as the General's wife."
"I know they are."
"I will prove you wrong, and do so with testimonies from five independent witnesses, each a scientist of international fame. Lady Victoria Blessington was a hysteric; so childishly dependent on a husband who found her unbearable that her doctor's visits were the happiest times of her week; so full of self-loathing that she gladly stupefied her mind with sedatives and yearned for her body to be surgically mutilated. Am I correct?"
"Yes, she gave the General hell," grumbled old Mr. Hattersley, "but you might have mentioned that in her worst fits she still acted like a perfect lady."
"She *relieved* her poor mind with sedatives," said the doctor, "and wished to be surgically *cured*. Apart from that your portrait of the unhappy lady is all too true."
"Yes, you know me wife well, Baxter," sneered the General.
"I never met your wife, Sir Aubrey. The drowned woman

who came to consciousness here is someone else. Tell the company, Dr. Prickett, who Charcot of Paris, Golgi of Pavia, Kraepelin of Würzburg, Breuer of Vienna and Korsakoff of Moscow are."

"They are alienists—specialists in diseases of the mind and nerves. I regard Charcot as a charlatan, but of course on the continent even he is highly regarded."

"On our world tour we visited them. Each examined the woman I call Bella Baxter and reported on her condition. These reports—signed and witnessed with English translations attached—lie on the table. Their terminology differs because they view the human mind from different standpoints, and Kraepelin and Korsakoff share Dr. Prickett's view of Charcot. But all are unanimous about Bella Baxter—she is sane, strong and cheerful, with a vigorously independent attitude to life, even though amnesia (caused by injury to her skull and the loss of an unborn child) has left her with no memories preceding her arrival here. Apart from that her balance, sensory discrimination, recollective and intuitive and logical powers are exceptionally keen. Charcot daringly suggests the amnesia has enlarged her intelligence by making her relearn things when old enough to think about them, which people who depend on childhood training hardly ever do. They agree that she shows no signs of mania, hysteria, phobia, dementia, melancholia, neurasthenia, aphasia, catatonia, algolagnia, necrophilia, coprophilia, folie de grandeur, nostalgie de la boue, lycanthropy, fetishism, Narcissism, Onanism, irrational belligerence, unhealthy reticence and is not obsessively Sapphic. They say her only obsessive trait is linguistic. These reports are based on tests carried out in the winter of 1880–81, when she was learning to read and had an enthusiasm for synonyms, assonance and alliteration which sometimes verged on echolalia. Kraepelin said this was an instinctive compensation for her poverty of sensory reminiscence. Charcot said it might make her a poet; Breuer that the obsession would diminish as she gained more memories. It has done so. Her speech is no longer eccentric. Charcot said she was unusually free of the insane prejudices which characterize her compatriots, which of course was an expression of national prejudice, but his final words sum up the verdict of the rest: Bella Baxter's most striking abnormality is her lack of it. Such a woman cannot be General Blessington's former wife. Please examine these proofs, Dr. Prickett, or take them away and verify them at your leisure."

"Don't waste your time, Prickett," said the General's solicitor. "They are irrelevant. They are quibbles."

"Explain, please," said Baxter patiently.

"I will, very easily. Suppose that a sickly unpleasant fellow escapes from London after stealing my cash. Suppose that three years later the police arrest him in Glasgow, and are about to lock him up when a doctor cries, 'Stop! I can prove this man is pleasanter and healthier since he stole your money, and has forgotten all about it.' The police would think that a quibble. Lady Blessington's erotomania made her a very miserable wife to the General, but neither he nor the laws of the land will allow her to commit bigamy and live happily ever after in a Scotch *ménage à trois*, simply because her happiness is sworn to by a horde of foreign brain doctors."

A noise like a quietly cackling hen was heard—the General was amused. Baxter sighed.

Sighed and said, "Sir Aubrey. Mr. Hattersley. This woman is studying to do useful work in the kindly art of medicine. Why drag her backward into a marriage which made herself and her husband miserable? If McCandless is my parasite, Harker and Prickett and Grimes are yours. Nobody in this room wants a scandal. The only person outside it who knows the truth, or some of it, is a certified lunatic. All I have said has been to persuade you it is honourable and possible to let this woman freely choose whether she returns to England with you or stays in Scotland with us—honourable and possible."

"Not possible," said the General heavily. "The gossip about me wife's disappearance has been increasin, not diminishin over the years. Half the London clubs think I got rid of me domestic problem like I got rid of the mutinous Indians and Ashanti. The damnable thing is, this time they disapprove.

The Prince of Wales cut me dead last week and the cad owes me several thou. Since I left the battlefields and went into Parliament the papers have started forgettin I was once the nation's darlin. A radical rag has started droppin hints, and unless I clap a libel writ on it the popular dailies will start callin me Bluebeard Blessington too. That arch-hypocrite Gladstone has suggested I *clear me name* by offerin a large reward for news of me wife's whereabouts, dead or alive. Has everyone here forgotten that a Scotch parson will soon sit down to Christmas dinner and blab to his family and friends about a weddin service I interrupted? No, Victoria. If I find this Baxter has taught you to behave sensibly I will pay him well for his trouble, but you must return south, whether you remember me or not."

"And think what you will have when you get home with him, Vicky!" cried old Mr. Hattersley growing very excited. "Sir Aubrey is three-quarters dead already and will not last more than another four years. That will give you time to squeeze at least one son out of him, then until the lad comes of age you can live how you like wherever you like: in the London town house or the estate in Loamshire or the other estate in Ireland! Think of those grand places, Vicky, all for you and me. Me! The grand-dad of a baronet! You owe me that, Vicky, because I gave you life. So be a sensible donkey. Honour and riches are the carrot heap ahead of you, a madhouse is the boot kicking you toward it. Yes, we can put you into an asylum for the insane! Who will care what a lot of foreign professors said two years ago when Dr. Prickett and an English specialist with a knighthood certify you are queer in the head? For you are queer Vicky, and the fact that you cannot remember your own dad proves it. Riches or a madhouse! Choose between em."

"Or divorce Sir Aubrey," said Baxter. "If he insists on taking a purely legal view of his marriage, so can you."

We stared at him.

Even the General opened his eyes and watched for a moment as Baxter returned to his seat at the table and

BLAYDON HATTERSLEY

rearranged the papers so that a different set lay on top. He glanced at the upper page and said, "On the 16th of February 1880 Lady Blessington, then in an advanced state of pregnancy, was visited by another heavily pregnant woman, a former kitchen-maid in Porchester Terrace who said she was Sir Aubrey's discarded mistress and begged for money. Sir Aubrey—"

"Take care sir!" barked the General but Baxter spoke louder: "Sir Aubrey broke in on them, flung the visitor into the street and locked his wife in a coal-cellar. Next morning Lady Blessington had disappeared."

"Mr. Baxter," said the solicitor swiftly, "you now pretend to know astonishing things about the past of a lady of whom, until this moment, you pretended to know nothing. If these allegations are not backed by eye-witnesses who will swear to their truth in a court of law—witnesses who will not collapse under the stress of skilful cross-examining—you will pay dearly for that slander."

"My information comes from Sergeant Cuff," said Baxter, "who you perhaps know of, Mr. Grimes?"

"Late of Scotland Yard?"

"Yes."

"A good man. Asks big money but gets results. Likes sniffin around the skirts of the aristocracy. Yooimploydim?"

"I employed him last month to find all he could about Lady Blessington, after a letter from Wedderburn told me Bella Baxter was a reincarnation of Victoria Blessington. Cuff's report here names many who will testify against the General in court, most of them servants who resigned or were dismissed from his service soon after Lady Blessington disappeared."

"No connection," said the General. "English servants are the worst in the world and none last more than two months with me. People say I dealt too savagely with the savage races, but the only man I can entirely trust is me Indian manservant. Odd thing, that."

"Servants who testify against their former employers," said the solicitor, "have very little credit in an English court of law."

"These will be believed," said Baxter. "Please, Mr. Harker, take this copy of the report back to your hotel and discuss it privately with the General. Go now, at once. Too many wounding things have been said here today. Tomorrow I will visit you in the St. Enoch's Hotel and hear what you decide to do."

"No God," said Bella in a firm, gloomy voice, "my past has grown too interesting. I want all the details now."

"Tell her, Baxter," said the General, yawning. "Play your word game to the end. It will change nothing."

Baxter sighed, shrugged and started summarizing the report while the solicitor, on a chair near the window, studied the copy he had been given. Baxter spoke straight to the General, however; not to Bella. Had he done so he would have been disturbed by the change the story made to her face and figure.

He said, "Dolly Perkins, a girl of sixteen, was your parlour-maid until the day before your wedding, Sir Aubrey, when you hired an apartment for her in a boarding-house near Seven Dials. You did not give your name to the landlady, Mrs. Gladys Moon, but she recognized you from your pictures in the *Illustrated London News*. She says you visited Miss Perkins regularly for two hours every Tuesday afternoon, and also on Friday afternoons when you paid the rent. This went on for four months, then one Friday while paying Mrs. Moon you told her, 'This is the last time I'm doing this, you won't see me again. Dolly Perkins is no use to anyone now. If you do not get rid of her she will give your house a bad name.' Mrs. Moon spoke to Miss Perkins who admitted she was penniless and pregnant. So she was told to leave."

"She was not pregnant by me," said the General coldly, "because me revels with Dolly never involved impregnation. Nobody will believe *that*, of course, so the greedy bitch tried to blackmail me into givin her money to give birth to the bastard, sayin she would tell me wife I had sired it if I refused. So I told the slut to go to hell and left her without a shillin."

"You queer sad old General," said Bella mournfully, "did you honestly think your wife a maniac because she wanted warmed by you more than an hour a week, while you regularly hugged a young girl for four?"

"I never *hugged* Dolly Perkins," said the General through tightly clenched teeth. "For God's sake tell her about MEN, Prickett. She has learned nothin about em in this place."

"I believe Sir Aubrey wiwiwishes me to say," said his doctor faintly, "that the strong men who lead and defend the BuBuBritish people must cucultivate their strength by satisfying the *animal* part of their natures by rererevelling with sluts, while maintaining the pupupurity of the mumumarriage bed and sanctity of the home where their sons and daughters are engendered. And that is why pupupupoor pupoor pupoor—" (here the General's doctor pulled out a handkerchief and dabbed his face) "—that is why poor Dolly *had* to be treated in that *tutututerrible* way."

"No need to blub about it, Prickett," murmured the General placidly. "You explained that very well. Now finish your story, Mr. Baxter, while rememberin I have done nothin I am ashamed of, indoors or out of it."

Baxter finished the story.

"On the 16th of February 1880 Dolly Perkins entered 19 Porchester Terrace by the servants' entrance. She was exhausted, ragged, penniless and hungry. The cook, Mrs. Blount, gave her a cup of tea, something to eat and a chair to rest in, then went on with her work. Shortly after she saw the chair was empty. Dolly Perkins had crept upstairs to the drawing-room, confronted Lady Blessington and told her story—"

"Mostly lies," said the General.

"—and begged for help. Lady Blessington was about to give her money when Sir Aubrey entered, called in his footmen who thrust Dolly Perkins out into the street, and with the help of his manservant dragged his wife upstairs—"

"Carried her upstairs. She had fainted," said the General.

"Then she soon recovered. You locked her in her bedroom but she flung up the window and started throwing things down to Dolly in the street outside: first a purse and jewellery then every small item of value in reach. By now, though it was a snowy day, a crowd of the poorer sort had gathered. I imagine—"

"What you imagine is not evidence," said the solicitor without looking up from the copy of the report he was reading.

"—her violent actions before an appreciative audience must have filled Lady Blessington with a kind of ecstasy. No wonder. They were probably the first decisive things she had ever done. She now flung out dressing-table sets, shoes, hats, gloves, stockings, corsets, dresses, pillows, bedding, fire-irons, clocks, mirrors, crystal and Chinese vases which smashed of course—"

"And a small oil portrait by Ingres of me mother as a girl," said the General drily. "A cab wheel ran over that one."

"At first Sir Aubrey thought the uproar in the street was caused solely by Dolly Perkins and a mob of her plebeian friends. When at last he learned the truth and rushed into the bedroom Lady Blessington was flinging out chairs and light tables. She was dragged down to the basement by his footmen and manservant—"

"Carried!" said the General firmly. "She was in a delicate condition, even if she had turned into a ravin lunatic. The basement was the only part of the house with barred windows."

"Yet you locked her in a windowless coal-cellar."

"Yes. I suddenly realized every damned room down there except the coal-cellar had keys I did not know about, and I did not trust the servants. Victoria had always been too friendly with em and I feared they would help her escape. Which happened. It took me three hours to collect Prickett and another doctor who would certify her, and find an insane asylum which would accept a pregnant lunatic, and was prepared to send along a padded ambulance with three stout nurses to manage her transport. When I got back she had flown the coop."

"Your former footman, Tim Blatchford, admits to smashing the cellar lock with a poker," said the solicitor, consulting the last page of the report Baxter had given him. "Your former cook, Mrs. Blount, says 'We all begged him to do it. The poor lady's sobs and frantic cries for help was heard all over. We feared she had gone into labour, and her terrible confinement might cause the deaths of two.' However, Lady Victoria emerged intact. Your former housekeeper, Mrs. Munnery, gave her clothing recovered from the street (it was cleaner than the coal-stained garments) and also the train fare to visit her father in Manchester."

"Victoria is goin mad again," said the General.

We looked at Bella and I heard old Mr. Hattersley moan in something like terror.

Her flesh had shrunk so close to the bones that her figure was now angular, but the horriblest change was in her face. The white sharp nose, hollow cheeks and sunken eye-sockets showed the skull all too clearly, yet within the sockets each black pupil had expanded to fill the whole eye, leaving just a tiny wee triangle of white in the corners. Her dark curling mass of hairs had also expanded, for the first inch of each one stood straight out from the head "like quills upon the fretful porcupine". I did not doubt that before me stood the emaciated form of Lady Victoria Blessington, exactly as she had emerged from the coal-cellar. But her voice, though sad, was distinctly Bella's.

"I feel how that poor thing felt," she said, "but it will not madden me. So I visited you in Manchester, Dad. What did you do to me?"

"The wrong thing! The wrong thing, Vicky," said the old man thumping the arms of the chair with his fists. "I should have kept you with me, sent for Sir Aubrey and thrashed out a better deal with him—a deal which would have benefited you as well as me. Instead I explained that a wife who abandons her husband is a truant in the eyes of man and God. I said you must fight the marital war on your own hearthstone or you would never win it. I told you to tell Sir Aubrey that if he lacked cash to bribe his cast-offs into holding their tongues he should send them to me—I know how to handle that sort of woman. All I said was *true*, Vicky, but I said it because I wanted you out of the house, out of my sight as soon as possible. I was afraid you would go into labour and I HATE women near me when they are whelping, hate the blood, screams and stinking mess they make, ugh, the thought of it makes me want to retch. So I took you back fast to the station and bought you a ticket for London. You were acting very calm and sensible, Vicky, and said I need not wait with you for the train, so I charged off in case you pupped on the platform. I was a coward, I admit, and I apologize. As soon as my back was turned you must have changed my first-class ticket to London for a third-class ticket to Glasgow. So here you are!"

"And here I stay," said Bella calmly, and as she spoke the lines of her figure and face relaxed into their proper softness, her hair began to settle, her eyes recovered their usual depth, size, and golden-brown warmth. She said, "Thank you for giving me life, Father, though from what you say my mother had most trouble making me and you took none at all. Besides, a life without freedom to choose is not worth having. Thank you, Sir Aubrey, for releasing me from my father, and thank you for driving me away from your house. Or perhaps I should thank Dolly Perkins for doing that. Without her it seems I would have gone on clinging to you. Thanks, Dr. Prickett, for trying to make life bearable for the poor silly creature I used to be. You cannot help being one still. Thank you, Mr. Grimes, for discovering and telling me how I had to travel through water to get my useless past washed off. Thank you for mending me, God, and giving me a home that is not a prison. I will continue living here. And Candle, how good to have a man I need not thank at all, who I cuddle and who cuddles me every night, is pleasant company in the mornings and evenings, and leaves me alone every day to get on with my work."

She smiled and came to me, embraced and kissed me and I could not resist her; though I was sorry to show our affections so openly before her first husband. He was a Liberal M.P. as well as a great soldier.

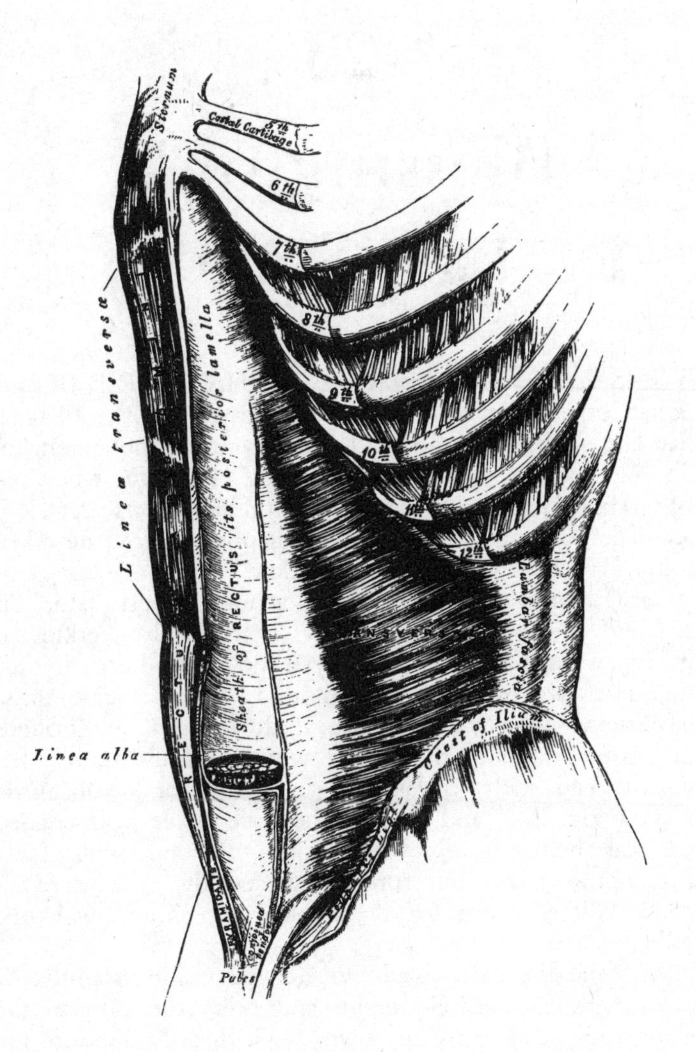

# 23

# Blessington's Last Stand

IT IS A REMARKABLE FACT THAT SINCE BELLA had pulled her hand so abruptly from his, the General had lain perfectly flat and still, apart from the movements of lips and tongue, eyelids and flickering eyes: thus when old Mr. Hattersley had called him "three-quarters dead" it seemed more of a diagnosis than an insult. Now he asked softly, "What is your opinion, Harker?"

"They cannot win a divorce action against you, Sir Aubrey. Your alleged adultery with Dolly Perkins is irrelevant. A husband's adultery is no ground for divorce unless it is unnatural—committed anally, incestuously, homosexually or with a beast. If they appeal on grounds of extreme cruelty their own witnesses must testify that you locked Lady Blessington in the cellar because she was raving mad, and to keep her safe while you fetched medical help. A divorce action will end with Lady Blessington taken into protective custody as a ward of court. Were it not for the scandal we should welcome it."

"No scandal, please," said the General smiling slightly. "I am leavin, Harker. Go down and bring the cabs to the front door. Make sure me own cab is directly opposite the

door, and send up Mahoun to help me downstairs. I find goin down harder than comin up."
The solicitor arose and left the room without a word.

A moment later General Blessington sat up, swung his legs to the floor and, placing his hands on his knees, looked smilingly round the room, nodding to each of us in turn. There was a sudden touch of colour in his cheeks, a mischievous brightness in his glance which I thought wonderful in a man accepting defeat.
"Would you like tea before you go?" asked Baxter. "Or something stronger?"
"No refreshments, thank you," said the General, "and I apologize, Mr. Baxter, for wastin so much of your time. Parliamentary methods always waste time. Are you ready Grimes?"
"Yessir," said Grimes with a promptness suggesting he had served in the army.
"See to McCandless," said the General, and taking a revolver from a pocket, clicked off the safety-catch and levelled it at Baxter.
"Sit down please, Mr. McCandless," said Grimes in a polite and friendly voice. I sat in the nearest chair, more hypnotized than terrified by the little black hole at the end of the weapon he so steadily showed me. I could not look away from it. I heard the General saying cheerfully, "There will be no killin Mr. Baxter, but if you do not stay where you are I promise to put a bullet into your groin. Are you ready with the chloroform, Prickett?"
"I—I—I do this with the gugugreatest—reluctance Sir Aubrey," said the doctor. He was sitting beside Grimes and I saw him struggle feebly to stand up while fumbling a bottle and cloth out of inner pockets.
"*Of course* you're reluctant, Prickett!" said the General with genial force, "but you'll do it because you are a good man and a good doctor and I trust you. Now Victoria, you love Mr. Baxter dearly because he saved your life and did you some other little services. Come and sit beside me and let Prickett put you to sleep. If you do not, I will disable Baxter

painfully with a bullet before stunnin you with the butt of this weapon GET OUT OF THE WAY WOMAN!"
I looked sideways.

And saw Bella had stepped between Baxter and Blessington and was going toward Blessington with her right hand outstretched for his gun. He slid along the sofa to aim at Baxter round her but with a light leap she landed before him, gripped the barrel and pointed it to the floor. It fired. I think the General was as shocked by this as everyone but Bella. She easily pulled the gun from his hand by the barrel and put the butt of it into her left. Like Baxter she was (is) ambidextrous, so naturally held the revolver as it was designed to be held, and this pointed it straight at the General's head.
"You silly soldier," she said, rubbing the palm of her right hand (scorched by the heat of the barrel) against the side of her wedding-dress, "you have shot me in the foot."
"The game is up, General," said Seymour Grimes, and with an apologetic shrug to me he locked the safety-catch of his revolver and pocketed it.
"Is the game *really* up, Grimes?" said the General, without taking his eyes off Bella's thoughtfully frowning face. "No, Grimes, I do not think the game is quite up yet."
With an effort he suddenly stood erect, to attention, like a soldier in a parade inspection, and now the point of the barrel pressed into the cloth of the coat over his heart and was an inch from it.
"Shoot!" he said, staring coldly ahead. A moment passed then he smiled benignly down at Bella who returned his look with wonder.
"Victoria me dear," he said in a soft, inviting voice, "squeeze the trigger. It is your husband's last request. Please oblige me."
Another moment passed then his face flushed crimson.
"SHOOT! I ORDER YOU TO SHOOT!" he cried, and to my ears the order rang backward in history through Balaclava, Waterloo, Culloden and Blenheim to Agincourt and Crécy. I realized General Blessington truly *wanted* to be

shot, had wanted it all his life, which was why he had been wounded so often. This historical command and passionate plea were so powerful that I imagined all the men killed in his battles rising from their graves to shoot him where he stood. Bella partly obeyed him. Half turning her body from the waist she fired the remaining five shots into the back of the fireplace. The detonations half stunned us; the smoke of it made my eyes water and other people cough. She blew fumes away from the reeking barrel in a gesture I later recognized when we went to see Buffalo Bill's circus during the Great Glasgow East End Exhibition of 1891. Then she put the revolver into the General's coat pocket and fainted.

After that several things happened quickly. Baxter lumbered across, lifted Bella up, laid her on the sofa and stripped shoe and stocking from the foot. Meanwhile I sprang to a cupboard containing a medical cabinet and brought it over to them. The bullet had luckily gone clean through into the carpet, puncturing the integument between the ulna and radius of the second and third metacarpals without even chipping a bone. Meanwhile old Mr. Hattersley was clapping his hands and shouting, "Eee she's a wonderful lass! Did you ever see anythink so brave? No never! A true daughter of Blaydon Hattersley, that's who *she* is!"

The door opened and two surprisingly different figures stood in it: Mrs. Dinwiddie and a tall brown turbaned man in an overcoat reaching from neck to ankles. I took this to be Mahoun, the General's manservant.

"Will I get the police Mr. Baxter?" asked our housekeeper.

"No, fetch some boiling water please, Mrs. Dinwiddie," said Baxter. "One of our visitors has just conducted an unsuccessful experiment, but done no great damage."

Mrs Dinwiddie left. The General stood to one side, gloomily tugging a corner of his heavy moustache.

"Time to leave, sir?" suggested Seymour Grimes smartly.

"O *please, please* let us leave!" begged Dr. Prickett, and had General Blessington left at once I believe he would have lived for several more years and been honoured with a state funeral and public monument.

I think what kept him beside us was his bafflement at being neither victorious nor wholly defeated. Bella, though not chloroformed, was now unconscious, and Baxter and I knelt with our backs to him behaving as if he did not exist. With the butt of the pistol in his pocket he could easily have stunned me and perhaps Baxter, and carried off Bella to the waiting cabs with the help of Mahoun. But that would have been a cowardly action and the General was no coward. Maybe he lingered because he was seeking a short, fierce, gentlemanly phrase to attract our attention before he strode out, for he was not used to being ignored. Meanwhile we gave Bella morphine, poured iodine into the wound and bound gauze round it. Suddenly she opened her eyes, looked at the General and said to him thoughtfully, "I remember you now, from the Dungeon Suite of the Hôtel de Notre-Dame, in Paris. You were the man in the mask—Monsieur Spankybot."

Then between bursts of laughter she cried aloud, "General Sir Aubrey de la Pole Spankybot V.C., how funny! Most brothel customers are quick squirts but you were the quickest of the lot! The things you paid the girls to do to stop you coming in the first half minute would make a hahahahaha make a cat laugh! Still, they liked you. General Spankybot paid well and did no harm—you never gave one of us the pox. I think the rottenest thing about you (apart from the killing you've done and the way you treat servants) is what Prickett calls the *pupurity of your mumarriage bed*. Fuck off, you poor daft silly queer rotten old fucker hahahahaha! Fuck off!"

I drew my breath in sharp. I have since been told that only in English is the word for bodily loving—whether used as noun, verb or adjective—an evil, unmentionable word. I had heard the hired men round the Whauphill farms use it from my earliest years, but both my mother and Scraffles would have knocked me senseless had they heard it from me. Yet Baxter now smiled as if at a magic word solving all our problems. The General's face went so pale that his grey moustache and beard looked dark against it. With half-shut eyes and gaping mouth he staggered sideways until he bumped into Prickett, reeled the other way until upheld by Grimes, then supported by both was moved on trembling legs toward the door which Mahoun held politely open for them. Mr. Hattersley followed with the dazed movements of a sleep-walker, but before Mahoun shut the door behind him he turned and in a sing-song moaning voice said, "That woman is no daughter of Blaydon Hattersley."

And then they were all gone.

"Good," said Baxter a moment later, having found Bella's pulse and temperature satisfactory. "I think the General will agree to a legal separation without the publicity of a divorce. Of course that means you and Bella cannot marry, but a divorce would seriously injure the career of woman doctor starting work in Scotland. A discreet private understanding will be the best thing for Bella and you until General Blessington dies of natural causes."

But two days later the papers announced that General Blessington had been found dead on the gun-room floor of his country house at Loamshire Downs. The revolver in his hand and angle of the bullet through his brain ruled out accident. The coroner said he had died "while the balance of his mind was disturbed", so he was given a Church of England burial service, but not a state funeral. The obituary in *The Times* of London said that perhaps political disappointment had made him choose "a Roman end", and implied that Gladstone was to blame.

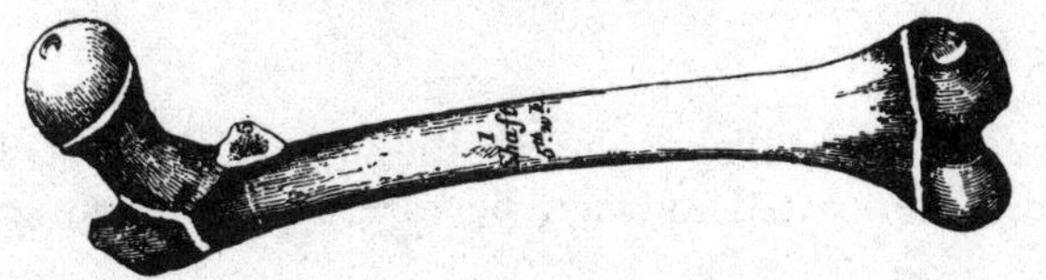

# 24

# Good-Bye

READER, SHE MARRIED ME AND I HAVE LITTLE more to tell. Our family prospers happily. Our public work is useful and noticed as such. Dr. Archibald McCandless is chairman of the Glasgow Civic Improvement Trust; Dr. Bella McCandless—through her management of the Godwin Baxter Natal Clinic, her Fabian pamphlets and promotion of female suffrage—has been invited to speak on platforms in nearly all the European capitals, while her old friend Dr. Hooker is currently organizing a lecture tour for her in America. When my friends in the Glasgow Arts Club twit me with my wife's greater fame I have a ready reply: "One famous McCandless is enough for any family." I believe our sons find their stolid father a welcome counterpoise to their brilliant, unconventional mother. I believe their mother finds me that too. She is the swelling sail, trim rigging and busy sunlit deck of our matrimonial yacht; I am the low hull with the invisible ballast and keel. This metaphor greatly contents me.

It is with a heavy heart that I now describe the last days of he who I will always consider the wisest and the best of men.

On the day after General Blessington's defeat Baxter's health deteriorated in ways he carefully hid from even his closest friends. He called us to his bedside, explained that he would need rest for a few weeks, and asked us to shift the apparatus for his feeding to a bench beside his bed. We did so. Happiness made Bell and I selfish, for we enjoyed our meals better without the queer smell from his end of the table and his sudden, disconcerting adjournments to the distillation plant. A week later our honeymoon took us abroad. When we returned Bella resumed her nurse's training in Duke Street Hospital, and I my doctoring in the Royal Infirmary, for the careers we aimed at were still beyond our reach. Each night before retiring we spent an hour or more by Baxter's bedside, I playing chess or cribbage with him while Bella discussed her work. It sometimes drove her into rages. Miss Nightingale has designed the British nursing service like the army it was first created to assist. The doctors correspond to superior officers, the matrons and sisters to sergeant-majors, the common nurses to private soldiers. Lower ranks seldom address the superiors unless ordered, since much of their intelligence is *deliberately* not employed. I saw the wisdom of this, but wisely did not say so, because Bella could not see it. Baxter told her, "Do not quarrel with the institution before you have seen through all its workings and understand them. Meanwhile use your free intelligence to plan better ways of doing things."

He also pointed out the flaws in what she planned, not to stop her seeking better ways, but to help her make them practical. The Godwin Baxter Natal Clinic is organized in ways they discussed through the spring of 1884. By then we took Baxter's bed-ridden state for granted. He had kept the mysteries of his metabolism a secret from us, so we were powerless to advise him.

One morning as I left for work Mrs. Dinwiddie gave me a note from him.

*Dear Archie, Please persuade someone to relieve you today, and return to see me as near noon as possible. I would like a private talk. Bella must not hear of it till afterwards. If you take this trouble, I will not trouble you again. Sincerely, G.*

I was disturbed by the tremulous and broken character of his pen strokes; also by his use of my Christian name. I could not remember him using it before. I returned prompt at noon and met Mrs. Dinwiddie in the lobby. She seemed to have been weeping, and said, "I have just helped Mr. Godwin dress and go into Sir Colin's old study. He needs you terribly, Dr. McCandless. Go quickly."
I ran.

As I entered the room I heard a mixture of thudding, buzzing and twanging in which I recognized the rhythm of a hugely amplified heart-beat. It came from Baxter who sat at the table, gripping the edge of it so tightly that the terrible vibration blurring the outlines of his face was not communicated to the arms.
"Quick! Do! Subcute!" he called in a blurred voice, writhing his head in a beckon. I saw a filled hypodermic syringe on a plate before him, a shirtsleeve rolled back from his forearm. I seized the syringe, gripped a fold of skin between thumb and forefinger and gave him a subcutaneous injection. A moment later the vibration ceased and the dreadful sound grew quieter. He sighed, mopped his face with a handkerchief, smiled and said, "Thank you, McCandless. I am glad you came. I am about to die."
I sat down and wept uncontrollably, for I could not pretend to misunderstand. He smiled even more at that and patted my shoulder saying, "Thank you again, McCandless, those tears console me. They mean I have been good for you."
"Can you not live longer?"
"Not without pain and indignity. Sir Colin told me from my earliest youth that my life depended on keeping a continuously even temper—strong feelings would lethally emphasize incompatibilities in my internal organs. When Bella told me she had engaged to marry you the agony damaged my respiration. On the night she returned from Paris she asked a frightening question from which my neural network never recovered. Six weeks later Blessington's solicitor so convulsed me with anger that my

alimentary canal was damaged beyond repair. You perhaps notice no great alteration to my apparent bulk, but I am starving to death, McCandless, and only derivatives of opium and cocaine have let me enjoy your evening visits with an appearance of ease. I had hoped to see April out with you, but when we separated last night I knew I had no time left. It is weak of me to want company in my last minutes but . . . I am weak!"

"I must fetch Bella," I cried, jumping up.

"No, Archie! I love Bella too much. If she begged me to live longer I could not refuse, and her last sight of me would be of an uncontrollably filthy, paralytic idiot. I will leave life while I can say Good-bye with dignity. But too much dignity is pompous. Let us share a *deoch an doruis*, a glass of my father's port together. I seem to remember two years ago locking up a decanter you had only half emptied. Wine is supposed to improve with keeping. Here is the key. You know the cupboard."

There was a cheerful zest in his speech which almost made me smile; yet I trembled as I brought out the ancient decanter and two delicate stemmed glasses. I dusted the glasses clean with my breast-pocket handkerchief, half filled them and we clinked them. He sniffed his curiously then said, "My will leaves all to Bella and you. Have children and teach them good behaviour and honest work by example. Never be violent with them, and never preach. Make sure Mrs. Dinwiddie and the other servants live comfortably here when they can no longer work, and be kind to my dogs. Finally—" (here he emptied the glass in one quick swallow) "—that is how wine tastes."

He put the glass down, gripped his gigantic knees with his gigantic fists, threw back his head and laughed. I had not heard him laugh before. The sound started small and swelled up huge, so huge that I flattened my hands over my ears, though the throbs and twangs of his heart-beat swelled loud too until it and the laughter stopped in a sudden sharp snap. Complete silence. He swayed neither forward nor back, but sat perfectly rigid.

A moment later I stepped over and, trying hard not to peer into the huge tooth-edged cavity which gaped so horribly at the ceiling, discovered his neck was broken and that *rigor mortis* had instantly ensued. Rather than break his joints in order to lay him out flat I ordered a cubical coffin four and a half feet wide, with a shelf inside on which he was placed, sitting. He sits like that to the present day, under the floor of the mausoleum Sir Colin acquired in the Necropolis overlooking Glasgow Cathedral and Royal Infirmary. In due course I and my wife (who was very upset by his death) will join him there, and so can all our children and grandchildren if they make room for themselves by getting cremated.

This record of our early struggles is dedicated to my wife, though I dare not show it to her since it tells of things neither she nor medical science dare yet believe. But scientific progress accelerates from year to year. In a short time the discovery may be made which Sir Colin Baxter communicated only to his son, and which will prove the factual ground of all I have written here.

FINIS

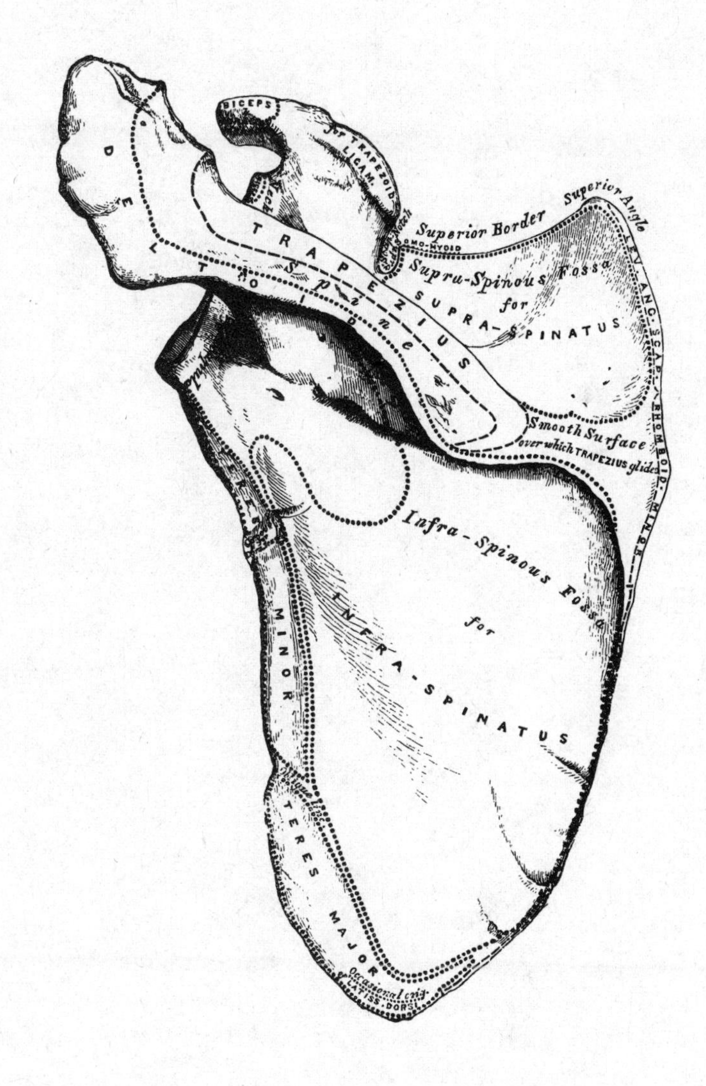
BICEPS
for TRAPEZOID LIGAM.
Neck
Supra-Scap. Notch
Superior Border
Superior Angle
OMO-HYOID
Supru-Spinous Fossa
for
SUPRA-SPINATUS
TRAPEZIUS
DELTOID
Spine
LEV. ANG. SCAP. RHOMBOID. MINOR
Smooth Surface
over which TRAPEZIUS glides
Infra-Spinous Fossa
for
INFRA-SPINATUS
TERES MINOR
TERES MAJOR
Occasional orig.
LATISS. DORSI

*Please remember me sometimes.*

*A letter from*
*Victoria McCandless M.D.*
*to her eldest surviving descendant*
*in 1974*
*correcting what she claims are errors*
*in*

EPISODES FROM
the EARLY LIFE
of a
SCOTTISH PUBLIC
HEALTH OFFICER

*by*
*her late husband*
*Archibald McCandless M.D.*
*b.1857 – d.1911*

*Dear Grand- or Great-Grandchild,*

*By 1974 my three strong, sprouting lads will be dead or senile, so all other surviving members of the McCandless dynasty will have two grandfathers or four great-grandfathers, and will easily laugh at the aberration of one. I cannot laugh at this book. I shudder at it and thank the Life Force that my late husband had just this single copy printed and bound. I have burned every scrap I could find of the original manuscript and would have burned this too, as he suggests in his verse on the fly-leaf; but alas! it is almost the only evidence left that the poor fool existed. He also paid a small fortune for it—enough to feed, clothe and educate twelve orphans for a year. The illustrations must have doubled the printing costs. The portrait of me is copied from one in an illustrated newspaper of 1896, and strikes me as a good likeness. If you ignore the Gainsborough hat and pretentious nickname it shows I am a plain, sensible woman, not the naïve Lucrezia Borgia and La Belle Dame Sans Merci described in the text. So I post the book to posterity. I do not care what posterity thinks of it, as long as nobody now living connects it with ME.*

*Having reread that first paragraph I notice it suggests my second husband was as repulsive as the first. Untrue. I married Archibald McCandless because he was convenient, and as the years slipped by I came to like and rely upon the man. He was not much use to anyone else. He calls his book "Episodes from the Early Life of a Scottish Public Health Officer"—he was a Glasgow municipal health officer for exactly eleven months, resigning from the job as soon as he became chairman of the Glasgow Civic Improvement Trust. Our investments, not his brilliant mind, got him that position. It required him to preside at certain meetings, but he had most of the week to himself. Not all this free time was wasted. He helped Mrs. Dinwiddie (my faithful housekeeper) with the early nurture of our children, taking them for walks, telling them stories, crawling about the floor with them, helping them build fantastical cities out of bricks and cardboard, and draw up fantastical maps and histories of invented continents. These tales and games gave them a rich variety of ideas and information. His scientific bent ensured that the queerest monsters had impeccable Darwinian-evolutionary pedigrees; the weirdest machines never contradicted the laws of thermo-dynamics. The education he gave them was very like the playful one I had been given by Godwin Baxter, and used many of the same toys, books and instruments. We still kept a small zoo in the back-garden, though the last of Godwin's dogs died five years after he did.*

*There is an old Scots proverb: "The shoemaker's bairns are aye the warst shod." It is a fact that I, the fearless advocate of homely cuddling and playful teaching, was kept out of the house by my clinical work for most of the week, while other responsibilities took me out of Glasgow for part of every year. My husband practised what I preached. I sometimes feared he was making early childhood too attractive for the lads so that their adult lives (like those of my first husband, and Bismarck, and Napoleon, and more commonplace criminals) would become bad boyish day dreams made real. I need not have feared. When they joined the society of other boys in Glasgow High School (founded in the twelfth century) they grew ashamed of their idle, dreamy fantastical father and emulated their practical, busy-in-the-world mother.*

*The eldest, Baxter McCandless, is our mathematician. He took an honours degree last year and now works in London for the Department of Imperial Statistics. Godwin, our engineer, moves so briskly between Gilmorehill and the Andersonian Institute that I never know where he is studying. He says steam and oil-fired engines are dangerous anachronisms, that we must prepare to draw energy electrically from the highland lochs and cataracts while gradually abandoning coal-mines and oil-wells whose wastes poison the air and soil the lungs. The youngest, Archibald, is in his last year at school and has two obsessions. One is painting garish water-colour landscapes, the other is commanding the Glasgow High School Army Cadet Corp. I hate military training, of course. The sight of young men marching in regular rows, each imitating the stiff movements of a clockwork doll while their movements are controlled by a single screaming sergeant—that sight sickens me even more than the sight of young women in a music-hall chorus-row, kicking up their heels in unison. However, I recognize that young Archie's love of uniformed comrades balances his Bohemian individualism. When these sides of his nature at last harmonize he too may become a fine public servant—perhaps the best of them.*

*In writing about my boys I have forgotten their father: always an easy thing to do in his later years. He spent more and more time in his study, scribbling books printed at his own expense since no publisher would pay for them. Every second year I would come down to breakfast and find another blue-black volume beside my plate, with a marker in the dedication page which always bore the message* TO SHE WHO MAKES MY LIFE

*WORTH LIVING. As I leafed through it, trying to show interest I could not possibly feel, he would watch my face with a maddening expression of timid hope and humorous resignation: an expression which made the soul of me want to grip him and shake him into useful activity. He would have been a decent general practitioner had he not used Baxter's money to buy the idleness he mistook for freedom. Having fulfilled his mother's ambition by joining the middle class he had no wish to reform it from inside, no wish to help the labouring class reform us (and themselves) from outside. But example is the best reproof I know. I would lay the book down, walk round the table, kiss him kindly, thank him and go off to work at my clinic.*

*In 1908 we found he had disseminated sclerosis (he diagnosed it himself) so it became easy to be kind. He relaxed into the disease, shifting his bed into the study and ordering a special table which let him write without getting up. He could easily have lived longer had he exercised, but he knew that and I would not bully him. I kept the marriage sweet by having a game of draughts, a light supper and a chat with him most nights before retiring. Increasingly our talk recalled our earlier days with Godwin Baxter. I also saw he was engaged on another book.*

*"Do you want to know about it?" he asked one night, with a kind of mischievous vivacity which he clearly attributed to creative inspiration and I to a mild fever caused by disease.*

*"Tell me if you want to," I said, smiling.*

*"Ah, but this time I want not to. I want you to read it with astonishment after I am gone. Promise to read it*

*through at least once. Promise not to bury it in my coffin."*
*I promised.*

*The bound volume at last arrived from the printers and gave him pleasure for many weeks. He slept with it under his pillow. He would lie on the sofa while the maid changed his sheets, turning pages forward or backward and chuckling over them. Later, as he weakened, a bitter impatience was what he mainly felt, and at the end he wanted nothing but the pressure of my hand on his brow, for he whimpered when I removed it. I stayed beside him though I could have done more good at other bed-sides. Never mind. I may want company during my own last days, so am glad I did not refuse it to him.*

*I read the book three years ago soon after the funeral and it made me unhappy for a fortnight. I am still unhappy when I remember it. To explain why I must tell my own life story as simply as possible.*

*The first home I remember was two small rooms and a kitchen where five of us lived, sometimes six when my father stayed with us. Our only water supply was a shared tap in a yard at the back. Father could have afforded a house with better sanitation. He was chief foreman (or works manager, as we call such nowadays) in a nearby Manchester foundry, and saving money was his major passion. He seldom gave my mother enough to buy proper food.*
*"I cannot give us a proper start in life before I control a good patent," he told us, "and that needs all the money I can get."*
*He treated his wife and children like he treated the workmen: as potential enemies who must be kept poor by*

*violence or the threat of it. He thought any remark which did not obviously flatter him was rebellion. When five years old I once watched him stand before the looking-glass in our dank little kitchen, adjusting his dark-green cravat and waistcoat with green velvet facings, for he spent money on his appearance though not on ours, and in a coarse way was something of a dandy. Impressed by the contrast between the colour of the clothes and his dark-red face I said, "You are a poppy, Dad."*

*I remember no more until I awoke in bed. He had clubbed me down with his fist, my head had struck the brick-cobbled floor, I had been bleeding and unconscious for several hours. I doubt if my mother had dared call a doctor. I still have an irregular three-inch-long scar above my left ear under the hair. It follows an abnormal widening of the squamosal suture, but apart from that period of unconsciousness it has never affected my memory. This is the crack my late husband describes as "mysteriously regular" and "ringing the entire skull under the hair line".*

*Of my mother I have only this to say: she was unselfish and hard-working, and taught me how useless these virtues are when separated from courage and intelligence. She felt positively wicked when not washing or darning clothes, scrubbing floors, beating carpets or making a gallon of soup out of scraps a butcher could not sell for cat-food. I do not know if she was able to read, but if she ever saw me with a book it was snatched away because "Girls need no excuses for idleness." I remember most clearly the misery of washing our bodies and clothes in cold water during the winter months, when we had no coal to heat it and hardly any soap. Life for Mother and me was mainly a struggle to keep the family and home clean, yet we never felt clean before my brothers died and Father (as if he had been waiting for that) shifted us into a three-storey house with a garden all round it, saying "I can afford this now."*

*I think he had afforded it for at least a year. It was richly furnished, with ten or twelve servants who took their orders from a fine-looking lady with yellow hair and a brighter dress than worn by housekeepers I met in later years. She was kind to us.*

*"Here is your private parlour," she said, showing us into a room with strongly patterned wallpaper and curtains, thickly carpeted floor, heavily upholstered furniture, the biggest fire I had ever seen and a bright brass scuttle of coal in the hearth.*

*"Here are biscuits, cake, sherry, port wine and spirits," she said, opening the door of a huge sideboard, "also a soda-water gazogene which is recharged by the handy-man in an outhouse. If you ever want anything pull that bell-rope twice and a maid will call for orders. What would you like just now? Will I send up tea?"*

*"What does HE want?" whispered Mother, tilting her head toward Father who stood on the hearth-rug smoking a cigar.*

*"Blaydon, your wife wants to know if you want tea!" said the lady, and we realized she was not afraid of Father.*

*"Not now, Mabel," he replied, yawning. "Give me a brandy. Give Mrs. Hattersley and young Vicky a sherry then go downstairs. I'll see you in ten minutes. For God's sake Mother sit down and stop twisting your hands together."*

*Mother obeyed and when the housekeeper left sipped the sherry uneasily and asked him, "You got it, then?"*

*"Got what?"*

*"Got patent."*

*"Got patent and heck of a lot more," said Father, chuckling. "Got a lot from your brother."*

*"My brother Elia?"*

*"Your brother Noah."*

*"Shall I see him then?"*

*"No, nobody sees Noah now," said Father, chuckling harder. "There is nothing much left of him to see. Take a word of advice, Mother. Don't ask visitors here until you can act ladylike. Ask Mabel to teach you how to sit and dress and stand and walk. And how to speak, of course. She knows a heck of a lot. She's taught ME a few new tricks. I'll leave you now. You've had to wait a while for this but it's solid. Depend on it."*

*He finished the brandy and walked out.*

*I met him a fortnight later on the stairs and said, "Father, Mother gets drunk every day. She has nothing else to do."*

*"Well, if she wants to kill herself by that particular road why should I object? As long as she does it quiet-like in her own parlour. What do you want from me?"*

*"I want to read books and learn about things."*

*"Things Mabel cannot teach?"*

*"Yes."*

*"All right then."*

*A week later I was taken to a convent school in Lausanne.*

*I will not describe my foreign education in detail. Mother had taught me to be a working man's domestic slave; the nuns taught me to be a rich man's domestic toy. When they sent me back Mother was dead and I could speak French, dance, play the piano, move like a lady and discuss events as Conservative newspapers reported them, for the nuns thought husbands might prefer wives who knew some things about the world. General Sir Aubrey de la Pole Blessington was indifferent to what I knew but waltzed beautifully in spite of his wounds. No doubt the uniform helped. I was tall but he taller and the other dancers stopped to gaze on us. I loved him for many reasons. Girls of my age were expected to have husbands, homes, babies. He was rich, famous and still handsome. Also I wanted to escape from my father, who had provided this escape route. I felt truly happy on my wedding-day. That night I discovered why "Thunderbolt" Blessington was called "The Arctic Pole" by his fellow officers, yet thought the fault was mine. Six months later I had my third hysterical pregnancy and was begging for a clitoridectomy. Dr. Prickett told me a skilful Scottish surgeon was in London and might "handle the job". So one afternoon I was visited by the only man I have truly loved, Godwin Baxter.*

*Why did my second husband describe Godwin as a monster whose appearance made babies scream, nursemaids flee and horses shy? God was a big sad-looking man, but so careful and alert and* unforcing *in all his movements that animals, small people, hurt and lonely people, all women (I repeat and emphasize it) ALL WOMEN AT FIRST SIGHT felt safe and at peace with him. He asked why I wanted the operation Dr. Prickett was arranging. I explained. He questioned my explanation. I told him about my childhood, my schooling, my marriage. After a long pause he said gently,*

*"My dear, you have been badly treated all your life by selfish, greedy, silly men. Yet they are not to blame. They too were horribly educated. Dr. Prickett really believes the operation the General wants for you will help you. It cannot. Have nothing to do with it. I will tell Prickett what I have just told you. He will not accept my opinion, but you have a right to know what it is."*

*I wept with grief and gratitude, knowing what he said was true. I had always felt it was true, but could not know it until I heard it said. I cried out to him, "They will drive me mad if I stay here. Where can I go?"*

*"If you have no friend to shelter you, no money and no experience of earning it," he said, "it will be suicide to leave your husband. I am sorry. I cannot help you."*

*I was inspired—by his kindness. I rushed across to the chair where he sat, knelt between his legs and raised my clasped hands to the level of his face.*

*"If!" I demanded, "one night several weeks from now, or months or years from now, a homeless desperate friendless woman comes to your home in Scotland and begs for shelter—a woman you have once treated kindly—could you turn her away?"*

*"I could not," he said, sighing and looking to the ceiling.*

*"That is all I need to know," I said, standing up, "apart from your address which I suppose I can find in a British medical directory."*

*"Yes," he murmured, standing up also, "but leave me alone if possible, Lady Blessington."*

*"Good-bye," I said, shaking his hand and nodding.*

*Was ever surgeon in this manner wooed? Was ever surgeon in this manner won?*

*The last possible moment came two months later, and I*

*was not pregnant, and had never considered leaping from a bridge when I arrived in Glasgow and took a cab to Park Circus and the house of the big dogs. I had just learned that the husband who would not give me a child was about to have one by a servant ten years my junior. Baxter received me without a single question. He led me to the room where Mrs. Dinwiddie sat (she must then have been forty-five years old, for he was thirty) and said, "Mother, this badly treated lady has come to us for a rest, and will stay here until she can afford a home of her own. Treat her as my sister."*

*Yes, 18 Park Circus had one thing in common with 29 Porchester Terrace. A master there had got a son by a servant: a woman he did not marry. But Godwin loved and acknowledged his mother, though she had not his father's name. The visitors Baxter most liked would be invited to drink tea with "my mother—Mrs. Dinwiddie". Tea with her was no cosy formality. A keen-minded woman with a strong sense of humour, she could hold her end in a conversation with anyone.*

*"What are you inventing now, Sir William?" she would ask the scientist who had been knighted for making the Atlantic Cable work, "and will it undo the damage of your last big job?"—for she pretended to think wars and the weather had worsened since the development of the telegraph. My own mother had made me Mancunian. The nuns had made me French. The friendship and conversation of Mrs. Dinwiddie gave me the voice and manners of an unprejudiced, straightforward Scotswoman. Colleagues who knew nothing of my early years still amuse me sometimes by saying how SCOTTISH I am.*

*God could be honest about his unmarried mother*

*because he was a bachelor with an unearned income. He could not be honest about sheltering the runaway wife of an English Baronet and Great British General. To save us from awkward questions he invented the South American married cousins, their death in a train crash and their amnesic daughter Bella Baxter, who was me. This was a good excuse for teaching me the important things I had never been taught, but he would not let me forget anything I had already learned.*

*"Forget nothing," he said; "your worst experiences in Manchester and Lausanne and Porchester Terrace will enlarge your mind if you remember them with intelligent interest. They will stop you thinking clearly if you cannot."*

*"I cannot!" I cried. "My fingers have ached scrubbing filthy clothes in a washtub of freezing water: they have ached playing Beethoven's Für Elise nineteen times without stopping on the piano because the teacher made me start again whenever I hit a wrong note. My head has ached because my dad cracked my skull with* his *fist; it has ached because I had to memorize passages of Fénelon's Télémaque, surely the dullest book ever. These things cannot be remembered intelligently—they belong to different worlds, God, and nothing connects them but pain I want to forget."*

*"No, Bella. They seem in different worlds because you met them far apart, but see me open the hinged front of this big doll's house and fold it back. Look into all the rooms. This is a type of house you will find by thousands in British cities, by hundreds in the towns, and tens in the villages. It could be Porchester Terrace or this house—my house. The servants live mostly in the*

*basement and attics: the coldest and most crowded floors with the smallest rooms. Their body heat, while they sleep, keeps their employers in the central floors more snug. This little female doll in the kitchen is a scullery-maid who will also do rough laundry work, scrubbing and mangling the clothes. She will have plenty of hot water to use if her master or mistress is generous, and may not be overworked if the servants set over her are kind, but we live in an age when thrift and hard competition are proclaimed as the foundations of the state, so if she is meanly and cruelly used nobody will remark upon it. Now look into the parlour on the first floor. Here is a piano with another little female doll sitting at it. If her dress and hair-style were changed for the scullery-maid's she might be the same girl, but that will not happen. She is probably trying to play Beethoven's Für Elise without a wrong note—her parents want her one day to attract a rich husband who will use her as a social ornament and breeder of his children. Tell me, Bella, what the scullery-maid and the master's daughter have in common, apart from their similar ages and bodies and this house."*

*"Both are used by other people," I said. "They are allowed to decide nothing for themselves."*

*"You see?" cried Baxter delightedly. "You know that at once because you remember your early education. Never forget it, Bella. Most people in England, and Scotland too, are taught not to know it at all—are* taught *to be tools."*

*Yes, Baxter taught freedom by surrounding me with toys I had never known as a child and by showing me how to work instruments (then called philosophical instruments) which his father had used to teach him. I cannot describe the heavenly feelings of power I enjoyed as I manipulated the terrestrial and celestial globes, the zoetrope, microscope, galvanic battery, camera obscura, regular solids and Napier's bones. Fine manipulations came easily to me because of my mother's needlework and the convent piano training. I also had botany, zoology, travel and history books with engraved and coloured pictures to brood over. Duncan Wedderburn, God's legal friend, sometimes took me out to theatres because God could not do that—he had a horror of crowds. I loved the theatre—even the high-kicking pantomime chorus-row struck me as carefree and happy! But I loved Shakespeare most. So I started reading him at home, starting with Lamb's Tales from Shakespeare, then the plays themselves. In the library (led on by the illustrations) I also discovered Andersen's Fairy Tales, Alice in Wonderland and The Arabian Nights (this last in a French translation which included the erotic passages). For a while Baxter got a tutor for me, Miss MacTavish. She did not last. I wanted nobody but God to teach me. With him learning was a surprising meal; with her it was a discipline. Around this time I first met young Archie McCandless.*

*It was a warm fresh pleasant afternoon and I may have looked slightly childish, kneeling on the tiny kitchen-garden green and peering into a hutch where Mopsy and Flopsy were copulating. Baxter and an awkward, ill-dressed lad whose ears stuck out entered from the lane. Baxter introduced us, but the boy was too shy to say a word, and this made me equally awkward. We went upstairs to take a cup of tea, but not with Mrs. Dinwiddie, so I knew Baxter did not consider McCandless a close friend. While tea was prepared Baxter chatted pleasantly about university medical matters but McCandless was staring so hard at me that he said not a word in reply. Embarrassing! So I went to the piano and played one of the simpler songs of Burns. It may have been The Bonnie Banks o' Loch Lomond, but I did not use the treadles of the pianola roll. I played with my fingers, and the timing was perfect. Besides, I distinctly remember that we acquired the pianola in the year of the Queen's Diamond Jubilee, 1897. I don't think the instrument had been invented before then. When McCandless left he insisted on kissing my hand. In Sir Aubrey's house this flowery continental gesture had never been practised even by our French and Italian guests. I was astonished, and probably stared at my fingertips afterward in a bemused way. Our visitor's salivation was extreme, and I did not want to dry my hand or touch my dress with it till he was out of sight. I did not see him again for a very long time, and certainly did not want to!*

*There was only one source of misery in those happy, happy days. God would not let me seduce him.*

*"Please do not fall in love with me, Bella," he said. "I am not a man, you see, I am a big intelligent dog who is shaped like a man. Apart from that I have only one undoggy trait. I want no master—and no mistress."*

*This was true, but I could not face that truth. I loved him with all my heart and all my mind and all my soul so wanted to convert him to humanity. One night, unable to sleep because of this desire, I took a candle in my hand and went naked into his bedroom. The dogs on the floor snarled jealously but I knew they would not bite. Alas, dogs were heaped beside him on the bed too and over his feet. They growled throatily.*

*"Victoria, I have no room for you," he murmured, opening his eyes.*

*"O please let me in for a little while God!" I begged him, weeping. "Give me just enough of you to make a child for us, a little child made from both of us who I can feed and love and cuddle forever."*

*"They grow up," he murmured, yawning, "and there is a medical reason why I must not father a child."*

*"You are sick?"*

*"Incurably sick."*

*"Then I will become a doctor and cure you! Doctors can do things surgeons cannot! I will be your doctor."*

*He made a clicking noise with his tongue. The two dogs on the floor nipped the calves of my legs gently between their great jaws and tugged me toward the door. I had to go.*

*Next day over breakfast God explained things fully, for he never made unnecessary mysteries. From his father, the great surgeon, he had inherited a syphilitic illness which would eventually cause insanity and general paralysis.*

*"I do not know exactly when the blow will fall," he said. "Perhaps in a few months; perhaps in a few years. But I am prepared for it. The only doctoring which can help me is painless poison, self-administered when the first symptoms appear. I always carry my medicine with me, so you need not become a doctor on my account."*

*"Then I will become a doctor on the world's account!" I declared between sobs. "I will save some people's lives, if not yours. I will replace you! I will become you!"*

*"That is a good idea, Victoria," he said gravely, "and if you hold to it your studies shall be directed that way. But*

*I would first like to see you equipped with a useful husband: an efficient, unselfish one who will help you do what you want while satisfying your amorous instincts—they have been terribly starved."*

*"Starvation shall be my husband if you will not!" I told him through clenched teeth. He smiled and shook his head. We had stopped thinking about my famous husband in England.*

*He took me on a world tour. The idea was mine—I wanted to get him away from his dogs. He did it (I now see) to extend my knowledge, but also to get rid of me. We visited hospitals or attended medical lectures in fourteen capital cities. A Viennese specialist taught me the most modern techniques of sexual hygiene and birth control, after which he kept pushing me into the company of other men whenever he could. But although the sensual appetite was strong in me I could not or would not split it off from the moral appetite to embrace the admirable, and who could I admire more than God? When we returned at last to Glasgow I had made him very miserable. My company deprived him of all freedom. I let him do nothing, go nowhere without me. I was more cheerful than he, because though unable to swallow him all up in a marriage I still had more of him than anybody else could get. And then, walking one day by the memorial fountain in the West End Park, we met McCandless again.*

*I have mentioned how animals, children and all small or awkward people felt safer when God was near them. McCandless had first met God in the university anatomy department where God gave demonstrations when the usual lecturer was off sick. Small, awkward McCandless fell as passionately in love with God as I had done. He loved me too, of course, but only because he saw me as God's female part—the part he could embrace and enter. But God was the first great love of his life, and the love was not returned. Long before I came to Park Circus McCandless had spied out the routes by which God took his dogs for their Sunday walk, and kept joining him on these. God was unable to be unkind to anybody, but once, when McCandless not only accompanied him home but had the insolence to force his way inside, my poor darling DID manage to say he needed more privacy than McCandless was allowing him. McCandless left God alone after that, unless they met by accident and God invited him home. Since God was infinitely good this sometimes happened, and that was how I had first met McCandless.*

*When we met the second time God positively thrust me onto the poor wee man. He sat on a bench, said he needed a rest and begged McCandless to take me a walk round the park. I see now (looking backward) that he wanted nothing but peace from the hideously talkative demanding creature I had become; but as I set off arm-in-arm through the shrubberies with McCandless I had another notion of his motives. Might he think McCandless was the useful, unselfish husband who would help me do what I wanted while satisfying my amorous et cetera? I realized such a man would have to be (in the eyes of the world and perhaps my own) a weakling, because he MUST NOT separate me from God. In fact, he would have to live with God and me, wanting no establishment of his own. While I pondered these things the vain little homunculus clinging to my arm babbled to me about the poverty of his childhood, his successes as a medical student and his wonderful achievements as a house doctor in the Royal Infirmary. Could THIS be the man I needed? I paused to stare at him more closely. He responded by kissing me, shyly at first, then with ardour. I had never been kissed by a man before. My only amorous pleasures had been a Sapphic affair with my piano teacher in Lausanne. I would have loved her till the end of time, but alas, she loved too many others for my selfish taste, so I had turned against her. I was amazed by the enjoyment I got from McCandless. When we separated I gazed at him with an emotion verging on respect. When he proposed marriage I agreed and said, "Let us tell God at once." There was no doubt in my mind that God would be overjoyed to get more privacy by sharing me with McCandless.*

*How astonishingly selfish I was in those days! I had no moral imagination, no intelligent sympathy for people. God wanted a good husband for me so that he might enjoy again the life I had interrupted; he had not expected my marriage to add ANOTHER person to his household! A person he did not greatly like! He nearly fainted when I told him the news. He begged us to consider the matter for at least a fortnight before making up our minds. We agreed, of course.*

*I hope the people of 1974 are less shocked by sexual facts than most of my late Victorian contemporaries. If not, this letter will be burned as soon as read.*

*In the following week the McCandless kiss filled my thoughts and daydreams. Was it because of McCandless, I wondered, or could any other man give me that feeling of exquisite power combined with exquisite helplessness? Perhaps (I even dared to think) ANOTHER MAN*

*MIGHT DO IT BETTER! To find out I seduced Duncan Wedderburn, a man I had never considered before and who (to be fair to him) had never considered me! He was a conventional soul, so completely devoted to a selfish mother that the notion of marriage never occurred to him before he and I became lovers. However, it occurred to him immediately after. I did not realize that the elopement he proposed was to involve marriage. I thought of it as a delicious experiment, a voyage to discover how suitable McCandless was. I explained this to God who said forlornly, "Go your ways, Victoria, I cannot teach you about love. But be gentle with poor Wedderburn, he has not a strong head. McCandless, too, will suffer when he hears about it."*

*"But you won't shut me out when I come back?" I asked him brightly.*

*"No. But I may not be alive."*

*"Yes you will," I said, kissing him. I no longer believed he had syphilis. I found it easier to believe he had invented that to prevent women like me twisting him round their little fingers.*

*Well, I enjoyed my Wedderburn while he lasted and was gentle with him when he fell apart. I still visit him once a month in the lunatic asylum. He is bright and cheerful, and always greets me with a mischievous wink and knowing grin. I am sure his insanity began as a pretence to evade imprisonment for embezzling clients' funds, but it is real enough now.*

*"How is your husband?" he asked me last week.*

*"Archie died in 1911," I told him.*

*"No, I mean your OTHER husband—Leviathan Pit-Bottomless Baxter de Babylon, surgical king of the*

*damned material universe."*
*"Dead also Wedder," I said with a heartfelt sigh.*
*"Teehee! That one will never die," he giggled. How I wish he had never died.*

*When I returned to Park Circus he was dying already. I saw it in his shrunk figure and trembling hand.*
*"O God!" I cried, "O God!" and kneeling down I embraced his legs and pressed my weeping face into them. He was sitting in Mrs. Dinwiddie's parlour, she on one side and McCandless standing behind. I was astonished to see my fiancé there, though of course I had kept in touch with him by letter. With the onset of the disease God had come to need medical help with some functions for which his mother's strength was too little. The nearness of death had also driven out his dislike of McCandless.*
*"Victoria," he murmured, "Bella-Victoria, you Beautiful Victory, my mind will soon be all gone, all gone, and you will no longer love me if our candle-maker friend does not give me a very strong medicine. But I am glad to see you before I drink it. Marry this candle, Bella-Victoria. All I own will be yours. Promise to look after my dogs for me, my poor poor lonely leaderless dogs. Poor dogs. Poor dogs."*
*His head began to shake and his mouth dribble.*
*McCandless bared his arm and gave him an injection. He became sensible for a few more minutes.*
*"Yes, take the dogs for their Sunday walks, Archie and Victoria. Go along the canal bank to Bowling then go by Strowan's Well to the Lang Crags above Dumbarton, cross the Stockiemuir to Carbeth, come back by way of Craigallion Loch, the Allander, Mugdock and Milngavie Waterworks. Or go up the Clyde to Rutherglen or*

*Cambuslang, mount the Cathkin Braes by the Dechmont and stroll by way of Gargunnock and the Malletsheugh to Neilston Pad. There are glorious walks around Glasgow, all leading easily to high places where you can look out upon glorious tracts of the world: mountains, lochs, pastured hills, woodlands and the great Firth, all framing this Glasgow which we do not love enough, for we would make it better if we did. Enjoy these things for me: the stepping stones by Cadder Kirk, clear Bardowie Loch, The Auld Wives' Lifts, The Devil's Pulpit, Dumgoyach and Dungoyne. If you have sons, please name one after me. Mummy will help you with them. Mummy! Mummy! Treat the McCandless bairns like grandchildren. I am sorry I could give you none. And try to forgive my father, Sir Colin. What a damnably foul old scoundrel the man was. He started more than he could see the end of. But we all do that haha. Quick, McCandless! The medicine!"*

*Archie brought forward the draught but it was I who took it from him and, after pressing my lips to my beloved's in the only kiss we ever shared, put my arm behind his head and helped him drink.*

*That is how Godwin Baxter died.*

*You, dear reader, have now two accounts to choose between and there can be no doubt which is most probable. My second husband's story positively stinks of all that was morbid in that most morbid of centuries, the nineteenth. He has made a sufficiently strange story stranger still by stirring into it episodes and phrases to be found in Hogg's Suicide's Grave with additional ghouleries from the works of Mary Shelley and Edgar Allan Poe. What morbid Victorian fantasy has he NOT filched from? I find traces of The Coming Race, Dr. Jekyll and Mr. Hyde, Dracula, Trilby, Rider Haggard's She, The Case-Book of Sherlock Holmes and, alas, Alice Through the Looking-Glass; a gloomier book than the sunlit Alice in Wonderland. He has even plagiarized work by two very dear friends: G. B. Shaw's Pygmalion and the scientific romances of Herbert George Wells. Ever since reading this infernal parody of my life-story I have been asking, WHY DID ARCHIE WRITE IT? I am now able to post this letter to posterity because I have at last found the answer.*

*As locomotive engines are driven by pressurized steam, so the mind of Archibald McCandless was driven by carefully hidden envy. His good fortune in later life never stopped him being at heart just "a poor bastard bairn". The envy the poor and exploited feel toward the wealthy is a good thing if it works toward reforming this unfairly ordered nation. That is why we Fabians think the trade unions and Labour Party are as much our allies as any honest public servant (Liberal or Tory) who wants a decent minimum wage, a sanitary house, proper working conditions and the vote for every British adult. Unluckily my Archie envied the only two people he loved, the only two who could tolerate him. He envied God for having a famous father and tender, loving mother. He resented my wealthy father, convent education and famous first husband, resented my superior social graces. Most of all he envied the care and company God gave me and the strength of my love for God, and hated the fact that the most we felt for him was friendly goodwill tempered (on my side) with sensual indulgence. So in his last months he soothed himself by imagining a world where he and*

*God and I existed in perfect equality. Having had a childhood which privileged people would have thought "no childhood" he wrote a book suggesting that God had none either—that God had always been as Archie knew him, because Sir Colin had manufactured God by the Frankenstein method. Then he deprived me of childhood and schooling by suggesting I was not mentally* me *when I first met him, but my baby daughter. Having invented this equality of deprivation for all of us he could then easily describe how I loved him at first sight, and how Godwin envied him! But of course, Archie was no lunatic. He knew his book was a cunning lie. When chuckling over it during his last few weeks what amused him was how cleverly his fiction outwitted the truth. Or so I believe.*

*Yet why did he not make it more convincing? In the twenty-second chapter, describing how my first husband shot me through the foot, he says "The bullet had luckily gone clean through into the carpet,* PUNCTURING THE INTEGUMENT BETWEEN THE ULNA AND RADIUS OF THE SECOND AND THIRD METACARPALS *without even chipping a bone." The capitalized words might just convince someone who knows nothing of anatomy but they are blethers, havers, claptrap, gibberish, gobbledygook, and since Archie cannot have forgotten his medical training to that extent he must have known it. He could easily have said "puncturing the tendon of the oblique head of adductor hallucis between the great and index proximal phalanges without chipping a bone", because that was what happened. But I have no time to go through every page separating fact from fiction. If you ignore what contradicts common sense and this letter you will find that this book records some actual events during a dismal era. As I said before, to my nostrils the book stinks of Victorianism. It is as sham-gothic as the Scott Monument, Glasgow University, St. Pancras Station and the Houses of Parliament. I hate such structures. Their useless over-ornamentation was paid for out of needlessly high profits: profits squeezed from the stunted lives of children, women and men working more than twelve hours a day, six days a week in NEEDLESSLY filthy factories; for by the nineteenth century we had the knowledge to make things cleanly. We did not use it. The huge profits of the owning classes were too sacred to be questioned. To me this book stinks as the interior of a poor woman's crinoline must have stunk after a cheap weekend railway excursion to the Crystal Palace. I realize I am taking it too seriously, but I am thankful to have survived into the twentieth century.*

*And so, dear grand- or great-grandchild, my thoughts turn to you because I cannot possibly imagine the world in which this message will be read—if it ever is read. Last month Herbert George Wells (that honey-smelling man!) published a book called* The War in the Air. *Set in the nineteen twenties or thirties it describes how a German air-fleet invades the U.S.A. and bombs New York. This draws the whole world into a conflict which destroys every major centre of civilized thought and skill. The survivors are left in a worse state than the Australian aborigines, for they lack the aboriginal skills of hunting and scavenging. H.G.'s book is a warning, of course, not a prediction. He and I and many others expect a better future because we are actively creating it. Glasgow is an exciting place for a dedicated Socialist. Even in its earlier Liberal phase it set the world an example through the municipal development of public resources. Our skilled labour force is now the best educated in Britain; the Co-operative movement is popular and expanding; the Glasgow telephone system is being adopted by the General Post-Office for extension over the United Kingdom. I know that the money which pays for our confidence and achievement has a dangerous source—huge war-ships built along Clydeside by government contract, in response to equally big destroyers being built by the Germans. So H. G. Wells' warnings should be heeded.*

*But the International Socialist Movement is as strong in Germany as in Britain. The labour and trade-union leaders in both countries have agreed that if their governments declare war they will immediately call a general strike. I almost hope our military and capitalistic leaders DO declare war! If the working classes immediately halt it by peaceful means then the moral and practical control of the great industrial nations will have passed from the owners to the makers of what we need, and the world YOU live in, dear child of the future, will be a saner and happier place. Bless you.*

*Victoria McCandless M.D.*

*18 Park Circus, Glasgow.*

*1st August, 1914.*

# NOTES CRITICAL AND HISTORICAL

by Alasdair Gray

CHAPTER 1, page 9. *Like most farm workers in those days my mother distrusted banks.*

This was not the superstition of an ignorant woman. Bank failures were frequent during the eighteenth and nineteenth centuries, and poorer folk suffered most by them, as the prosperous were better informed as to which financial houses were unsound, or becoming so. In twentieth-century Britain such injustices only happen with pension funds.

CHAPTER 2, page 15. *This was the only son of Colin Baxter, the first medical man to be knighted by Queen Victoria.*

In his history *The Royal Doctors* (published by Macmillan, 1963) Gervaise Thring gives most space to Godwin's progenitor, Sir Colin Baxter, but says: "Between 1864 and 1869 his less well-known yet equally gifted son was attendant consultant during the delivery of three princes and a princess royal, and probably saved the life of the Duke of Clarence. For reasons perhaps connected with his precarious health Godwin Baxter withdrew into private life and died in obscurity a few years later." In Register House, Edinburgh, there is no record of his birth, and on the death certificate of 1884 there are blanks in the spaces reserved for age and mother's name.

Page 17. *They drove poor Semmelweis mad, he committed suicide through trying to broadcast the truth.*

Semmelweis was a Hungarian obstetrician. Appalled by the high death rate in the Viennese maternity hospital where he worked, he used antiseptics and cut the death rate from 12 to 1¼ per cent. His superiors refused to accept his conclusions and forced him out. He deliberately contracted septicaemia in a finger and in 1865 died in a mental hospital of the disease he had spent his life combating.

Page 17. *Our nurses are now the truest practitioners of the healing art. If every Scottish, Welsh and English doctor and surgeon dropped suddenly dead, eighty per cent of those admitted to our hospitals would recover if the nursing continued.*

The following extract on this subject is from "Women and Medicine", an entry by Johanna Geyer-Kordesch in the *Encyclopaedia of Medical History*, edited by W.F. Bynum: "Florence Nightingale once wrote that she didn't wish women to become doctors at all, because they would become like their male colleagues. Nightingale's objectives were breathtakingly broad. She wanted no less than a medical reform so thorough in prevention and care that doctors might become redundant."

CHAPTER 3, page 22. *A narrow garden between high walls.*

Michael Donnelly, indefatigable in his efforts to prove this history a work of fiction, points out that the garden here described does not mention a coach-house on the far side of it. He has visited Baxter's old home (18 Park Circus) and asserts that the space between back entrance and coach-house is too small and sunken to have ever been more than a drying-yard. This, of course, only proves that the coach-house was built at a later date.

CHAPTER 4, page 27. *A fine, fine woman, McCandless, who owes her life to these fingers of mine — these skeely, skeely fingers!*

"Skeely" means "skilful", as in the old Scots ballad *Sir Patrick Spens*:

> The King sits in Dumfermline toun,
> Drinking the bluid-red wine.
> "O whaur will I find a skeely skipper
> To sail this new ship o' mine?"

Page 29. *Kobolds Discovering the Skeleton of Ichthyosaurus in a Cavern under the Harz Mountains.*

The first ichthyosaurus was discovered by Mary Anning (the Fossil Woman of Lyme Regis) in 1810. The illustration here referred to is in Pouchet's *The Universe*, a popular nineteenth-century introduction to natural history.

CHAPTER 5, page 32. *Geordie Geddes is an employee of the Humane Society who lives in a rent-free house on Glasgow Green.*

*DWARFS OF GERMAN LEGEND BARING THE ICHTHYOSAURUS*
*From The Universe, or, The Infinitely Great and the Infinitely Small by F.A. Pouchet, M.D.: the 9th edition published in 1886 by Blackie & Son, Old Bailey, E.C.; Glasgow and Edinburgh.*

The Glasgow Humane Society for the Rescue and Recovery of Drowning Persons was founded by the Glasgow Faculty of Surgeons in 1790, and the first boat-house and house built for its officers on Glasgow Green in 1796. George Geddes, the first full-time officer, was employed from 1859 to 1889; his son (the second George Geddes) worked from 1889 to 1932. The job then went to the equally famous Ben Parsonage, whose son (July 1992) now occupies the Humane Society House near the end of the suspension bridge.

St. Andrew's Suspension Bridge, upstream from the wharf, was always a favourite place for suicides. It is a foot-bridge with very little traffic, and an iron lattice-work parapet which (though now covered by a fine mesh grille) was once easily climbed. The grandson of the first George Geddes was drowned while attempting to save the life of a man who jumped from St. Andrew's Bridge in 1928.

CHAPTER 7, page 44. *I strolled to the Loch Katrine memorial fountain.*

The proper name is The Stewart Memorial Fountain, since it was erected to commemorate the work of Mr. Stewart of Murdostoun, Lord Provost of Glasgow in 1854. Against strong opposition from the private water companies he got an Act of Parliament passed which enabled Glasgow Corporation to turn Loch Katrine, thirty-three miles away in the depths of the Trossach mountains, into the city's main public water supply.

However, Dr. McCandless's mistake is understandable. Designed by James Sellars I.A. and erected by the Water Commissioners in 1872, the fountain is elaborately carved with creatures found on the Loch Katrine islands: heron, otter, weasel and owl. On the summit is set the graceful figure of Helen, the Lady of the Lake herself. Oar in hand she stands erect behind the prow of a delicately imagined bark, exactly as Fitz-James beheld her in the most famous poetical work of Sir Walter Scott.

Around 1970 the authorities turned the water off and made the stonework a children's climbing frame. The sculptures got broken. In 1989, as Glasgow prepared to become the European Cultural Capital, it was fully repaired and set flowing again. In July 1992 it is waterless once more. A high timber wall surrounds it.

Page 49. *She retrieved her parasol and cheerfully waved it to some starers on a terrace of the hillside above.*

The steeply raked terraces of Glasgow's West End Park were designed in the early 1850s by Joseph Paxton, who also designed Queen's Park and the Botanic Gardens. The acute angle of the slope made it useful to Percy Pilcher when testing one of the gliders which eventually led to his death in 1899, but established the main structure of the aeroplane as it has developed to this day, and even gave the 'aeroplane' its name. The Pilcher connection may have led H. G. Wells to use the West End Park in his novel *The War in the Air*, published a month before the 1914–18 war. Wells describes Britain's first successful airman flying from London to Glasgow and back without stopping. As he circles above the park on a level with the highest terrace he shouts to the astonished crowds there, "Me muver was Scotch!" and is wildly applauded.

Page 52. *When the scream came the whole sky seemed screaming.*

Weather reports show that 29th June 1882 was abnormally hot and sultry. At sunset most Glaswegians were disturbed by a noise whose cause was discussed in the local press through the following fortnight. Most folk assumed it had an industrial origin and came from very far away. At Saracen Cross in the north-west folk thought something had exploded at Parkhead Forge; around Parkhead to the south-east it was thought a disaster in the Saracen Head Ornamental, Hygienic and Sanitary Iron Works. In Govan to the south-west folk thought a new kind of steam whistle was being tested in the north-east locomotive works; in the north-east it was assumed that a boiler had burst in a ship on Clydeside. A scientific correspondent in *The Glasgow Herald* said the phenomenon had been "more like an electrical shock than a noise", and perhaps had "a meteorological source in an abnormal weather condition combining with fumes in the atmosphere". A humorous periodical called *The Bailie* pointed out that the West End Park and University were at the centre of the area over which the noise was heard, and suggested that Professor Thomson was experimenting with a new kind of telegraph which went through air instead of through wires. A final facetious letter in *The Scotsman* (an Edinburgh journal) suggested that a Glasgow tinker had been playing a new kind of bagpipe.

CHAPTER 9, page 60. *When the gloaming comes so will he, stepping quietly from the lane through that door in the far-away wall.*

Michael Donnelly has shown me the original plans of Park Circus, designed by Charles Wilson in the 1850s, plans which show a coach-house dividing the backyard of 18 Park Circus from the lane. But the fact that an architect designed such a feature would not prevent it being built till much later. The builders of the gothic cathedrals took centuries to complete their architects' designs. The National Monument in Edinburgh, though designed to commemorate the Scots soldiers who died fighting Napoleon, is still little more than a façade.

CHAPTER 12, page 82. *For when we boarded the London train on that soft summer evening I had arranged to break our journey at Kilmarnock.*

Railway timetables from the 1880s show that it was possible to get off the first Midland Line night train from Glasgow to London at Kilmarnock and continue the journey on the second train which left an hour later.

Page 88. *I arranged to sell my Scottish Widows and Orphans shares.*

It was improvident of Wedderburn to do so since this insurance company (now called Scottish Widows) is still a highly flourishing concern. In March 1992, as part of

Conservative publicity preceding a General Election, the chairman of Scottish Widows announced that if Scotland achieved an independent parliament the company's head office would move to England.

CHAPTER 14, page 109. *Do you remember taking me to see / the Glasgow Stock Exchange? It looked like that.*

The Royal Exchange, in Queen Street, was erected and opened on 3rd September 1829. It was built by subscription at an expense of £60,000, and was not only a lasting monument of the wealth of the Glasgow merchants, but the noblest institution of the kind in Britain for many decades afterward. This splendid structure is built in the Grecian style of architecture from designs by David Hamilton. The building is entered by a majestic portico, surmounted by a beautiful lantern tower. The great roof is 130 feet in length and 60 in breadth; the roof, supported by Corinthian pillars, is 30 feet in height. The interior is now occupied by Stirling's Public Lending Library, and as magnificent as ever.

Page 115. *It is wide enough to march an army down, but otherwise like the steps down to the West End Park near our house.*

Most visitors to Odessa know the great flight of stairs down the cliff to the harbour front. The granite stairway in Glasgow's West End Park (erected in 1854 at a cost of £10,000) is equally substantial and handsome, but unfortunately in a corner where it is seldom seen and not much used by the public. Had it been erected nearer the central slope from Park Terrace it would have confronted Glasgow University across the narrow valley, and appeared to greater advantage.

Page 122. The Russian gambler's speech which starts: *"Well," he said with a rueful smile*, and ends: *"bed bugs too must have their unique visions of the world,"* shows he was steeped in the novellas of Fyodor Dostoyevsky. Bella could not have known this, as the great novelist had died the year before (1881) and was not yet translated into English.

CHAPTER 15, page 134. *Movement turns . . . flour butter sugar an egg and a tablespoonful of milk into Abernethy biscuits.*

According to *The Scots Kitchen* (by Marian McNeill, Blackie and Son, Bishopbriggs, 1929) this recipe omits two vital ingredients: half a teaspoonful of baking powder and a moderate amount of heat.

CHAPTER 16, page 164. *Your offer does not tempt me, Harry Astley, because I do not love you.*

A meticulous search through the public records and newspapers of the period has unearthed no evidence that "Harry" Astley ever existed. All Scottish and several English readers will have raised their eyebrows on reading that he claimed to be a cousin of "Lord Pibroch". *Pibroch* is the Gaelic name for *bagpipe*, and the Scottish College of Arms, like the English, insists that all titles are taken from place names. To a foreign ear, however, all decidedly Scottish names sound equally plausible, which indicates Astley was an impostor. No firm of sugar refiners called Lovel and Co. is listed in the commercial registers of the period. Who could Astley have been? Our only clue is in his undoubted links with Russia and his history lectures to Bella. These prove that behind his English façade lay no love of the British Empire. He was probably a Tsarist agent, visiting London to spy on the emigré Russian revolutionaries who sheltered there. Herzen and (much later) Lenin were the most famous of these. It is a good thing Bella refused Astley's offer of marriage.

Page 165. *We are going to Paris . . . Hand me over to the midinettes.*

A midinette is a French work girl, especially a young milliner or dressmaker. Their wages were low but they often knew how to dress well, so moneyed men regarded their class as a source of cheap mistresses.

CHAPTER 17, page 168. *Do you remember . . . how we . . . visited Professor Charcot at the Salpêtrière?*

Charcot, Jean Martin (1825–93), French physician, born in Paris. He graduated as M.D. of Paris University in 1853, and three years later he became physician of the Central Hospital Bureau. In 1860 he was appointed professor of pathological anatomy in the medical world of Paris, and in 1862 he began his connection with the Salpêtrière which lasted all his life. He was elected to the Academy of Medicine in 1873, and in 1883 was made a member of the Institute. He was a good linguist and had an excellent knowledge of the literature of other countries as well as his own. He was a great clinical observer and pathologist. He spent much of his time in studying obscure morbid conditions such as hysteria in relation to hypnotism. His work at the Salpêtrière was chiefly in the study of nervous diseases, but besides his labours in the field of nerves he also published many able works on the subjects of liver and kidney diseases, gout, et cetera. His complete works came out in nine volumes between 1886 and 1890. He was extraordinarily successful as a teacher, and his many followers were most enthusiastic in their work. Dr. S. Freud was among his pupils.

*Everyman's Encyclopaedia*, 1949, editor Athelstan Ridgway

Page 170. *"Hoist with my own petard ha ha ha ha ha."*

This phrase means 'blown up by my own bomb'. Shakespeare used it.

CHAPTER 18, page 184. *I said . . . she should think of my loving embraces, not imaginary owls.*

Bella misunderstood Mme Cronquebil's dialect. The poor lady probably said 'hole'.

CHAPTER 21, page 200. *The Park Church was nearest but I did not want the neighbours' children scrambling at the door, so chose Lansdowne United Presbyterian, less than ten minutes' walk away beside Great Western Road.*

A scramble is a Scottish custom which operated thus: children would gather outside a house from which a bride or groom would be leaving to get married. When they did so the bride's escort or the groom was expected to fling a handful of money into the crowd—if they did not the crowd would chant "Hard up! Hard up!" indicating that the person who had disappointed them was too poor to do the right thing. If a handful of coin was flung a wild crush would follow in which the strongest, most violent and ruthless children would grab the money and the weakest and smallest be left weeping with trampled fingers. This custom still prevails in parts of Scotland. Some modern conservative philosophers will think it good training for the world of adult competition.

Anyone who cares to try the experiment can easily walk from 18 Park Circus to Lansdowne Church in less than ten minutes by way of the park. The building (designed by John Honeyman) is of cream sandstone in the French Gothic style, with the most slender spire (in proportion to its height) in Europe. The sight of it so impressed John Ruskin that he burst into tears. The interior retains an unusual arrangement of boxed pews, and has two important stained glass windows by Alfred Webster relating biblical scenes to contemporary Glasgow. Both church and congregation date from 1863.

CHAPTER 22, page 212. *George Geddes a popular and respected person in this city) says he recovered a dead body.*

The popularity of George Geddes is proved by a comic song once performed in Glasgow music-halls. It describes a disastrous outing on a Clyde pleasure-steamer and ends with the line: "*Send for Geordie Geddes 'cause the boat's gawn doon.*"

Page 213. *It is on record that in the 1820s one of your sort animated the corpse of a hanged criminal, who sat up and spoke. Public scandal was only prevented by one of the demonstrators severing the subject's jugular with a scalpel.*

This story has been told and retold in so many nineteenth-century anecdotal histories of Glasgow that the original sources have themselves become the subject of an exhaustive monograph by Professor Heinrich Heuschrecke: *War Frankenstein Schotte?*, Stillschweigen Verlag, Weissnichtwo, 1929. Those who cannot read German will find the argument neatly summarized in Frank Kuppner's *Garscadden's Gash*, Molendinar Press, Glasgow, 1987.

CHAPTER 23, page 239. *But two days later the papers announced that General Blessington had been found dead on the gun-room floor of his country house at Loamshire Downs.*

The career of this once famous soldier began as well as ended under a cloud. At Sandhurst in 1846 a fellow student fell to his death in a prank Blessington initiated, though it was probably not he who untied the victim's boot-laces. His family connections with the Duke of Wellington perhaps led to him being reprimanded instead of expelled. In 1848 the Duke was Lord High Constable of England and organizing the military against the Chartists in London. He employed Blessington as an aide, but found him unsuitable. Rigby in his *Memoirs* records the Duke saying to Lord Monmouth: "Aubrey is a brave and clever soldier, but only feels alive when killing people. Unluckily most soldiering is spent waiting to do that. We must send him to frontiers as far from England as possible. We should keep him there."

The Duke died in 1852 but his advice was heeded. Blessington's frontier victories (often won with the help of native troops) delighted the British newspapers. George Augustus Sala called him "Thunderbolt Blessington" in *The Daily Telegraph*. Though not popular with his own social class he was honoured by the Queen: in other words, Palmerston and Gladstone and Disraeli recommended him for honours. Meanwhile Parliament voted him thanks and money, though a radical M.P. sometimes suggested that he "pacified" territories with undue ferocity. Most writers liked him. Carlyle called him:

> *a lean skyward-pointing pine tree of a man, scraped branchless by storm yet every straight inch of him stretched heavenward because rooted in Fact. Good wood for a lance! Words are less than wind to him.*

*Not strange, then, to find him dispraised in the pow-wows of the Westminster talking-shop. Would that the lance became a lancet to cut open the boil of putrescent parliamentary verbifaction and relieve the body politic of fever-inducing poisons!*

Tennyson met him at a public banquet in support of Governor Eyre and was so impressed that he wrote *The Eagle.* Though many people know it, few realize it is a romantic portrait of the author's friend:

*THE EAGLE*

*He clasps the crag with crooked hands;*
*Close to the sun in lonely lands,*
*Ring'd with the azure world, he stands.*

*The wrinkled sea beneath him crawls;*
*He watches from his mountain walls,*
*And like a thunderbolt he falls.*

But the finest poetic tribute to Blessington is by Rudyard Kipling, who believed the General had been hounded to his death by parliamentary criticism:

*THE END OF THE THUNDERBOLT*

*The trappers round the Hudson Bay*
*don't fear the half-breeds now.*
*In peaceful Patagonia the farmers drive their plough.*
*The wily Chinese traders pursue their gains in peace*
*Under justice dealt out cleanly by unbribable police;*
*While the founder of this industry, the giver of this gain,*
*LIES DEAD UPON THE GUN-ROOM FLOOR—*
*A BULLET IN HIS BRAIN.*

*There's always room in parliament*
*for nincompoop and knave,*
*And sentimental radicals who do not love the brave.*
*A host of lukewarm "realists" like things the way they are,*
*But feel the men responsible have "often gone too far".*
*Then there are men responsible,*
*the men who get things done,*

*And some, like Kitchener, we cheer;*
*some curse, like Blessington!*
*Let radical and "realist" sleep soundly in their bed.*
*BLESSINGTON'S ON THE GUN-ROOM FLOOR—*
*A BULLET IN HIS HEAD.*

*Many a peaceful settlement that Englishmen call home*
*Was once a howling wilderness where nomads used to roam.*
*Many a half-tamed tribesman*
*mines ore, shears sheep, breaks colt*
*Because his savage forebears were struck by Thunderbolt.*
*Yes, we scorched them with The Thunderbolt*
*but would not sniff the reek.*
*We lashed them with The Thunderbolt*
*but did not like the shriek.*
*We split them with The Thunderbolt and,*
*deafened by the crash,*
*We smashed them with The Thunderbolt.*
*Some shuddered at the smash.*
*Our kindly English stay-at-homes*
*like things genteel and fair;*
*They prefer the Danes to Nelson,*
*the blacks to Governor Eyre.*
*But argosies are bringing England*
*meat, wool, ore and grain.*
*SIR AUBREY'S ON THE GUN-ROOM FLOOR—*
*A BULLET IN HIS BRAIN.*

After such eulogy it is not unfair to quote two less friendly references to him. Dickens was writing *Dombey and Son* in 1846 when he heard about Blessington's lethal Sandhurst prank. It gave a hint for the conversation on the front at Brighton where Major Bagstock asks Dombey if he will send his son to public school:

> *"I am not quite decided," said Mr. Dombey. "I think not. He is delicate."*
>
> *"If he's delicate, Sir," said the Major, "you are right. None but the tough fellows could live through it, Sir, at Sandhurst. We put each other to the*

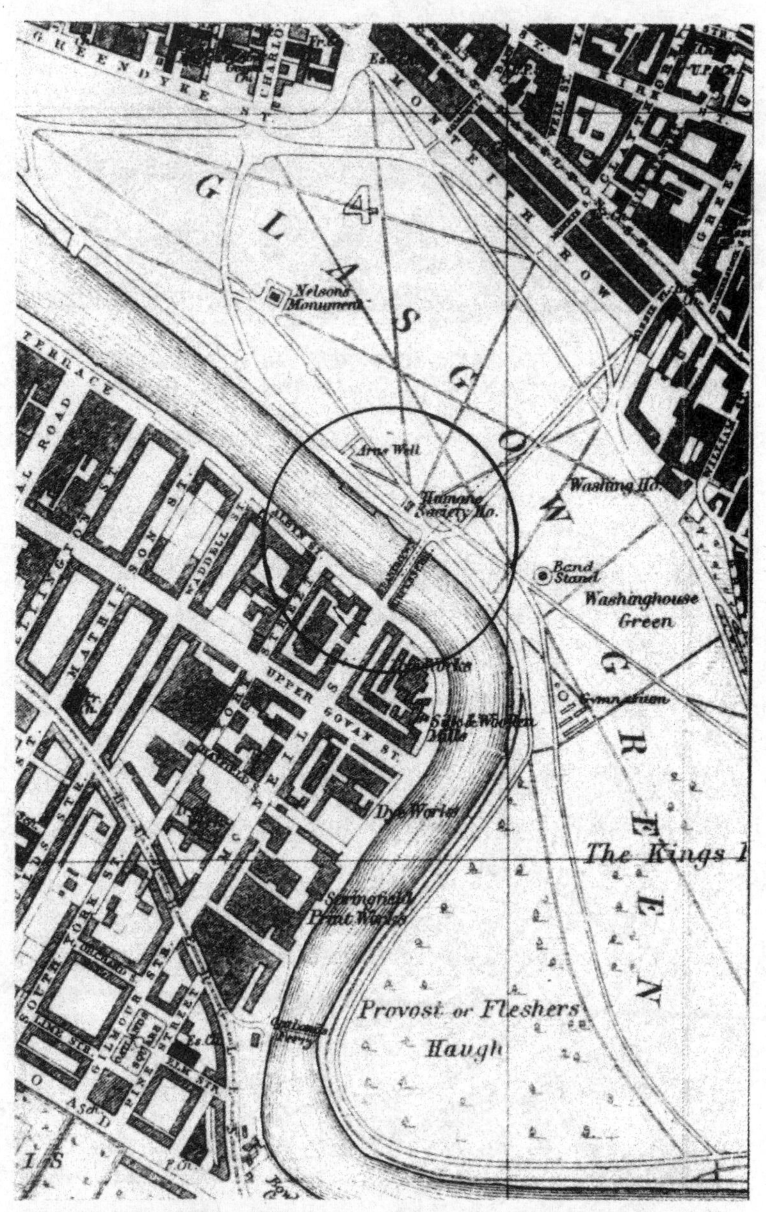


*GLASGOW GREEN, 1880. The circle surrounds the spot where Lady Victoria Blessington drowned herself: also the bridge from which she leapt; the wharf where Geddes saw her drown; the Humane Society House where Godwin Baxter examined her corpse.*

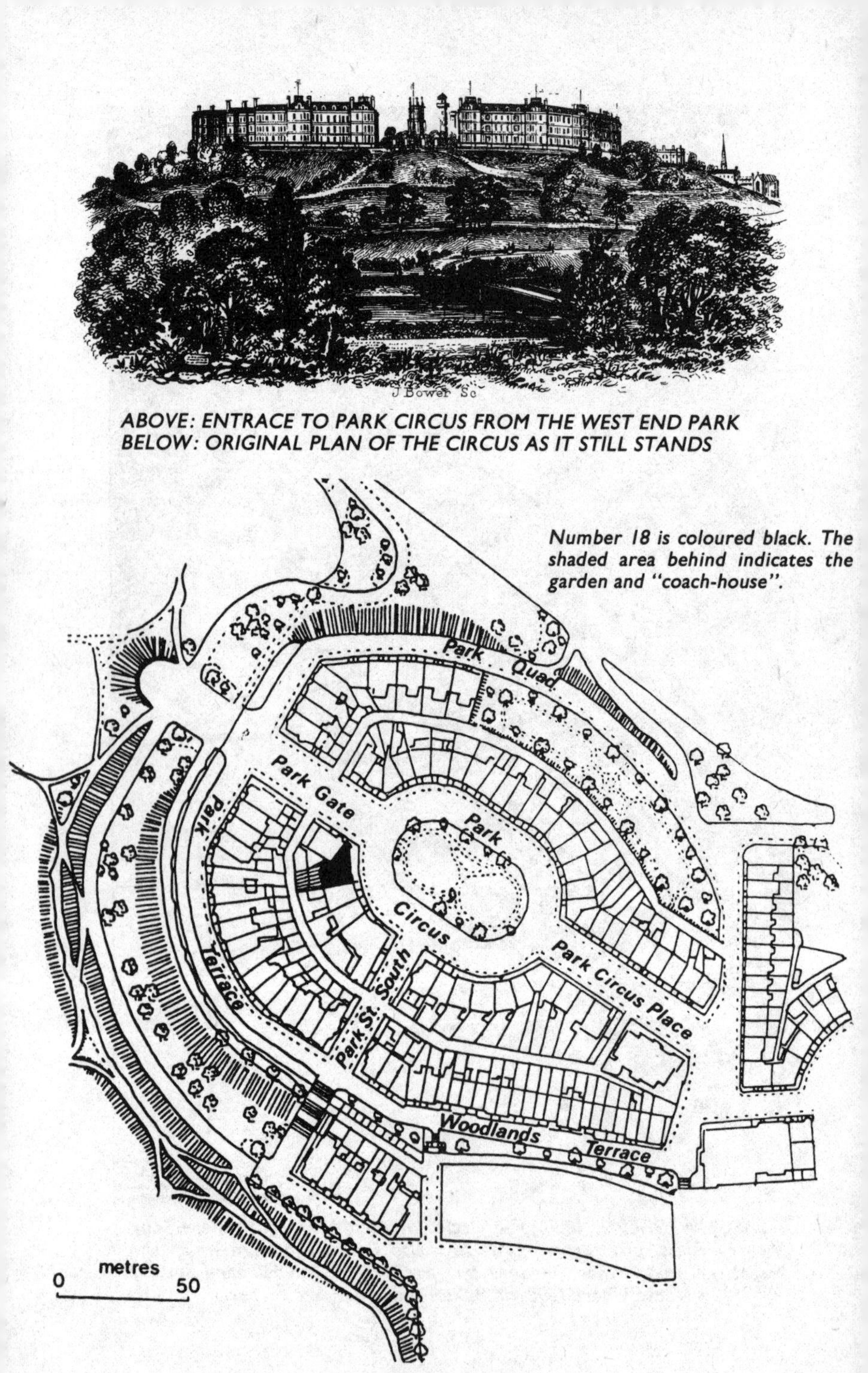


ABOVE: ENTRACE TO PARK CIRCUS FROM THE WEST END PARK
BELOW: ORIGINAL PLAN OF THE CIRCUS AS IT STILL STANDS

*Number 18 is coloured black. The shaded area behind indicates the garden and "coach-house".*

*ABOVE: The Stewart Memorial Fountain with Glasgow University to the left, Park Circus right. BELOW: The Midland Hotel, St Pancras, where Bella and Wedderburn spent the second night of their elopement.*

*LEFT: Lansdown United Presbyterian Church, where a wedding ceremony was interrupted on Christmas Day 1883.*

*OPPOSITE: Events in General Blessington's career as shown and reported in the Graphic Illustrated Weekly News.*

*BELOW: The kind of cab in which General Blessington planned to abduct his drugged "wife", Bella Baxter.*

*AUCTIONING LOOT IN MANDALAY AFTER BURMESE EXPEDITION*
*"'Thunderbolt' Blessington believes that the common soldier who preserves the peace of the Empire deserves more than mere wages."*

*KING PREMPEH'S HUMILIATION: "One of the Governor's demands made after the Ashanti rebellion was that King Prempeh should make abject submission in accordance with native custom. The King removed his crown and sandals, came forward with the Queen Mother to perform the act of humiliation, and reached the platform on which was seated Sir Francis Scott, General Blessington and Mr Maxwell. They knelt and embraced the Englishmen's legs and booted feet, while the Ashantis looked on with astonishment at their King's abasement."*

*MURDER IN NORTHERN INDIA: "The punitive expedition against the Lushai Hill tribes has found the gun of the late Lieut. Stewart in the grave of the Chief Howsata. It had been reported from other villages that if Howsata had murdered Lieut. Stewart, the gun would be in the Chief's grave. This was opened. Howsata's embalmed body was found lying with the gun beside it: conclusive proof that General Blessington had been right to burn the homes of the guilty tribesmen."*

*torture there, Sir. We roasted the new fellows at a slow fire, and hung 'em out of a three pair of stairs window, with their heads downward. Joseph Bagstock, Sir, was held out of the window by the heels of his boots, for thirteen minutes by the college clock."*

Lastly, Hilaire Belloc's caricature of an empire builder—Captain Blood—was based as much upon General Blessington as upon Cecil Rhodes:

*Blood understood the native mind.*
*He said: "We must be firm but kind."*
*A mutiny resulted.*
*I never will forget the way*
*That Blood upon this awful day*
*Preserved us all from death.*
*He stood upon a little mound,*
*Cast his lethargic eyes around*
*And said beneath his breath:*
*"Whatever happens we have got*
*The Maxim gun, and they have not."*

CHAPTER 24, page 244. *Rather than break his joints in order to lay him out flat I ordered a cubical coffin.*

Had Dr. McCandless waited patiently until putrefaction had set in, his friend Baxter would have lost the *rigor mortis*, and in such a flaccid state could have fitted comfortably into a conventional coffin. But perhaps Baxter's odd metabolism defied the normal process of decay.

A LETTER BY VICTORIA McCANDLESS, page 253. *He spent more and more time in his study, scribbling books printed at his own expense since no publisher would pay for them.*

Four books by Dr. McCandless apart from this one were printed in his lifetime at his own expense. Unlike *Poor Things* he sent copies of the following works to the Scottish National Library in Edinburgh where they are catalogued under his pseudonym, "A Gallowa' Loon".

1886 *Whaur We Twa Wandered*
Verses inspired by places in Glasgow associated with the courtship of his wife. One of these (headed "The West End Park Loch Katrine Waterworks Memorial Fountain") is quoted in Chapter 7 of *Poor Things* and is by far the best.

1892 *The Resurrectionists*
This five-act play about the Burke and Hare murders is no better than the many other nineteenth-century melodramas based on the same very popular theme. Robert Knox, the surgeon who bought the corpses, is treated more sympathetically than usual, so the play may have influenced James Bridie's *The Anatomist.*

1897 *Whauphill Days*
Reminiscences of childhood on a Galloway farm. Though purporting to be autobiography, this says so little about the author's father, mother and friends that the reader is left with the impression that he never had any. The only character to be described in affectionate detail is an atrociously harsh "dominie" whose approval of the author's scholastic abilities never mitigated the severity of the beatings inflicted on him. The bulk of the book describes the delights of "guddling" trout, "running down" rabbits and smaller vermin, and "harrying" birds' nests.

1905 *The Testament of Sawney Bean*
This long poem in "Habbie" stanzas opens with Bean lying in the heather on the summit of the Merrick, from which he surveys the nation which has both enticed and driven him into cannibalism. The year is 1603, shortly before the union of the crowns. Bean is suffering from food poisoning, for he has recently eaten part of an Episcopalian tax-collector on top of a Calvinist gaberlunzie. The symbolism, not the comedy of this intestinal broil is emphasized. In his delirium Bean harangues apparitions of every Scottish monarch from Calgacus to James the Sixth. Figures from Scotland's past *and* future appear: Fingal, Jenny Geddes, James Watt, William Ewart Gladstone et cetera, with finally, "a poet of futuritee,

| Who loses, seeks, finds Scotland just like me, | Upon that day." Here it becomes plain that Bean and his hungry family (soon to be arrested by the royal army and burned alive in the Grassmarket, Edinburgh) symbolize the Scottish people. The main difficulty with the poem (apart from its great length and dull language) is knowing what the cannibalism symbolizes. It may represent bad eating-habits which Dr. McCandless thought were once common in Scotland, for he addresses the reader as if the Bean clan had existed. A little research would have shown him it is neither in Scottish history or legend, folk tale or fiction. It first appeared in the *Newgate Calendar or Bloody Malefactors' Register* printed in London around 1775. The other stories in the book were factual accounts of gruesome English murders committed in what was then living memory. The Sawney Bean story was told in the same factual style but set upon a wild Scottish coast nearly two centuries earlier. It was a fiction based on *English* folk tales: tales told by the English about the Scots during centuries when these peoples were at war with each other, or on the verge of it.

I have described these four worthless books in detail to discourage others from wasting time on them. They do, however, prove that Dr. McCandless had no creative imagination or ear for dialogue, so must have copied *Poor Things* out of highly detailed diary notes. The manuscript burned by his wife would certainly have proved this.

Page 256. *Life for mother and me was mainly a struggle to keep the family and home clean, yet we never felt clean before . . . father . . . shifted us into a three-storey house . . . saying "I can afford this now." I think he had afforded it for at least a year.*

There is reason to think he had afforded it for fourteen years. In Chapter 22 Blaydon Hattersley is quoted as boasting that he was "employing half the skilled work-force of Manchester and Birmingham" ten years after he "smashed King Hudson". George Hudson—known as the Railway King—was a very successful shares and property speculator until the railway mania of 1847–8 plunged him into ruin. This means Bella's father became a millionaire when she was three.

Page 258. *"Got what?" "Got patent." "Got patent and heck of a lot more."*

The patent of the MacGregor Shand twin reciprocating gubernator sockets gave Blaydon Hattersley's Steam Traction Company a lead over its competitors which lasted until 1889 when the Belfrage popper valve made gubernators obsolete. MacGregor Shand died of consumption in the charity ward of Manchester Royal Lunatic Asylum in 1856.

Page 265. *I . . . played one of the simpler songs of Burns. It may have been "The Bonnie Banks o' Loch Lomond".*

Dr. Victoria is mistaken. This anonymous folksong was neither written nor collected by Robert Burns.

Page 274. *Yet why did he not make it more convincing? In the twenty-second chapter . . . he says "The bullet had luckily gone clean through into the carpet,* puncturing the integument between the ulna and radius of the second and third metacarpals *without even chipping a bone." The . . . words . . . are blethers, havers, claptrap, gibberish and gobbledygook.*

If Dr. Victoria had loved her husband more she would easily have seen why he wrote this claptrap. Archibald McCandless obviously wanted her to edit his book for publication. This, the only part of it which she had the experience and medical training to correct, was his way of asking for her collaboration. But she could not see it.

Page 275. *I am thankful to have survived into the twentieth century.*

Bella Baxter's later life was passed under the name Victoria, for in 1886 she used that name to enrol in the Jex-Blake women's medical school of Edinburgh, and was made a Doctor of Medicine under that name by Glasgow University in 1890. In 1890 she also opened the Godwin

Baxter Natal Clinic in Dobbie's Loan near the Cowcaddens. It was a purely charitable foundation, and she ran it with a small staff of local women trained by herself. These were continually leaving and being replaced, for she employed nobody more than a year after she had trained them. To a devoted employee who did not want to leave she said, "You are a great help to me but there is nothing more I can teach you. I enjoy teaching my helpers. Go away and help your neighbours, or work for a doctor who can teach you something new."

Several of her helpers enrolled as nurses in the city hospitals, but not many did well because (as one ward sister said) "They ask too many questions."

Between 1892 and 1898 Dr. Victoria bore three sons at two-yearly intervals, each time continuing her clinical work until the last two or three days of her pregnancies and starting again very soon after. She said, "That's how the poor women I treat have to do it—they cannot afford to be horizontalists. And I am luckier than most of them. I have a very good wife in my husband."

The Fabian Society published her pamphlet on public health in 1899. It was called *Against Horizontalism*, and said that many doctors wanted patients laid flat because it made the doctors, not the patients, feel stronger. She agreed that rest in bed was essential to the healing of many diseases, but said childbirth, though painful, was not a disease, and came more easily in a squatting posture. She advocated birthing-stools of a sort used in the eighteenth century. She also said horizontalism was a mental as much as a bodily state. It assumed that the inner workings of the body were sacred mysteries only doctors could understand, so good patients should have unquestioning faith in them. She said:

> *When priests and politicians ask for unquestioning faith we know they are thinking first of themselves. Why should we with scientific training ALSO want the people we serve to remove their thinking apparatus and bow down before us? But patients will only stand up properly for doctors—doctors will only stand up*

*properly for patients—when all know the common-sense daily foundations of the healing art.*

She wanted all children to be taught basic nursing in their primary schools ("where they can learn it as a game") and basic medical training in secondary schools. In this way all would learn not only how and when doctors could help them, but how to live more healthily, how to care for each other better, and why they should not tolerate housing and working conditions which damaged the health of themselves, their children and community. Here are some typical reactions from the journals of the period:

*It would seem that Dr. Victoria McCandless proposes to turn every British school—yes, even the infant schools!—into training grounds for revolutionary socialists.* The Times

*We hear that Dr. Victoria McCandless is a married woman with three sons. This is astonishing news—we can hardly believe it! From her writing alone we would have deduced that she was one of those stick-like, unwomanly women who would benefit from a course of "horizontalism"! Under the circumstances we can only offer her husband our hearty sympathies.*
The Daily Telegraph

*We do not doubt the adequacy of Victoria McCandless M.D.'s training, nor do we doubt the kindness of her heart. Her clinic is in a very poor part of Glasgow, and probably does more good than harm to the unfortunates who attend it. But that clinic is her hobby—she does not live by what it pays. We who earn our livings by the stethoscope and scalpel should smile tolerantly on her Utopian schemes, and return to our mundane task of healing the sick.* The Lancet

*Dr. McCandless wants the world to stop being a battlefield and become a sanatorium where everybody takes a turn of being doctor and patient, as in a children's game. It is surely obvious that in such a*

*world the only thing to flourish would be—disease!*

The Scots Observer

From 1900 onwards Dr. Vic (as the papers started calling her) was an active suffragette, and her work for the movement can be read in histories of it. The war of 1914 shocked her in a way from which she never recovered. She wanted working people and the soldiers to end it by going on strike, but her two youngest sons joined the army almost at once and were killed on the Somme soon after. She split with the Fabians because of what she called "their lukewarm tolerance of criminal carnage", and appeared on platforms with Keir Hardie, Jimmy Maxton, John Maclean and other Clydeside Socialists (and advocates of Scottish home rule) who opposed the war. She quarrelled with Baxter, her eldest son, who supported the war effort from his desk in the Department of Imperial Statistics. In a letter to Patrick Geddes she wrote:

*Baxter performs miracles of falsification, proving that the huge number being killed and maimed in France is less horrifying than the publicity suggests, since it contains many thousands who would have been killed and maimed by accidents in peace time. This comforts the shareholders and profiteers who draw unearned incomes from our war industry. It means that millions of dead young soldiers will soon be as forgotten as those who die in factory and road accidents.*

It is ironical that Baxter McCandless died without issue in 1919 at the age of twenty-seven, knocked down by a Paris taxi-cab while attending Lloyd George to the Versailles peace conference.

Like many at that time she thought long and hard about why the world's richest nations—nations who had prided themselves on being the most civilized because the most industrialized—had just fought the biggest and cruellest war in history. What puzzled her was why millions of men who, taken singly were neither bloodthirsty or stupid (she was thinking of her sons) had obeyed governments which ordered them to kill and be killed to such a suicidal extent. She accepted Tolstoy's view that human animals are prone to epidemics of insanity, like many thousands of Frenchmen going into Russia with Napoleon and dying there, when their country would have been no better off if they had conquered it. However, being a doctor she knew epidemics can be prevented if the causes are discovered. She knew that people who live and work in overcrowded quarters are as liable to epidemics of belligerence as any overcrowded creatures, but at least a quarter of those who fought and died in the Great War were prosperous with spacious homes, and to this class belonged nearly all who had ordered and officered the carnage. She decided that although the Great War had been started by the same national and commercial rivalries which had caused the British wars with France, Spain, Holland, France, the United States and France, she believed the men fighting and supporting it had succumbed to "an epidemic of suicidal obedience" because bad mothering and fathering had left most of them with a heartfelt belief that their lives were valueless:

> *What men who respected their bodies could bear to queue naked in rows and have their genitals examined by another clothed man? What man who respected his mind could bear to make money by doing such a thing? Yet the medical inspection was nothing but baptism into the religion of man-killing, in which the best soldier was he who regarded his own body as the least sensitive machine—not even his own machine, but a machine steered by remote controllers. My two youngest sons willingly became such machines and let their beautiful bodies be mangled and crushed into mud. My oldest made his mind, not his body part of the war machine. I now think him as much a victim of self-disrespect as his brothers. Yet for the first ten years of their lives these three young men lived in a clean spacious home and were shaped by the care and example of loving, educated and adventurous parents. I was (as I am) a radical Socialist. My husband was a*

*Liberal. Our boys were all preparing to be peaceful professional Scottish public servants, using the most humane modern ideas to tackle what we knew to be the great task of the twentieth century—to make a Britain where everyone has a good clean home and is well paid for useful work. Yet when war was declared my three boys AT ONCE behaved like sons of an English fox-hunting Tory. They* knew *I thought this was wicked behaviour. Why did they* feel *it was right? I refuse to seek the answer in the inherent depravity of human nature or the human male. Nor can I blame the militaristic histories they were taught at school, because that was certainly counteracted by the reading and teaching they got at home. I am forced to seek the reason in myself. For the first six or seven years of their lives I had total power over these boys, for I had plenty of money and a loving husband. Yet I did not give them the self-respect to resist that epidemic of self-abasement which was the 14–18 war. How did I fail? If I cannot find the root of the illness in myself I am no use to others. But I have found it. Please read on.*

The previous passage summarizes and quotes from the introduction to a booklet she published in 1920 at her own expense: *A Loving Economy—A Mother's Recipe for the End of All National and Class Warfare*. On the title-page is also printed: *The Godwin Baxter Peace Press, Volume I*. There never was a second volume. It received no serious attention although she posted copies to the leaders and secretaries of all the British trade union branches, in envelopes with *and your Wife* written after the names of the men, with *and your Husband* after the few women. She sent it to every doctor, clergyman, soldier, writer, civil servant and member of parliament in *Who's Who*. She also posted two thousand copies to equivalent people in North America, but they were seized and burned by the United States customs. In a letter to George Bernard Shaw, who was then on holiday in Italy, Beatrice Webb wrote:

> *When you come home you will find Dr. Vic's latest pamphlet awaiting you. It is an insane blend of ideas culled from Malthus, D. H. Lawrence and Marie Stopes. She blames herself for the Great War because she bore too many sons and did not* cuddle *them enough. She asks working-class parents to reduce future armies by having only one child. She wants them to make it feel infinitely precious by having it share their bed where it will learn all about love-making and birth control by practical example. In this way (she thinks) it will grow up free of the Oedipus complex, penis envy and other diseases discovered or invented by Doctor Freud, and instead of fighting with siblings will play husband-and-wife with a neighbour's child. She is now quite sex-mad—an erotomaniac, to use the older term—and tries to hide it under prim language which shows she is still, at heart, a subject of Queen Victoria.* Cuddles *is her word for love-making, she calls fornication* wedding. *Yet she once had an excellent mind. I wish her poor little husband had not died. I think he kept her stable between her embarrassing affairs with Wells and Ford Madox Hueffer. And of course the loss of her sons hit her hard. The last six years have damaged all but the strongest minds.*

The Clydeside Independent Labour Party socialists also disliked *A Loving Economy*. Tom Johnston, reviewing it in *Forward*, said:

> *Victoria McCandless M.D. wants working-class parents to increase the value of their children's labour by going on a limited form of birth strike. In this year of lock-outs and reduced wages—a year when working-class movements everywhere are pressing the government to abolish unemployment by work rationing—such a demand from a good comrade is a frivolous distraction. Hunger and homelessness must be tackled now, not postponed to a future generation.*

Clergymen of every Christian church denounced the book for the birth control proposals, but it annoyed advocates of birth control by saying commercial contraceptives were unhealthy. Said Dr. Victoria:

> *They fix the minds of the users upon the genitals, so distract them from cuddling. Cuddling is like milk. It can, and should, nourish our health from birth to death. Wedding is the cream of cuddling, the main delight of our middle years (if we are lucky) but it is not different from cuddling. Yet all our teaching—alas, even the teaching of the good Marie Stopes—*makes *it different by separating it and advertising it as a rare commodity. That is why uncuddled men fear sexual love or treat it as a smash-and-grab business.*

So although Victoria McCandless placed advertisements for *A Loving Economy* in the major British newspapers it had only two favourable notices: one by Guy Aldred in an anarchist periodical, one in *The New Age* by the stone-carver and typographer, Eric Gill. Beaverbrook took a hint from the churches and enlarged the circulation of the *Daily Express* by a successful campaign to deprive Victoria McCandless of her clinic. Here is an extract from an article headed LADY DOCTOR ORDERS INCEST:

> *We all know what a mother's boy is—an effeminate little pansy who wants everyone to admire him yet is too cowardly to strike a blow in his own defence. If Dr. Vic has her way all British boys from now onward will be turned into exactly that sort of whining cissy, but before she corrupts our children she must corrupt their parents. This is exactly what she is trying to do.*

Two days later this appeared:

> *DOCTOR VICTORIA PRESCRIBES NATIONAL SUICIDE*
>
> *If the Dr. Vic's "sex through a sheet" method becomes popular (and it may—she has spent a fortune advertising it) in a few years every British male of*

*military age will be outnumbered by the Catholic Irish. If it becomes fashionable throughout the civilized world we will be overwhelmed by the Bolsheviks, the Chinese and the Negroes. It cannot be coincidence that she is a close friend of John Maclean, the Bolshevik Consul General in Britain. It cannot be coincidence that she was one of the "pacifist" harpies who would have been awarded an Iron Cross by Kaiser Wilhelm if his hordes had succeeded in placing him on the British throne.*

Soon after came:

*DR. VIC'S BOLSHEVIK CHARITY!*

*The most sinister figures in the twentieth century are people with unearned incomes who, under the guise of socialism, use their money-bags to spread discontent and evil practices among the poor. The* Express *has discovered that for the last thirty years Victoria McCandless, the Bolshevik doctor, has been secretly teaching what she now openly preaches. At her so-called "charity" clinic in a Glasgow slum she has taught thousands of poor women to defy nature, the Christian faith and the law of the land: we refer to something graver than her ridiculous "sex through a sheet" idea. We mean abortion. That is what her "Loving Economy" comes to in the end.*

The *Express* reporters had no proof that Dr. Victoria performed abortions. They did, however, produce two former employees of the clinic who swore she had trained women to perform abortions on each other, and this resulted in a public prosecution. The prosecution failed (or did not completely succeed) because it was proved that the two employees had been to some extent bribed by the *Daily Express*, and were also mentally retarded. Campbell Hogg, the procurator fiscal, tried to make something of this last point during his cross-examination, and very nearly succeeded:

*CAMPBELL HOGG: Doctor McCandless! Have you trained many mentally retarded women to assist you?*
*VICTORIA McCANDLESS: As many as I could.*
*CAMPBELL HOGG: Why?*
*VICTORIA McCANDLESS: For reasons of economy.*
*CAMPBELL HOGG: Oho! You got them cheaper?*
*VICTORIA McCANDLESS: No. The accounts of the clinic show they were paid as much as cleverer nurses. I was not talking about financial economy but social economy—loving economy. Many people with damaged brains are far more affectionate, if given the chance, than many we classify as "normal". They can often be taught to perform the most essential nursing tasks more efficiently than cleverer people—people who want to be doing more ambitious things.*
*CAMPBELL HOGG: Things like writing books on Loving Economy?*
*VICTORIA McCANDLESS: No. Things like acting the buffoon in a court drama set up for the amusement of the gutter press.*
*(Laughter in court. The sheriff warns the accused that she is in danger of being held in contempt of court.)*
*CAMPBELL HOGG (forcibly): I suggest that you deliberately choose cretins for your helpers because sane people are unlikely to believe what these say about your clinic!*
*VICTORIA McCANDLESS: You are wrong.*
*CAMPBELL HOGG: Doctor McCandless, have you* never *(think hard before you answer) have you* never *given your patients instruction which would help them abort an unwanted baby?*
*VICTORIA McCANDLESS: I have never given instructions which could hurt their mind or body.*
*CAMPBELL HOGG: The answer I want is "yes" or "no".*
*VICTORIA McCANDLESS: You will get no more answers from me, young man. Go and teach another older person their job. Try an unemployed engineer—one who fought in the war.*

*(The sheriff warns accused that she must answer the procurator, but can choose her own words.)*
*VICTORIA McCANDLESS: I see. Then I repeat that I have taught nothing which can hurt mind or body.*

Since the trial was in Scotland the jury was able to bring in a verdict of not proven, and did. Dr. Vic was not struck off the British medical register, but not declared guiltless.

When Victoria and Archibald opened the Natal Clinic in 1890 they put all Baxter's money into the fund supporting it. The managing committee contained Sir Patrick Geddes and Principal John Caird of Glasgow University. By 1920 these had been replaced by weaker people who now bowed before the storm of unfriendly publicity. They sacked Victoria and gave the clinic to Oakbank Hospital as an out-patients department. Dr. Victoria had spent her savings printing, distributing and advertising *A Loving Economy*, so her only remaining property was 18 Park Circus. All Baxter's old servants were dead by now. She let the upper rooms to university students and withdrew to the basement where she continued what she still called *The Godwin Baxter Natal Clinic* on a much smaller scale.

From then until 1923 she was chiefly noticed for her support of John Maclean. In a letter to C. M. Grieve (Hugh MacDiarmid) she wrote:

*I cannot like the orthodox communists. They have one simple answer to every question and believe (like the fascists) that they can forcibly simplify what they do not understand. In any discussion with one I feel I am facing a bad school teacher who wants to shut me up. Maclean is a good school teacher.*

When Maclean did not join the newly formed British Communist Party but founded the Scottish Workers' Republican Party she offered him her home as a meeting place. When he died of overwork and pneumonia in 1923 she made a short speech by his graveside. His daughter,

Nan Milton, recorded it in a letter, and Archie Hind quotes it at the end of his play about Maclean, *Shoulder to Shoulder*:

> *John was not a Zapata, galloping on horseback over the corn-fields. He was of the peasantry who fed Zapata. He was not a Lenin, working to move his office into the Kremlin. He was of the Kronstadt sailors whose mutiny gave Lenin the chance. John was not the sort who lead revolutions. He was the sort who make them.*

The *Daily Express* put another reporter onto her two years later, perhaps hoping to find more conclusive evidence of illegal abortions, but the article which came out of this was a short character sketch, probably because nearly everyone who now remembered "Dr. Vic" thought she was dead. The reporter learned that children of the area called her The Dog Lady, because she walked around the West End Park accompanied by dogs of many sizes, some of them bandaged. The clinic was entered from the back lane, and the ground on each side of the path was overgrown with rhubarb plants. The waiting-room was crammed with heavy mid-Victorian seating, particularly a huge horse-hair-covered sofa. The only wall decorations were old posters for the Scottish Workers' Republican Party. There was also a heavy padlocked box with a slit in the lid and a notice pinned to the side saying *Put what you can afford in here—it will not be wasted. If you are hungry please do not steal this but speak to me in the surgery—hunger is curable.* Half the people waiting looked very poor and old. The rest seemed to be children with animals, mostly dogs. There was only one pregnant woman.

When the reporter was admitted to the surgery he found it was a huge gas-lit kitchen with a pot of soup simmering on the fire range, various animals reclining in corners, and a tall, straight-backed woman sitting at a kitchen table laden with books, papers and medical instruments. She wore a white apron which covered her body from neck to ankles, with white celluloid cuffs attached to the black sleeves of her dress. Her strangely unlined face could have been any age between forty and eighty. When the journalist sat down facing her she said at once, "You look like a newspaper reporter. Is it the *Daily Express*?"

He said yes, and hoped she would not mind answering some questions. She said, "Of course not, if you pay for my time on the way out."

He asked her if all her patients paid her in that voluntary way. She said, "Yes. They are poor people, or children. How can I judge what they are able to pay me without hurting themselves?"

He asked if she always gave money to hungry beggars. She said, "No. I give them soup."

He asked if her veterinary work had not reduced her number of human patients. She said, "Undoubtedly. The human animal is prone to silly prejudices."

He asked if she preferred dogs to human beings. She said, "No, I am not that kind of sentimentalist. I will always feel tenderness toward my own silly prejudiced species. But nowadays folk with sick animals shun me less than sick humans."

He asked if there was anything in her life she sincerely regretted. She said, "The Great War."

He told her she had misunderstood him—he meant, did she regret something for which she felt personally responsible? She said, "Yes. The Great War."

He asked what she thought about de Valera's Irish republic, the short length of young women's skirts, *Mairzy Doats and Dozy Doats* (a popular song of the time) and Trotsky's expulsion from the Russian Communist Party. She said, "Nothing. I no longer read newspapers."

He asked if she had a message to give to British youth. She smiled brightly and said that for five pounds she would give him a very quick little answer summing up all she thought good in life, but she wanted the money first. He gave her five pounds. From a pile at her elbow she handed over a little hardbound copy of *A Loving Economy*, bade him good-bye and ushered him out.

That article is the only record of Victoria McCandless between 1925 and 1941, apart from her name and address in Kelly's street directory.

The Second World War revived for a while both the industrial and intellectual life on Clydeside. Glasgow was the main transit port between Britain and the U.S.A. The bombing of south Britain inclined many to the northern industrial capital. The painter J. D. Fergusson returned here with his wife, Margaret Morris. They had known Dr. Victoria in her younger days, and Margaret Morris rented an upper floor of 18 Park Circus as a rehearsal space for her Celtic Ballet Company. Until 1945 the house became one of several unofficial little arts centres flourishing on or near Sauchiehall Street. The painters Robert Colquhoun, Stanley Spencer and Jankel Adler briefly lodged in it or visited it. So did the poets Hamish Henderson, Sidney Graham and Christopher Murray Grieve, better known as Hugh MacDiarmid. In his autobiography *The Company I've Kept* (published in 1966 by Hutchinson & Co.) MacDiarmid says:

> *I seem to have been the only one there who knew that the queer old landlady lurking in the basement was the one female Scottish healer—apart from Long Mairi of the Glens—whose name could have been proudly inscribed beside Madame Curie, Elizabeth Blackwell and Sophia Jex-Blake. Perhaps her pets' hospital frightened away the lily-livered, but her Scotch broth was excellent, and ladled freely out with a lavish hand.*

He reviles:

> *our cowardly Scottish medical establishment which could easily have given her a university lectureship in gynaecology, but was scared out of its wits by the English gutter press led by that analphabetic hoodlum, Beaverbrook.*

This last statement is perfectly true, but would have been more persuasive if expressed more politely. We must be grateful to MacDiarmid, however, for quoting in full a letter she wrote shortly before her death. A lesser man would have suppressed it, as it said things he certainly did not like. Though undated it was obviously written soon after the 1945 general election.

*Dear Chris,*

*So at last, for the first time this century, we have a Labour government with an overall working majority! I will start reading the newspapers again. Britain is suddenly an exciting country. The anti-trade-union laws of 1927 are being repealed and it seems we WILL get social welfare and national health care for all, and Fuel and Power and Transport and Iron and Steel WILL become Public Property! As Public as broadcasting, telephones, tap-water and the air we breathe! And we WILL jettison that millstone round our necks, the British Empire! Do you not feel a little happier, Chris? I feel a lot happier. We are setting the world a finer example than the Soviet Union ever did. I feel that everything between 1914 and the present day has been proved a hideous detour, a swerving from the good path of social progress whose last fixed point was the Lloyd George budget which abolished poor-houses by the old-age pension, and started breaking up the enormous estates by death duties. It seems John Maclean was wrong. A workers' co-operative nation will be created from London, without an independent Scotland showing the way.*

*I know (you thrawn old Devil) that you will not believe a word of this, and think I have a heart "too easily made glad". I know you are even now reaching for your pen to describe for me all the obviously vicious worms gnawing at the roots of Blooming Britain. Leave that pen alone! I am going to die happy.*

*If you have read my publications (but has anyone alive ever done that?) if you have read* A Loving Economy *(which should be read as a poem, just as your worst poems should be read as treatises) if you have skimmed through even a paragraph of my poor neglected little* magnum opus *you will know I am unusually acquaint with my inner workings. No wonder! I was introduced to them by a genius. A cerebral haemorrhage will release me from this mortal coil in early December. I am winding down the little clinic which was launched so bravely and richly fifty-six years ago. Easily done! My patients now are some children's pets and two elderly hypochondriacs who feel slightly happier after talking breathlessly to me for an hour about things only Sigmund Freud could understand. I have found homes for all my dogs except Archie, the Newfoundland. He has a home waiting for him, but will not be led off to it until the friend who calls on me after breakfast (Nell Todd, a courageous Sapphist who defies the Glasgow police in male attire) uses the basement key I have given her, and finds me* out. *Completely. I would have preferred a warm steady man at the last, but there has only been one in my life, and he died thirty-five years ago. Not that I disliked the fly-by-nights—some of them were great fun. But steady heat is what I need now, and my Archie will provide it.*

*If you insult me by offering to provide it I will never speak to you again. My love to Valda.*

*Sincerely,*

*Victoria McCandless.*

Dr. Victoria McCandless was found dead of a cerebral stroke on 3rd December 1946. Reckoning from the birth of her brain in the Humane Society mortuary on Glasgow Green, 18th February 1880, she was exactly sixty-six years, forty weeks and four days old. Reckoning from the birth of her body in a Manchester slum in 1854, she was ninety-two.

*The Necropolis of Glasgow where the three principal characters of this book are interred in the Baxter Mausoleum – the Romanesque rotunda on the far right.*